DETECTIVE SWEET PEA

THE CASE OF THE
GOLDEN BONE

SARA VARON

:01

First Second

NEW YORK

In memory of my mom, Elise Varon,
who encouraged and enabled me to become an artist,
and who always had a treat for Sweet Pea.
—SV

First Second

Published by First Second
First Second is an imprint of Roaring Brook Press,
a division of Holtzbrinck Publishing Holdings Limited Partnership
120 Broadway, New York, NY 10271
firstsecondbooks.com
mackids.com

Library of Congress Control Number: 2023940549

Our books may be purchased in bulk for promotional, educational, or business use.
Please contact your local bookseller or the Macmillan Corporate and Premium Sales Department
at (800) 221-7945 ext. 5442 or by email at MacmillanSpecialMarkets@macmillan.com.

First edition, 2024
Edited by Mark Siegel and Tess Banta
Cover design and interior book design by Molly Johanson
Production editing by Dawn Ryan

Penciled in Clip Studio Paint on an iPad. Inked with a Pentel Pocket Brush pen on Bristol paper.
Colored digitally in Photoshop. Lettered with a font based on the author's handwriting.

Printed in China by RR Donnelley Asia Printing Solutions Ltd., Dongguan City, Guangdong Province

ISBN 978-1-250-34840-1 (paperback)
1 3 5 7 9 10 8 6 4 2

ISBN 978-1-250-23637-1 (hardcover)
1 3 5 7 9 10 8 6 4 2

Don't miss your next favorite book from First Second!
For the latest updates go to firstsecondnewsletter.com and sign up for our enewsletter.

Chapter 1

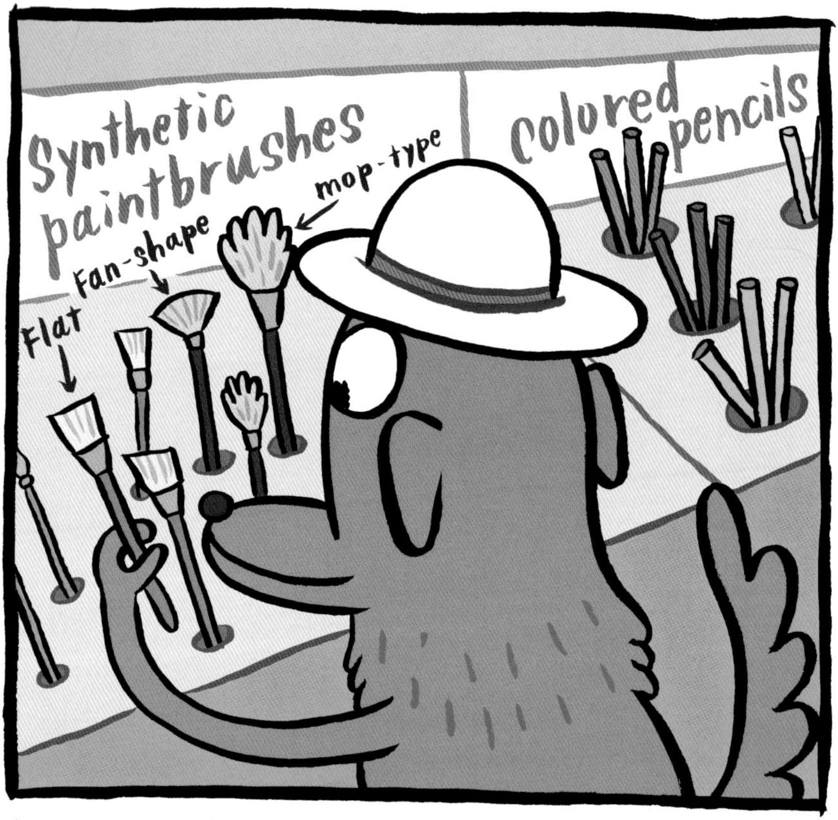
Synthetic paintbrushes
Colored pencils
mop-type
Fan-shape
Flat

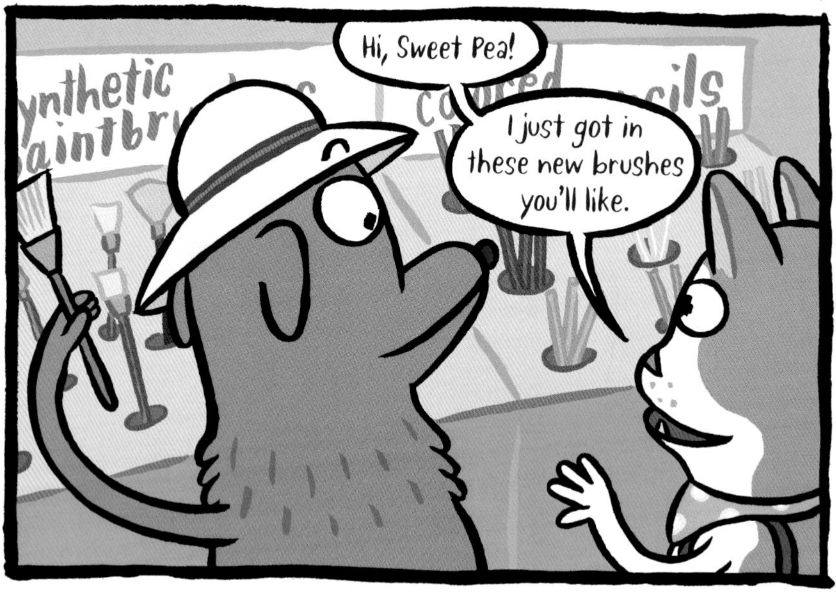
Hi, Sweet Pea!
I just got in these new brushes you'll like.

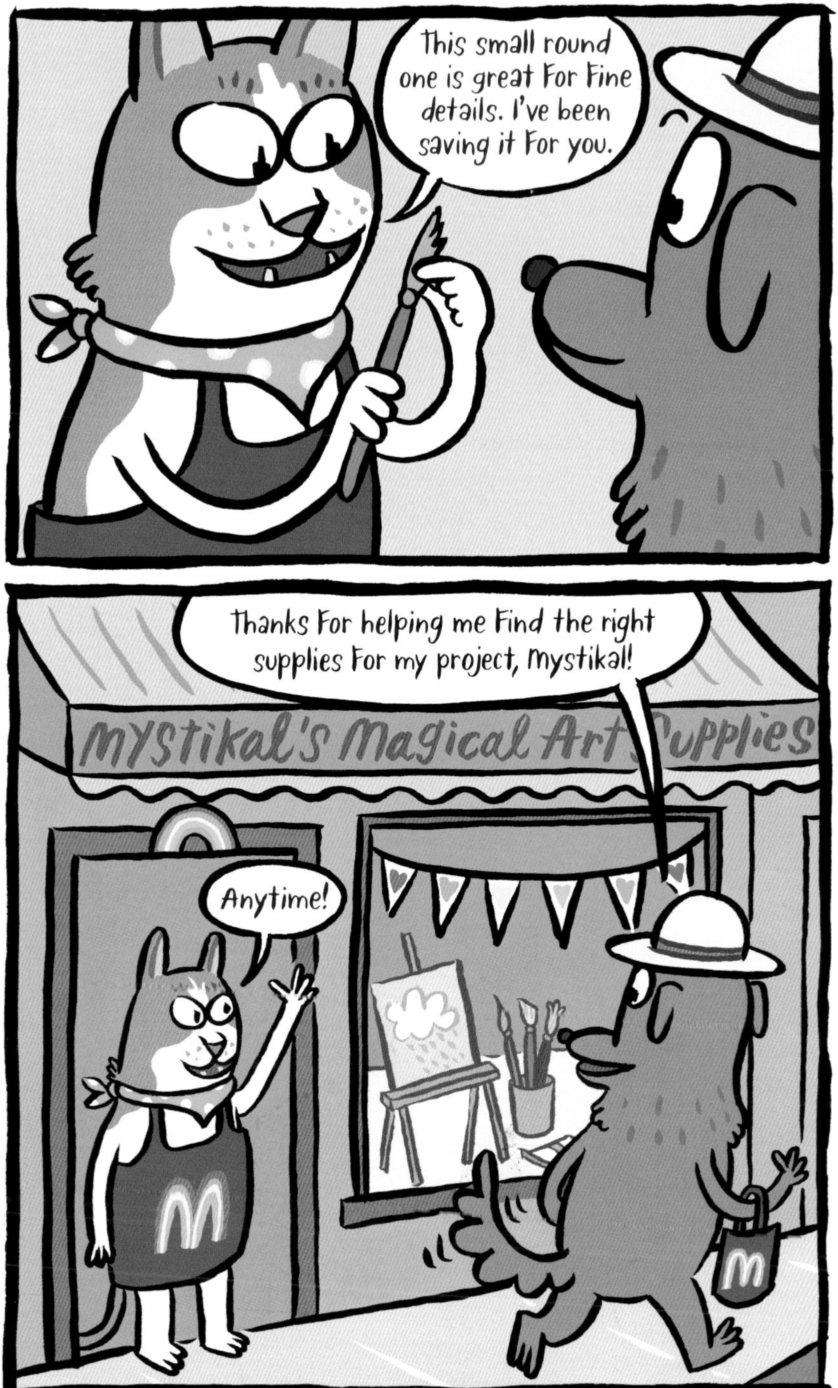
This small round one is great for fine details. I've been saving it for you.
Thanks for helping me find the right supplies for my project, Mystikal!
Mystikal's Magical Art Supplies
Anytime!

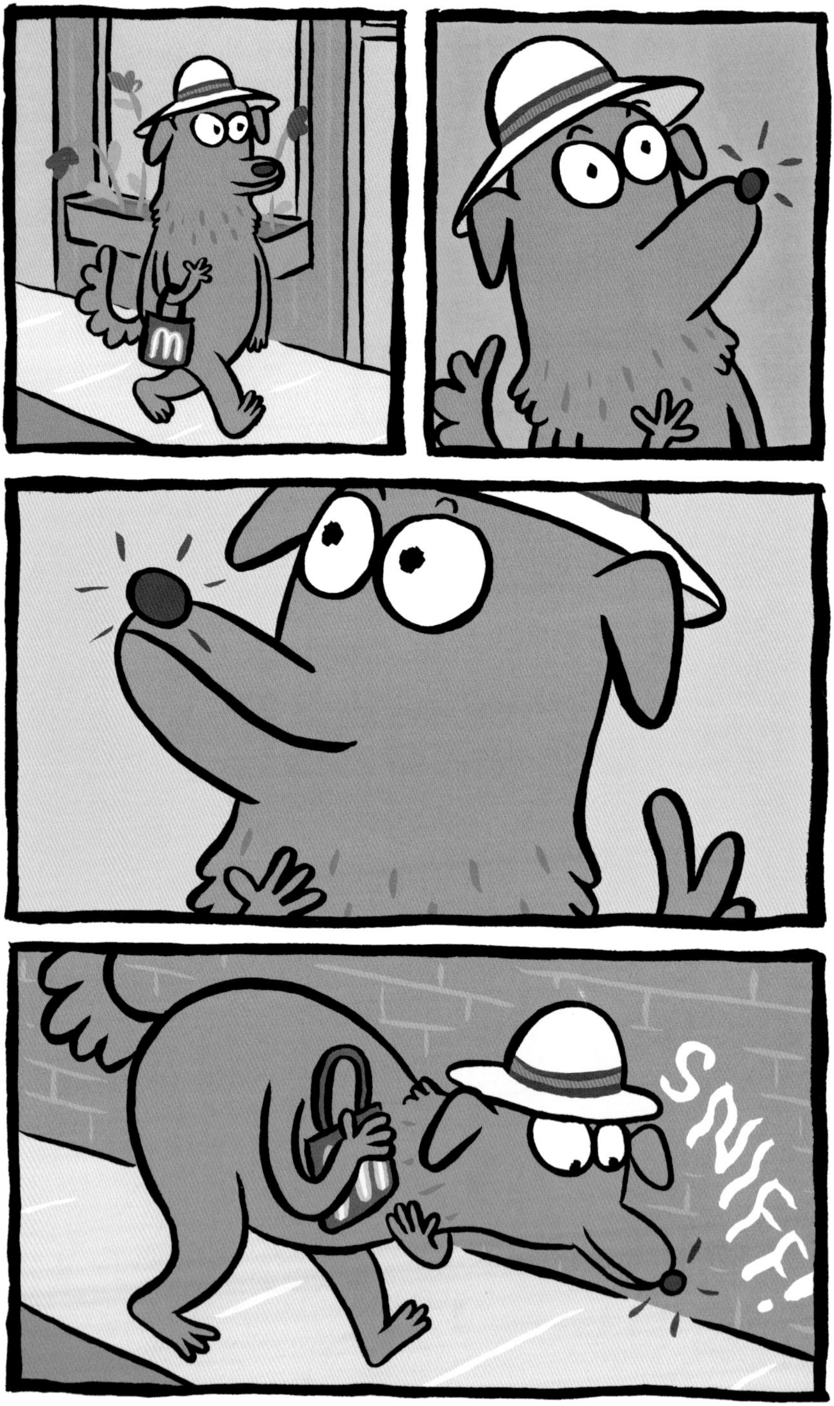

SNIFF!

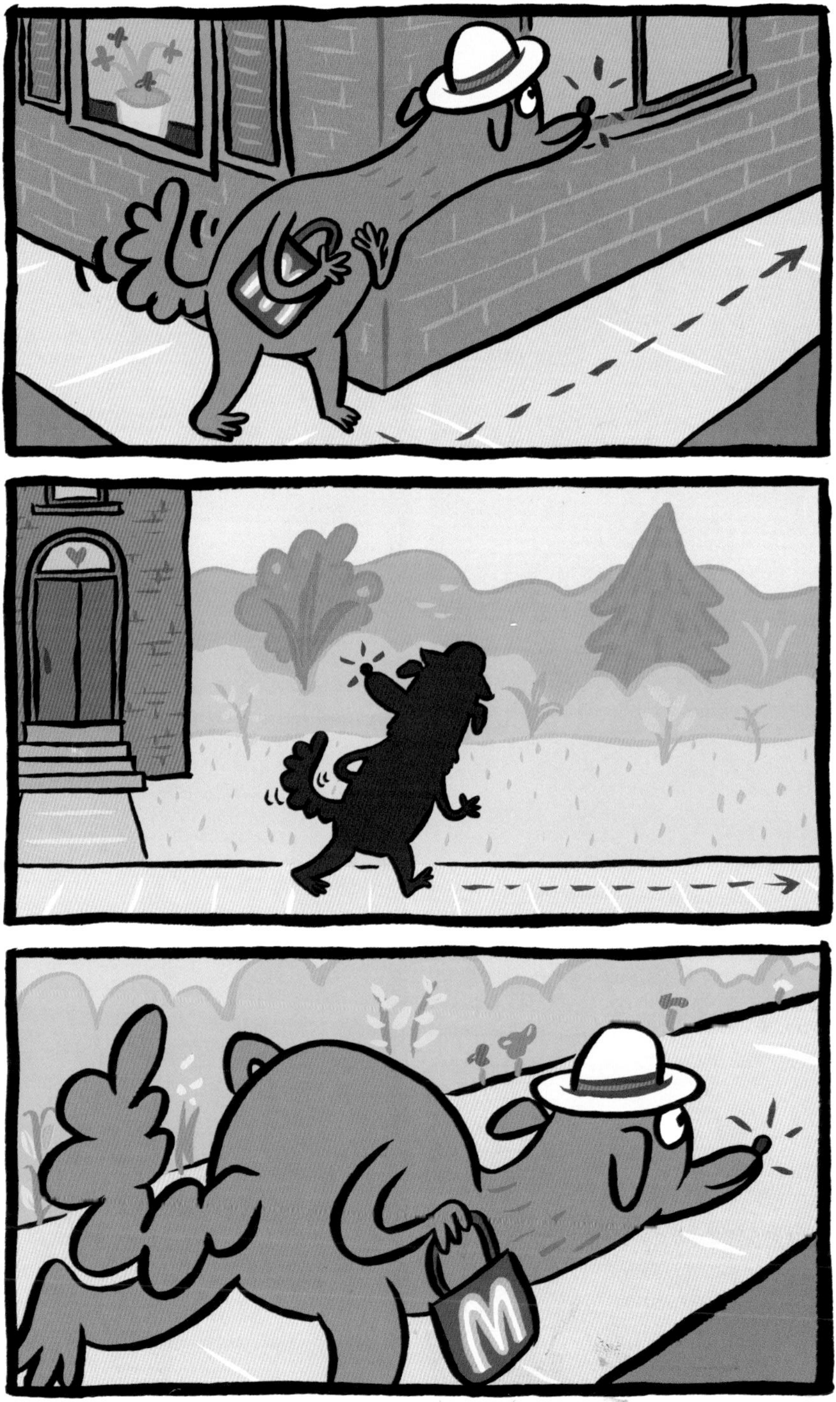
M

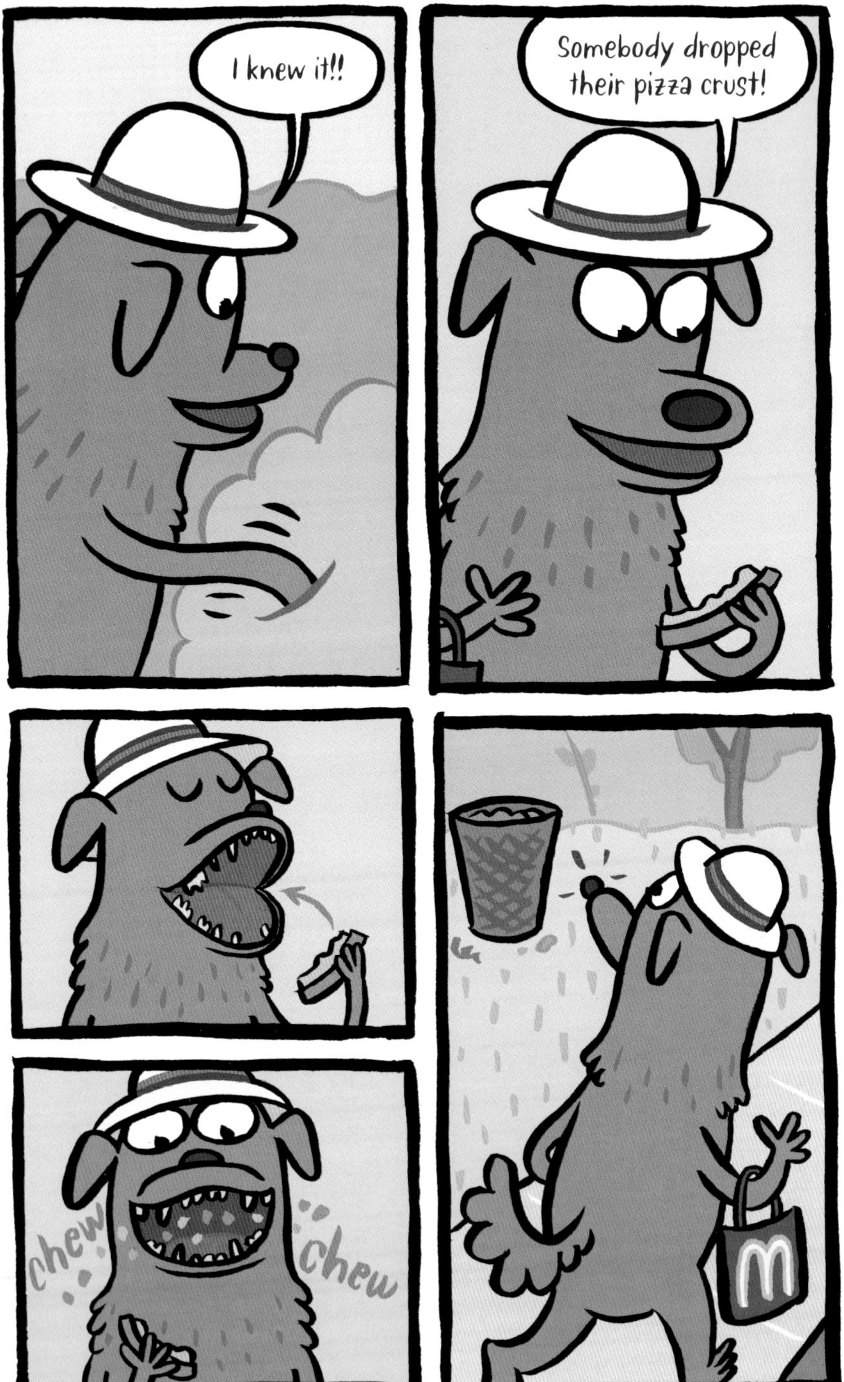
I knew it!!
Somebody dropped their pizza crust!
chew
chew

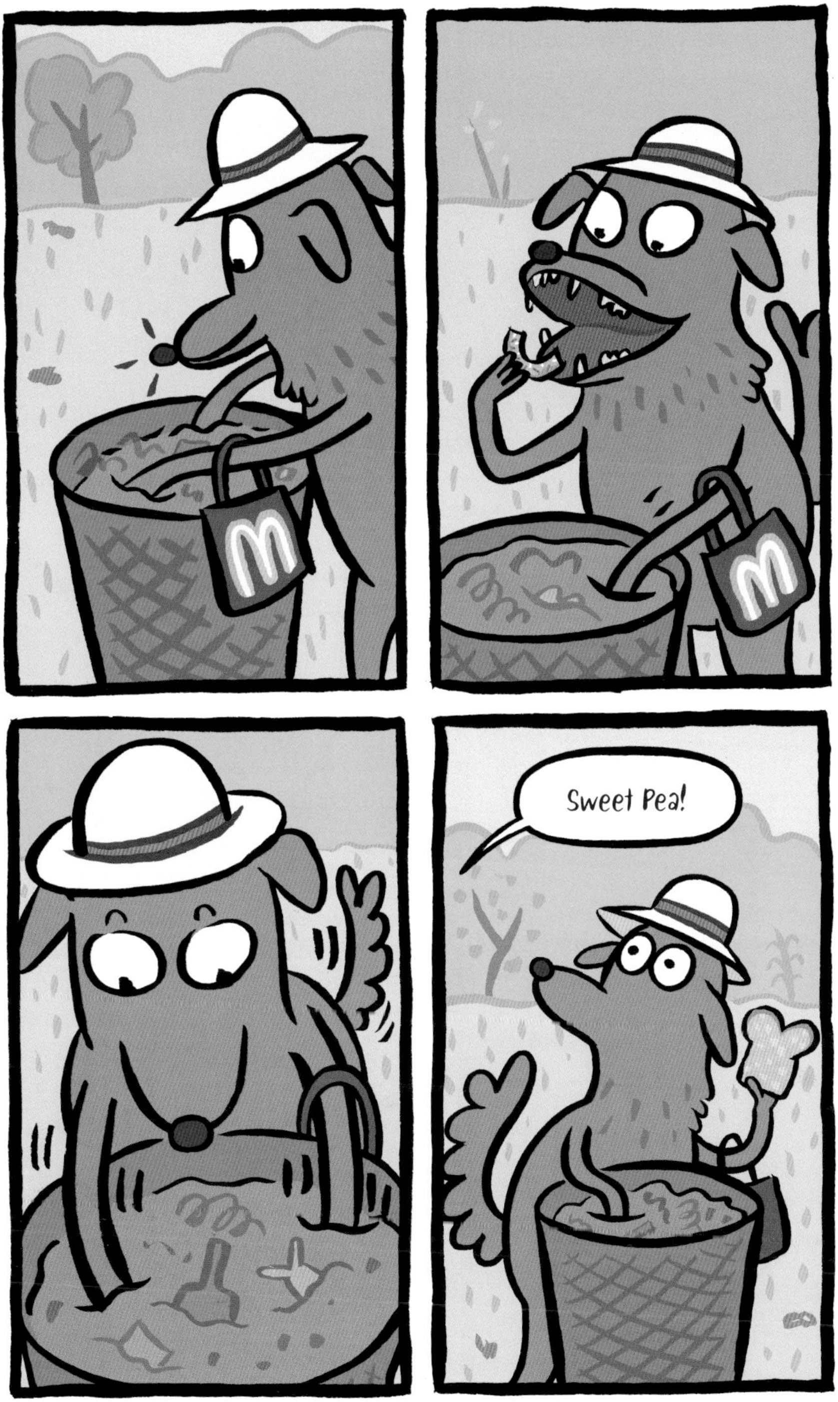
Sweet Pea!

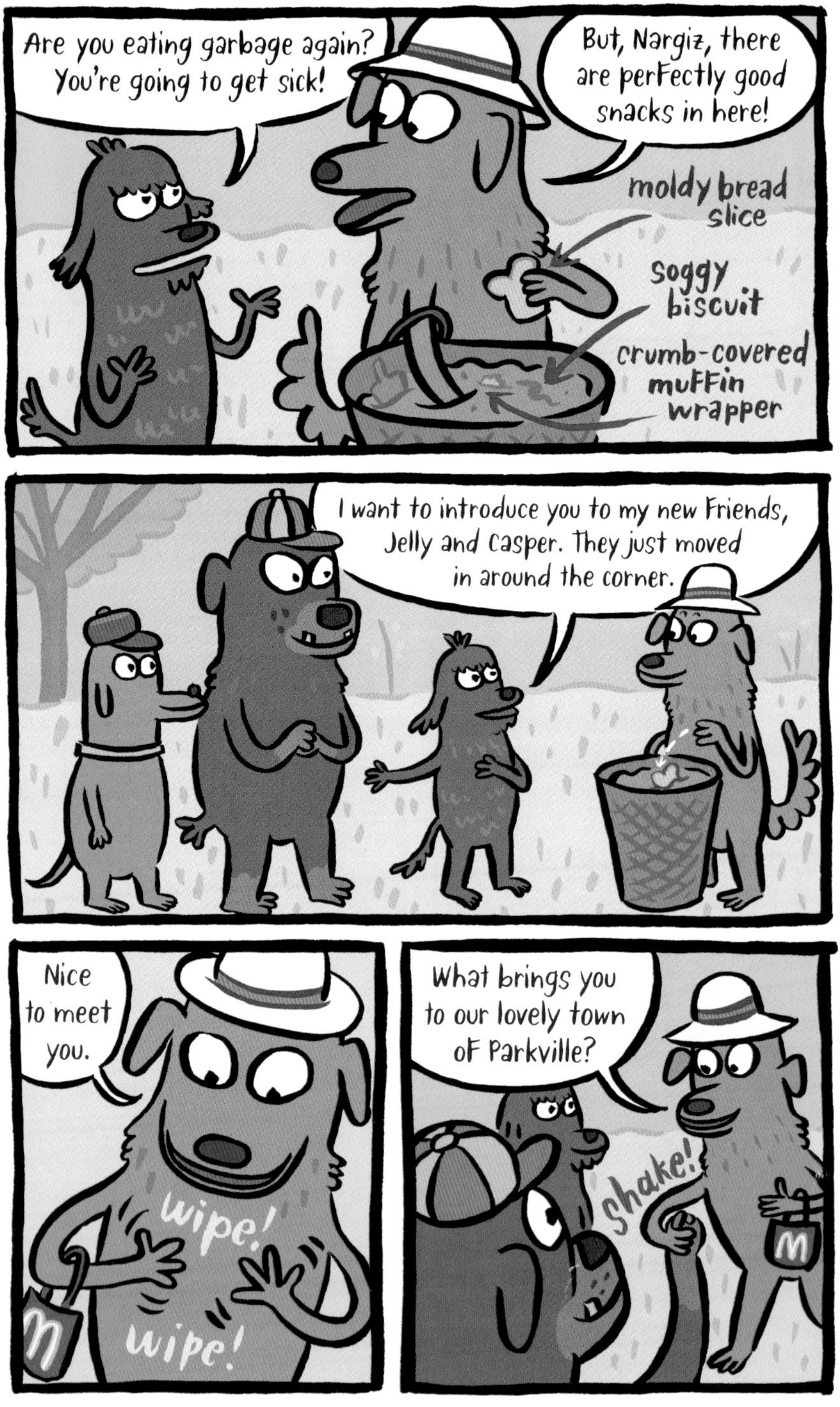
Are you eating garbage again? You're going to get sick!
But, Nargiz, there are perfectly good snacks in here!
moldy bread slice
soggy biscuit
crumb-covered muffin wrapper
I want to introduce you to my new friends, Jelly and Casper. They just moved in around the corner.
Nice to meet you.
wipe!
wipe!
What brings you to our lovely town of Parkville?
shake!

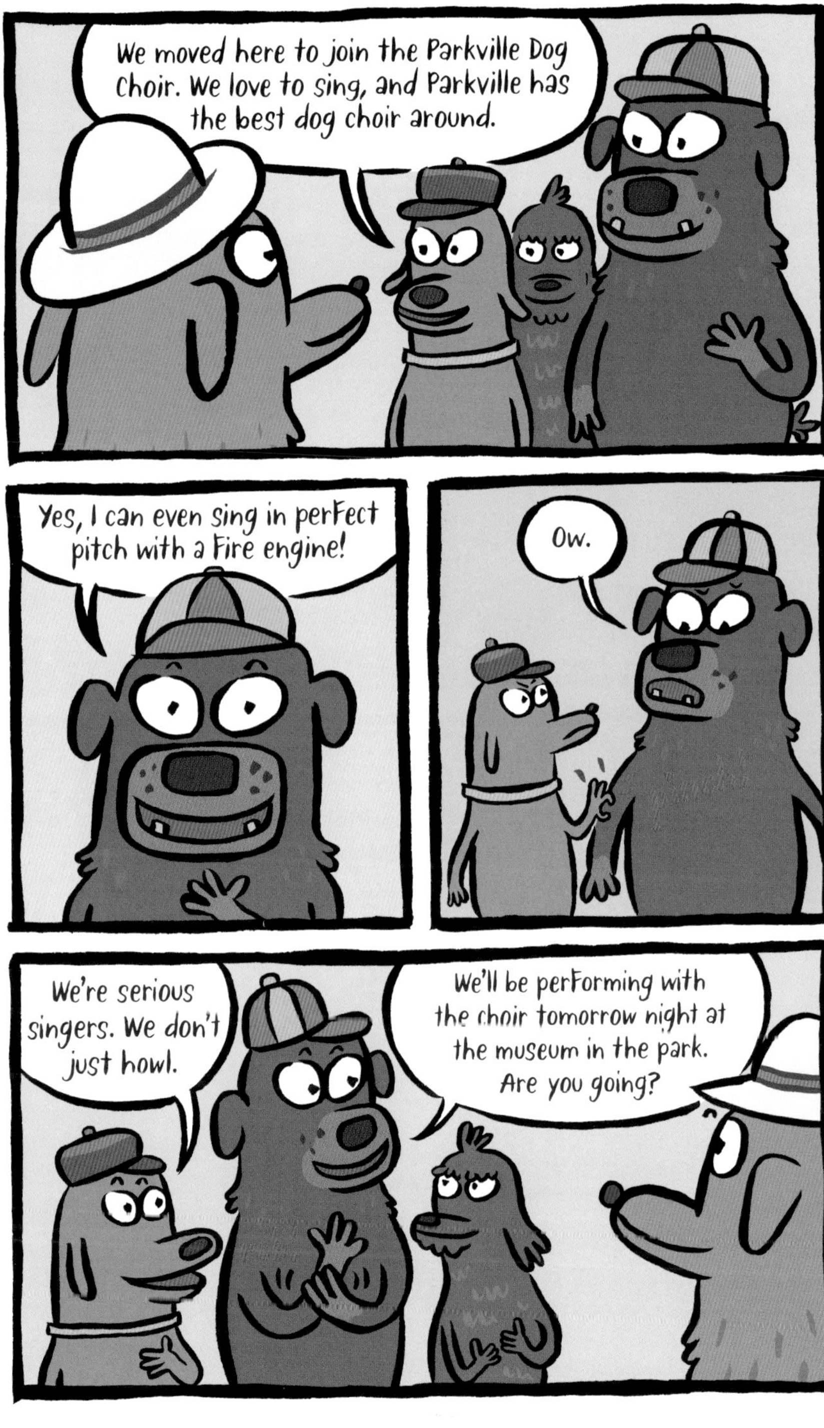
We moved here to join the Parkville Dog Choir. We love to sing, and Parkville has the best dog choir around.
Yes, I can even sing in perfect pitch with a fire engine!
Ow.
We're serious singers. We don't just howl.
We'll be performing with the choir tomorrow night at the museum in the park. Are you going?

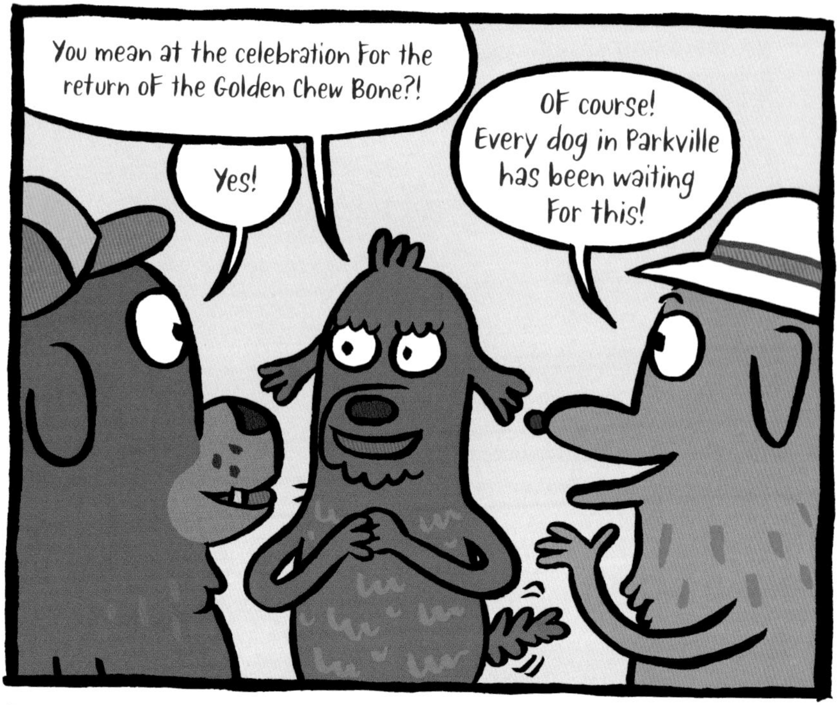
You mean at the celebration For the return oF the Golden Chew Bone?!
Yes!
OF course! Every dog in Parkville has been waiting For this!

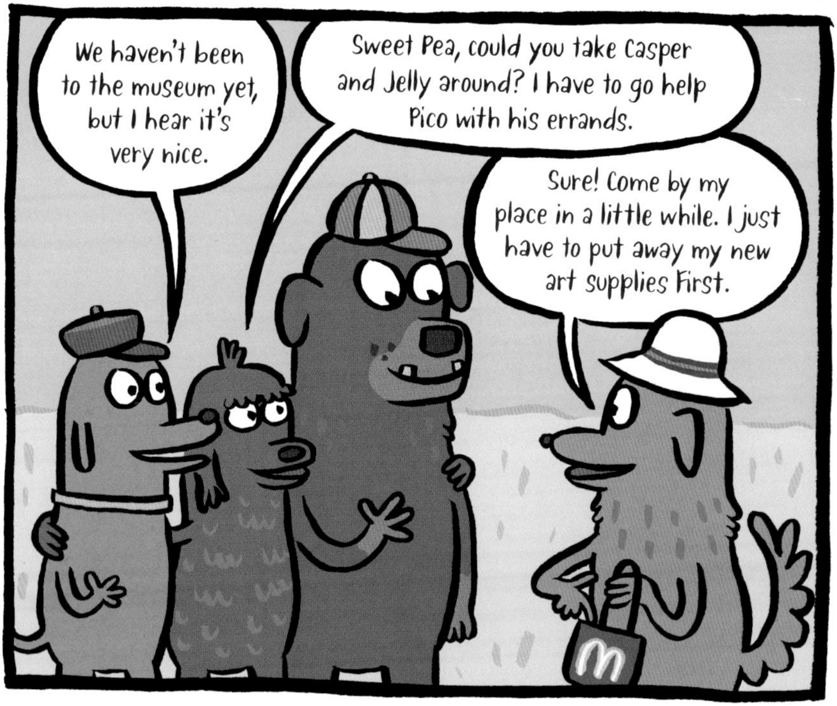
We haven't been to the museum yet, but I hear it's very nice.
Sweet Pea, could you take Casper and Jelly around? I have to go help Pico with his errands.
Sure! Come by my place in a little while. I just have to put away my new art supplies First.

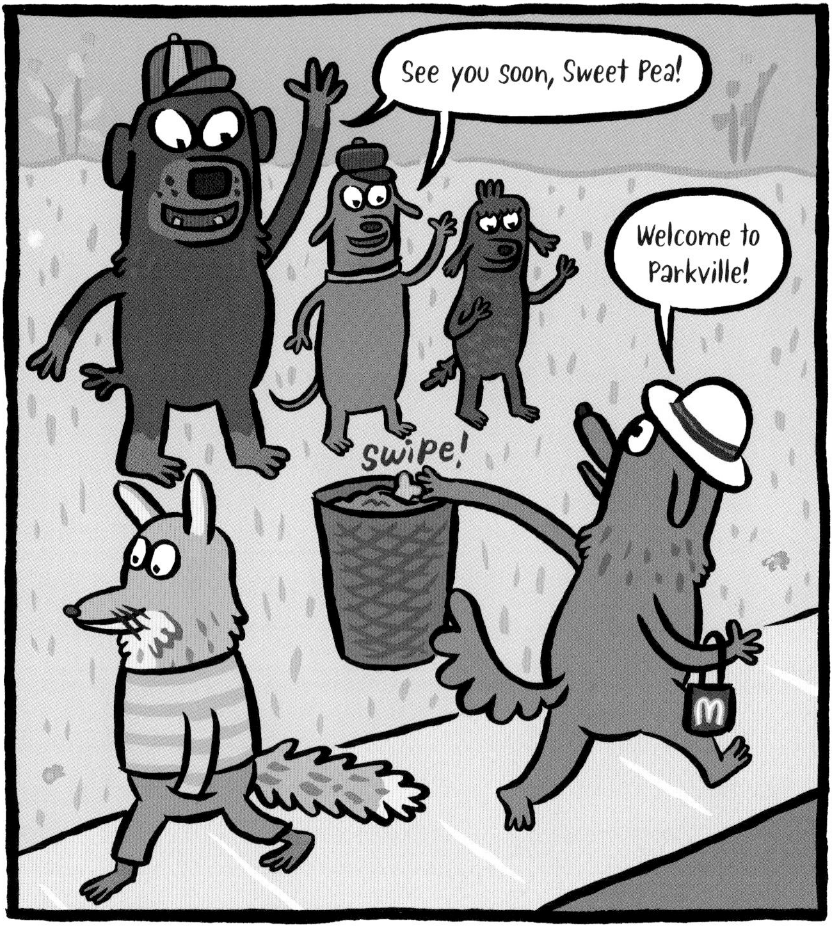
See you soon, Sweet Pea!
Welcome to Parkville!
swipe!

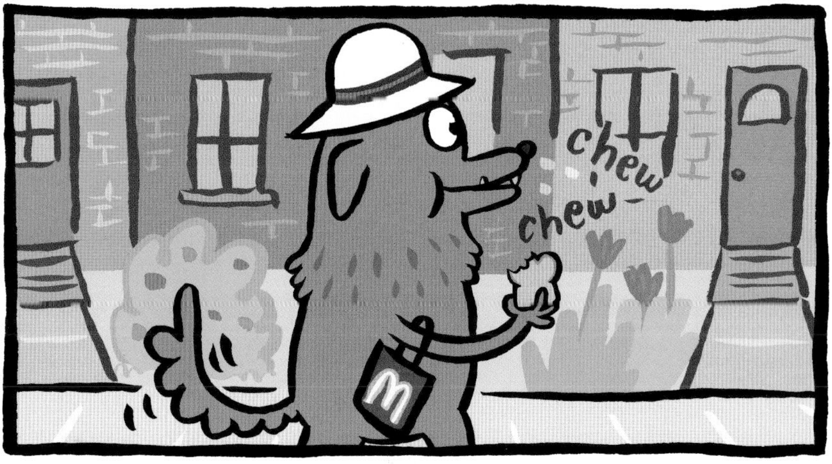
chew
chew

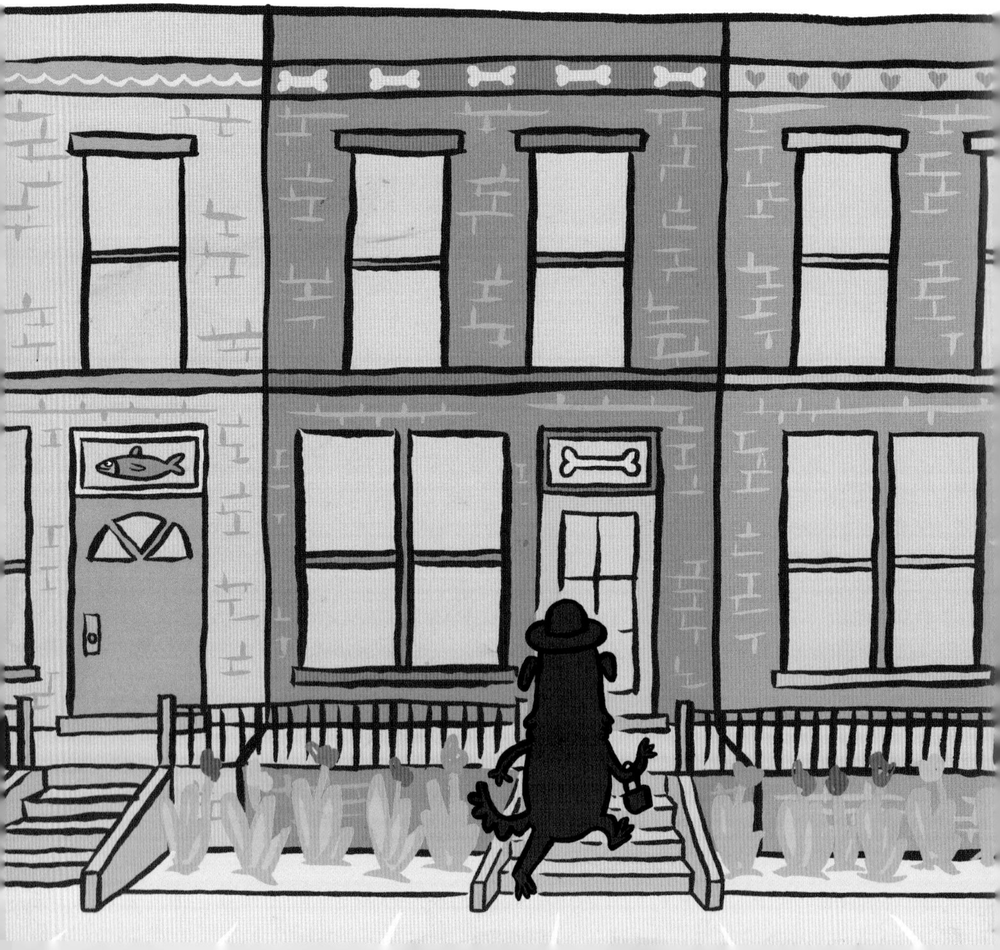

Chapter 2

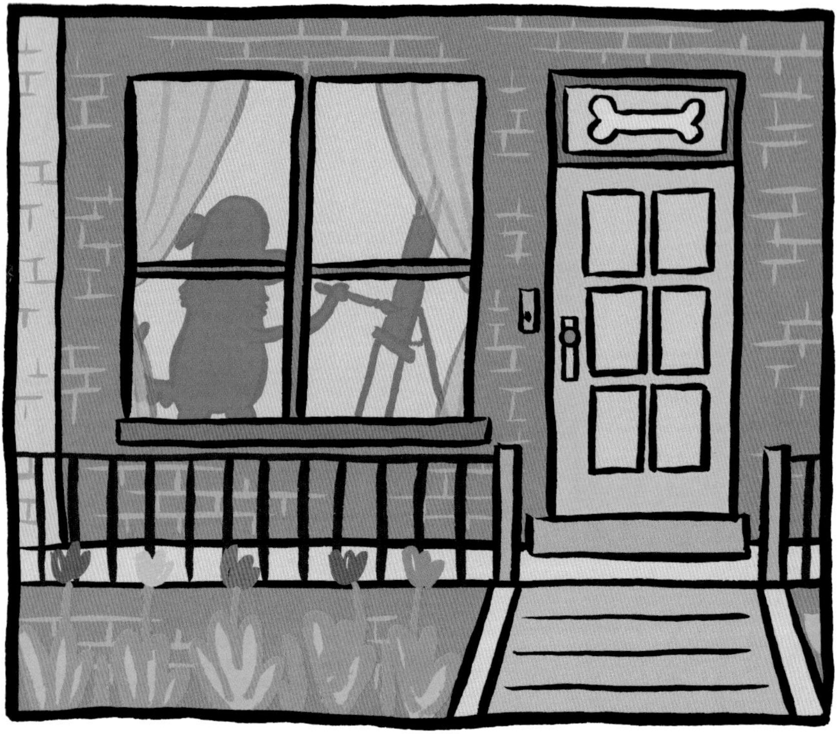

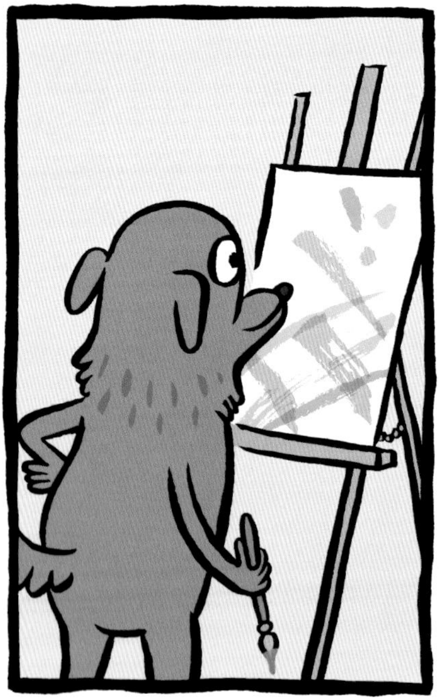

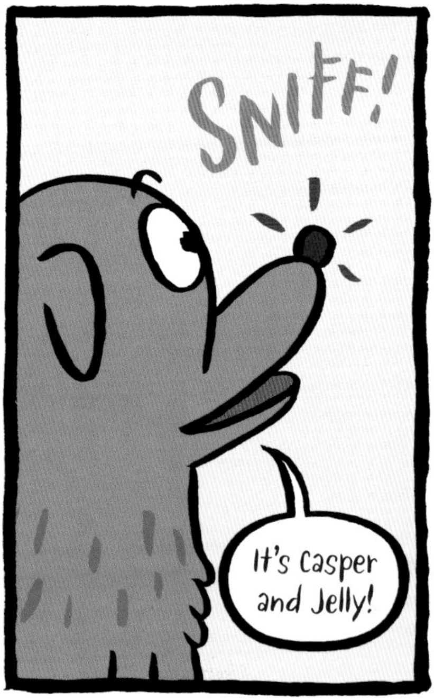
SNIFF!
It's Casper and Jelly!

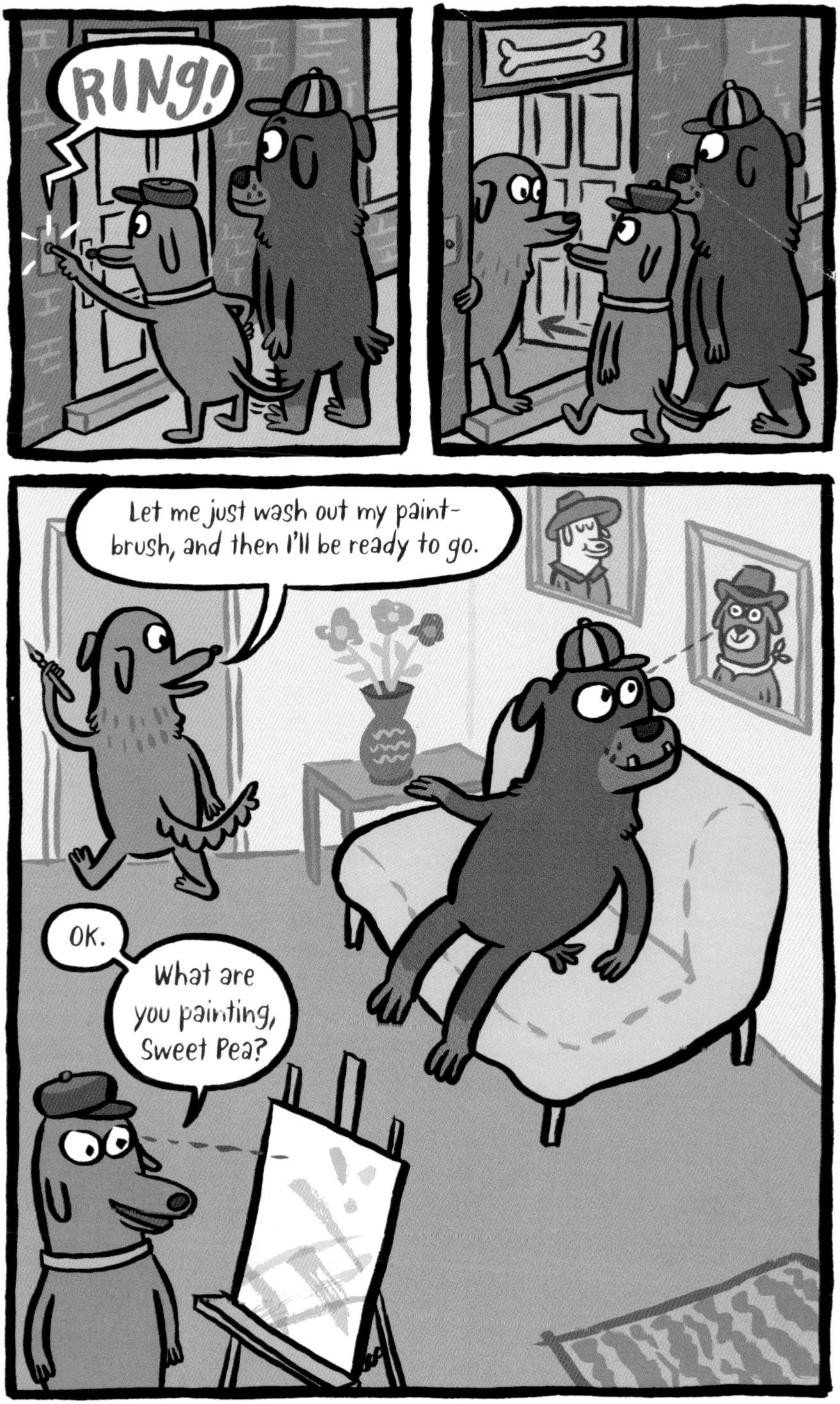
RING!
Let me just wash out my paint-brush, and then I'll be ready to go.
OK.
What are you painting, Sweet Pea?

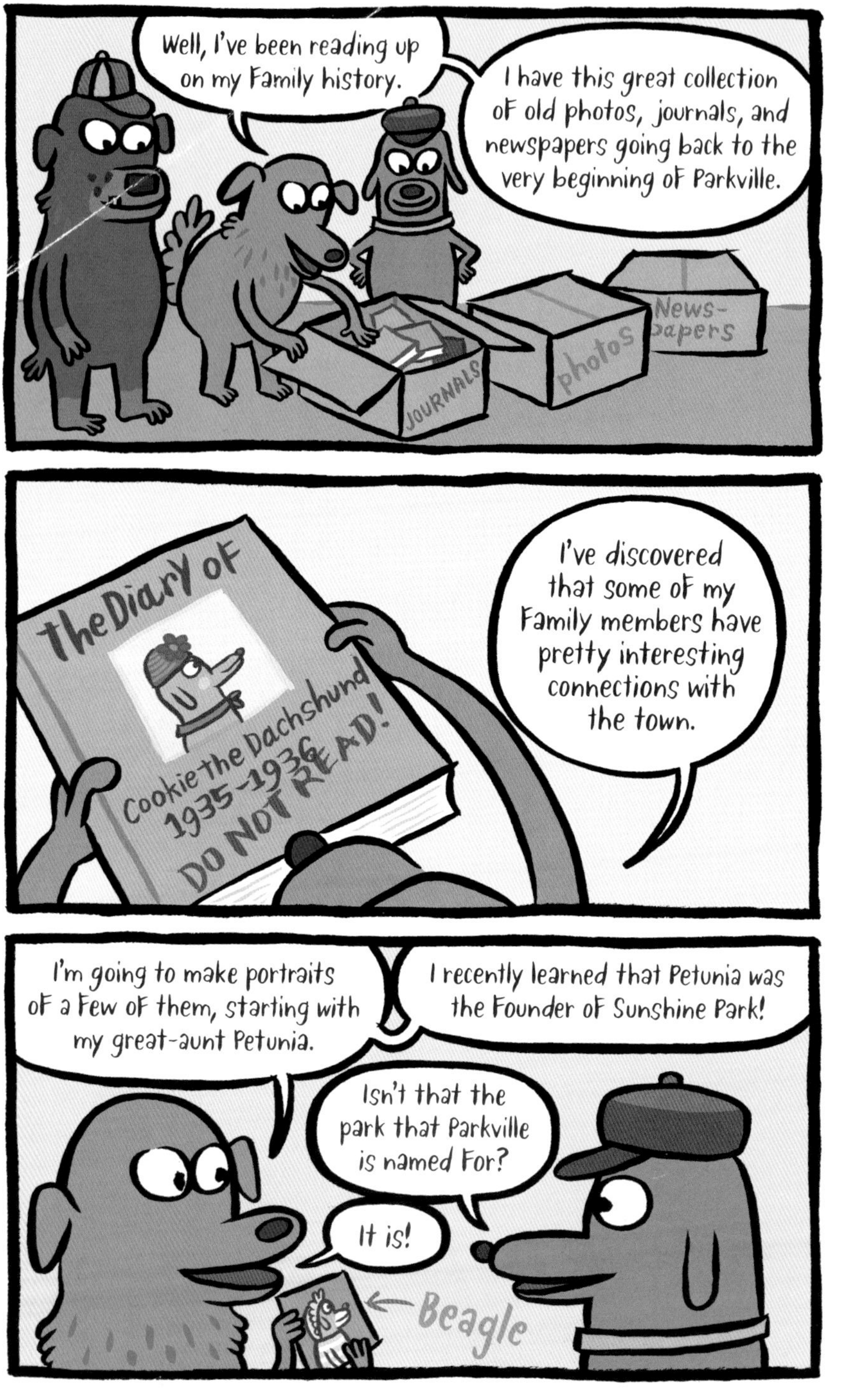
Well, I've been reading up on my Family history.
I have this great collection of old photos, journals, and newspapers going back to the very beginning of Parkville.
JOURNALS
photos
News-papers
The Diary of Cookie the Dachshund 1935-1936 DO NOT READ!
I've discovered that some of my Family members have pretty interesting connections with the town.
I'm going to make portraits of a Few of them, starting with my great-aunt Petunia.
I recently learned that Petunia was the Founder of Sunshine Park!
Isn't that the park that Parkville is named For?
It is!
Beagle

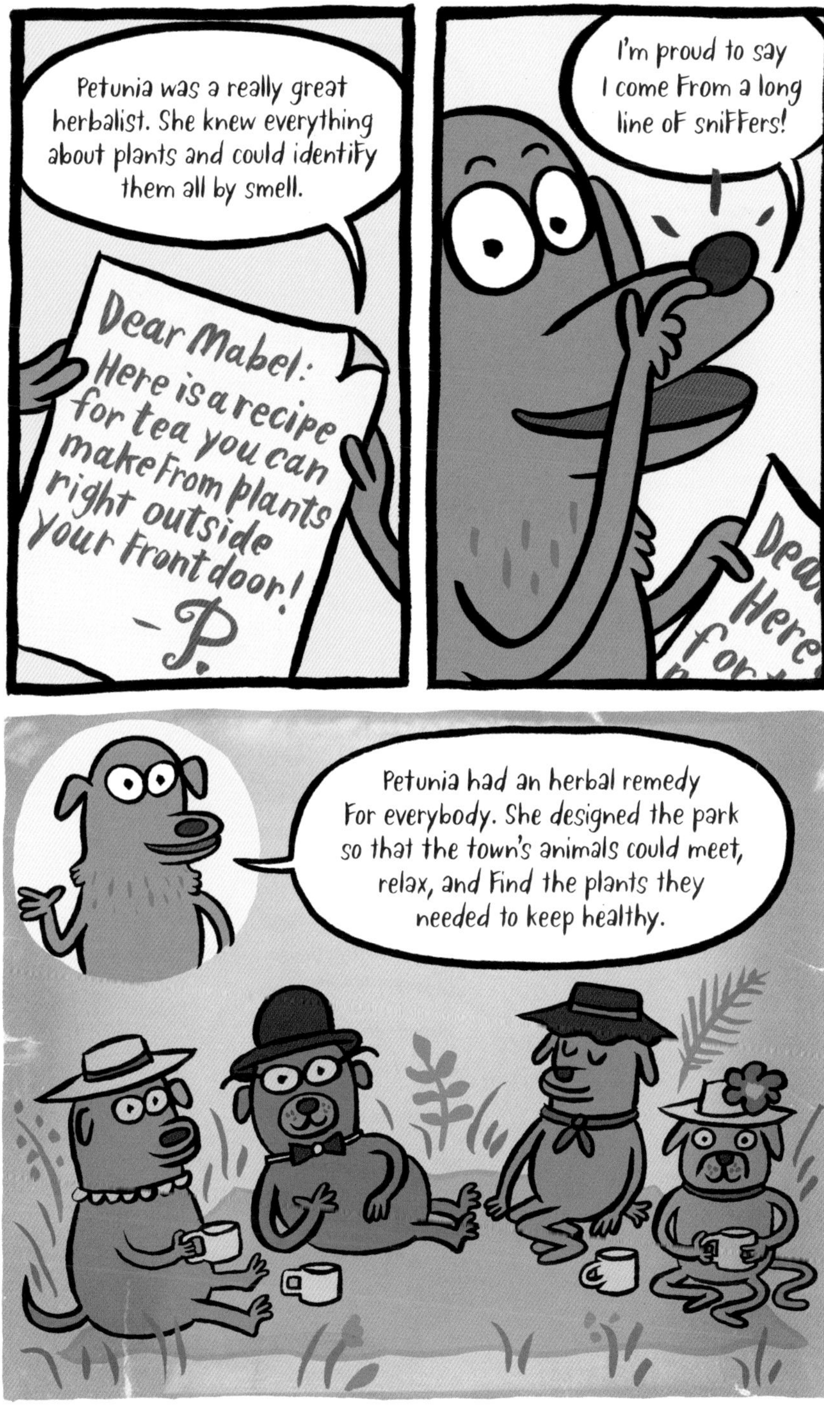
Petunia was a really great herbalist. She knew everything about plants and could identify them all by smell.
Dear Mabel: Here is a recipe for tea you can make from plants right outside your front door! -P.
I'm proud to say I come from a long line of sniffers!
Petunia had an herbal remedy for everybody. She designed the park so that the town's animals could meet, relax, and find the plants they needed to keep healthy.

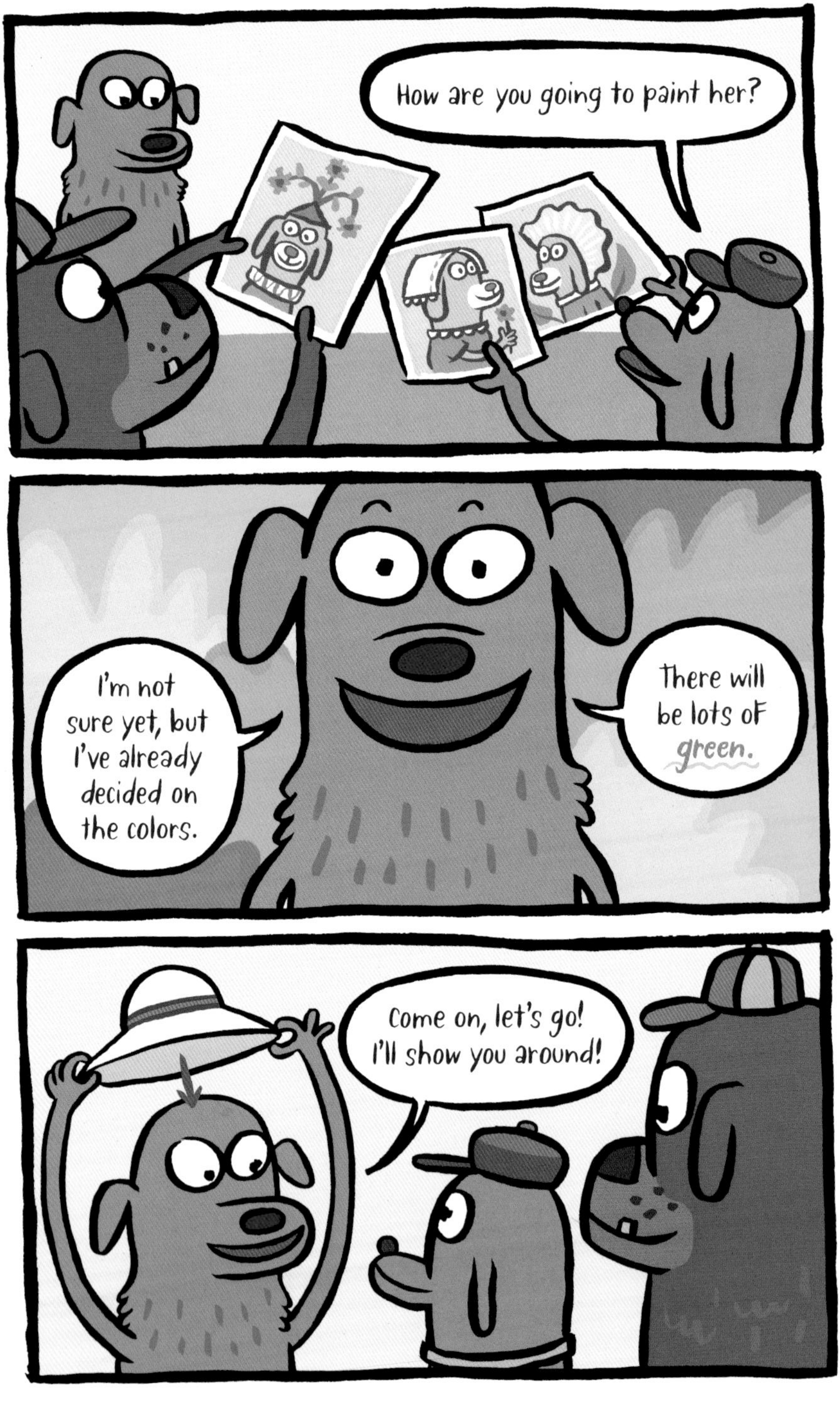
How are you going to paint her?
I'm not sure yet, but I've already decided on the colors.
There will be lots of green.
Come on, let's go! I'll show you around!

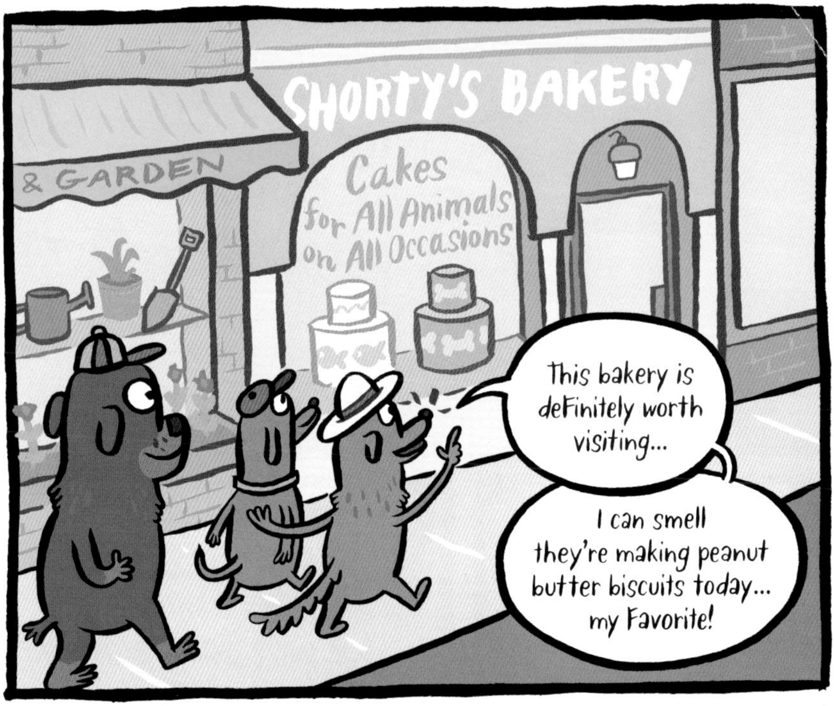
SHORTY'S BAKERY
& GARDEN
Cakes for All Animals on All Occasions
This bakery is definitely worth visiting...
I can smell they're making peanut butter biscuits today... my favorite!

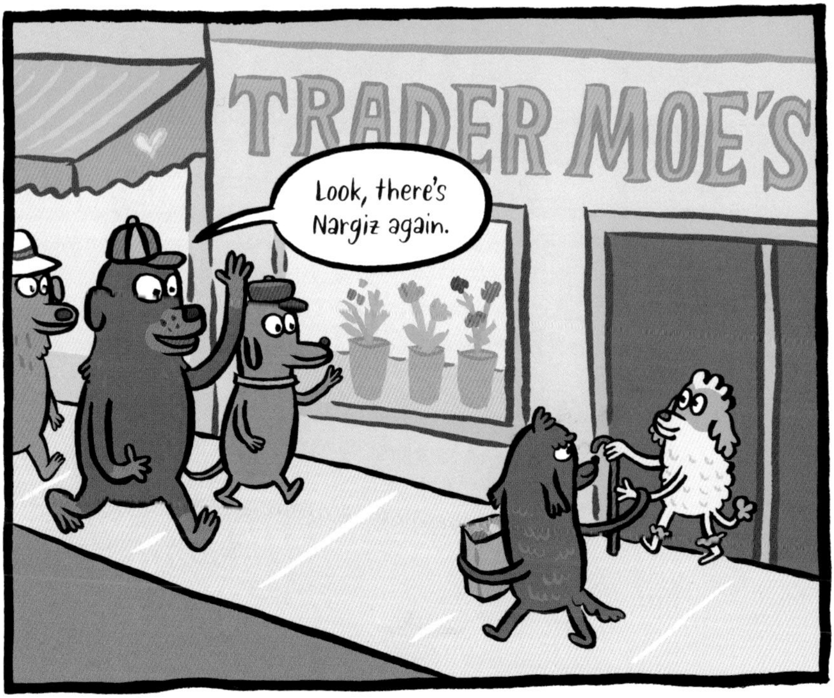
TRADER MOE'S
Look, there's Nargiz again.

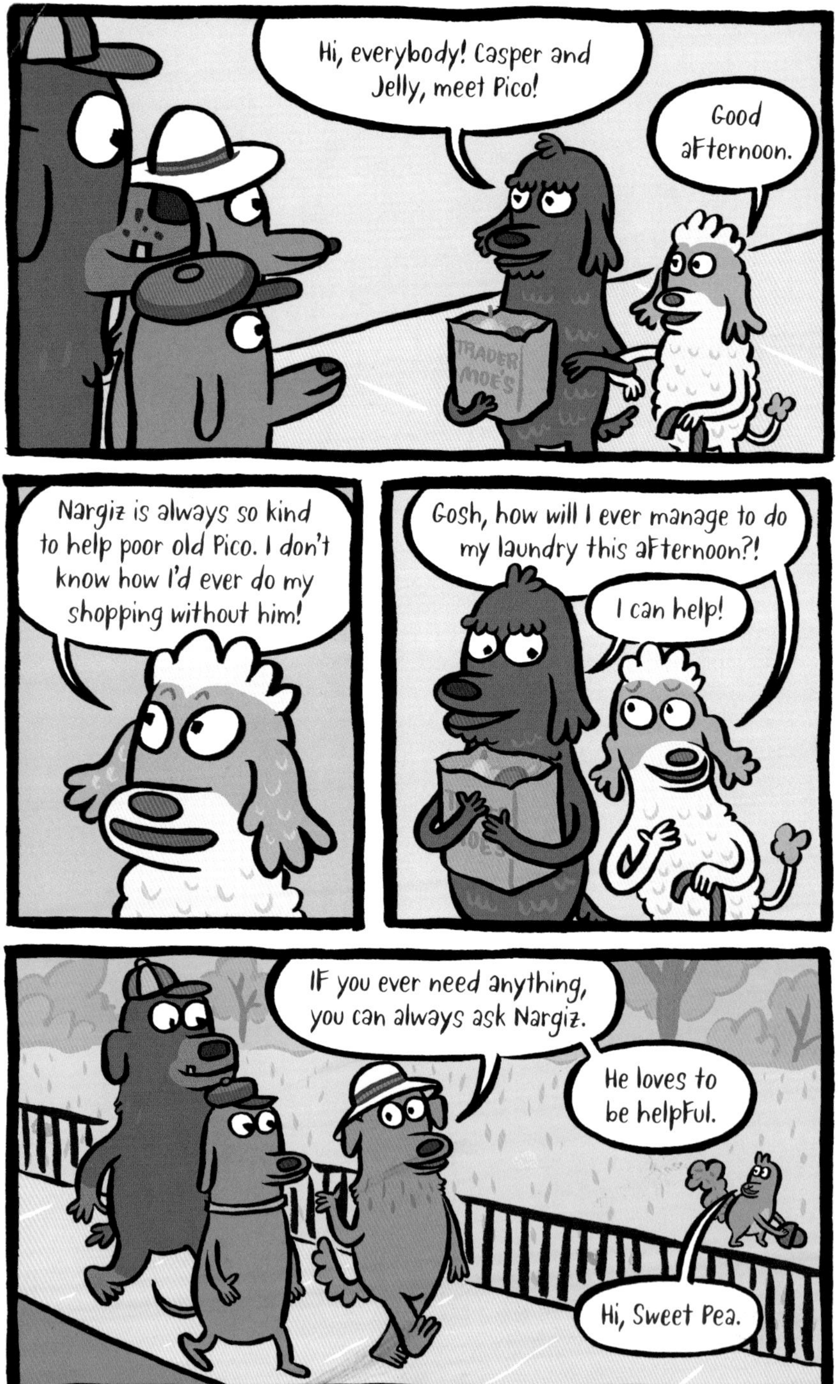

Hi, everybody! Casper and Jelly, meet Pico!
Good afternoon.
TRADER MOE'S
Nargiz is always so kind to help poor old Pico. I don't know how I'd ever do my shopping without him!
Gosh, how will I ever manage to do my laundry this afternoon?!
I can help!
If you ever need anything, you can always ask Nargiz.
He loves to be helpful.
Hi, Sweet Pea.

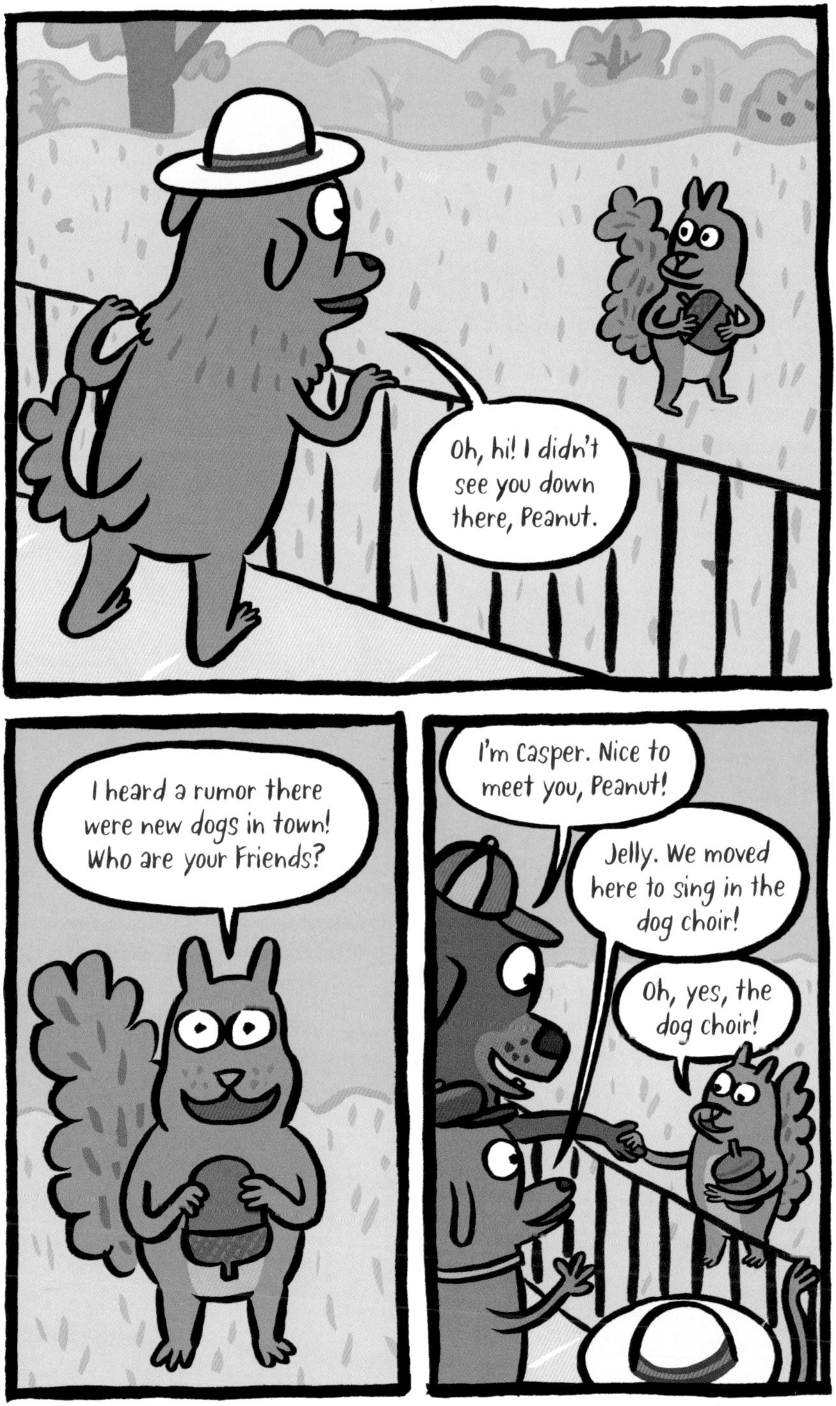

Oh, hi! I didn't see you down there, Peanut.
I heard a rumor there were new dogs in town! Who are your friends?
I'm Casper. Nice to meet you, Peanut!
Jelly. We moved here to sing in the dog choir!
Oh, yes, the dog choir!

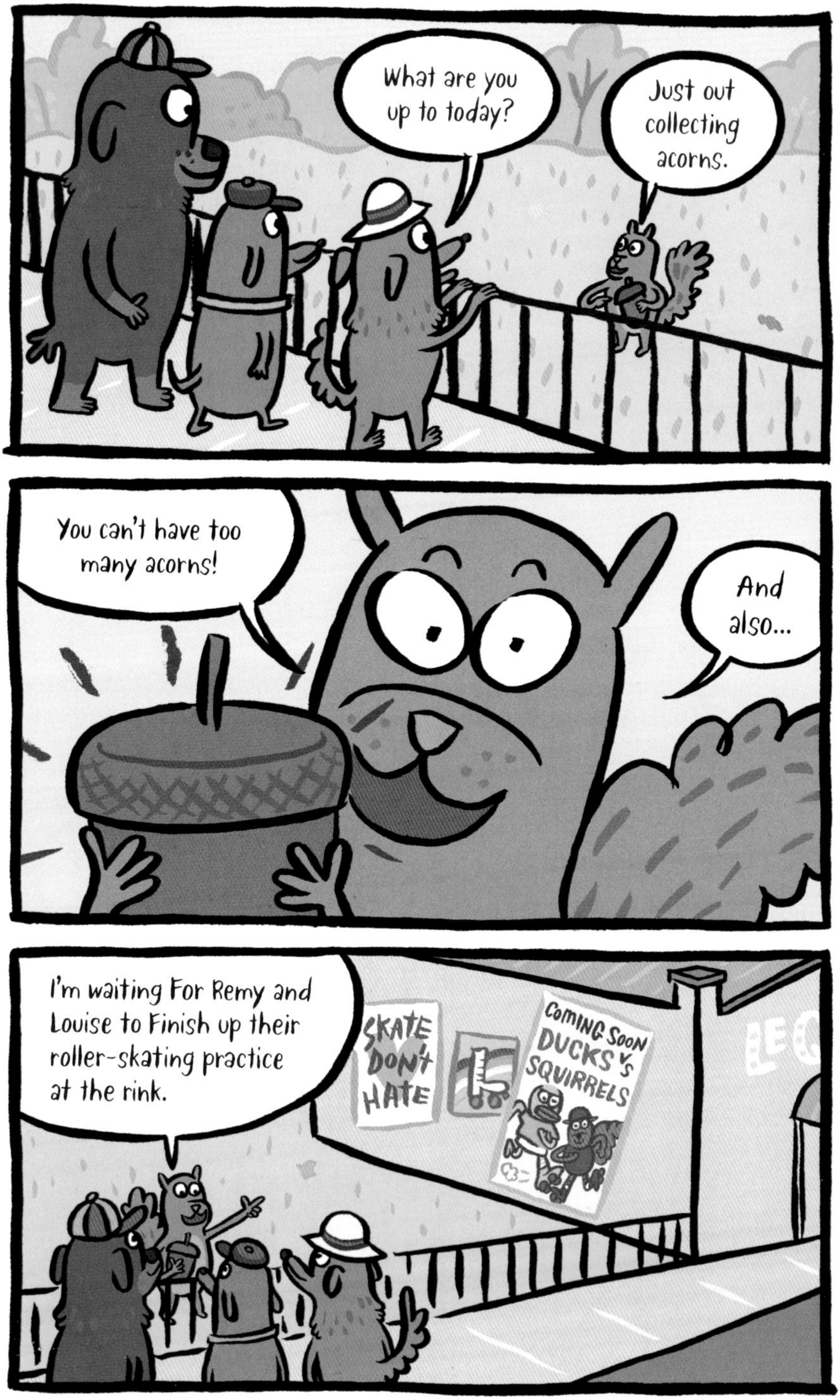
What are you up to today?
Just out collecting acorns.
You can't have too many acorns!
And also...
I'm waiting For Remy and Louise to Finish up their roller-skating practice at the rink.
SKATE, DON'T HATE
COMING SOON DUCKS VS SQUIRRELS

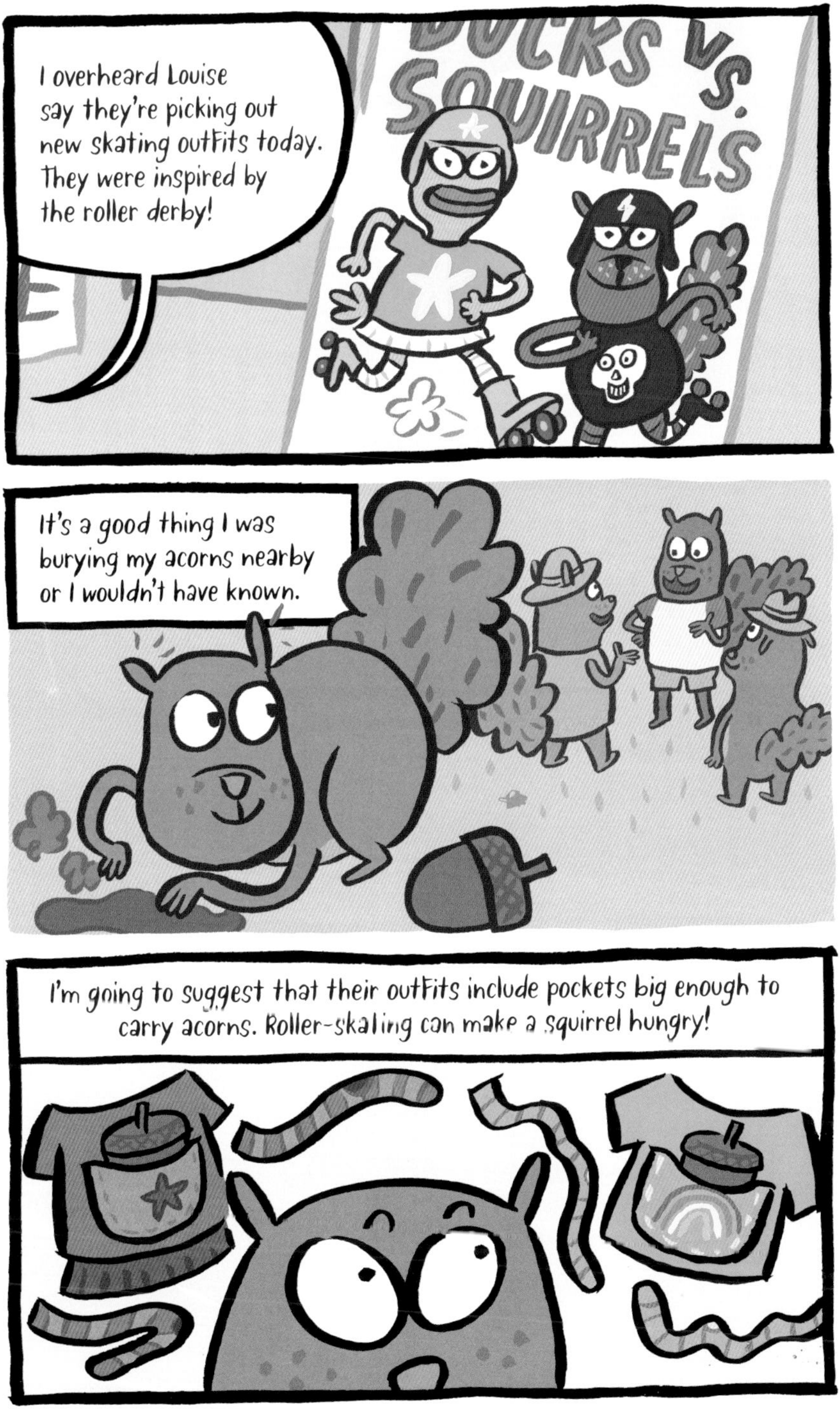
I overheard Louise say they're picking out new skating outfits today. They were inspired by the roller derby!
DUCKS VS. SQUIRRELS
It's a good thing I was burying my acorns nearby or I wouldn't have known.
I'm going to suggest that their outfits include pockets big enough to carry acorns. Roller-skating can make a squirrel hungry!

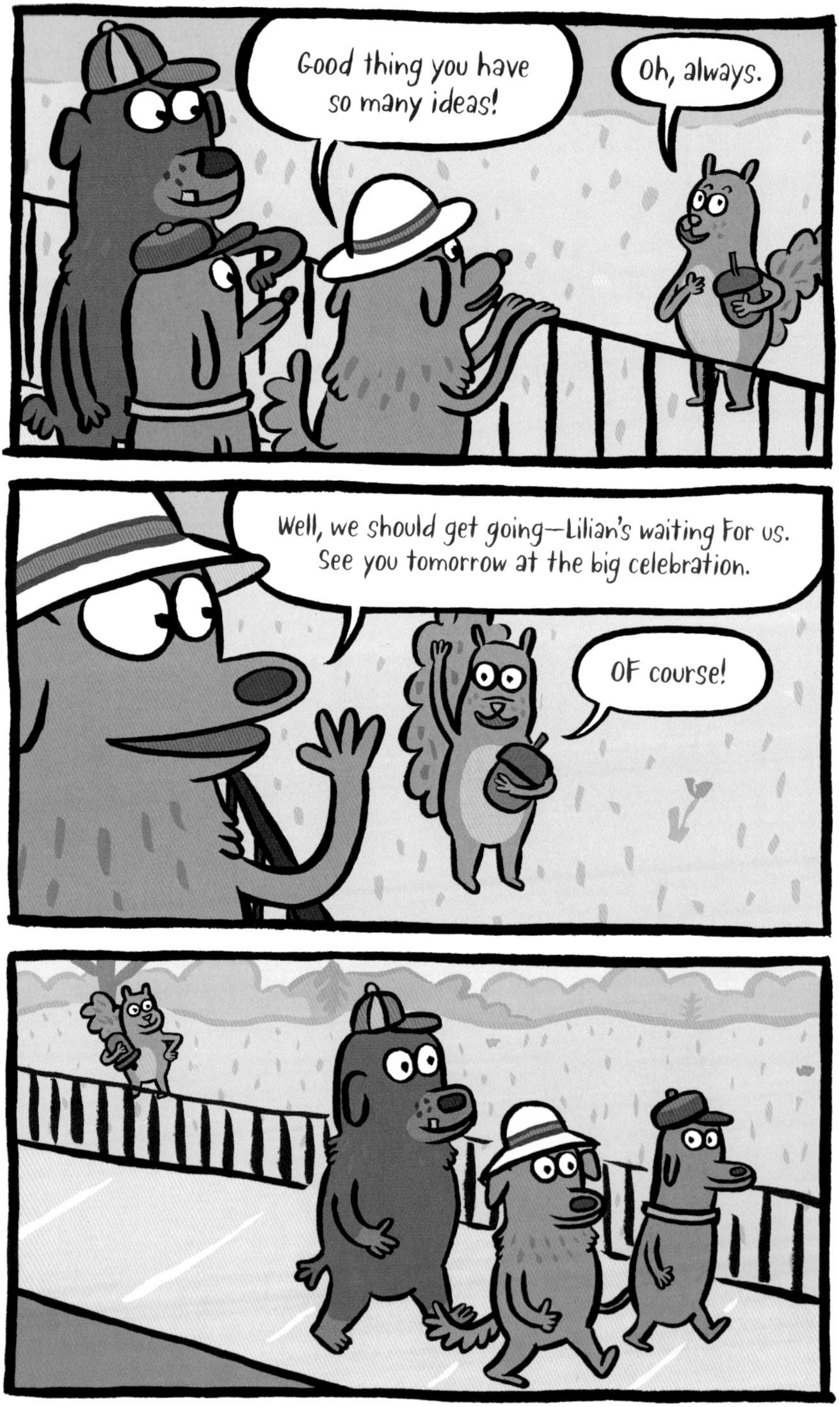
Good thing you have so many ideas!
Oh, always.
Well, we should get going—Lilian's waiting for us. See you tomorrow at the big celebration.
Of course!

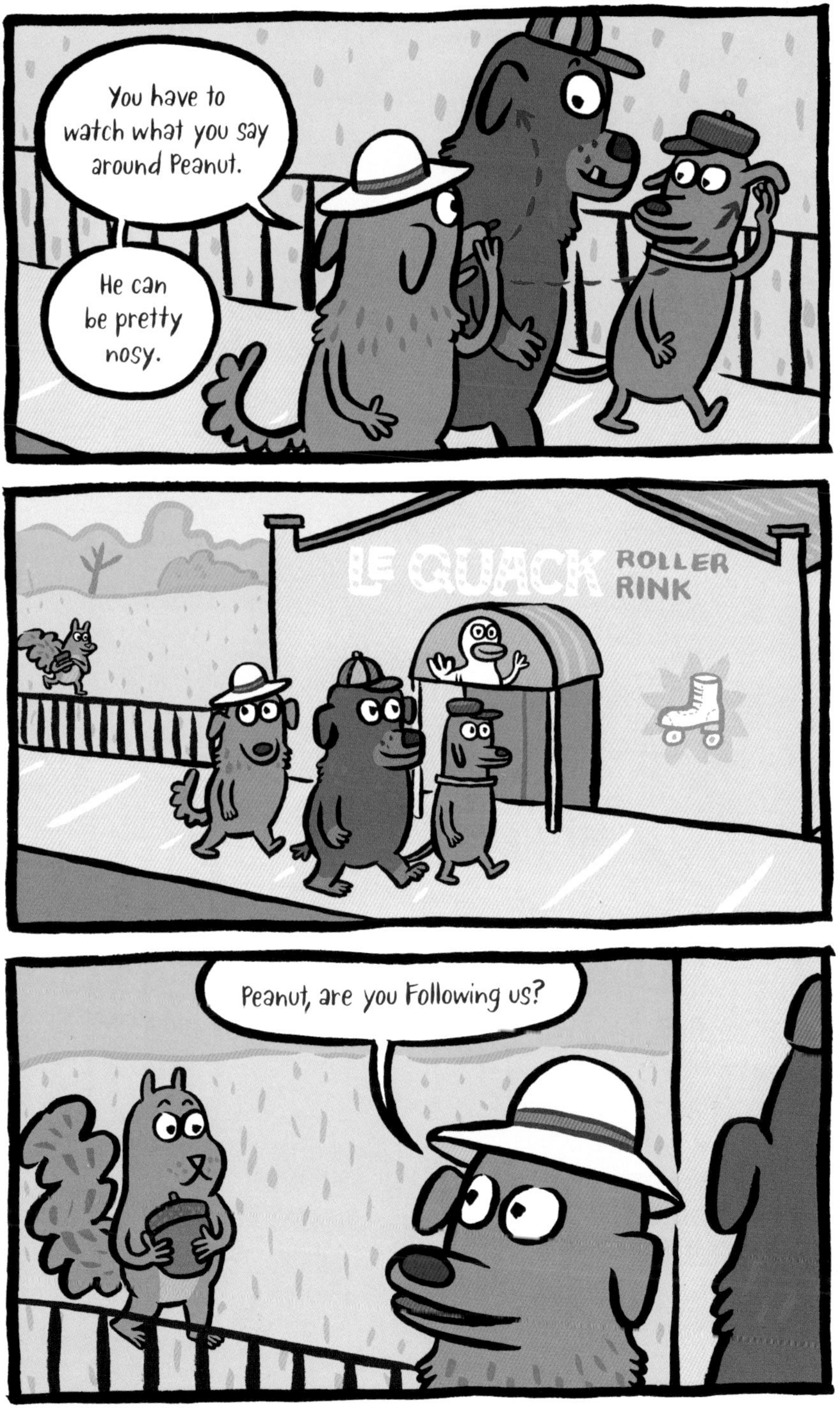
You have to watch what you say around Peanut.
He can be pretty nosy.
LE QUACK ROLLER RINK
Peanut, are you following us?

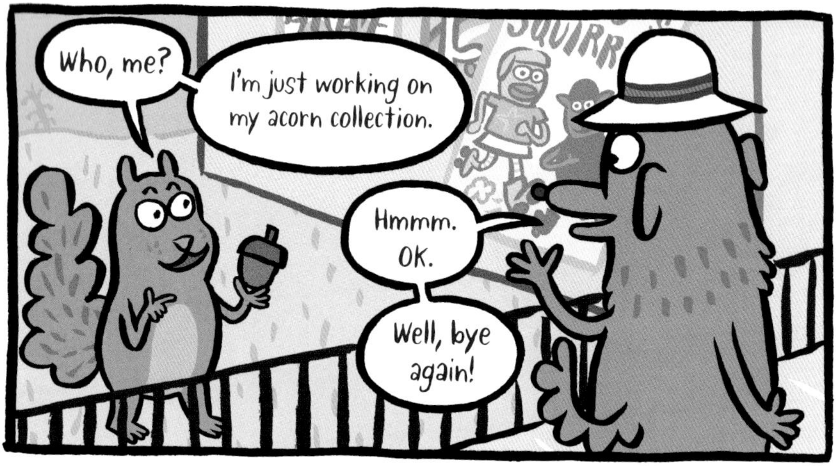
Who, me?
I'm just working on my acorn collection.
Hmmm. OK.
Well, bye again!

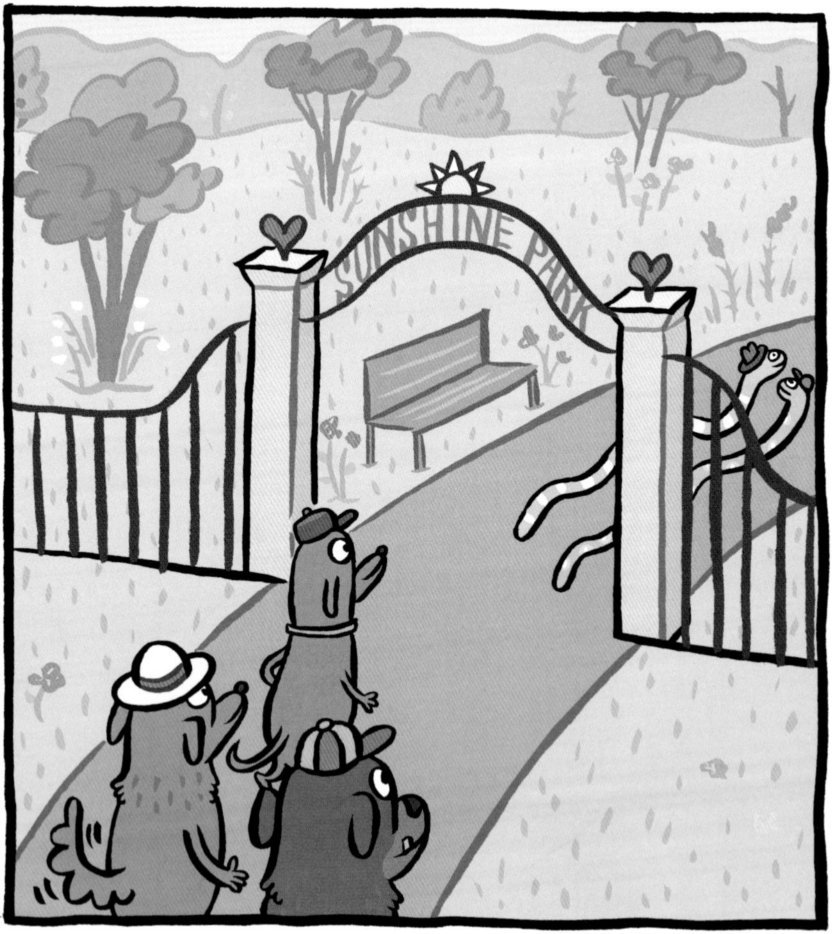
SUNSHINE PARK

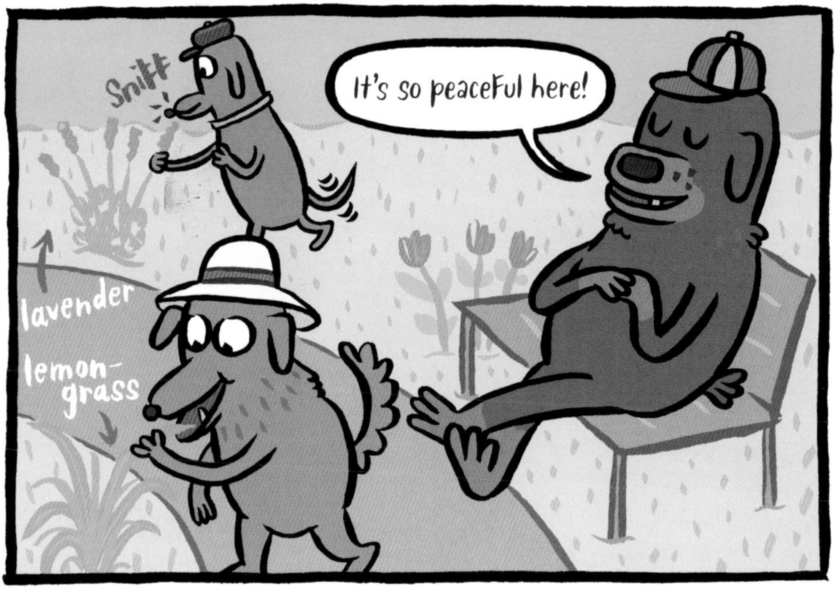
Sniff
It's so peaceful here!
lavender
lemon-grass

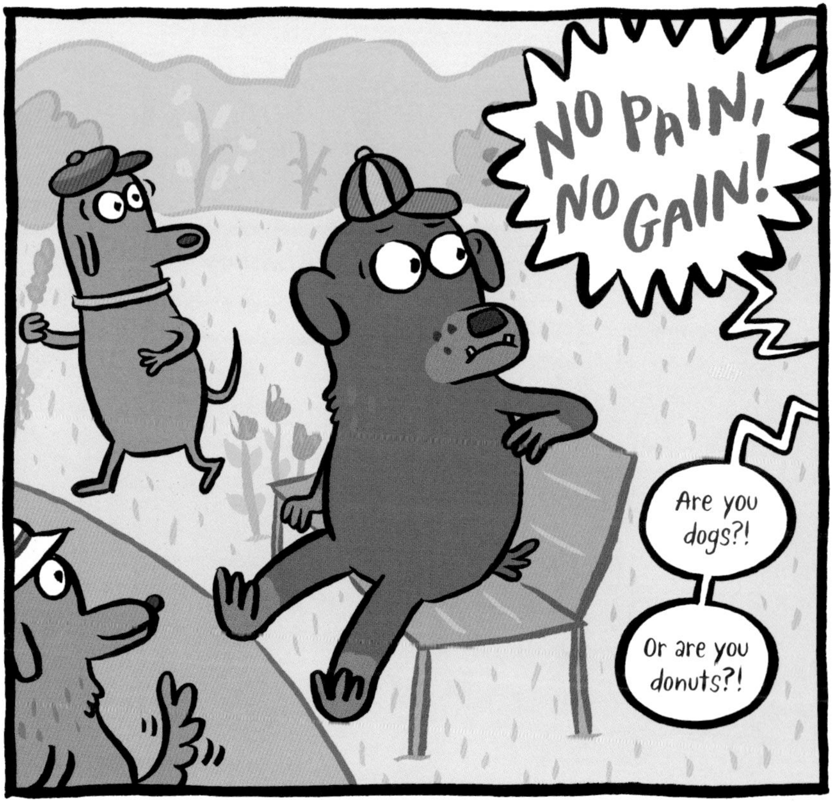
NO PAIN, NO GAIN!
Are you dogs?!
Or are you donuts?!

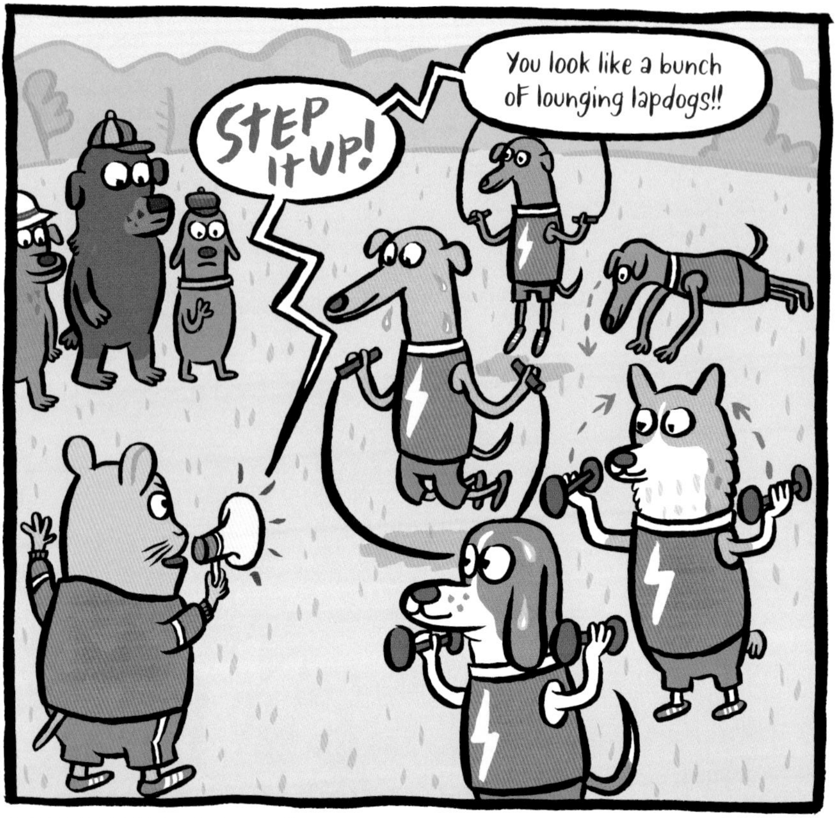
STEP IT UP!
You look like a bunch of lounging lapdogs!!

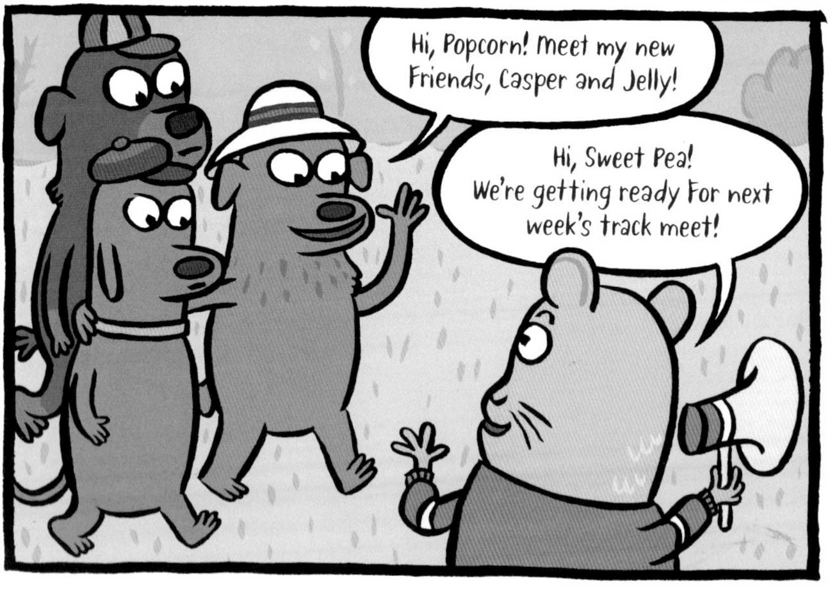
Hi, Popcorn! Meet my new Friends, Casper and Jelly!
Hi, Sweet Pea! We're getting ready For next week's track meet!

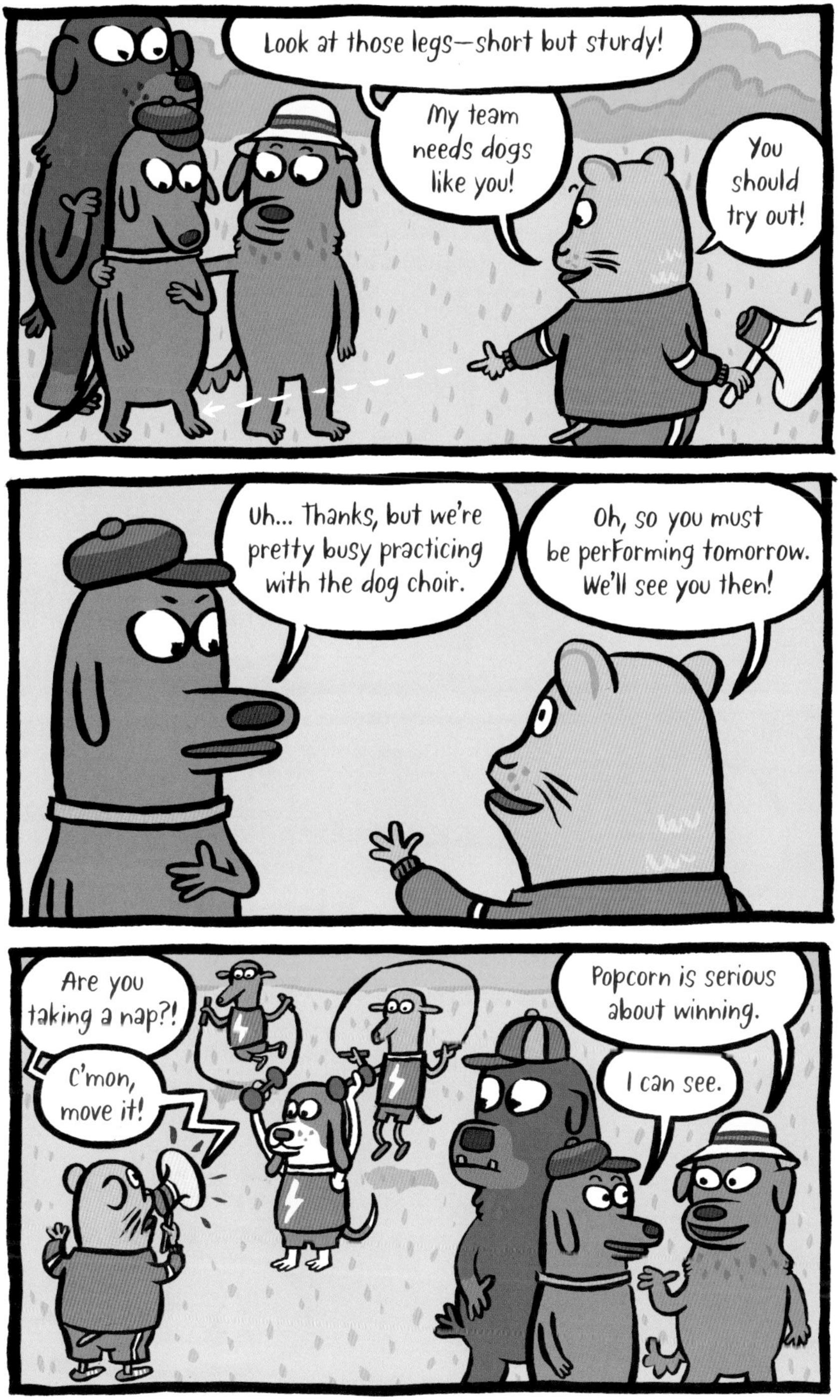
Look at those legs—short but sturdy!
My team needs dogs like you!
You should try out!
Uh... Thanks, but we're pretty busy practicing with the dog choir.
Oh, so you must be performing tomorrow. We'll see you then!
Are you taking a nap?!
C'mon, move it!
Popcorn is serious about winning.
I can see.

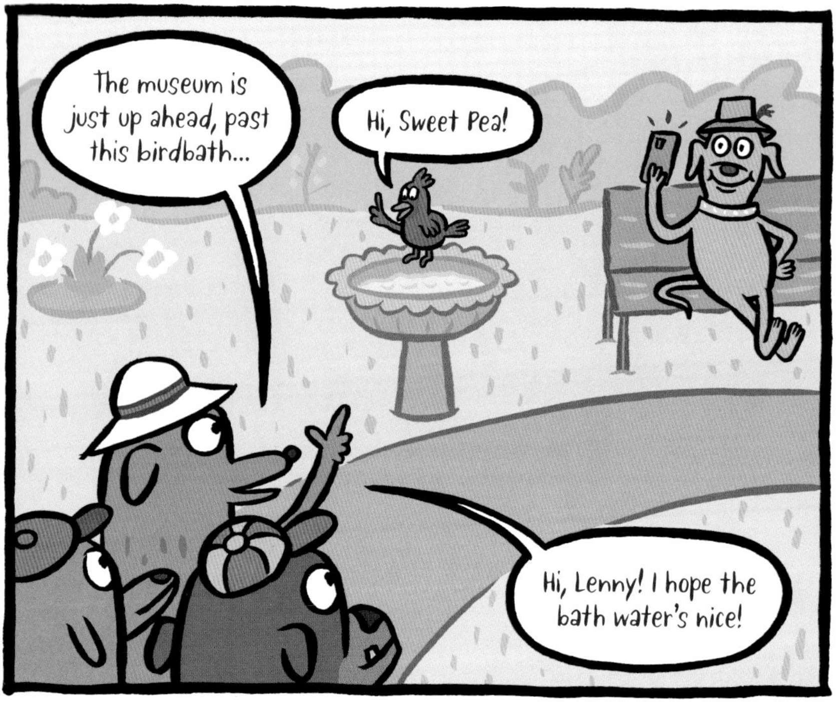
The museum is just up ahead, past this birdbath...
Hi, Sweet Pea!
Hi, Lenny! I hope the bath water's nice!

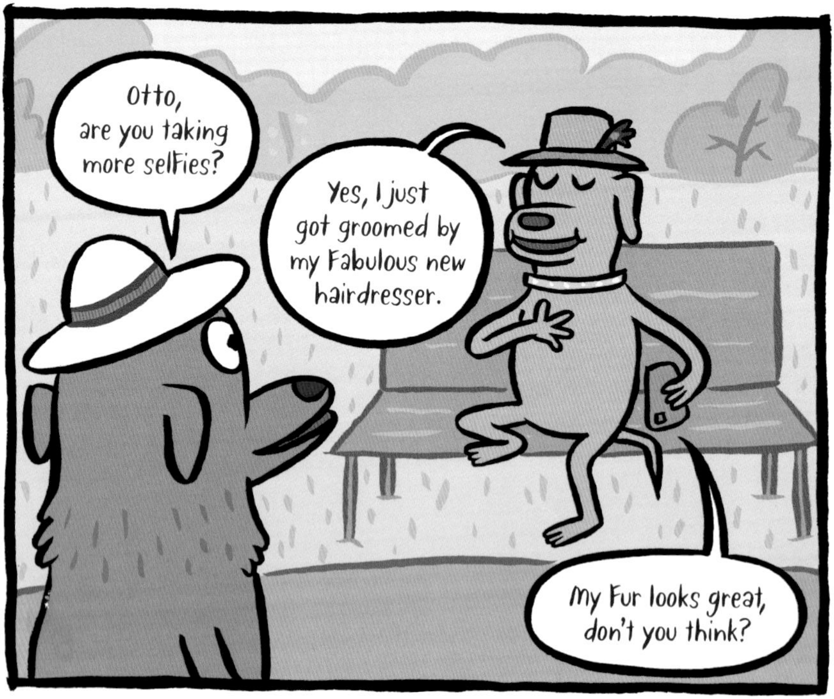
Otto, are you taking more selfies?
Yes, I just got groomed by my fabulous new hairdresser.
My fur looks great, don't you think?

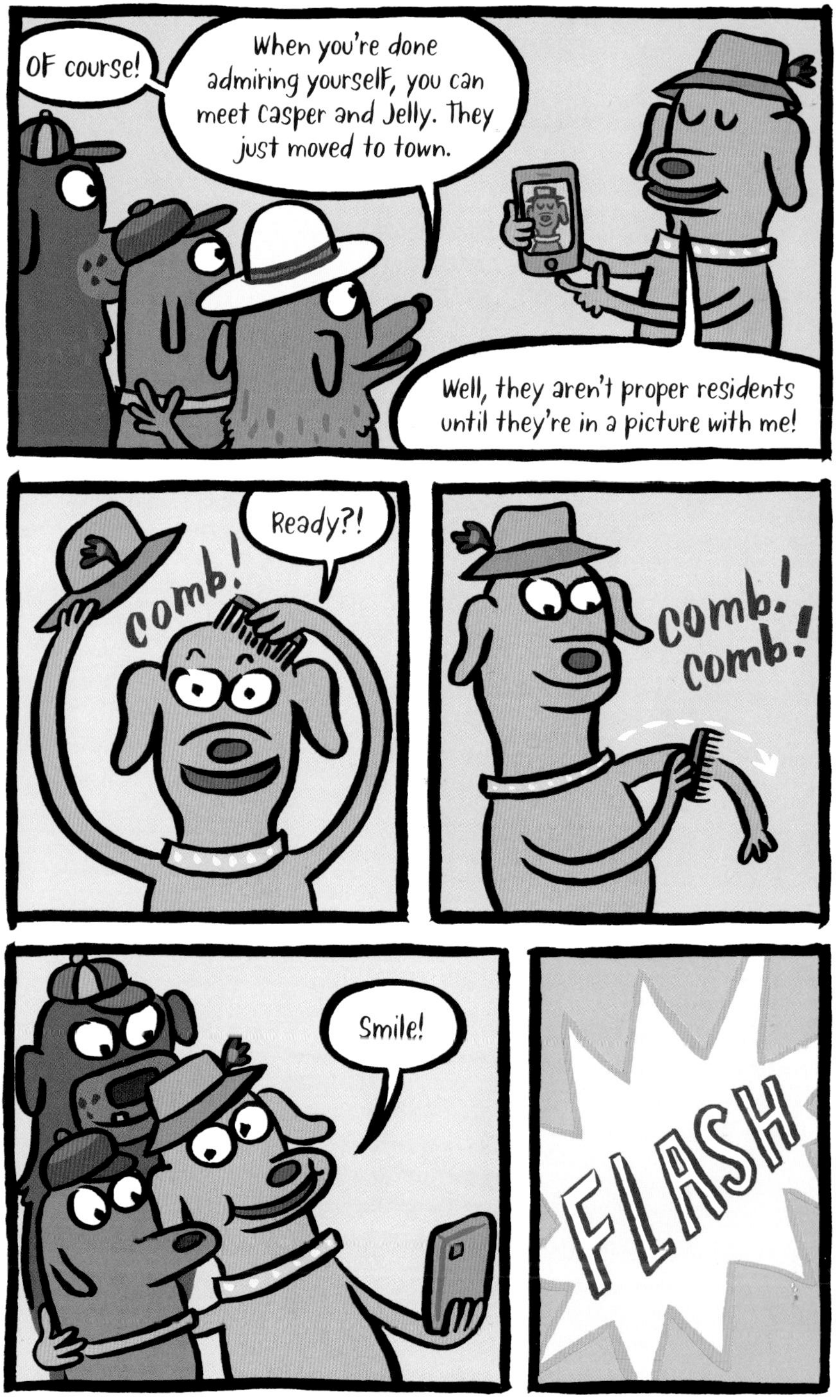
OF course!
When you're done admiring yourself, you can meet Casper and Jelly. They just moved to town.
Well, they aren't proper residents until they're in a picture with me!
Ready?!
comb!
comb!
comb!
Smile!
FLASH

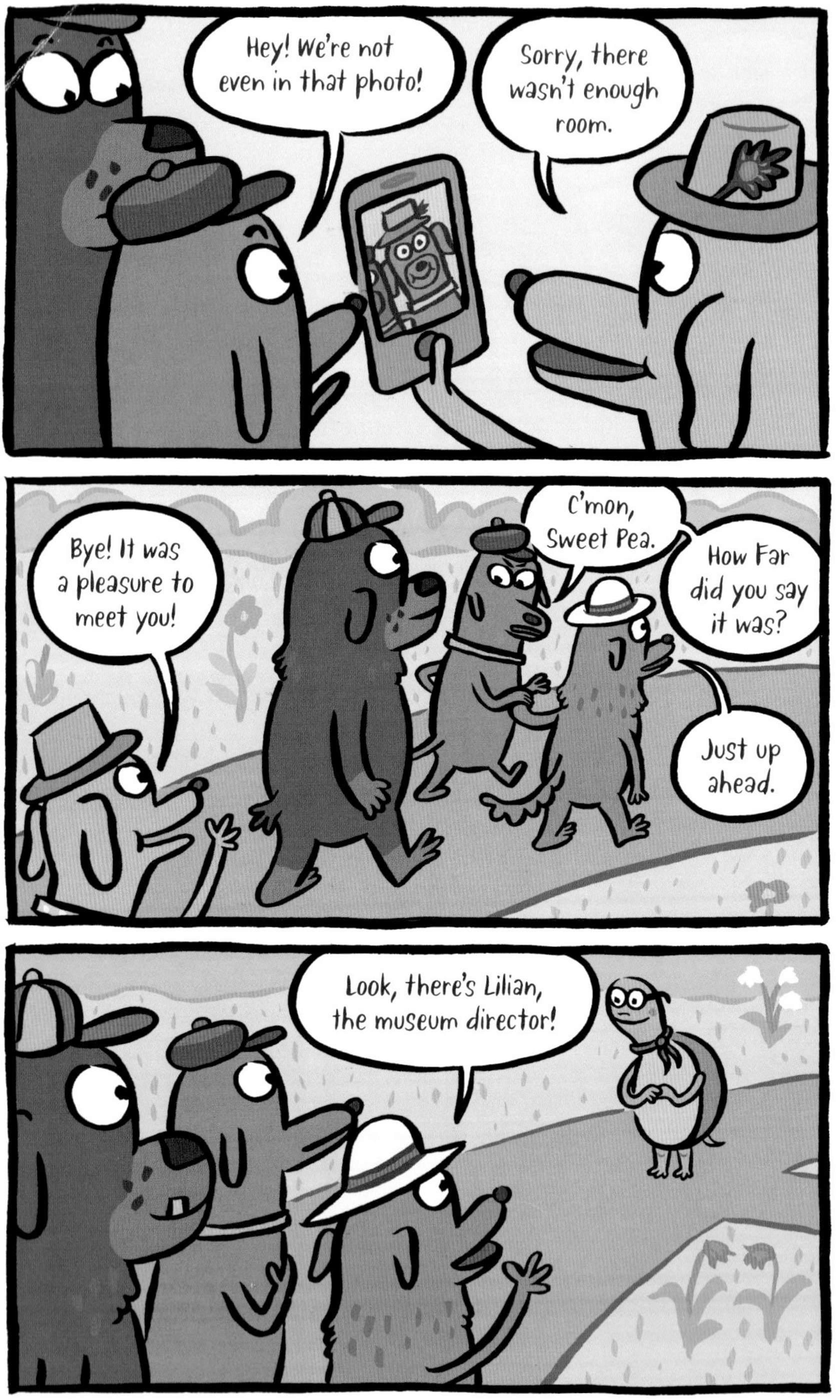
Hey! We're not even in that photo!
Sorry, there wasn't enough room.
Bye! It was a pleasure to meet you!
C'mon, Sweet Pea.
How Far did you say it was?
Just up ahead.
Look, there's Lilian, the museum director!

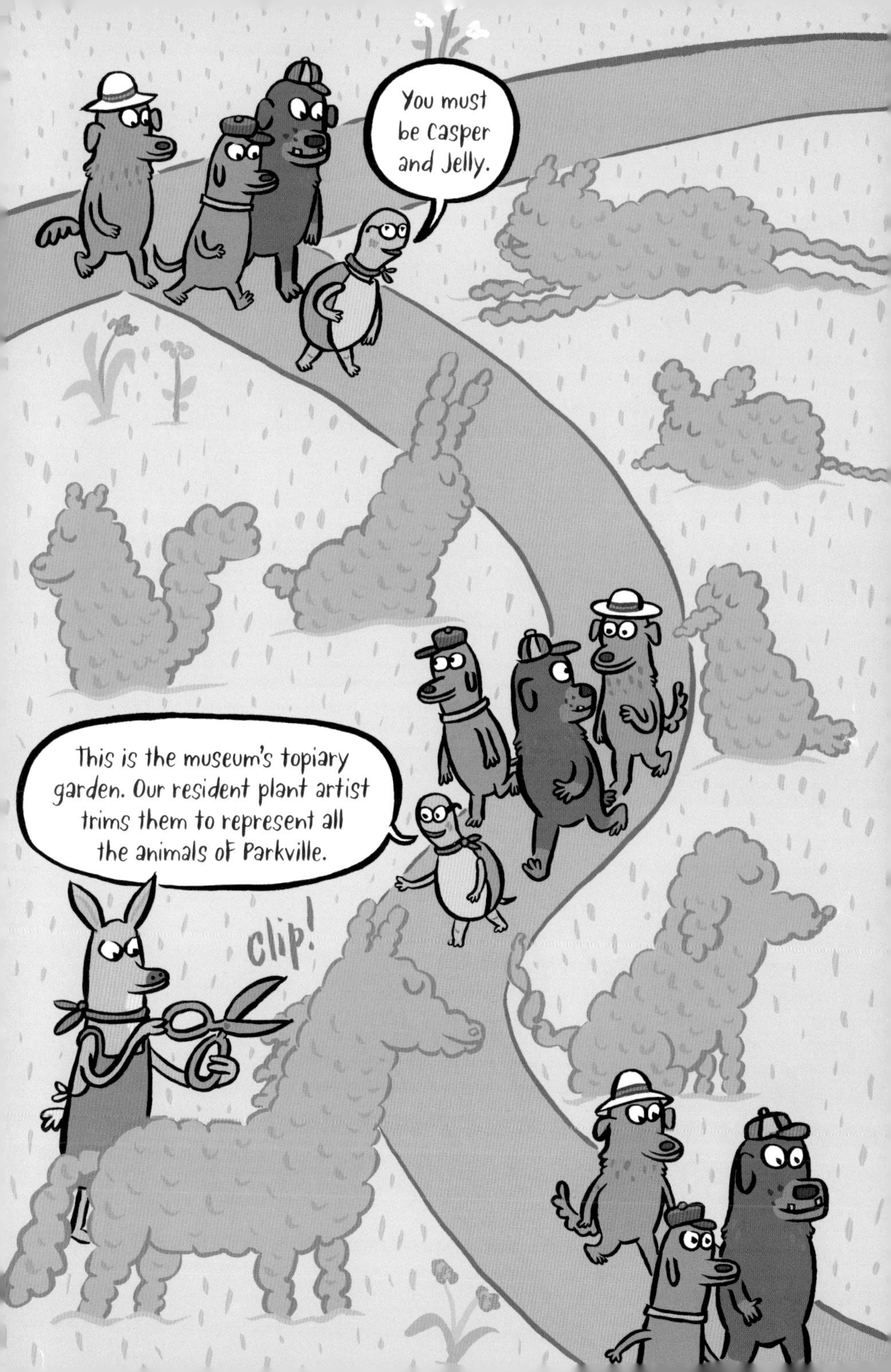
You must be Casper and Jelly.
This is the museum's topiary garden. Our resident plant artist trims them to represent all the animals of Parkville.
clip!

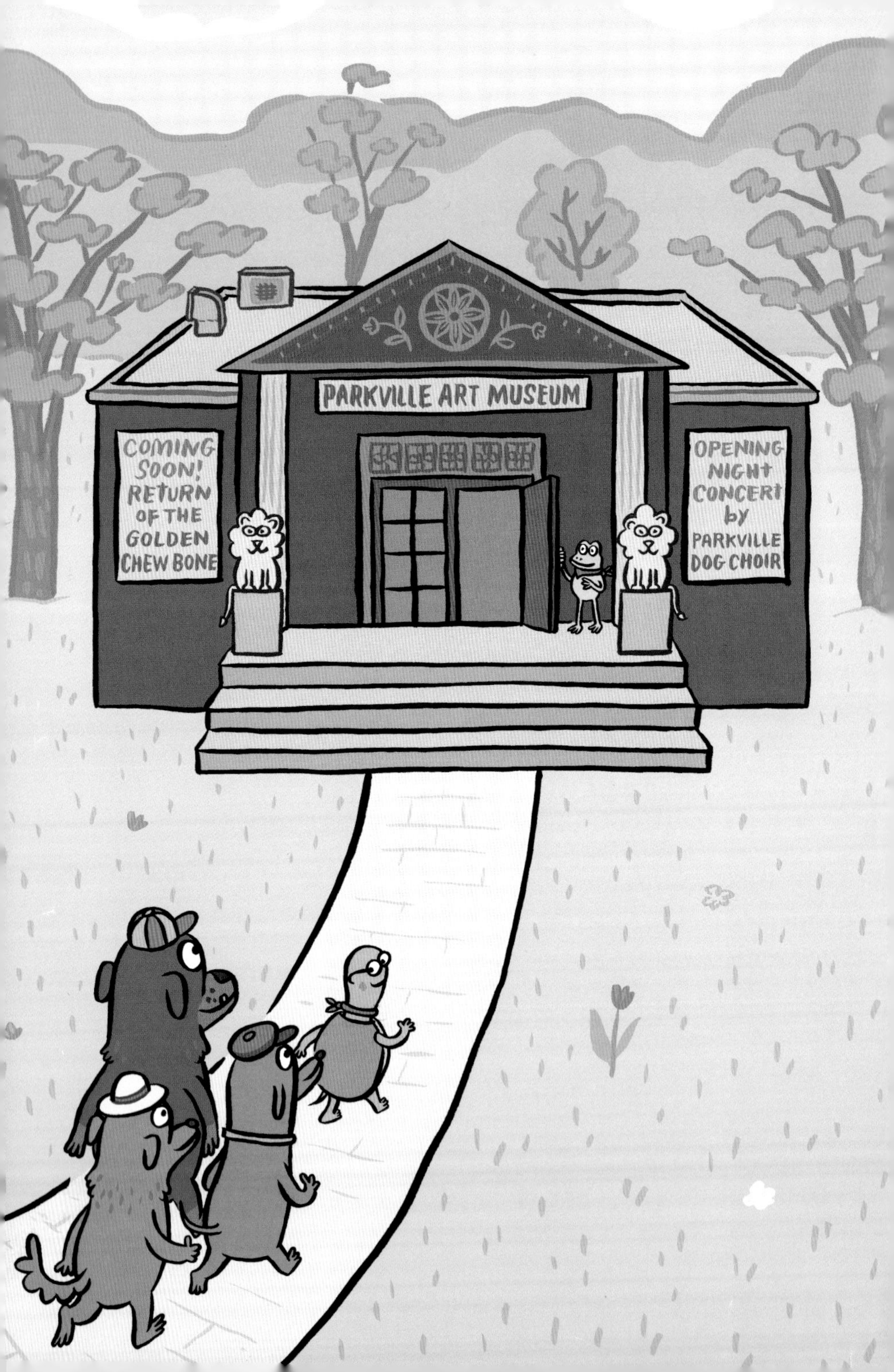
PARKVILLE ART MUSEUM
COMING SOON! RETURN OF THE GOLDEN CHEW BONE
OPENING NIGHT CONCERT by PARKVILLE DOG CHOIR

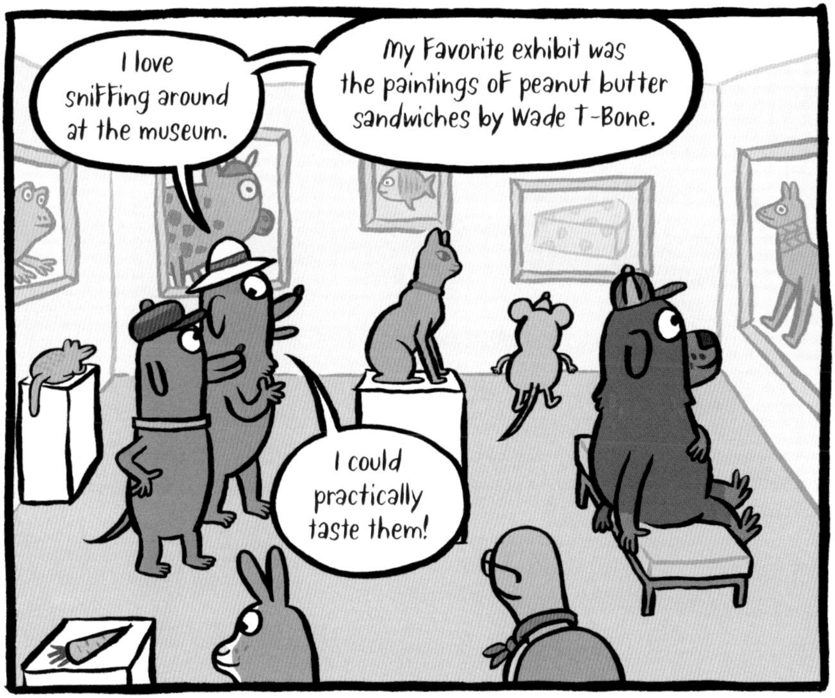
I love sniffing around at the museum.
My favorite exhibit was the paintings of peanut butter sandwiches by Wade T-Bone.
I could practically taste them!

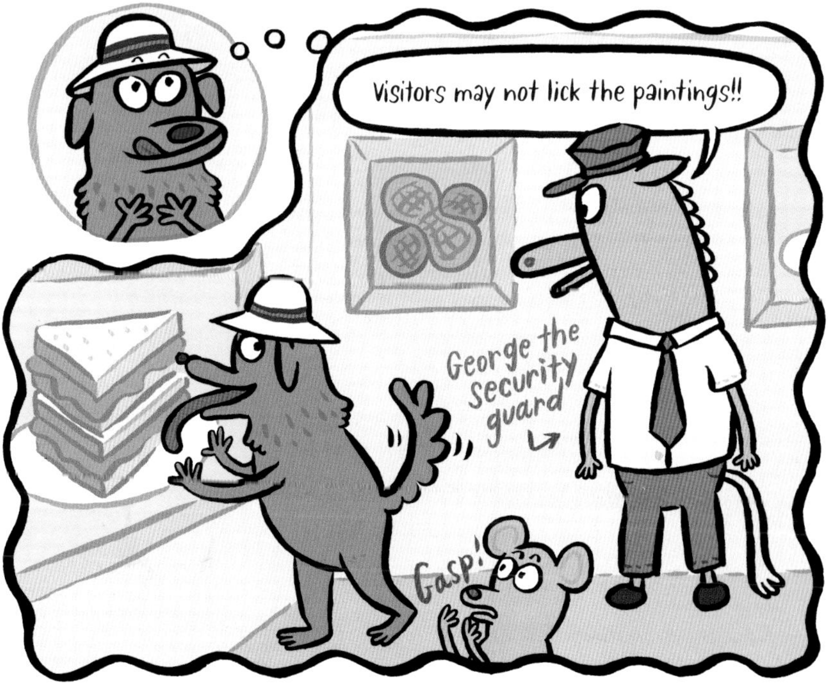
Visitors may not lick the paintings!!
George the security guard
Gasp!

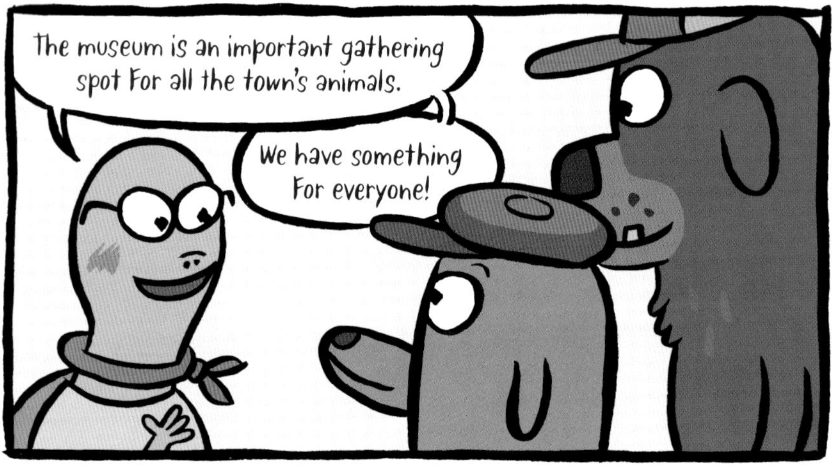
The museum is an important gathering spot for all the town's animals.
We have something for everyone!

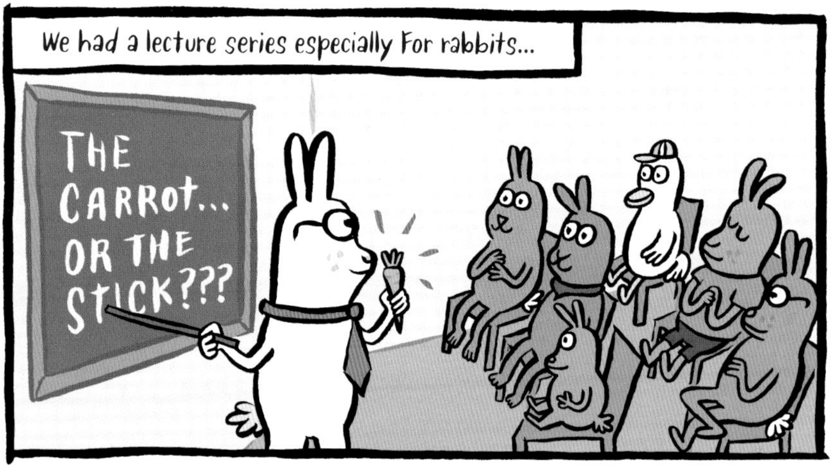
We had a lecture series especially for rabbits...
THE CARROT... OR THE STICK???

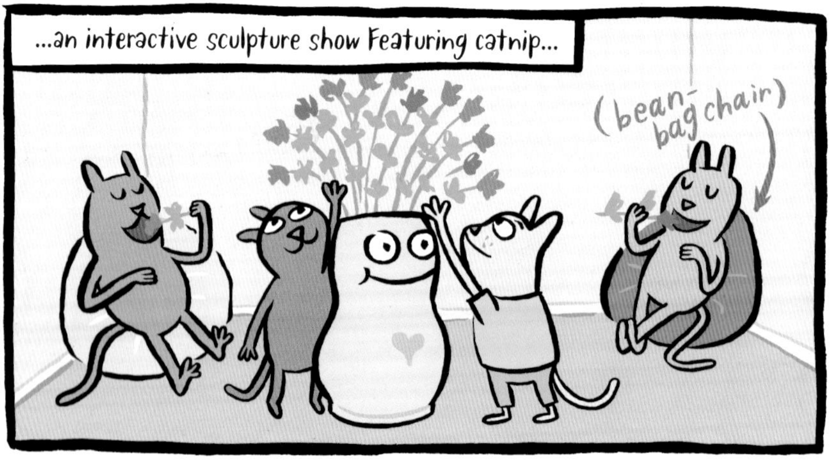
...an interactive sculpture show featuring catnip...
(bean-bag chair)

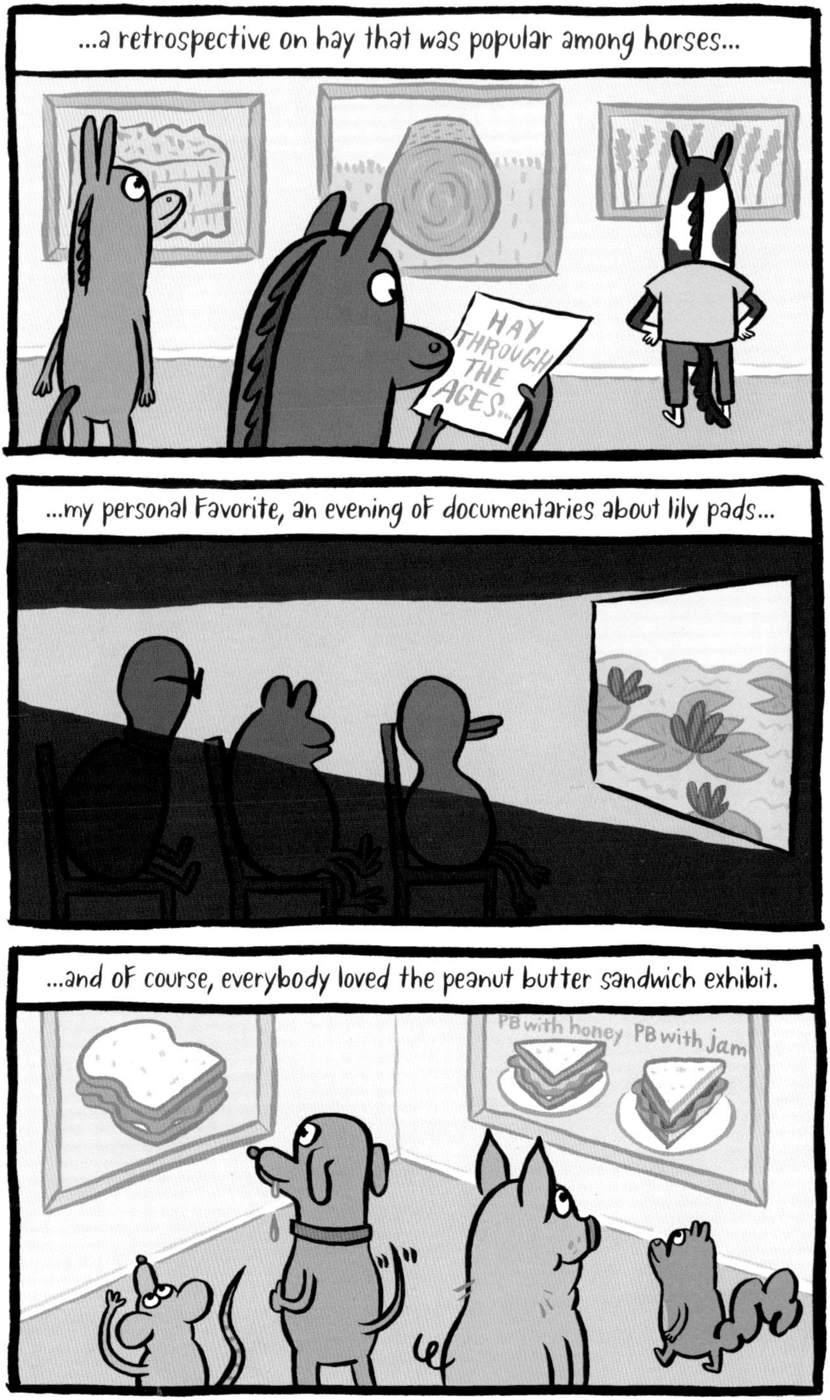
...a retrospective on hay that was popular among horses...
HAY THROUGH THE AGES...
...my personal favorite, an evening of documentaries about lily pads...
...and of course, everybody loved the peanut butter sandwich exhibit.
PB with honey
PB with jam

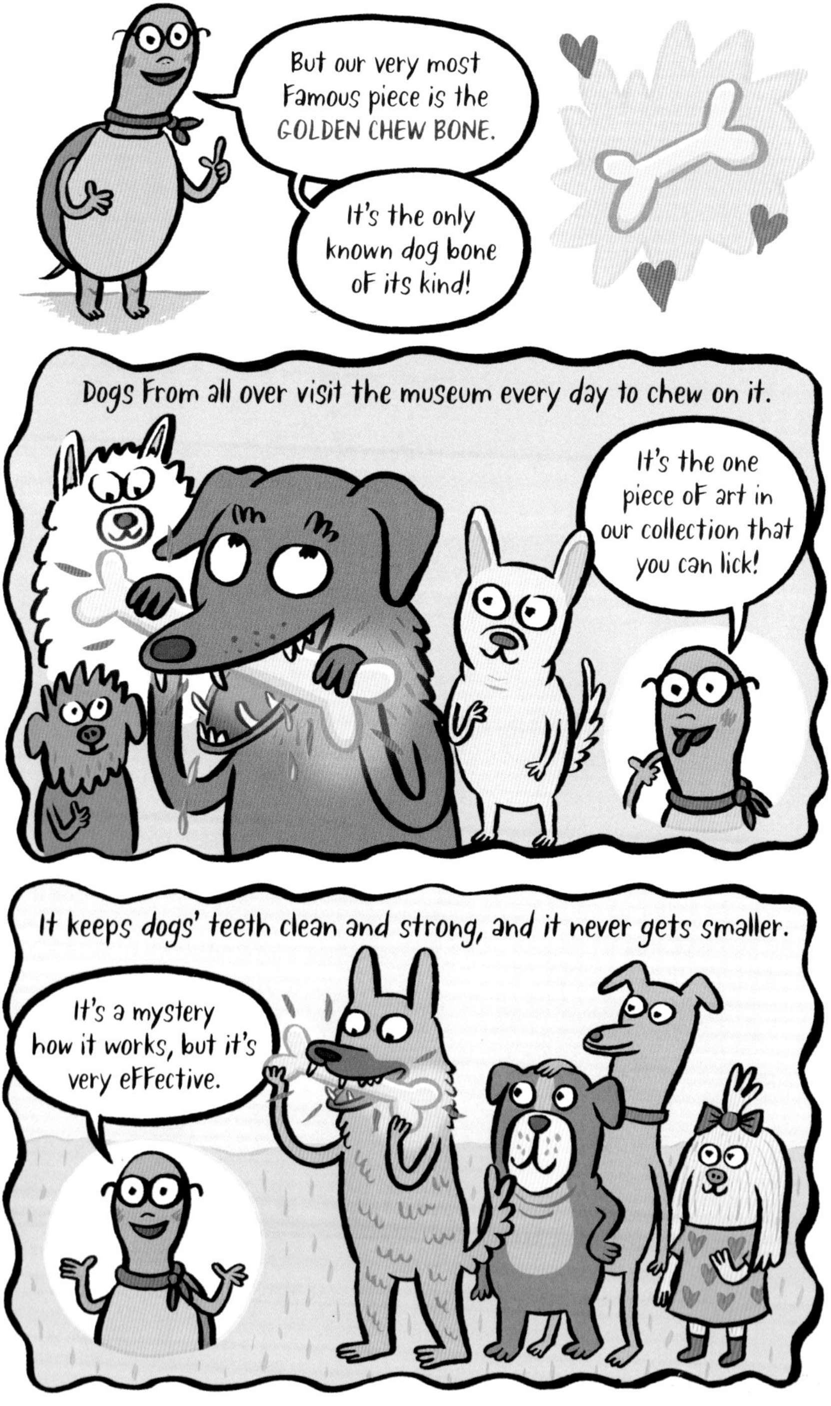
But our very most Famous piece is the GOLDEN CHEW BONE.
It's the only known dog bone oF its kind!
Dogs From all over visit the museum every day to chew on it.
It's the one piece oF art in our collection that you can lick!
It keeps dogs' teeth clean and strong, and it never gets smaller.
It's a mystery how it works, but it's very eFFective.

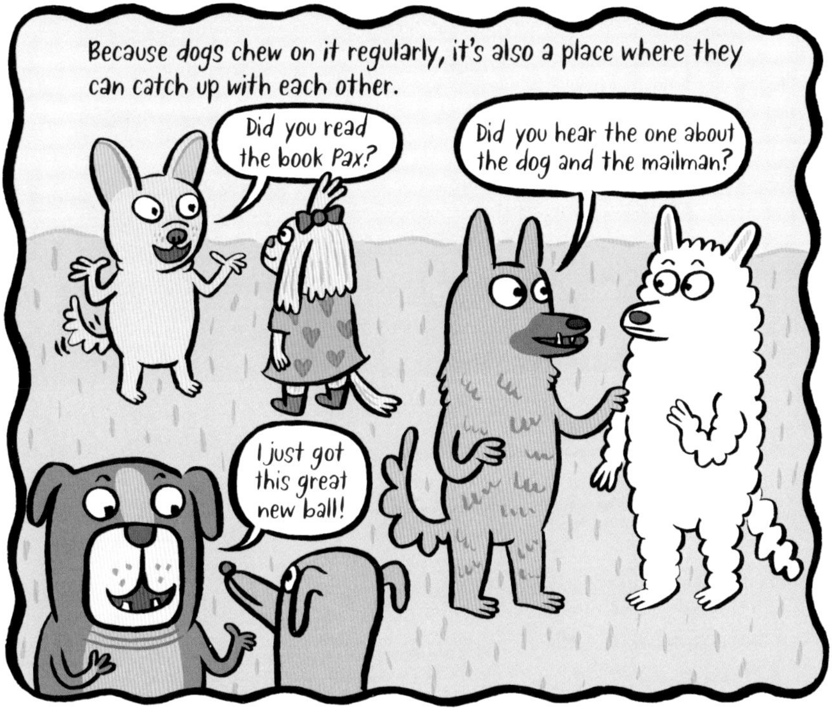
Because dogs chew on it regularly, it's also a place where they can catch up with each other.
Did you read the book Pax?
Did you hear the one about the dog and the mailman?
I just got this great new ball!

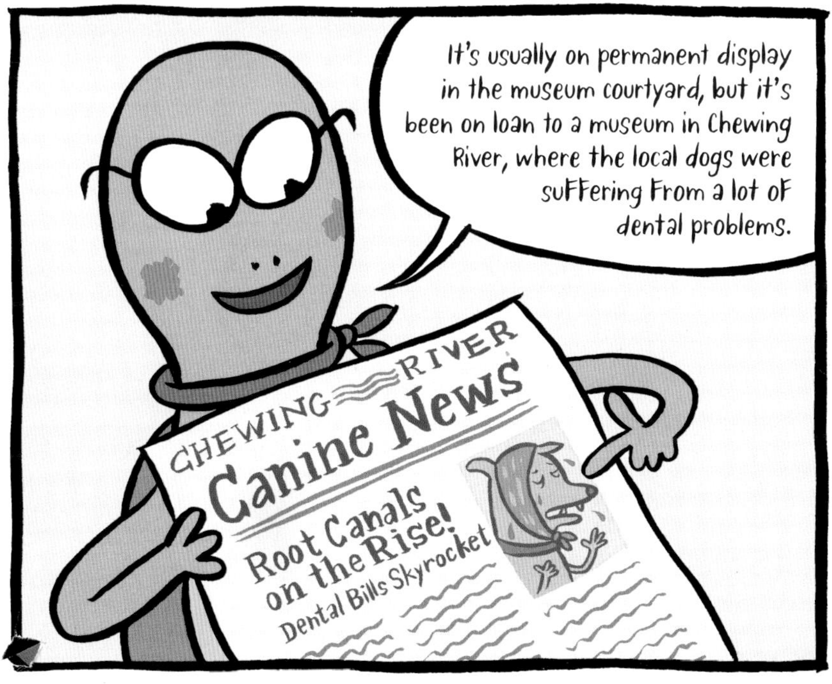
It's usually on permanent display in the museum courtyard, but it's been on loan to a museum in Chewing River, where the local dogs were suffering from a lot of dental problems.
CHEWING RIVER
Canine News
Root Canals on the Rise!
Dental Bills Skyrocket

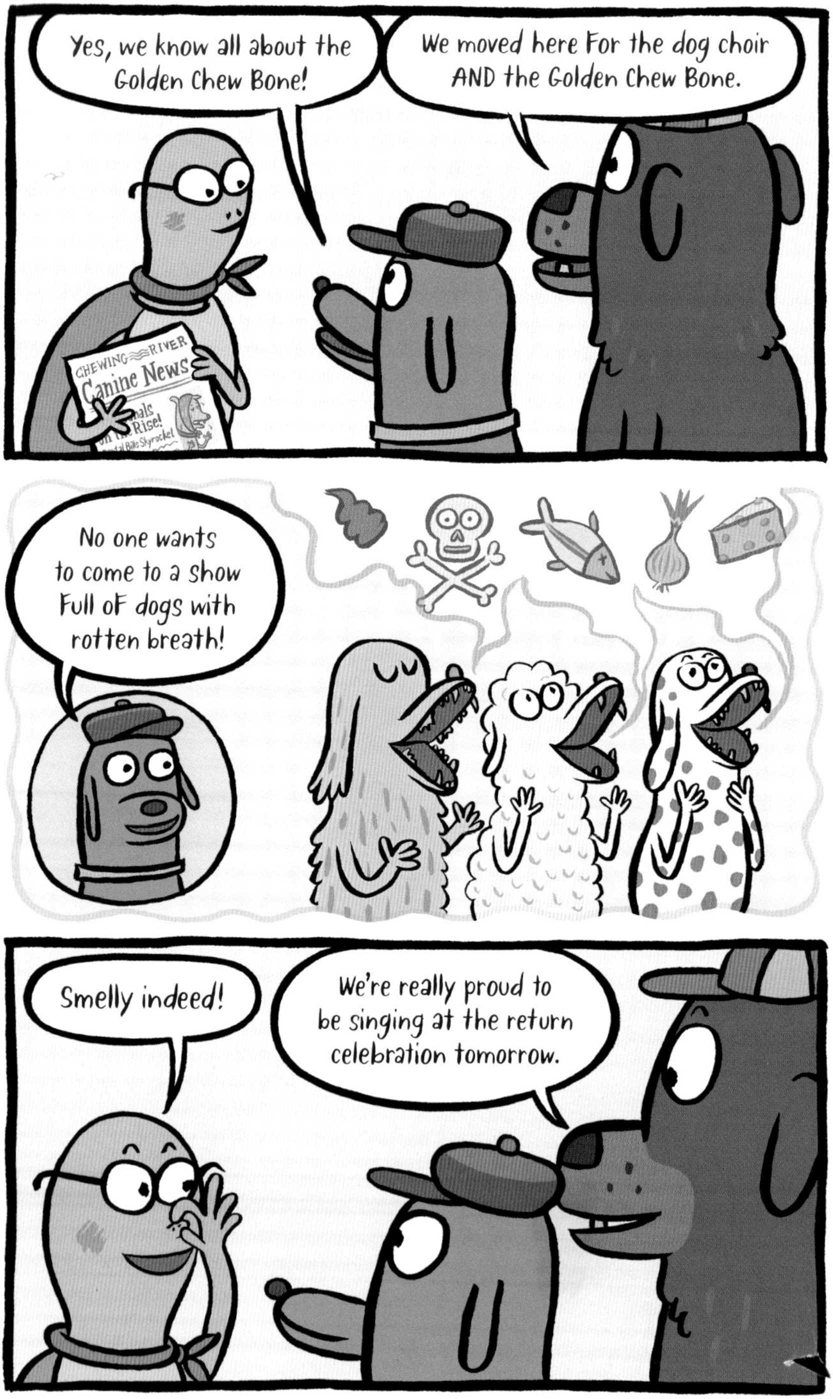
Yes, we know all about the Golden Chew Bone!
We moved here for the dog choir AND the Golden Chew Bone.
CHEWING RIVER
Canine News
No one wants to come to a show full of dogs with rotten breath!
Smelly indeed!
We're really proud to be singing at the return celebration tomorrow.

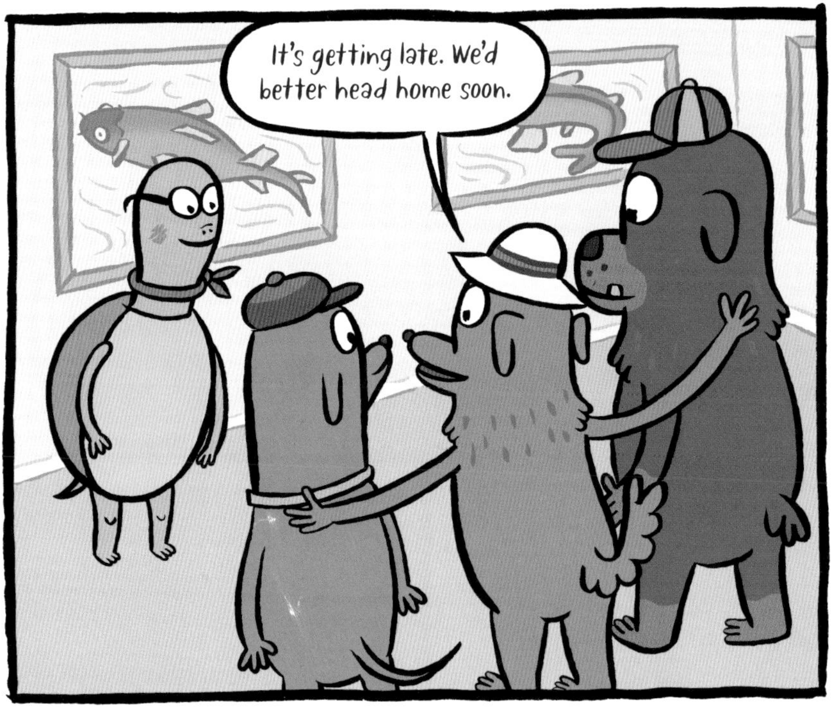
It's getting late. We'd better head home soon.

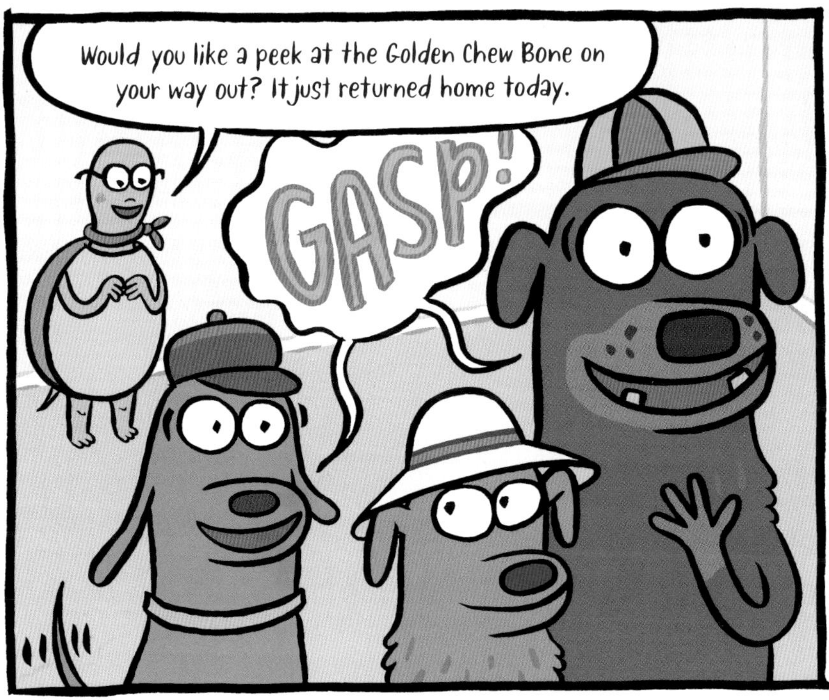
Would you like a peek at the Golden Chew Bone on your way out? It just returned home today.
GASP!

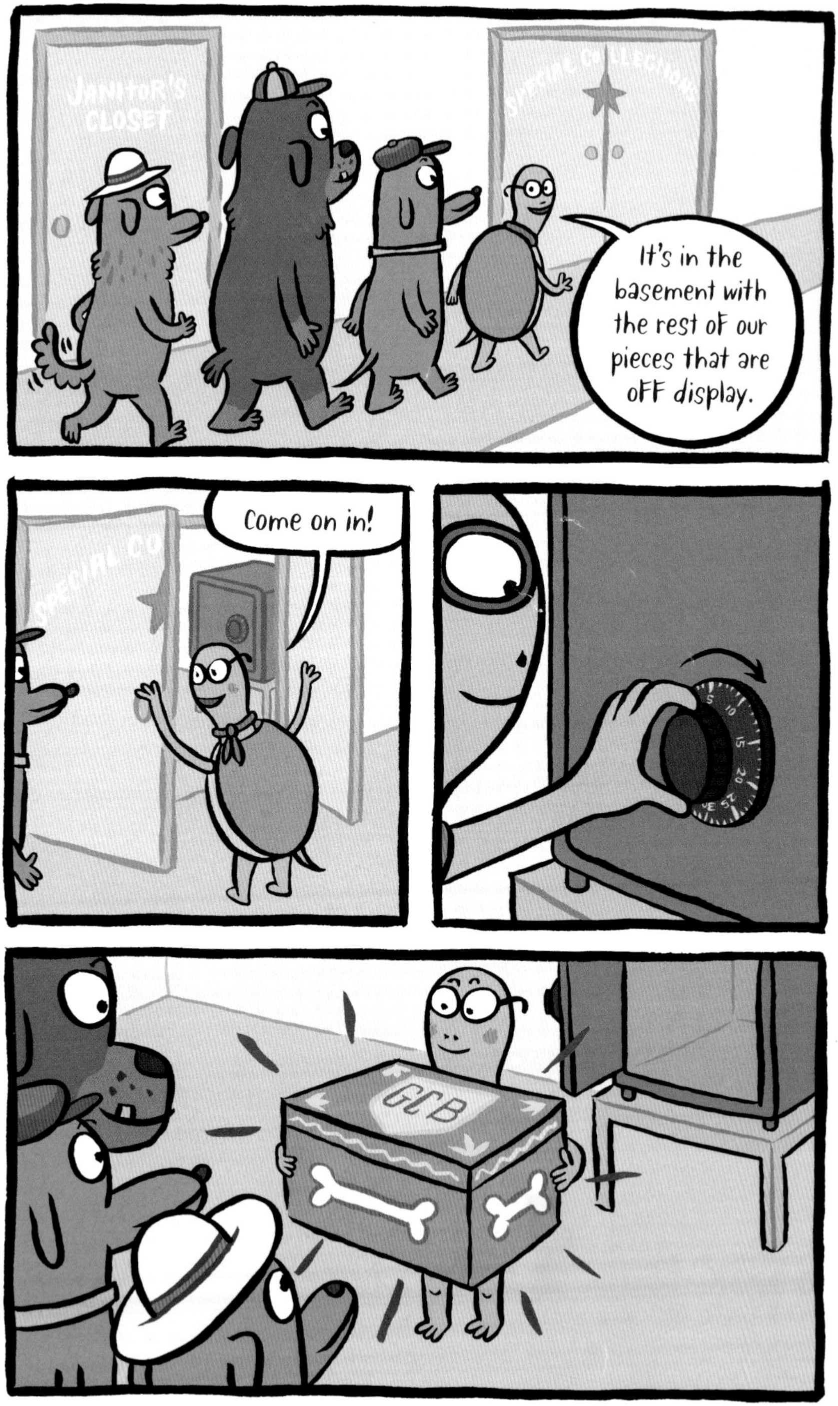
JANITOR'S CLOSET
SPECIAL COLLECTIONS
It's in the basement with the rest of our pieces that are off display.
SPECIAL CO
Come on in!
GCB

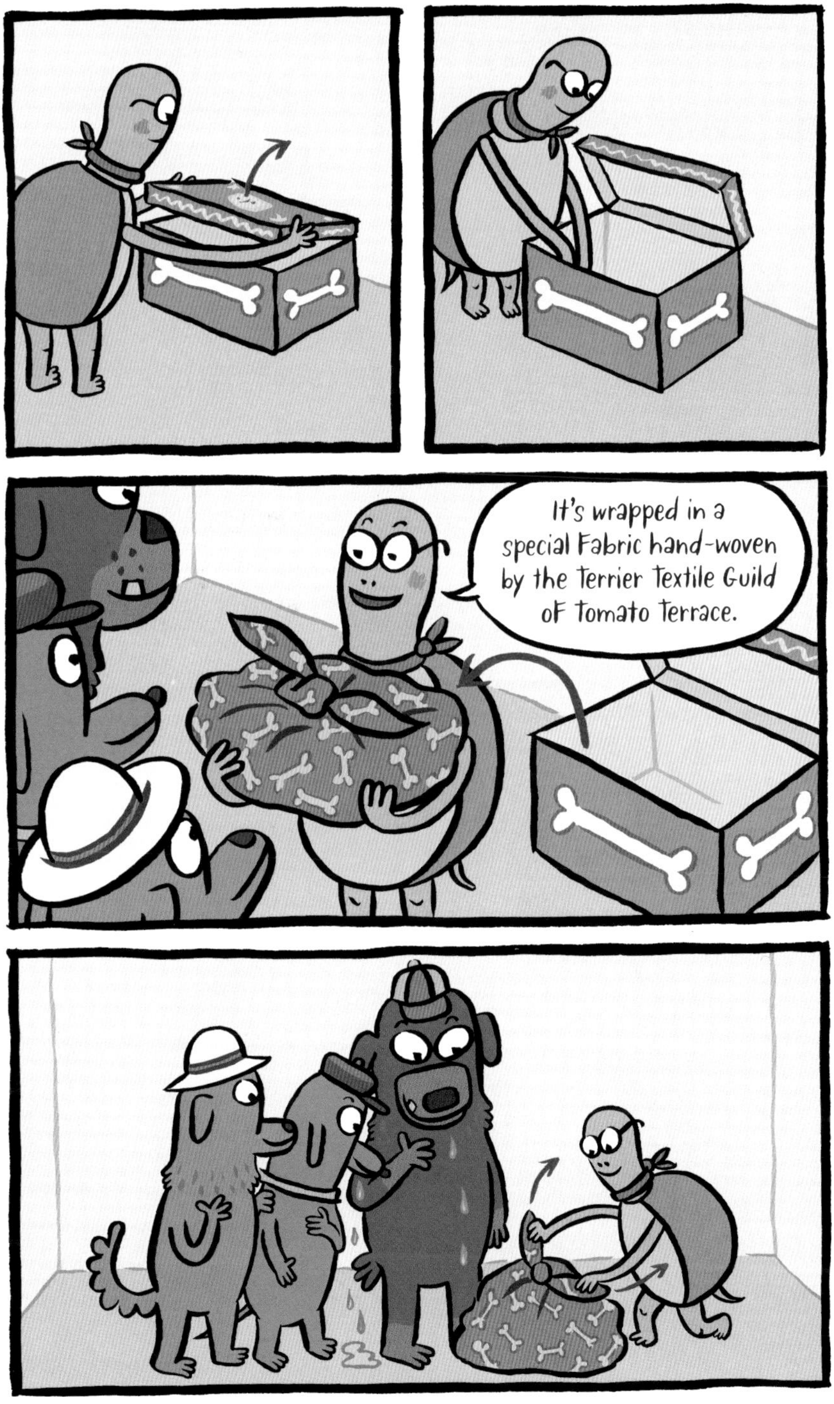
It's wrapped in a special Fabric hand-woven by the Terrier Textile Guild oF Tomato Terrace.

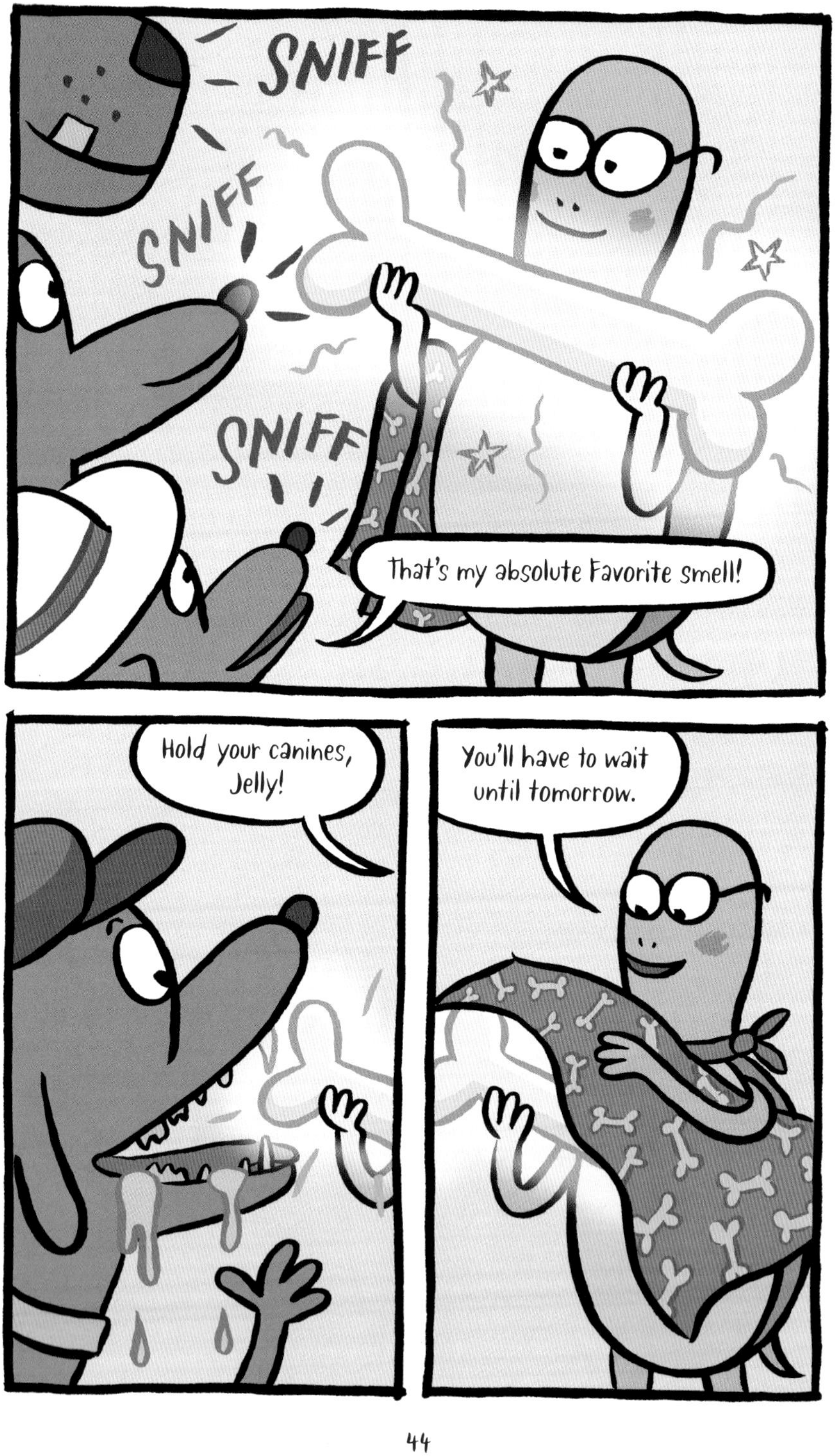
SNIFF
SNIFF
SNIFF
That's my absolute Favorite smell!
Hold your canines, Jelly!
You'll have to wait until tomorrow.

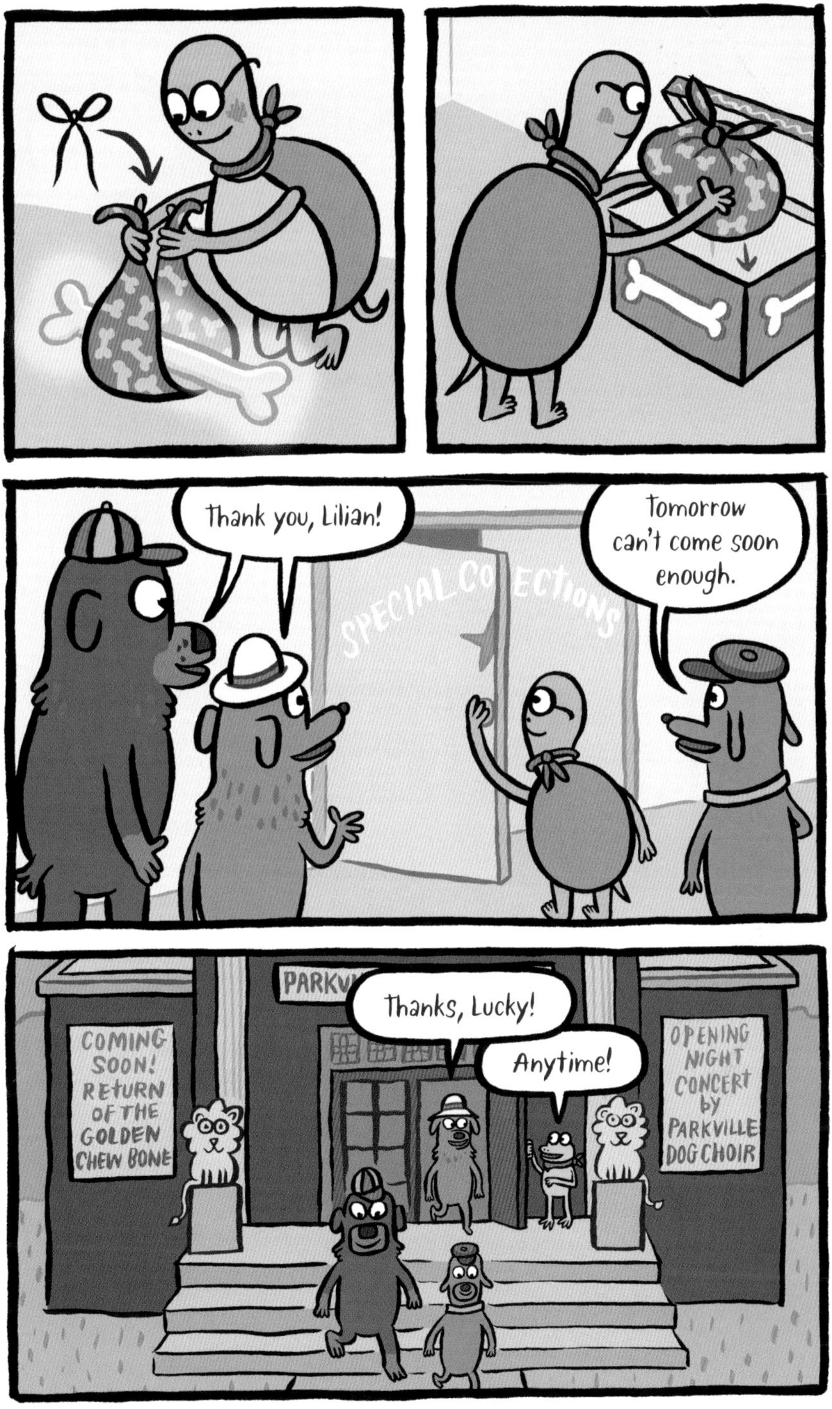
Thank you, Lilian!
SPECIAL CO ECTIONS
Tomorrow can't come soon enough.
PARKV
COMING SOON! RETURN OF THE GOLDEN CHEW BONE
Thanks, Lucky!
Anytime!
OPENING NIGHT CONCERT by PARKVILLE DOG CHOIR

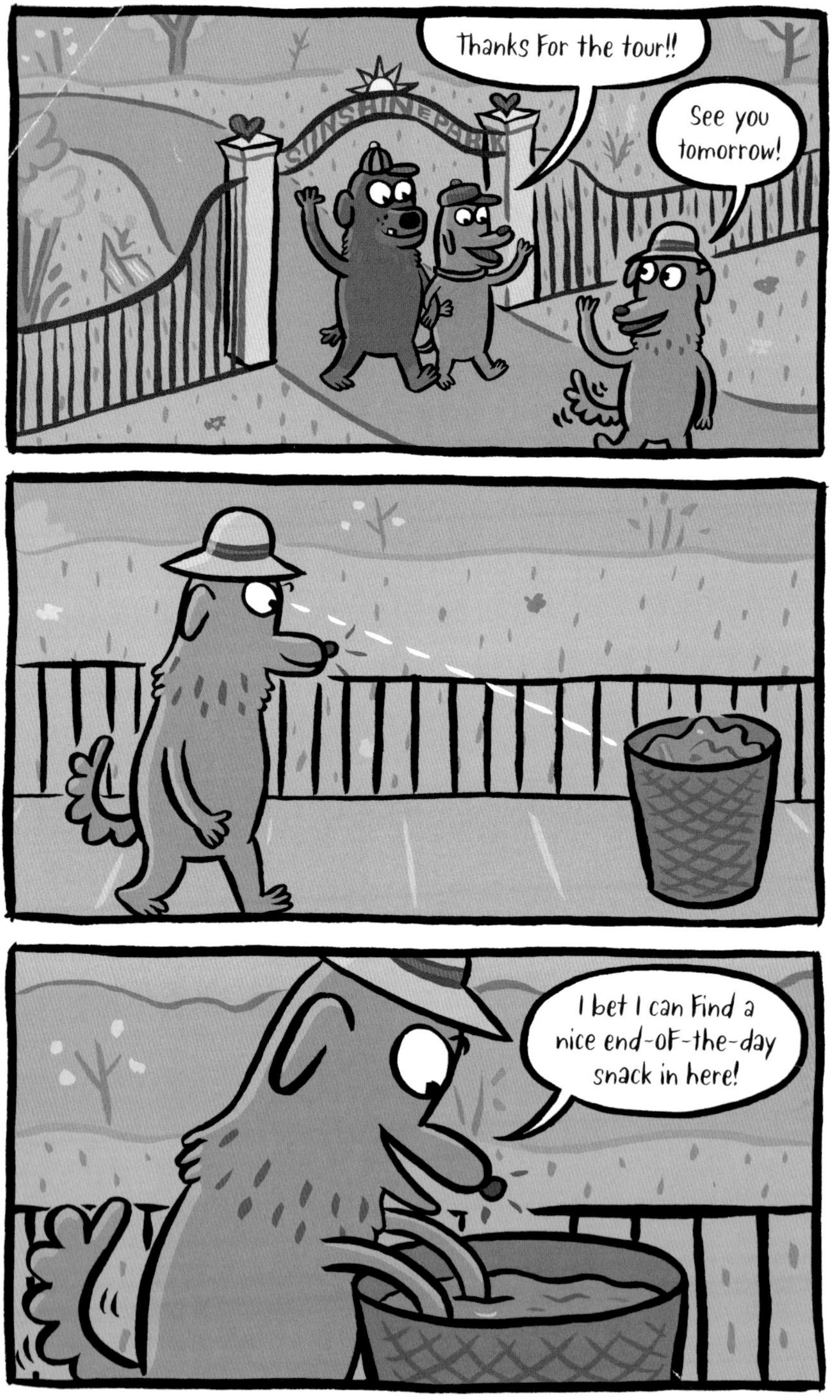

SUNSHINE PARK
Thanks For the tour!!
See you tomorrow!
I bet I can Find a nice end-oF-the-day snack in here!

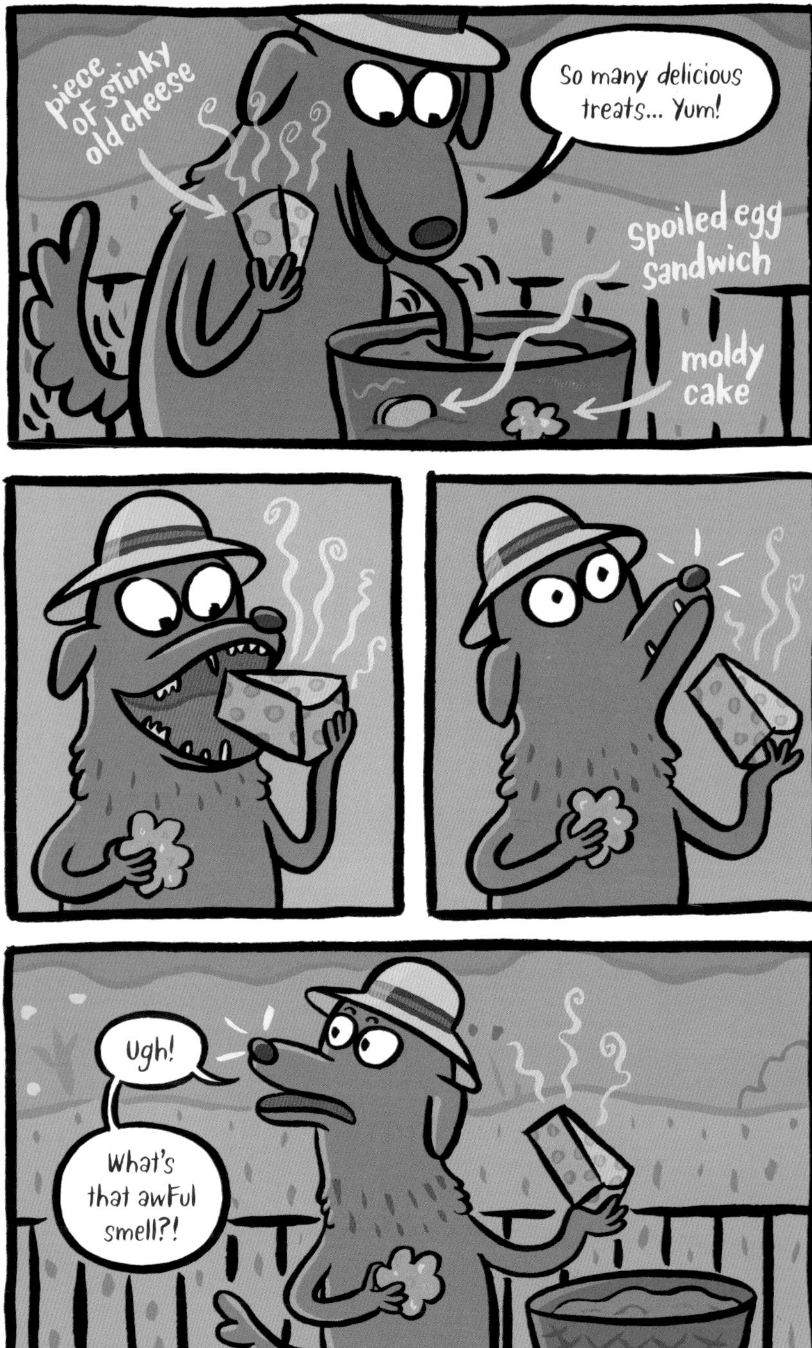
piece of stinky old cheese
So many delicious treats... Yum!
spoiled egg sandwich
moldy cake
Ugh!
What's that awful smell?!

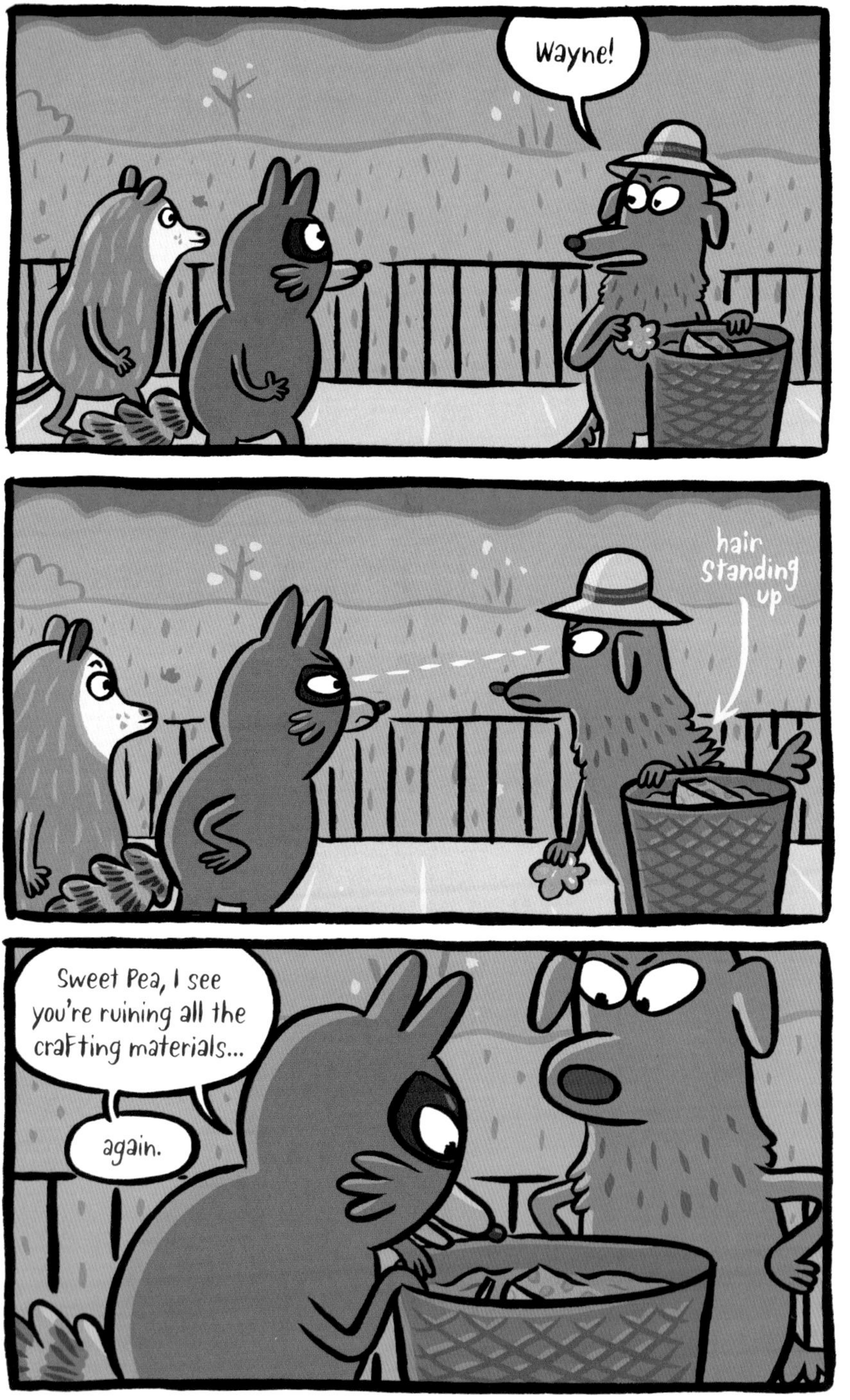
Wayne!
hair standing up
Sweet Pea, I see you're ruining all the crafting materials...
again.

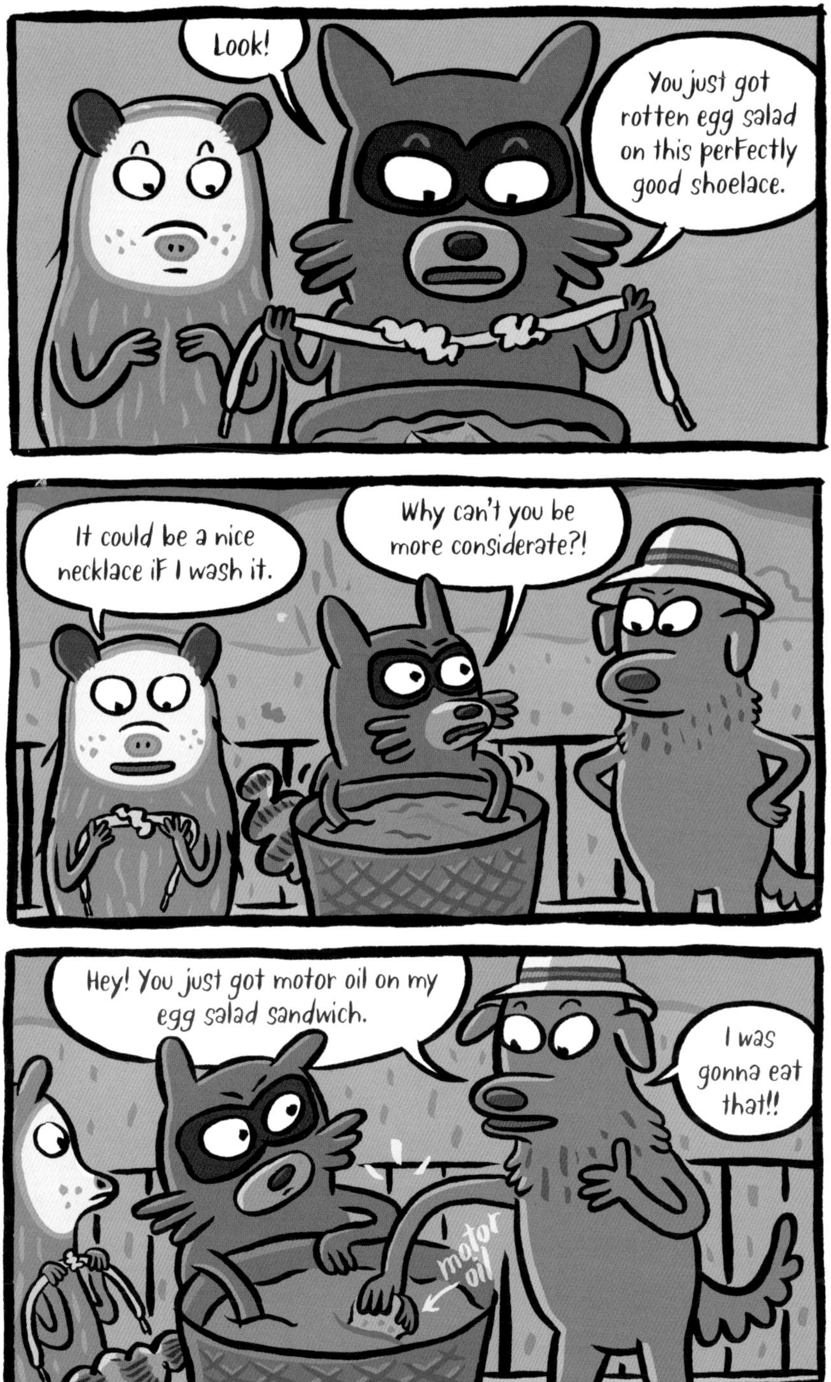
Look!
You just got rotten egg salad on this perfectly good shoelace.
It could be a nice necklace if I wash it.
Why can't you be more considerate?!
Hey! You just got motor oil on my egg salad sandwich.
I was gonna eat that!!
motor oil

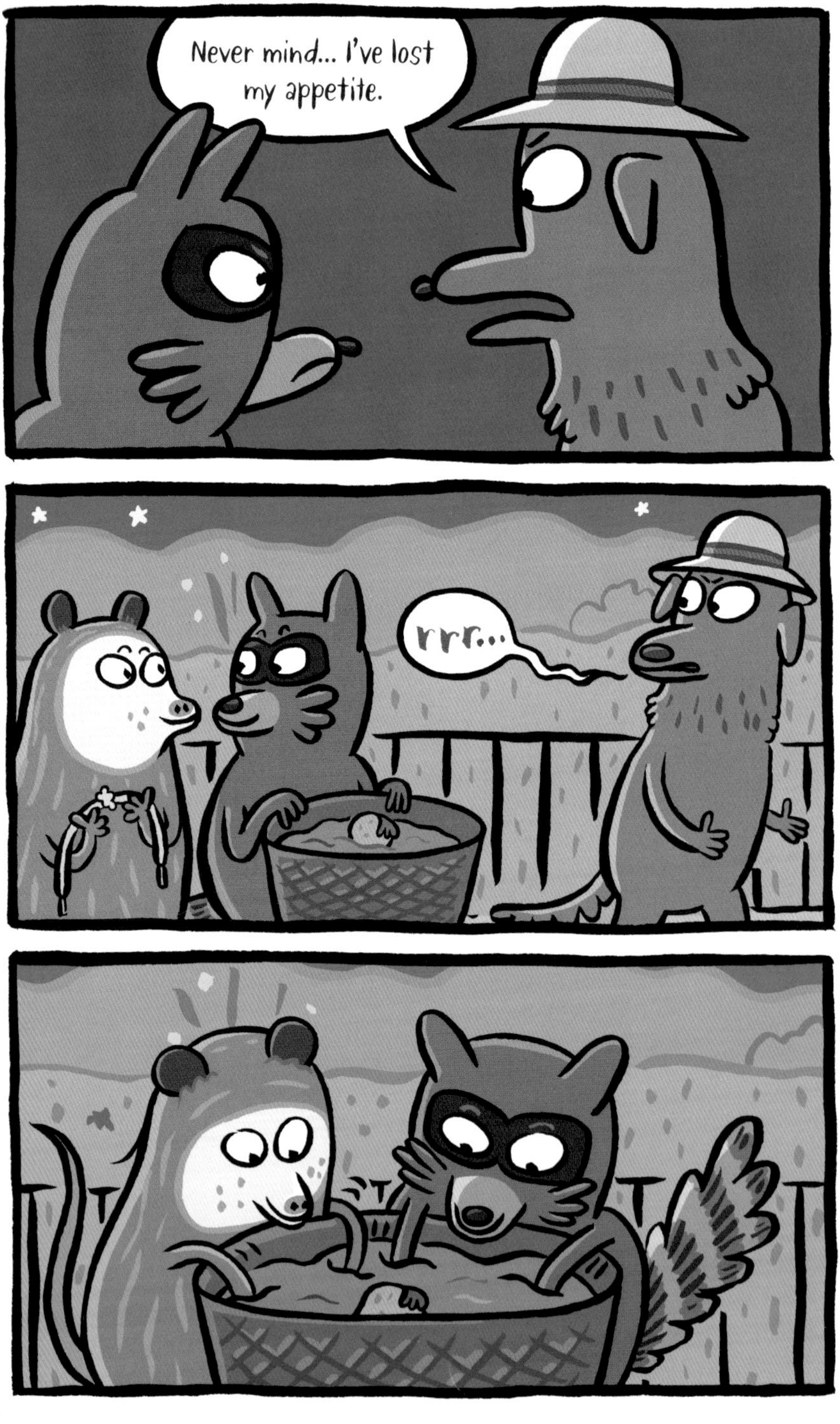
Never mind... I've lost my appetite.
rrr...

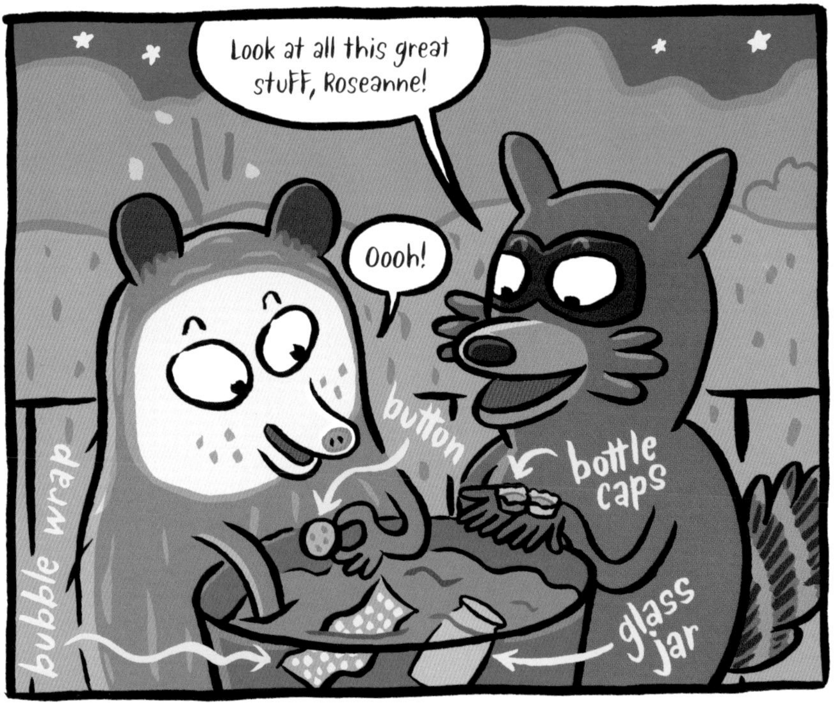
Look at all this great stuFF, Roseanne!
Oooh!
button
bottle caps
bubble wrap
glass jar

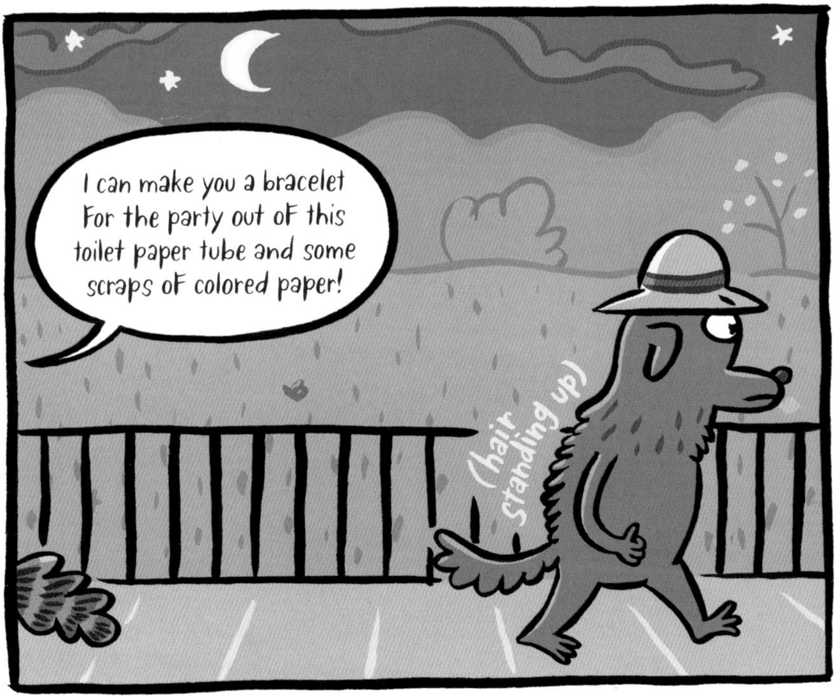
I can make you a bracelet For the party out oF this toilet paper tube and some scraps oF colored paper!
(hair standing up)

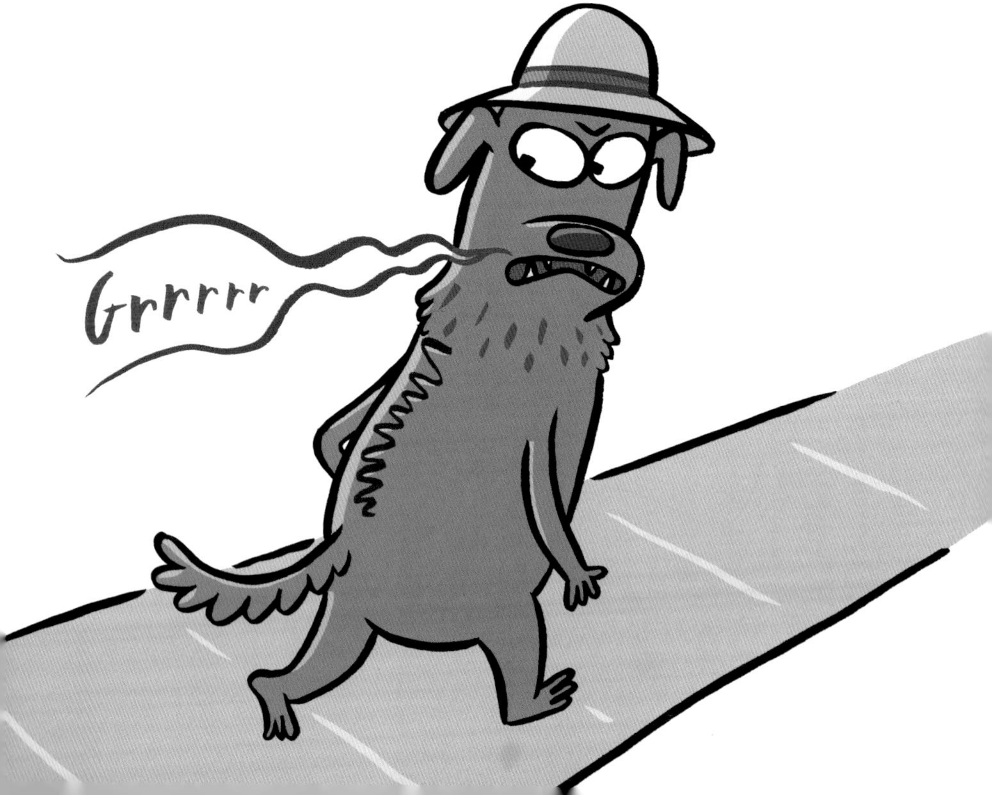
Grrrrr

Chapter 3

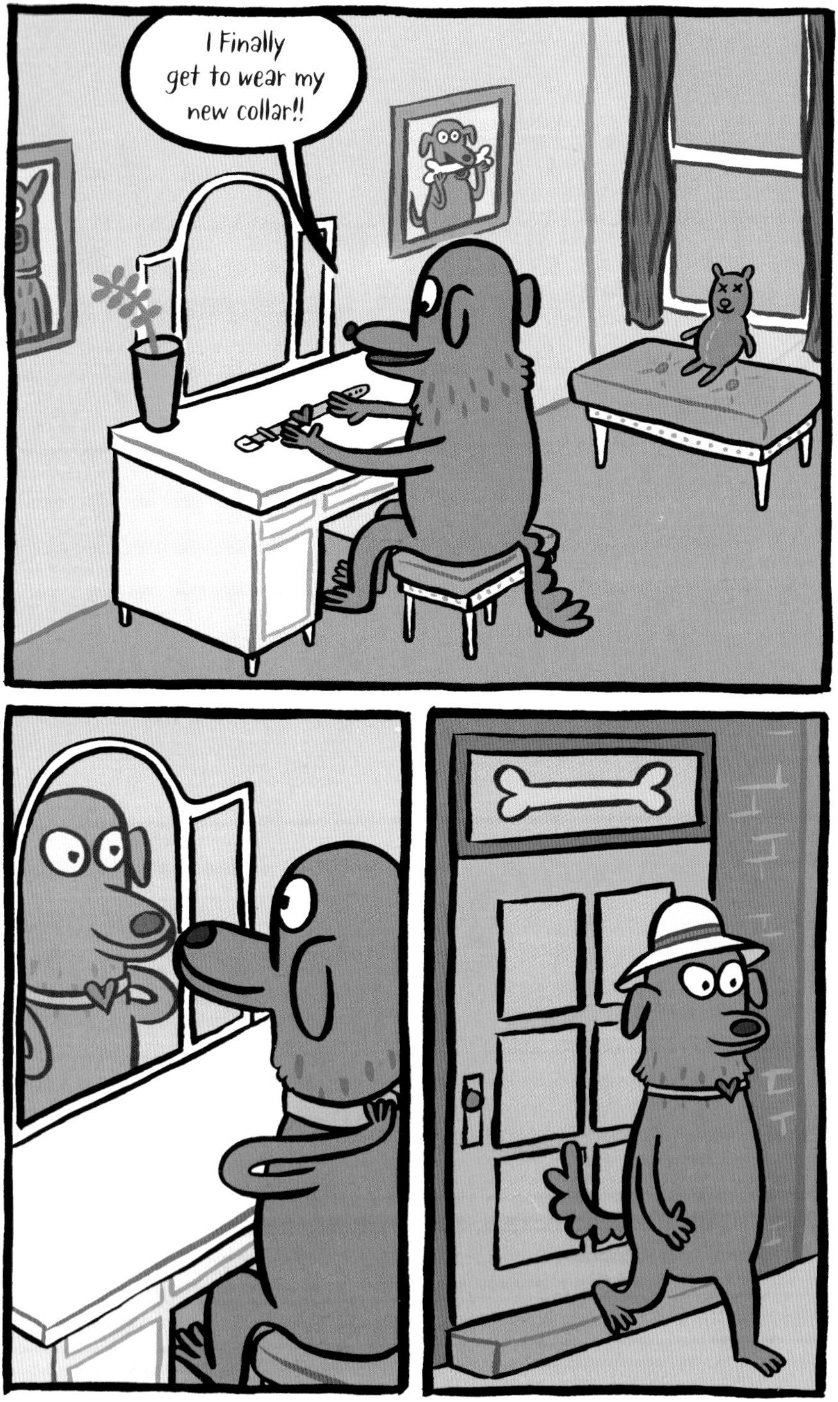
I Finally get to wear my new collar!!

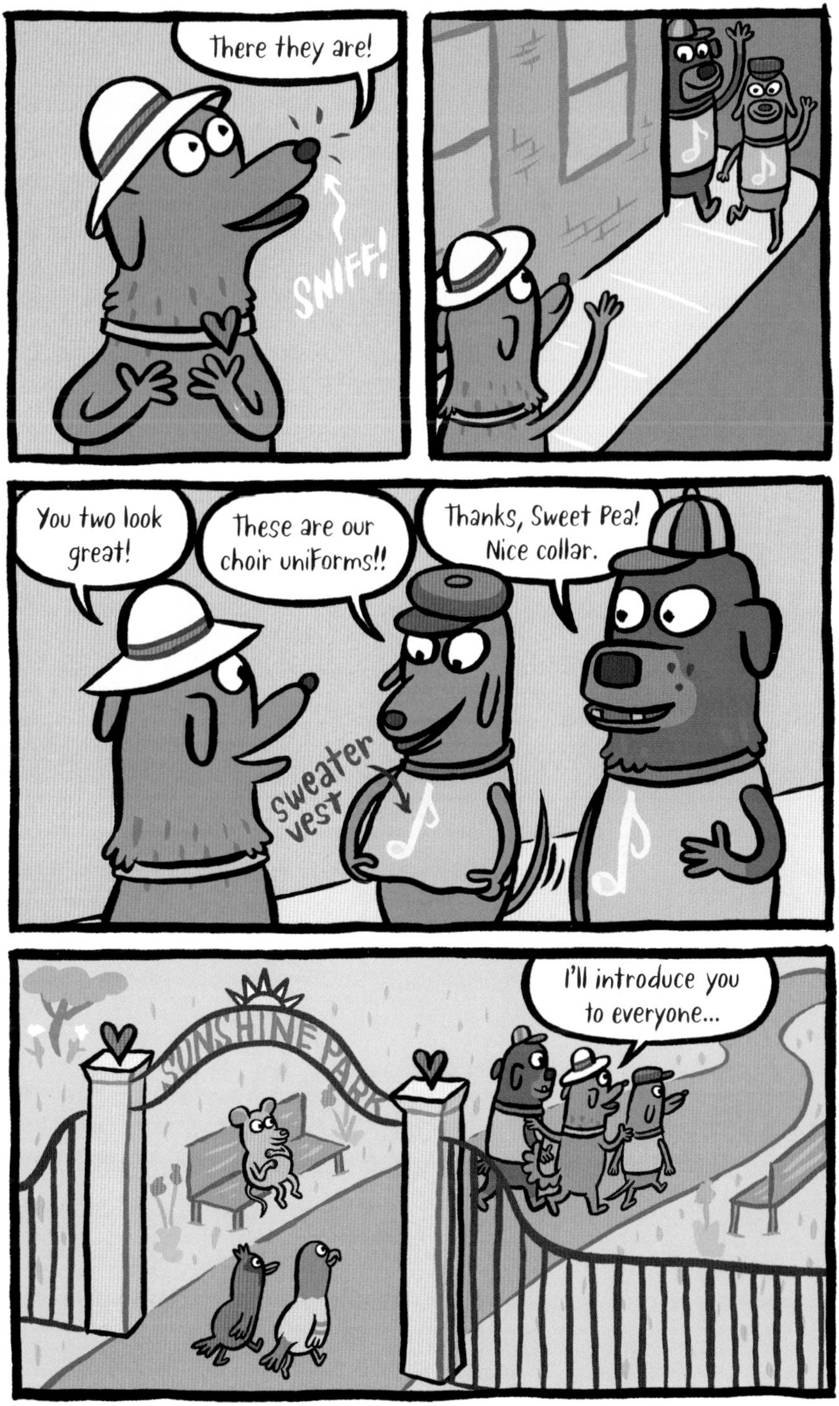
There they are!
SNIFF!
You two look great!
These are our choir uniforms!!
Thanks, Sweet Pea! Nice collar.
sweater vest
SUNSHINE PARK
I'll introduce you to everyone...

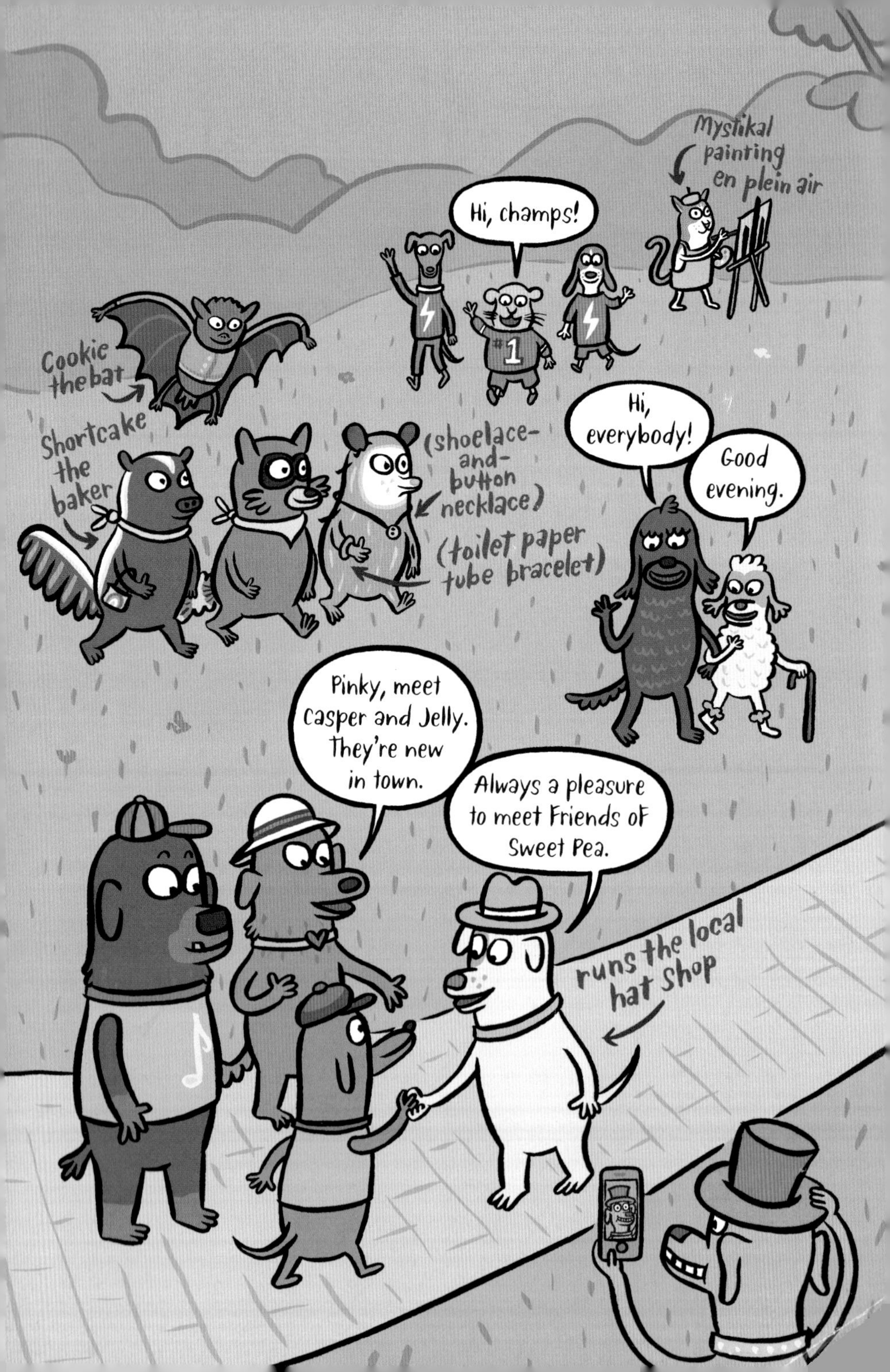
Mystikal painting en plein air
Hi, champs!
Cookie the bat
Shortcake the baker
(shoelace-and-button necklace)
(toilet paper tube bracelet)
Hi, everybody!
Good evening.
Pinky, meet Casper and Jelly. They're new in town.
Always a pleasure to meet Friends of Sweet Pea.
runs the local hat shop

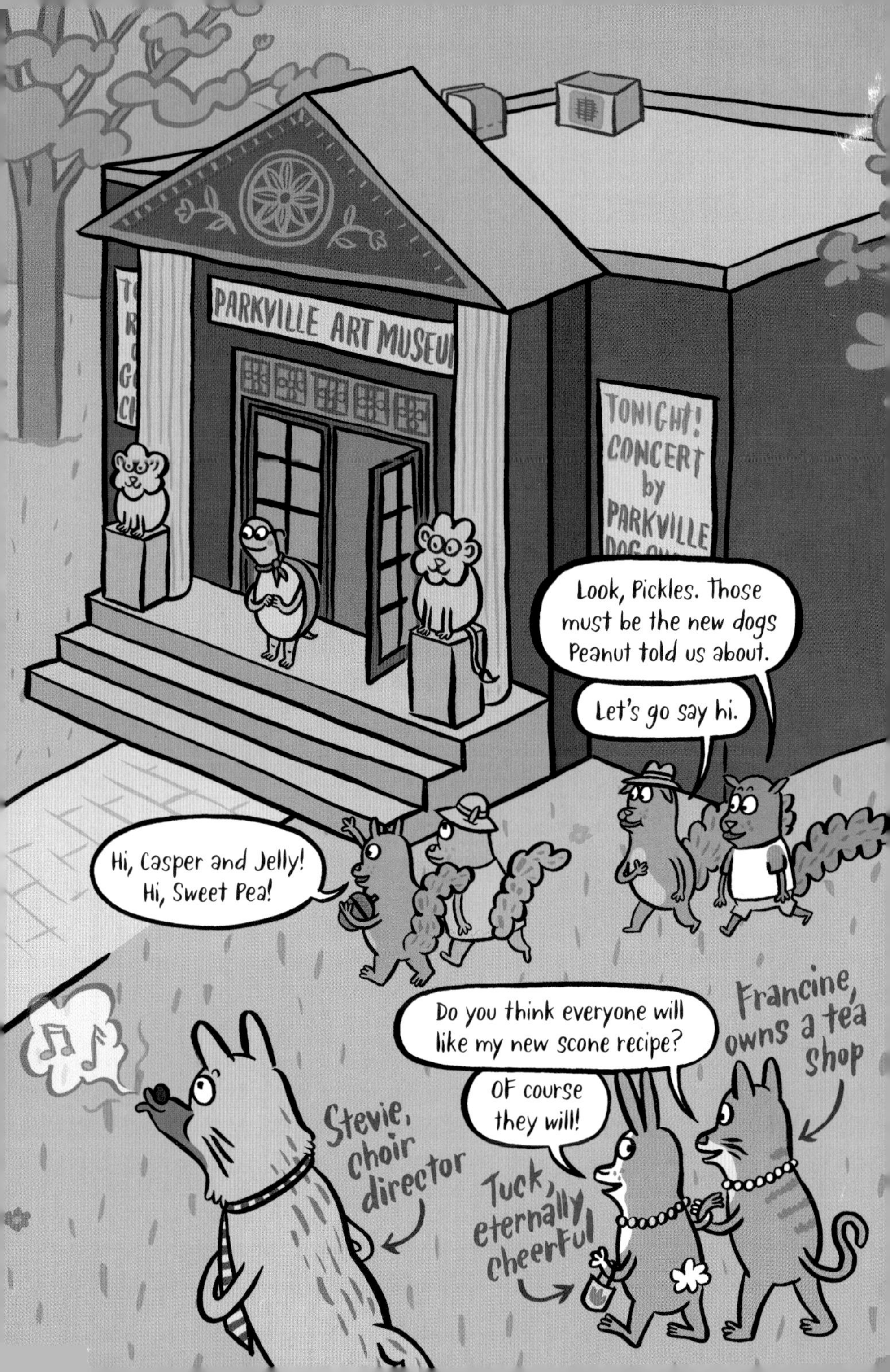
PARKVILLE ART MUSEU
TONIGHT! CONCERT by PARKVILLE
Look, Pickles. Those must be the new dogs Peanut told us about.
Let's go say hi.
Hi, Casper and Jelly! Hi, Sweet Pea!
Do you think everyone will like my new scone recipe?
Of course they will!
Stevie, choir director
Tuck, eternally cheerful
Francine, owns a tea shop

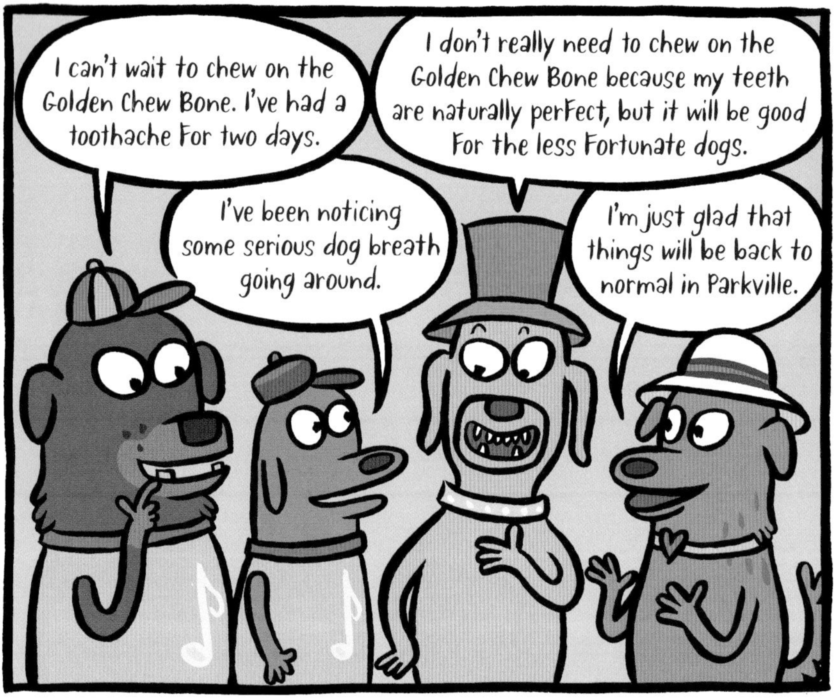
I can't wait to chew on the Golden Chew Bone. I've had a toothache for two days.
I don't really need to chew on the Golden Chew Bone because my teeth are naturally perfect, but it will be good for the less fortunate dogs.
I've been noticing some serious dog breath going around.
I'm just glad that things will be back to normal in Parkville.

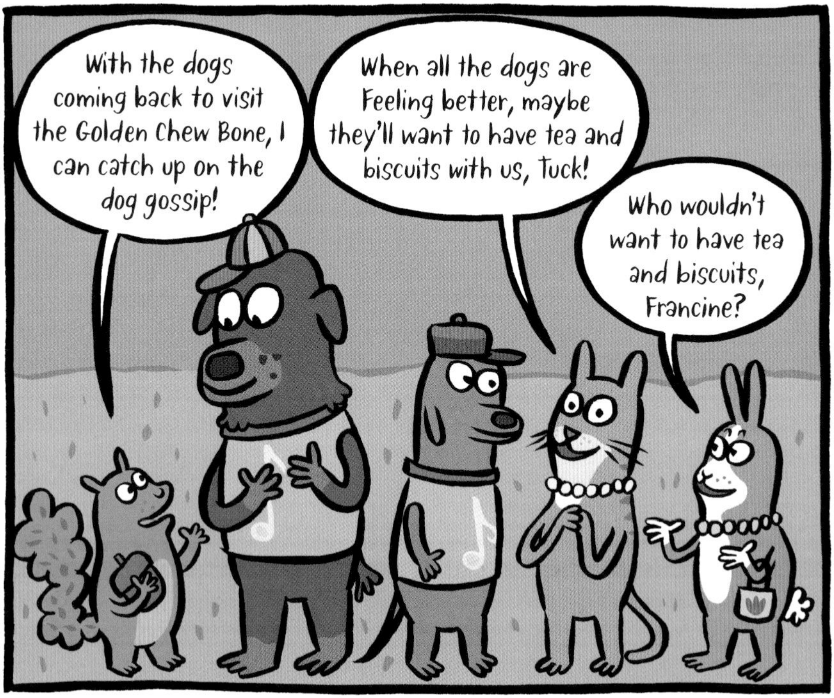
With the dogs coming back to visit the Golden Chew Bone, I can catch up on the dog gossip!
When all the dogs are feeling better, maybe they'll want to have tea and biscuits with us, Tuck!
Who wouldn't want to have tea and biscuits, Francine?

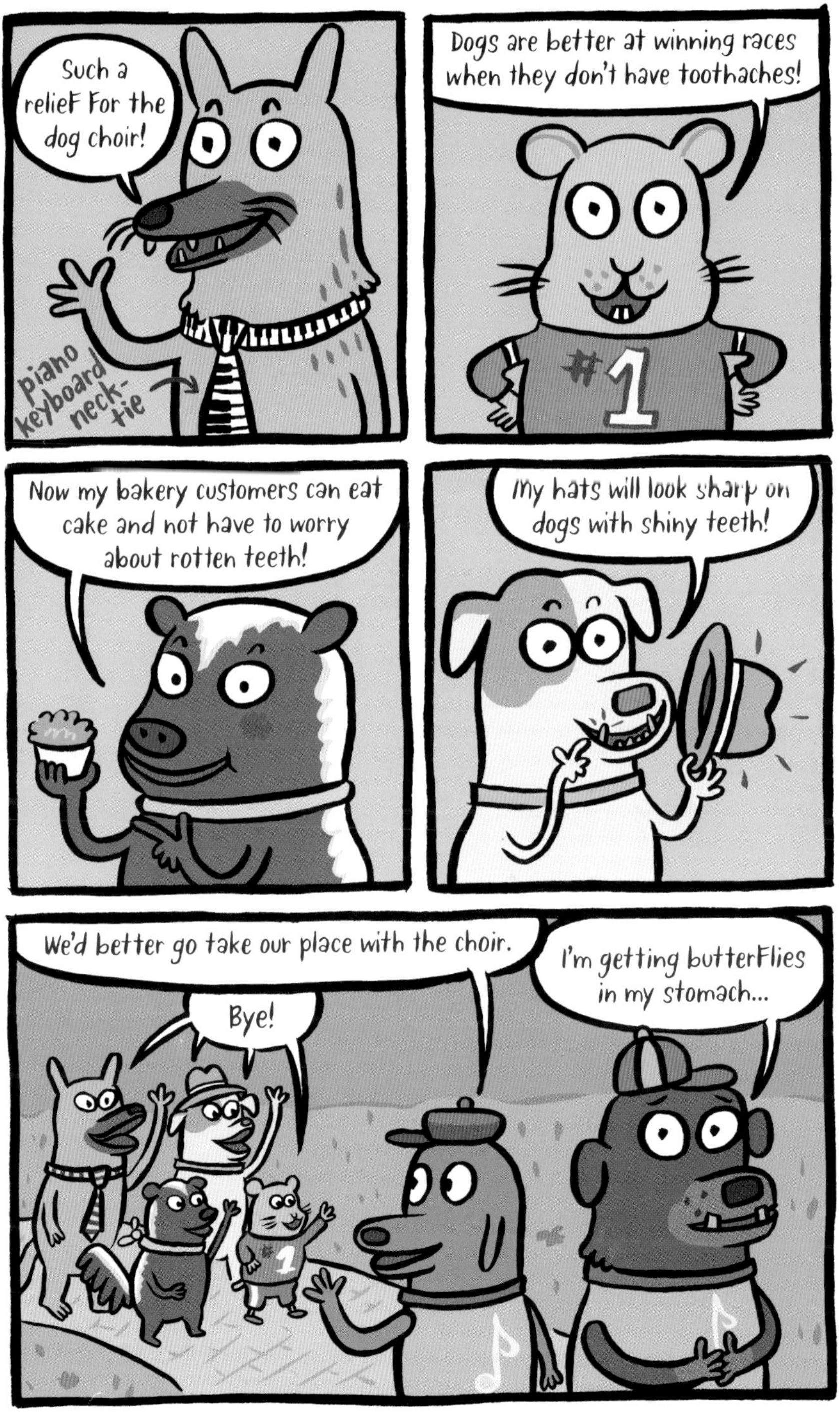
Such a relief For the dog choir!
piano keyboard neck-tie
Dogs are better at winning races when they don't have toothaches!
Now my bakery customers can eat cake and not have to worry about rotten teeth!
My hats will look sharp on dogs with shiny teeth!
We'd better go take our place with the choir.
Bye!
I'm getting butterFlies in my stomach...

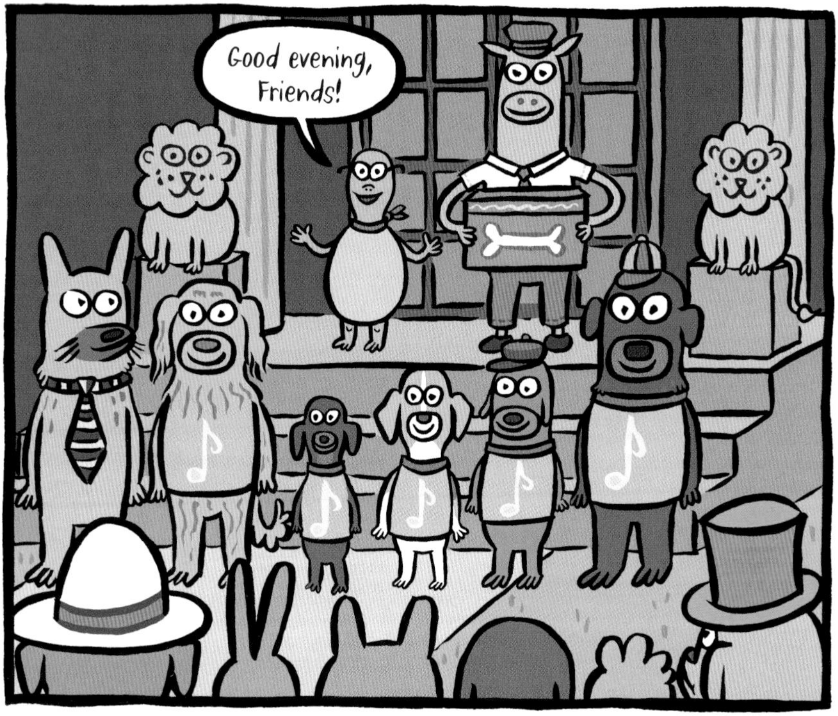
Good evening, Friends!

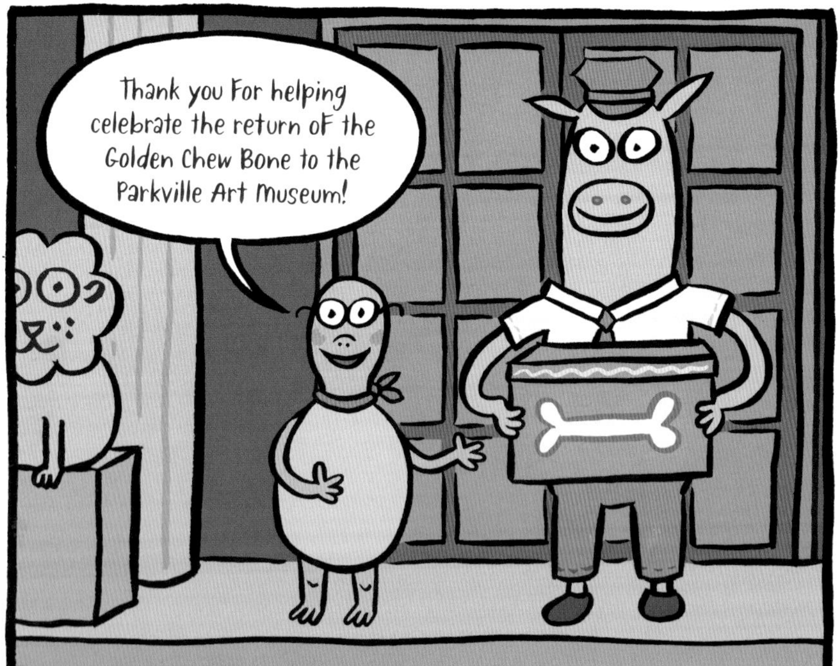
Thank you For helping celebrate the return oF the Golden Chew Bone to the Parkville Art Museum!

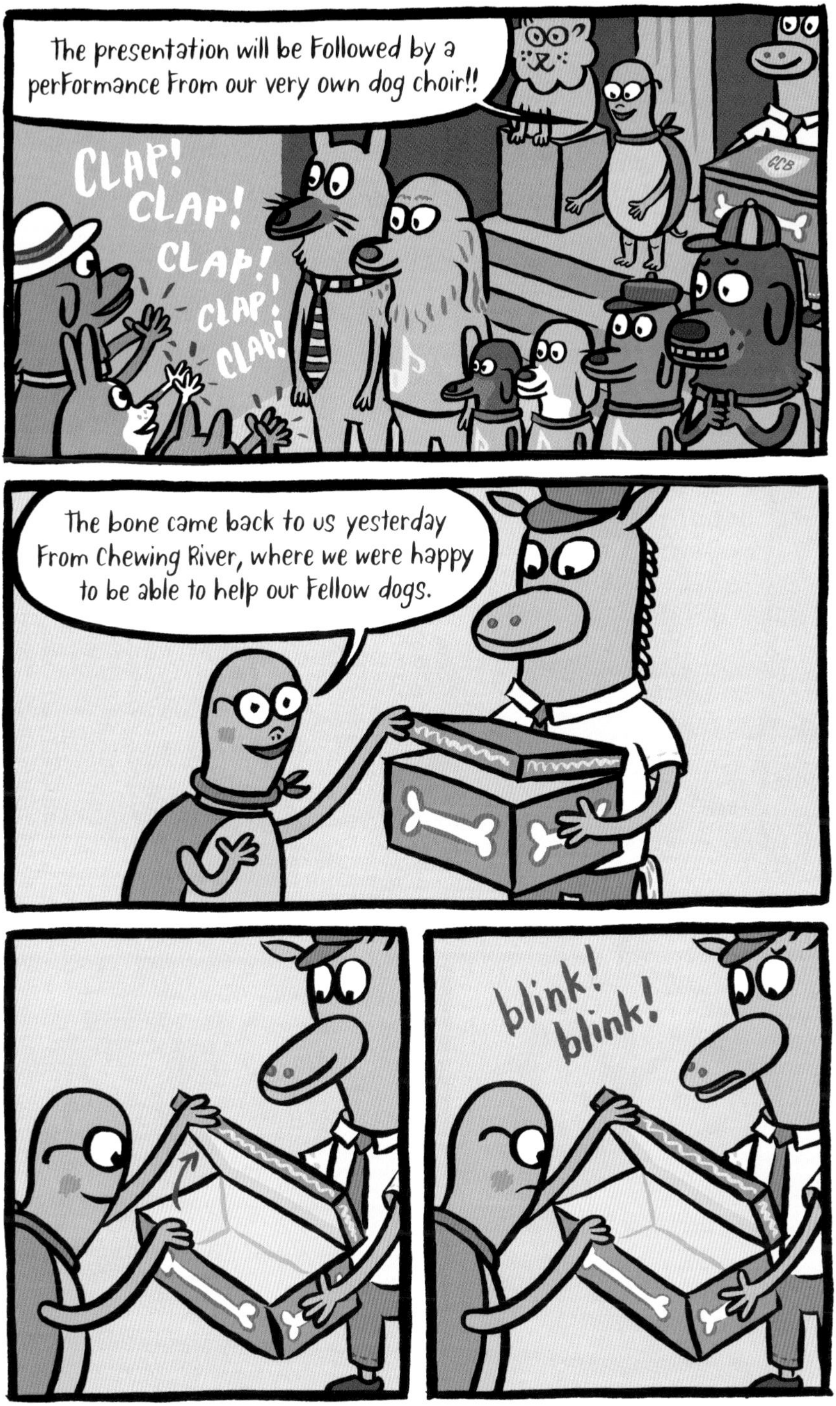
The presentation will be Followed by a performance From our very own dog choir!!
CLAP!
CLAP!
CLAP!
CLAP!
CLAP!
GCB
The bone came back to us yesterday From Chewing River, where we were happy to be able to help our Fellow dogs.
blink! blink!

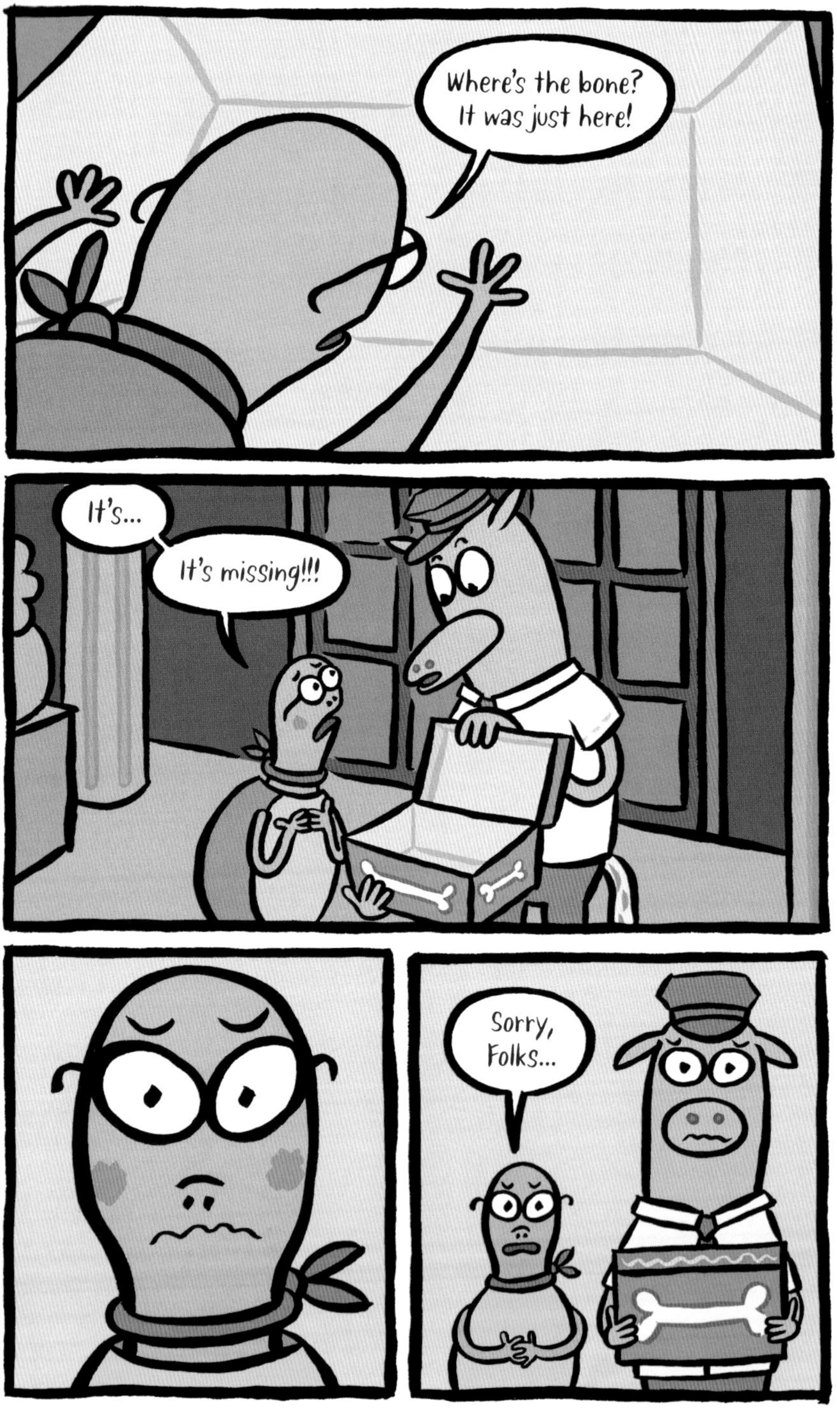
Where's the bone? It was just here!
It's...
It's missing!!!
Sorry, Folks...

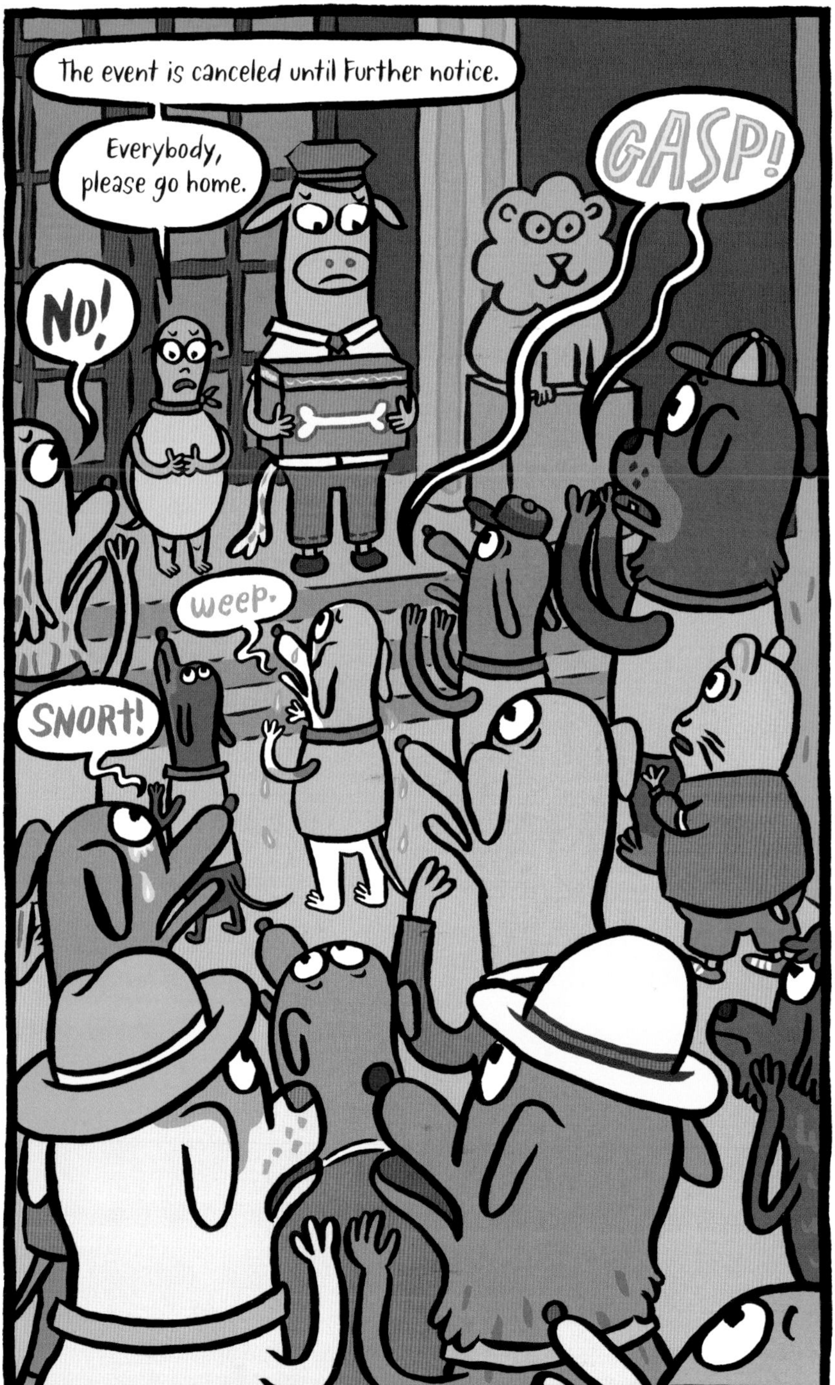
The event is canceled until further notice.
Everybody, please go home.
NO!
GASP!
weep.
SNORT!

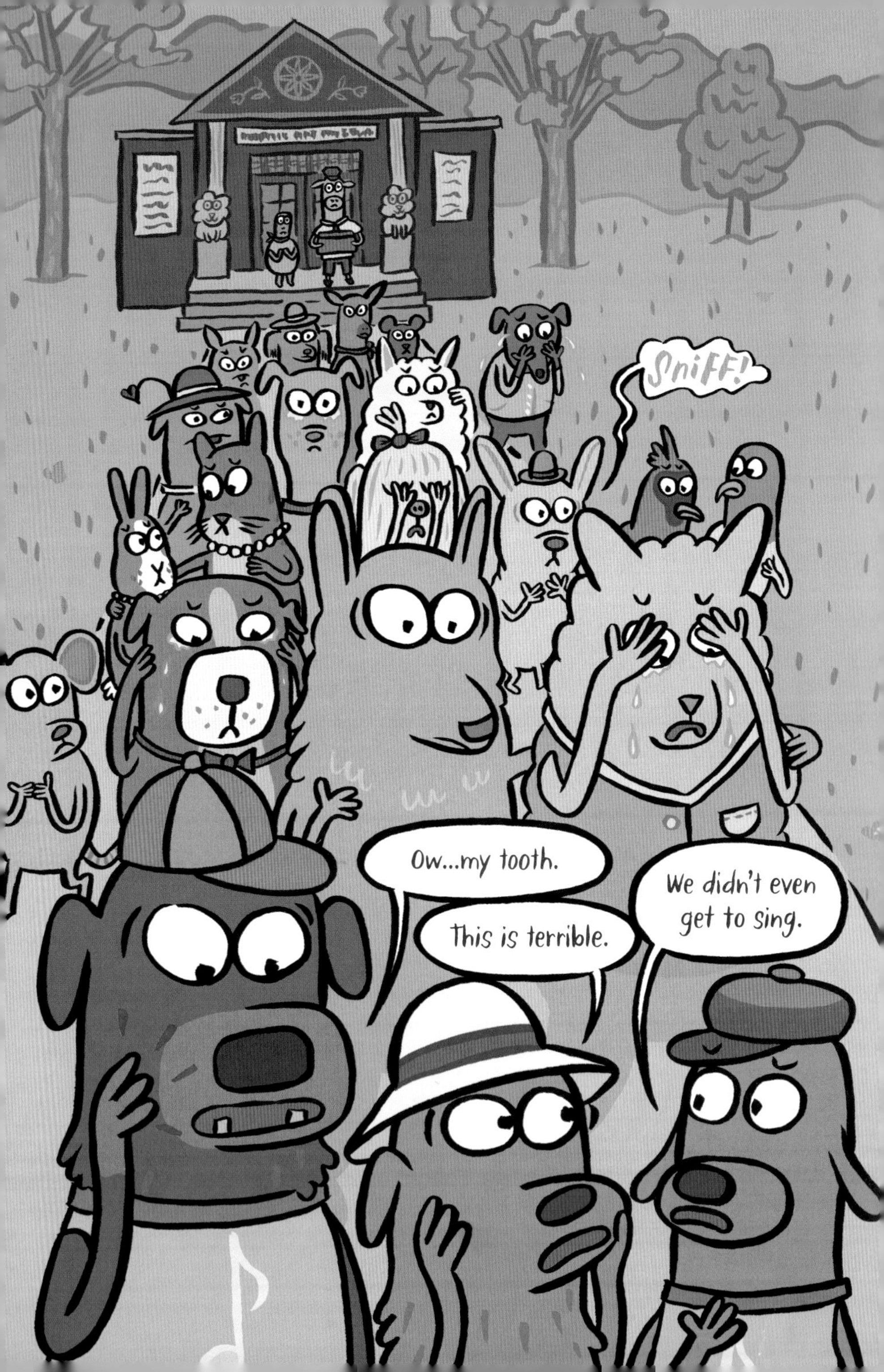
SniFF!
Ow...my tooth.
This is terrible.
We didn't even get to sing.

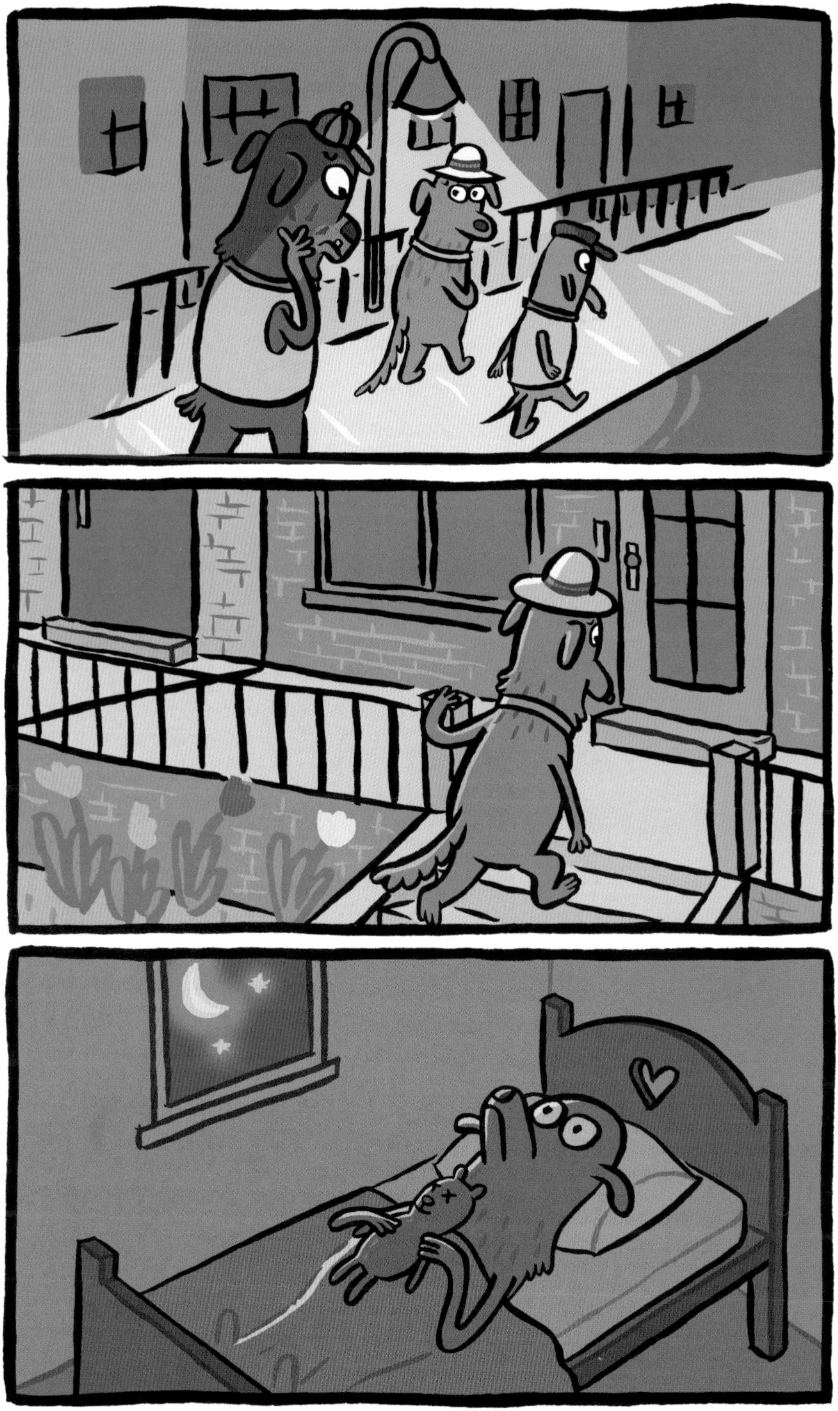

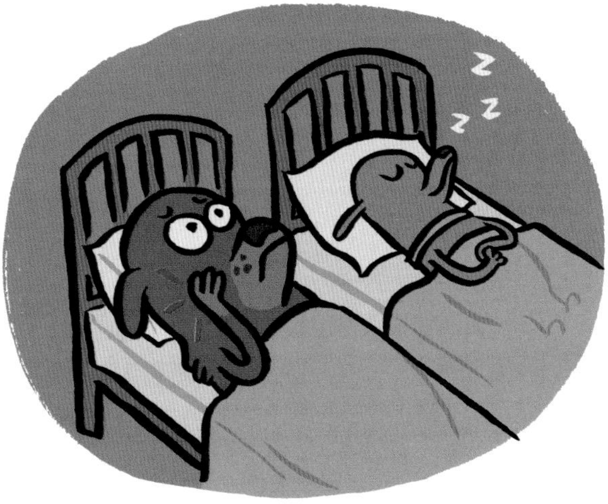
Z Z Z

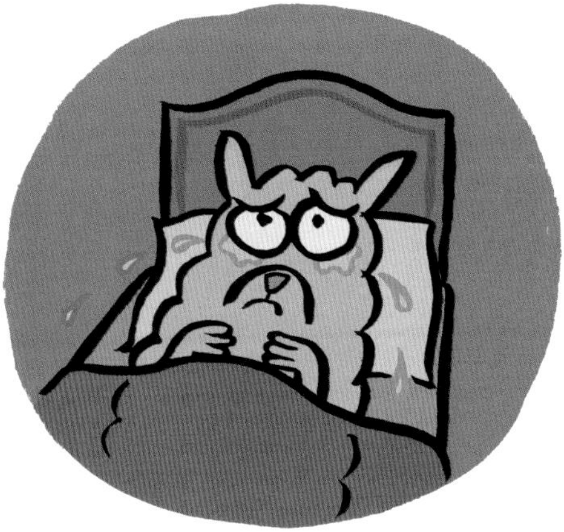

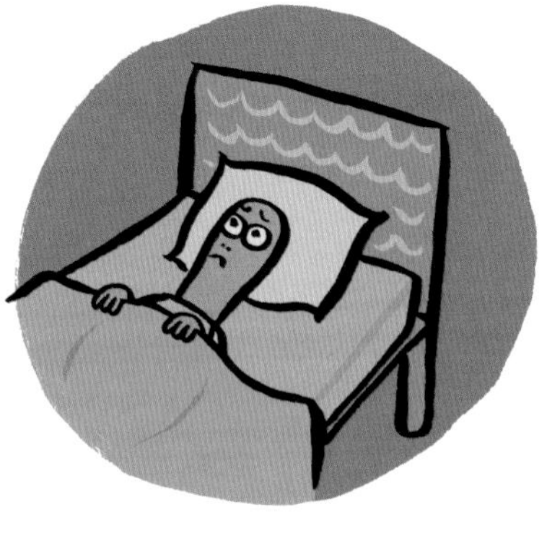

Chapter 4

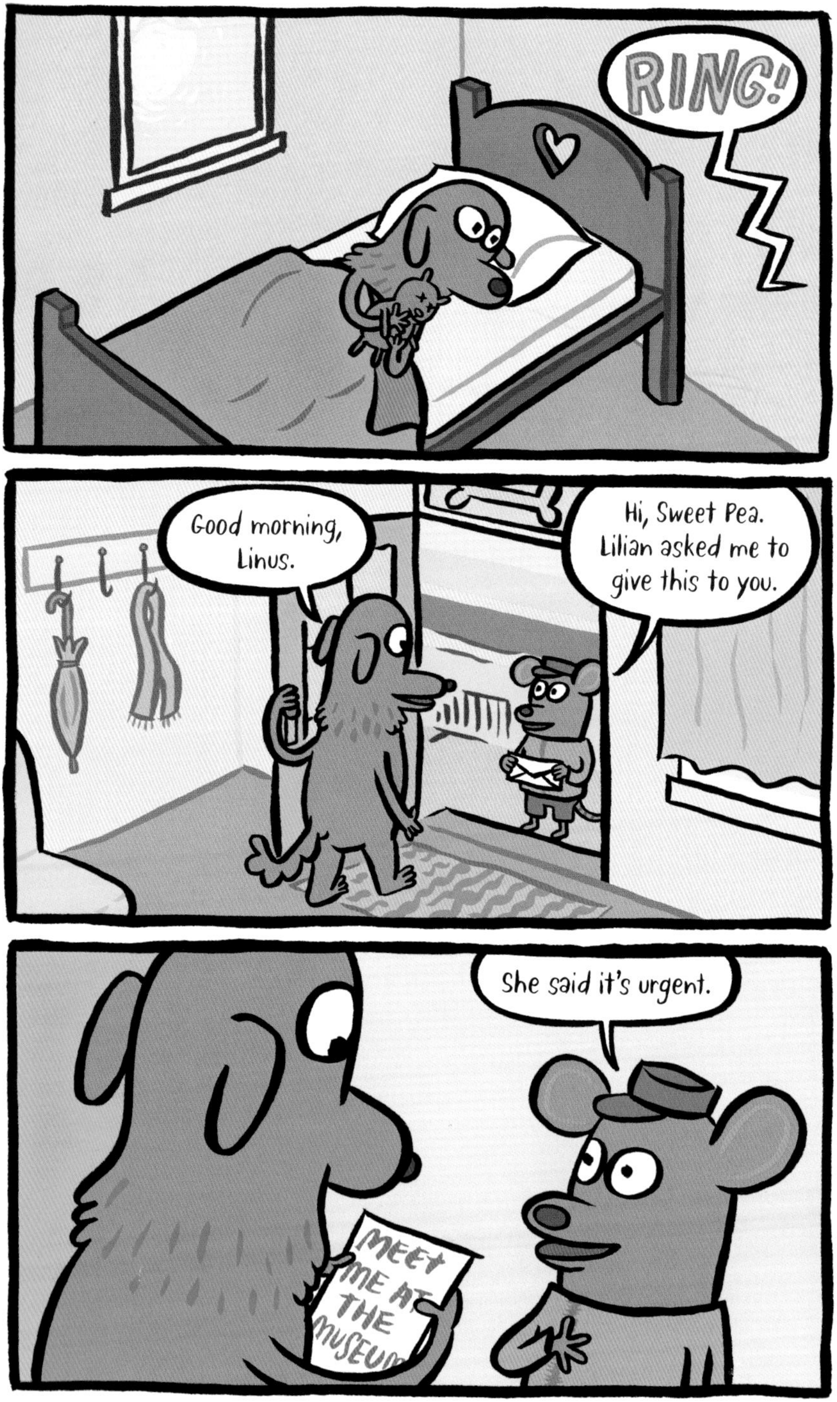
RING!
Good morning, Linus.
Hi, Sweet Pea. Lilian asked me to give this to you.
She said it's urgent.
MEET ME AT THE MUSEU

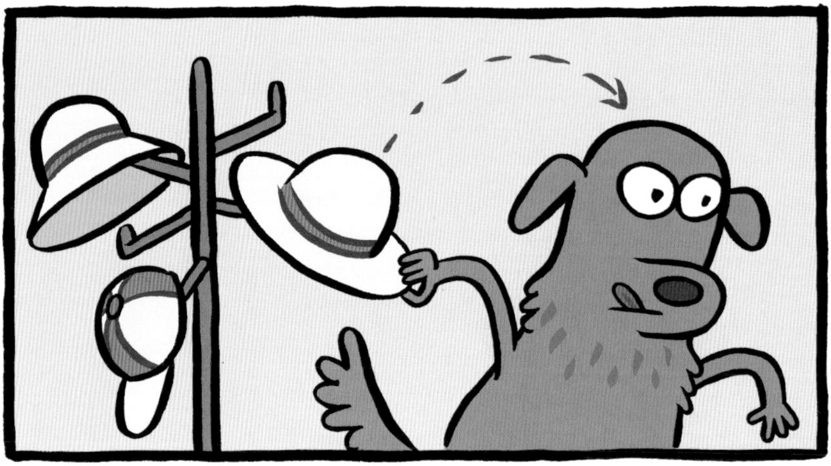

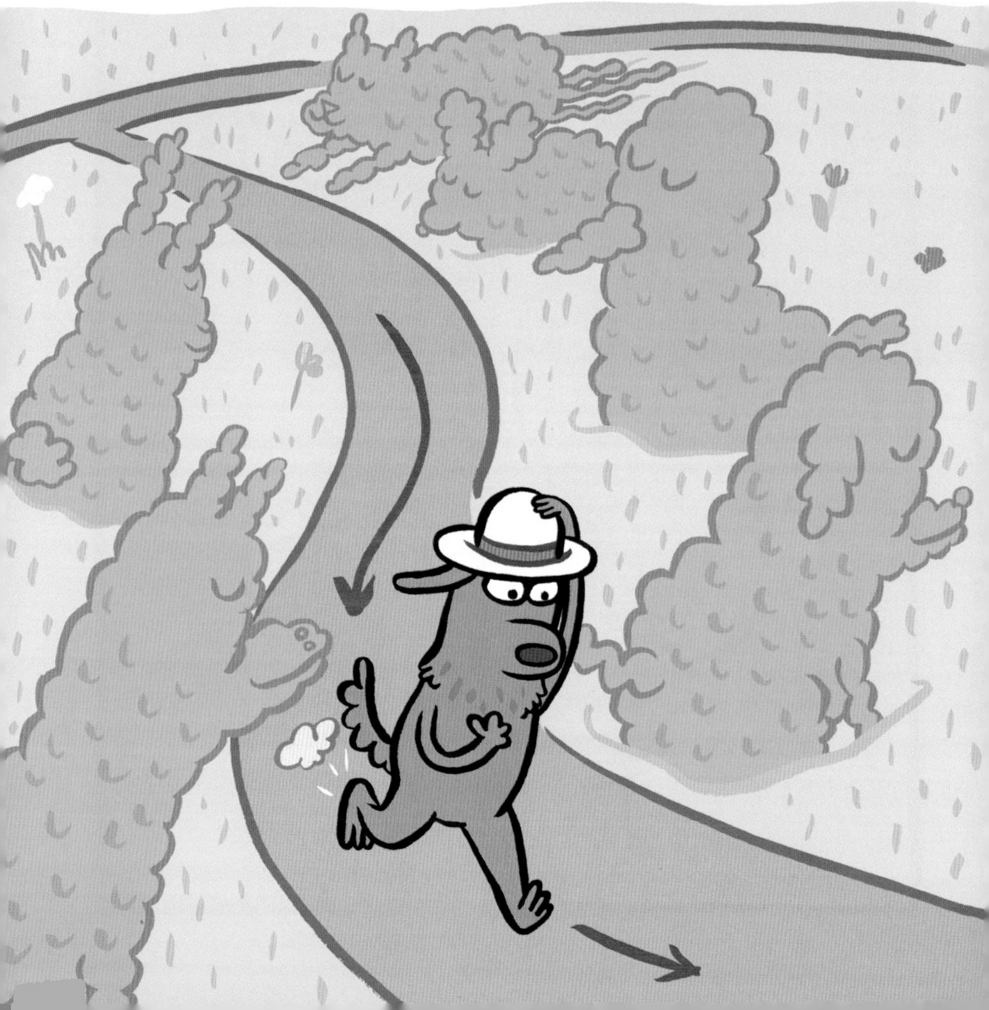

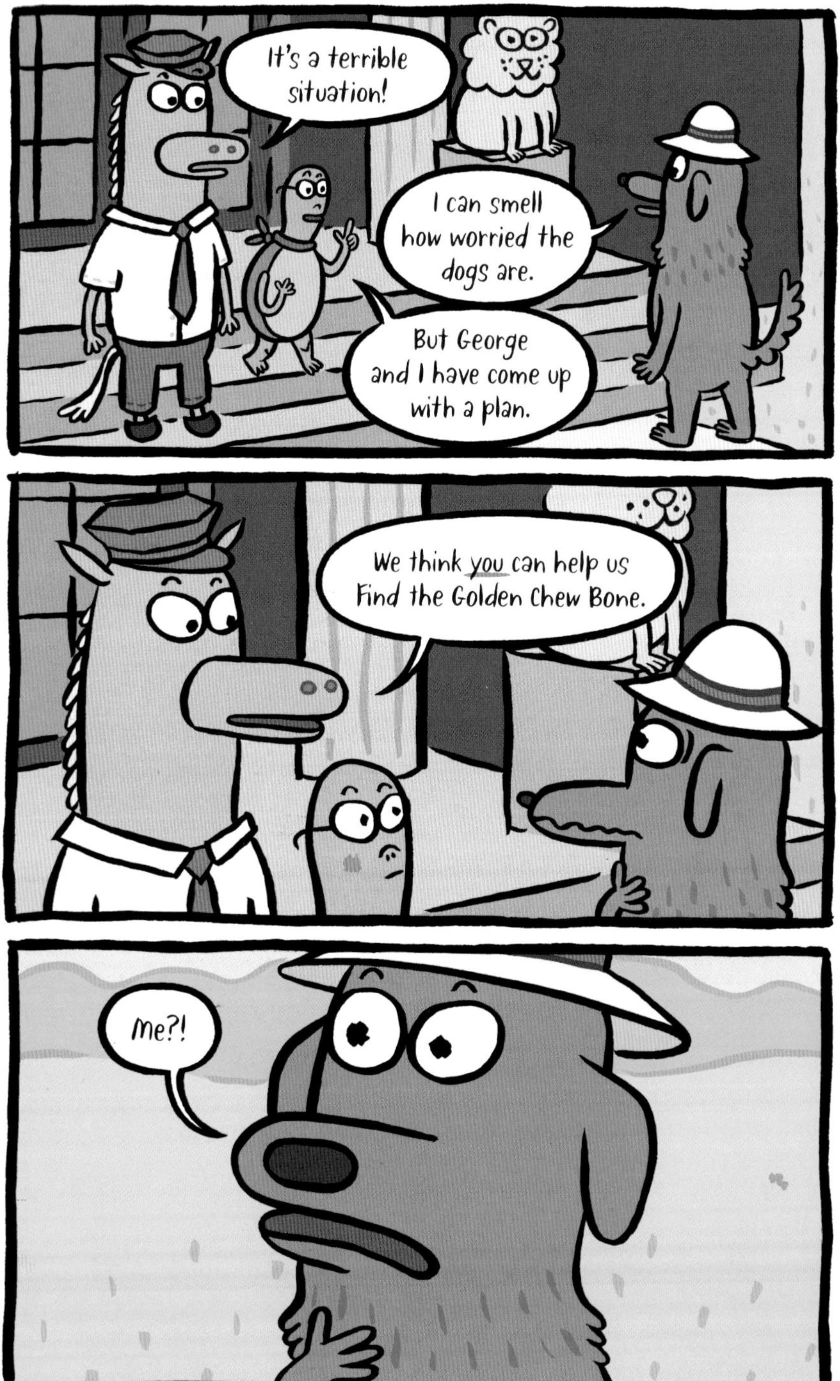
It's a terrible situation!
I can smell how worried the dogs are.
But George and I have come up with a plan.
We think you can help us find the Golden Chew Bone.
Me?!

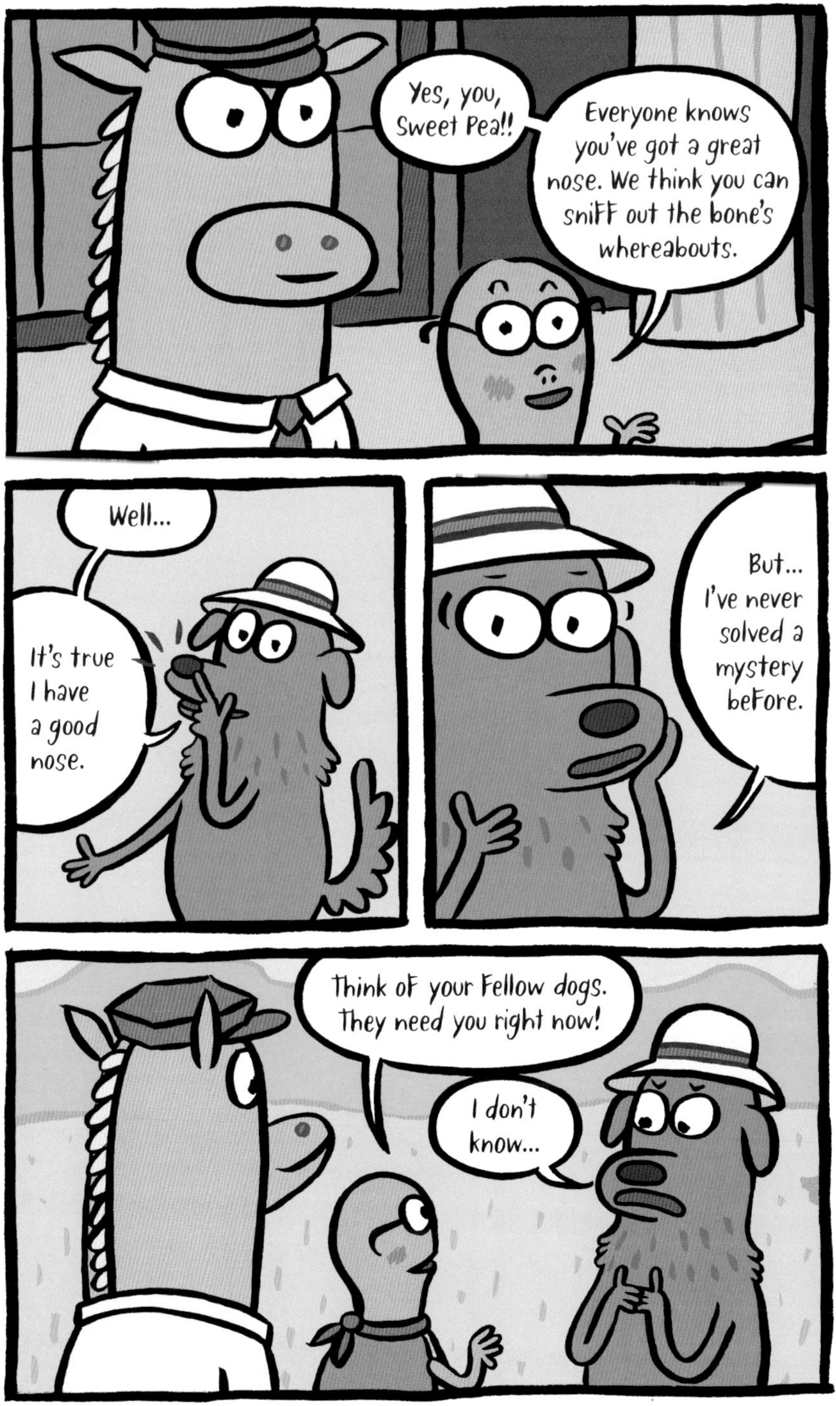
Yes, you, Sweet Pea!!
Everyone knows you've got a great nose. We think you can sniff out the bone's whereabouts.
Well...
It's true I have a good nose.
But... I've never solved a mystery before.
Think of your fellow dogs. They need you right now!
I don't know...

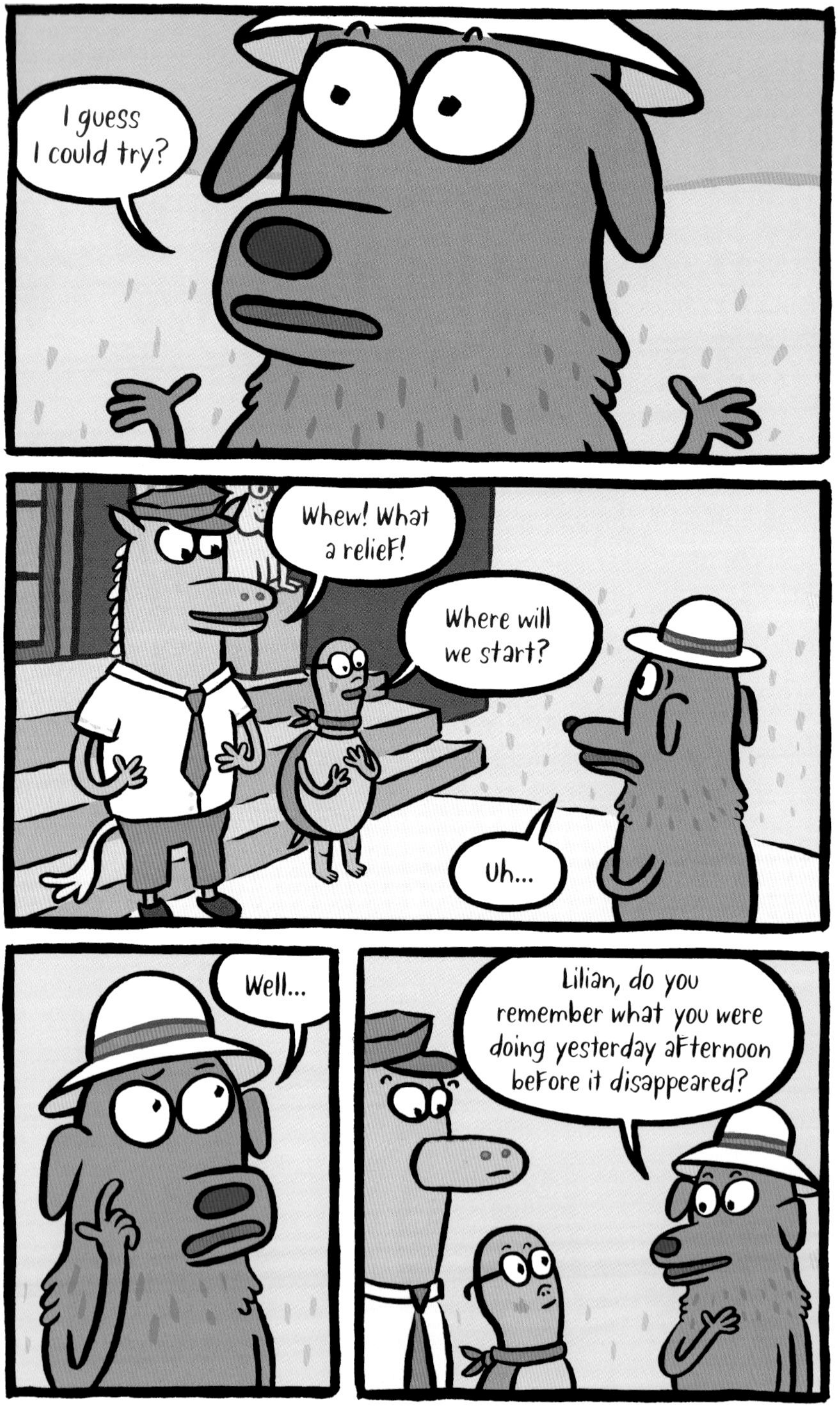
I guess I could try?
Whew! What a relief!
Where will we start?
Uh...
Well...
Lilian, do you remember what you were doing yesterday afternoon before it disappeared?

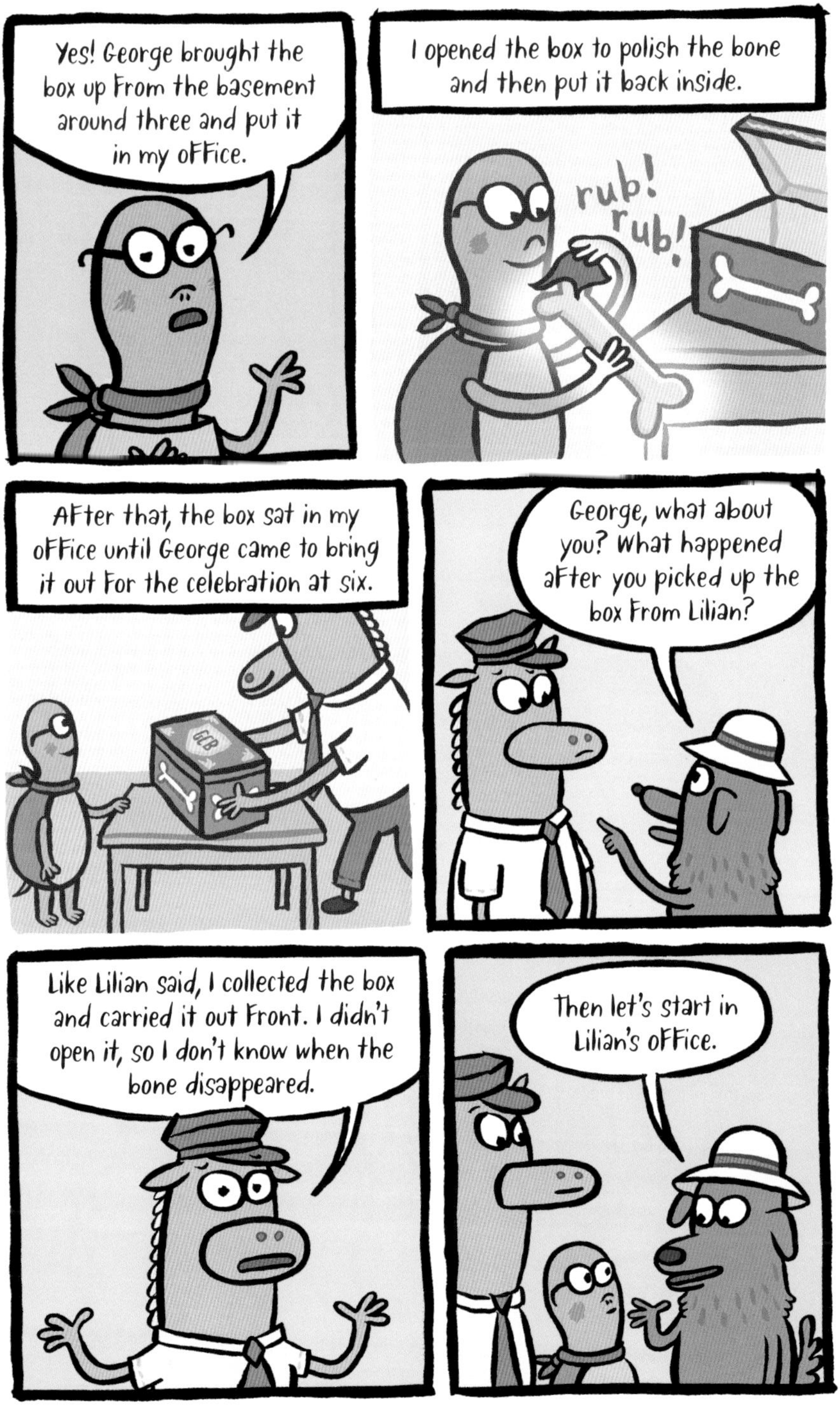

Yes! George brought the box up From the basement around three and put it in my oFFice.
I opened the box to polish the bone and then put it back inside.
rub! rub!
AFter that, the box sat in my oFFice until George came to bring it out For the celebration at six.
GCB
George, what about you? What happened aFter you picked up the box From Lilian?
Like Lilian said, I collected the box and carried it out Front. I didn't open it, so I don't know when the bone disappeared.
Then let's start in Lilian's oFFice.

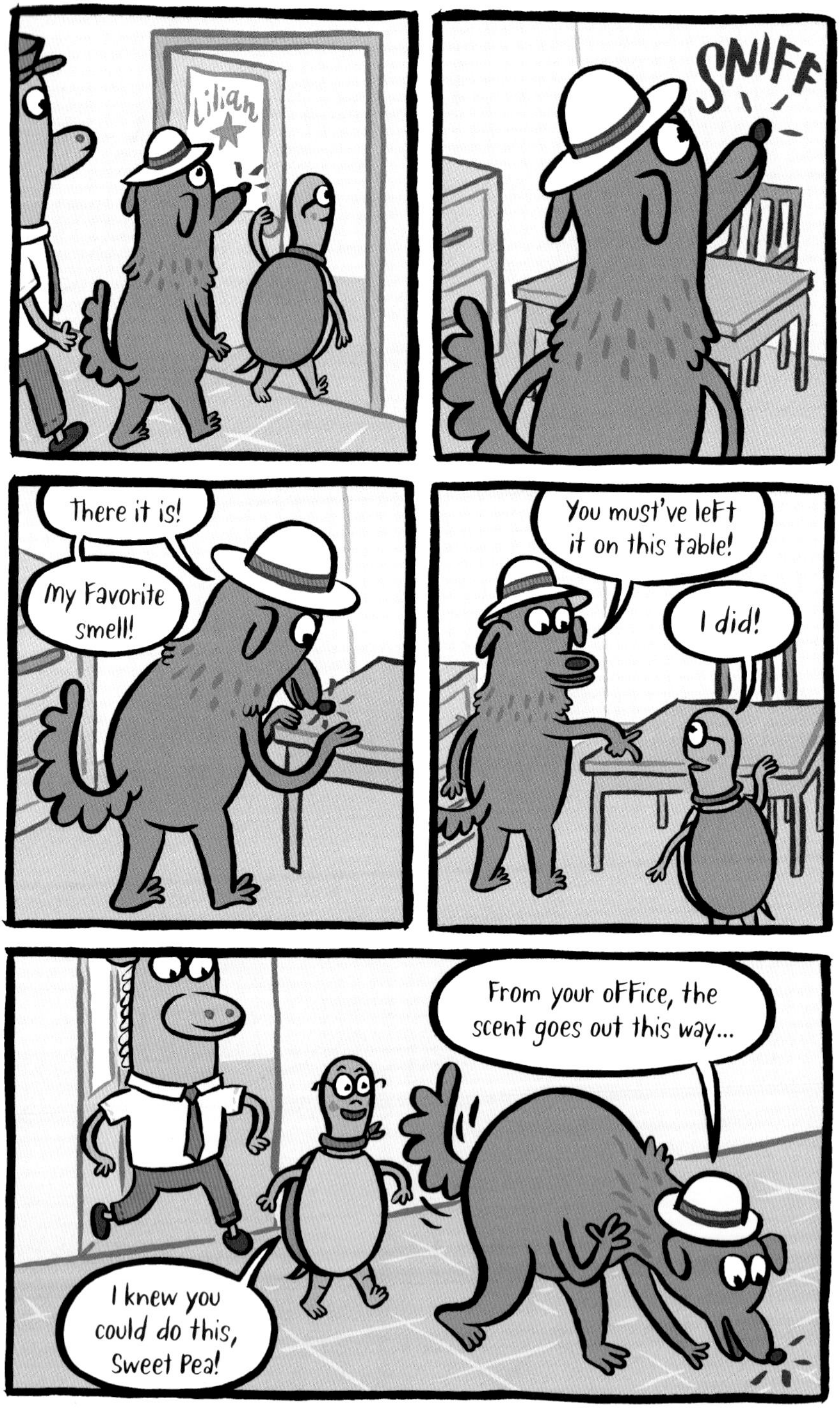
Lilian
SNIFF
There it is!
My favorite smell!
You must've left it on this table!
I did!
From your office, the scent goes out this way...
I knew you could do this, Sweet Pea!

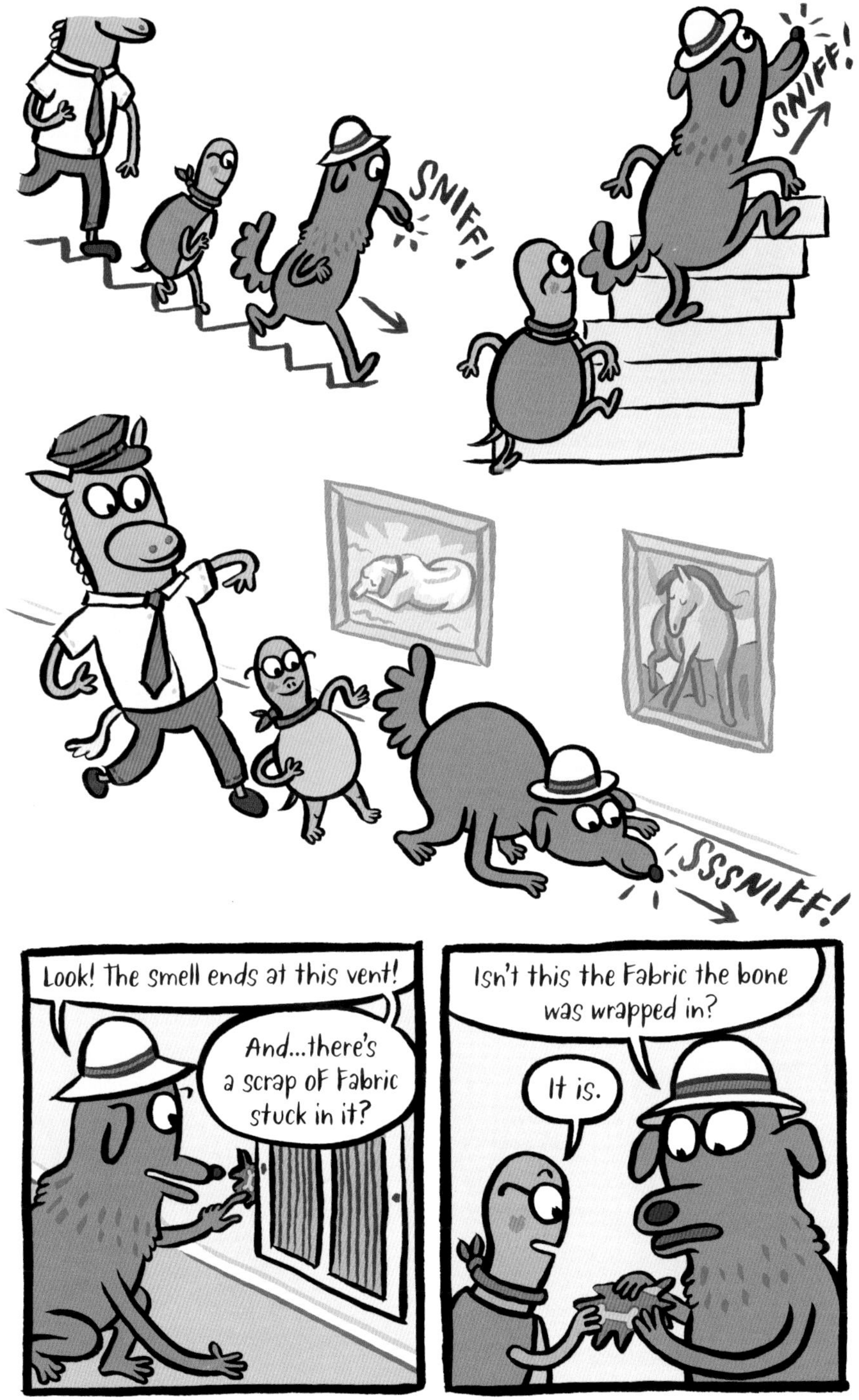
SNIFF!
SNIFF!
SSSNIFF!
Look! The smell ends at this vent!
And...there's a scrap of fabric stuck in it?
Isn't this the fabric the bone was wrapped in?
It is.

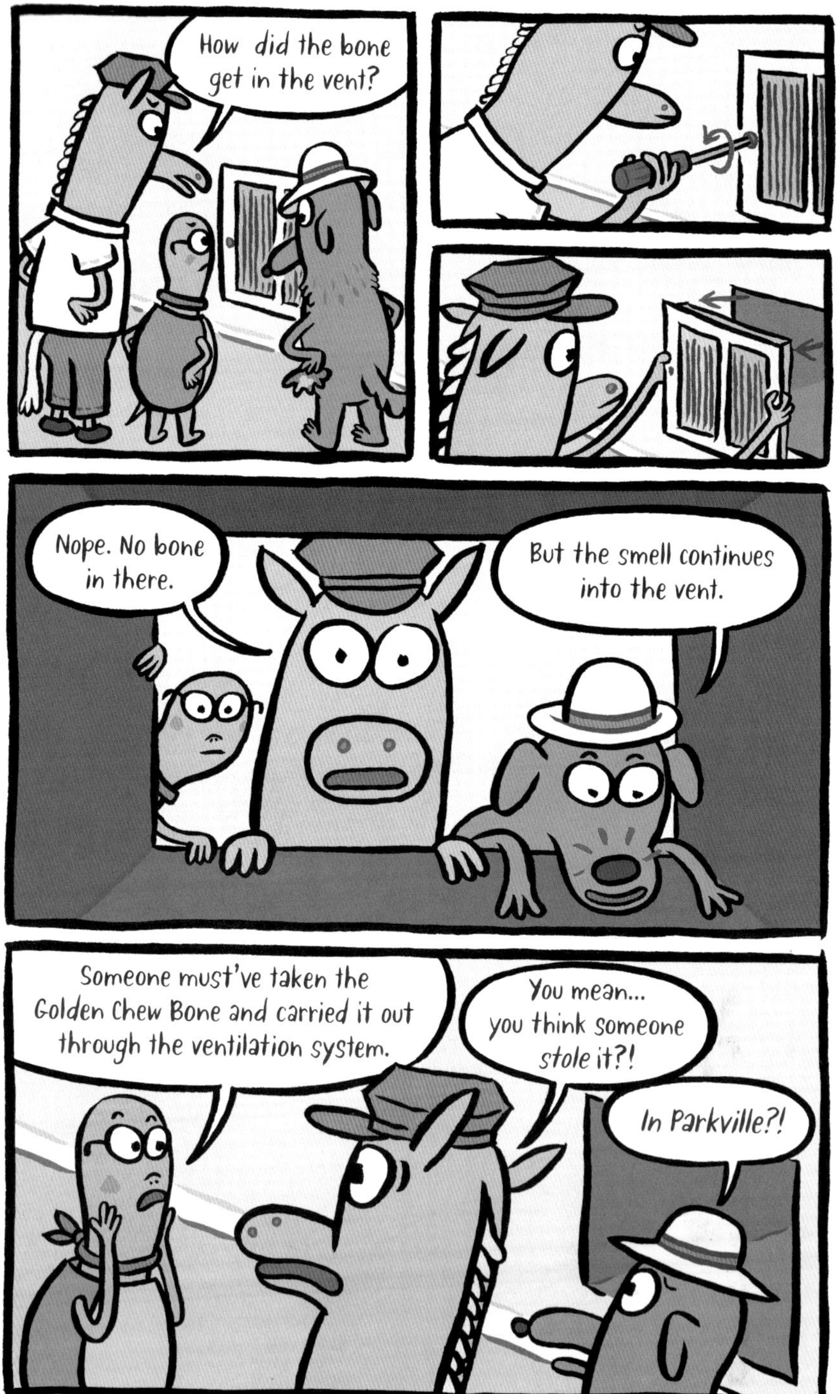
How did the bone get in the vent?
Nope. No bone in there.
But the smell continues into the vent.
Someone must've taken the Golden Chew Bone and carried it out through the ventilation system.
You mean... you think someone stole it?!
In Parkville?!

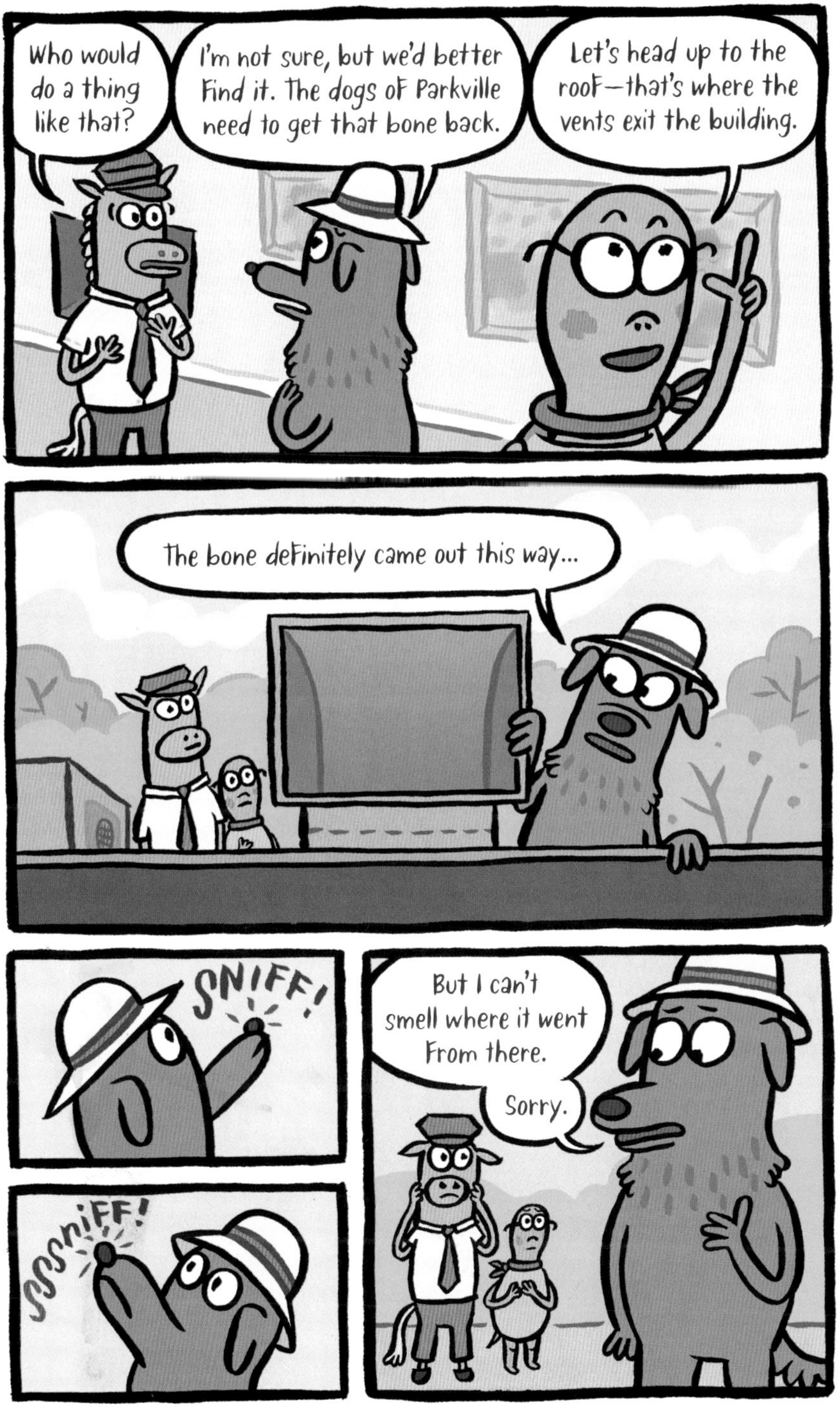
Who would do a thing like that?
I'm not sure, but we'd better find it. The dogs of Parkville need to get that bone back.
Let's head up to the roof—that's where the vents exit the building.
The bone definitely came out this way...
SNIFF!
SSSniFF!
But I can't smell where it went from there.
Sorry.

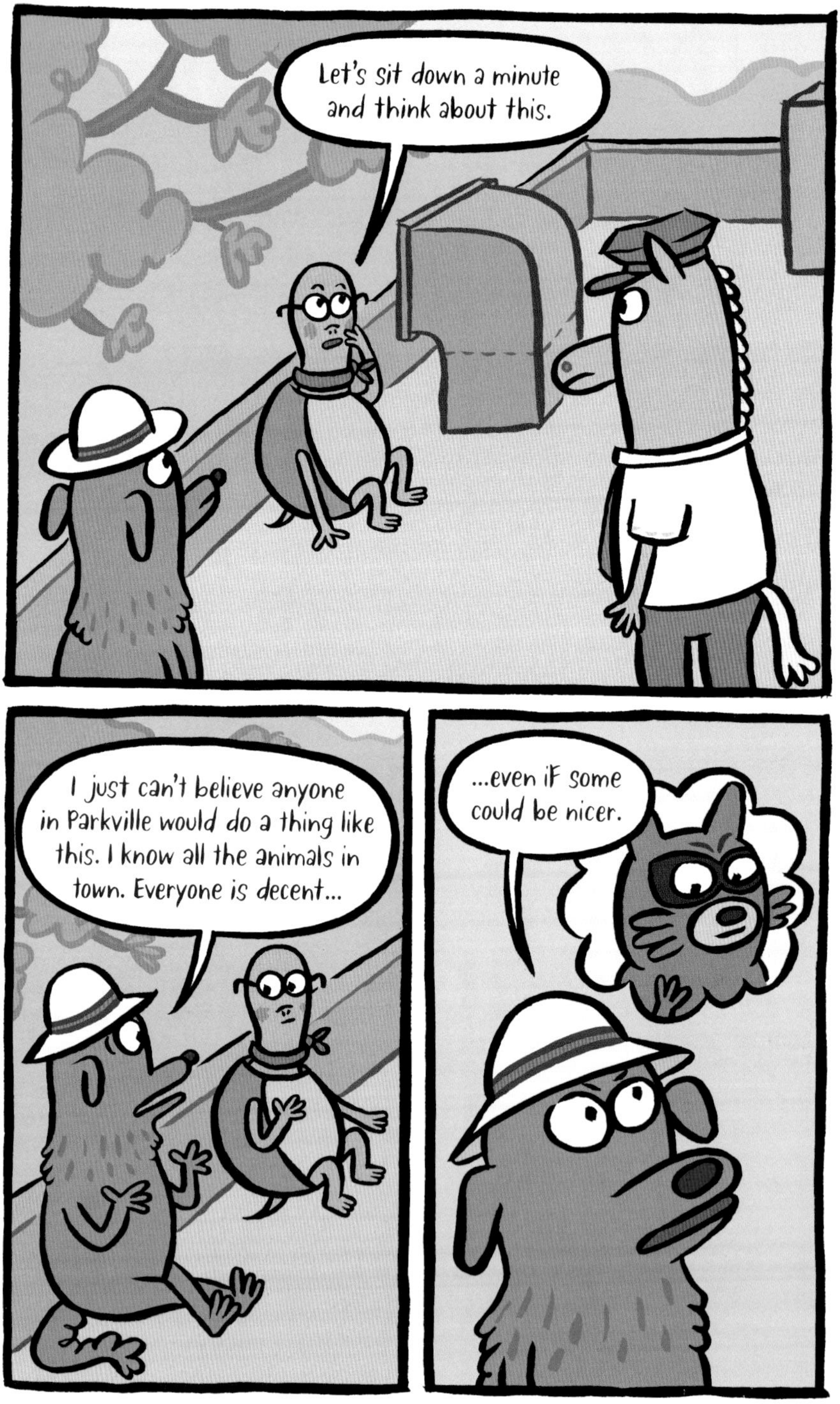
Let's sit down a minute and think about this.
I just can't believe anyone in Parkville would do a thing like this. I know all the animals in town. Everyone is decent...
...even if some could be nicer.

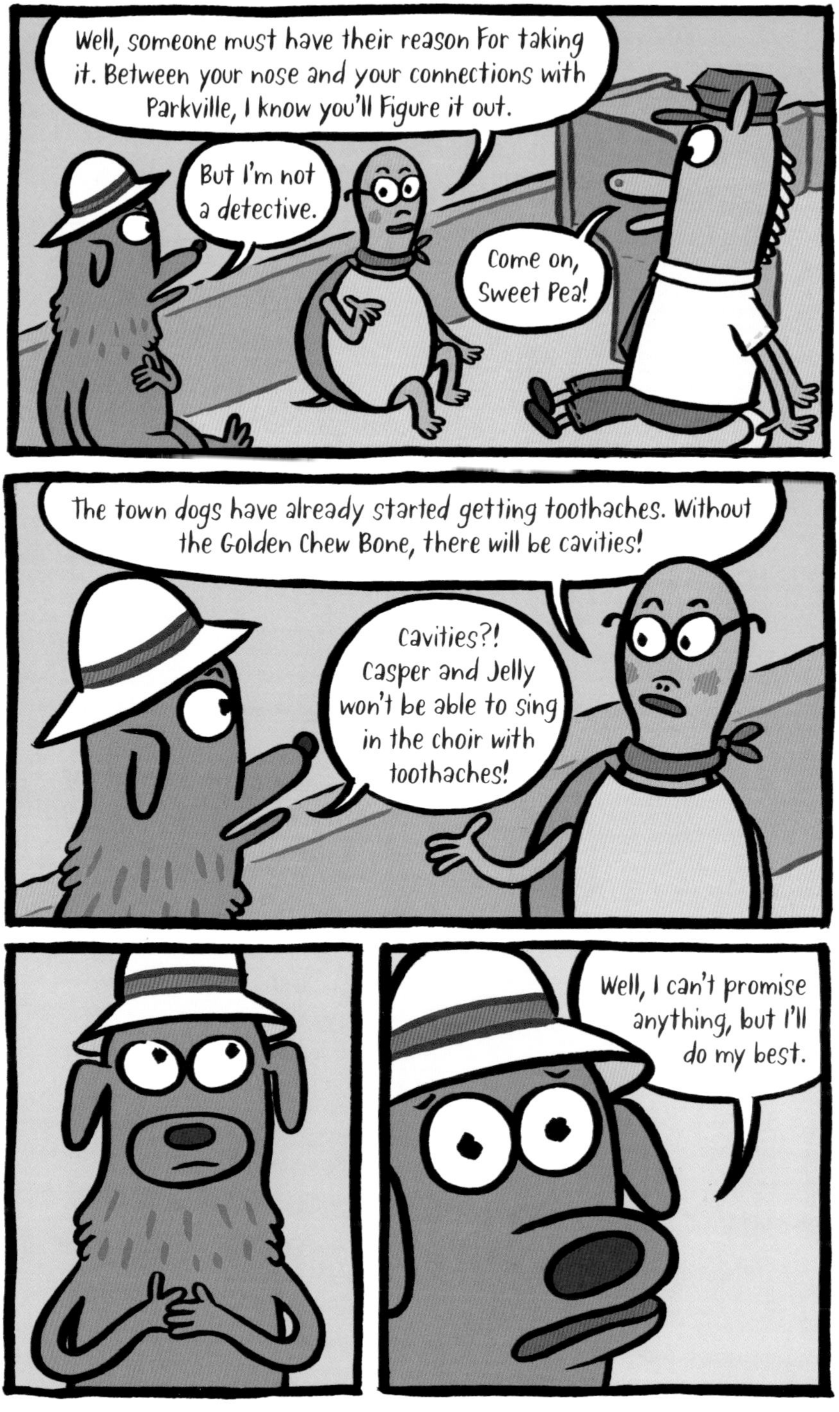
Well, someone must have their reason For taking it. Between your nose and your connections with Parkville, I know you'll Figure it out.
But I'm not a detective.
Come on, Sweet Pea!
The town dogs have already started getting toothaches. Without the Golden Chew Bone, there will be cavities!
Cavities?! Casper and Jelly won't be able to sing in the choir with toothaches!
Well, I can't promise anything, but I'll do my best.

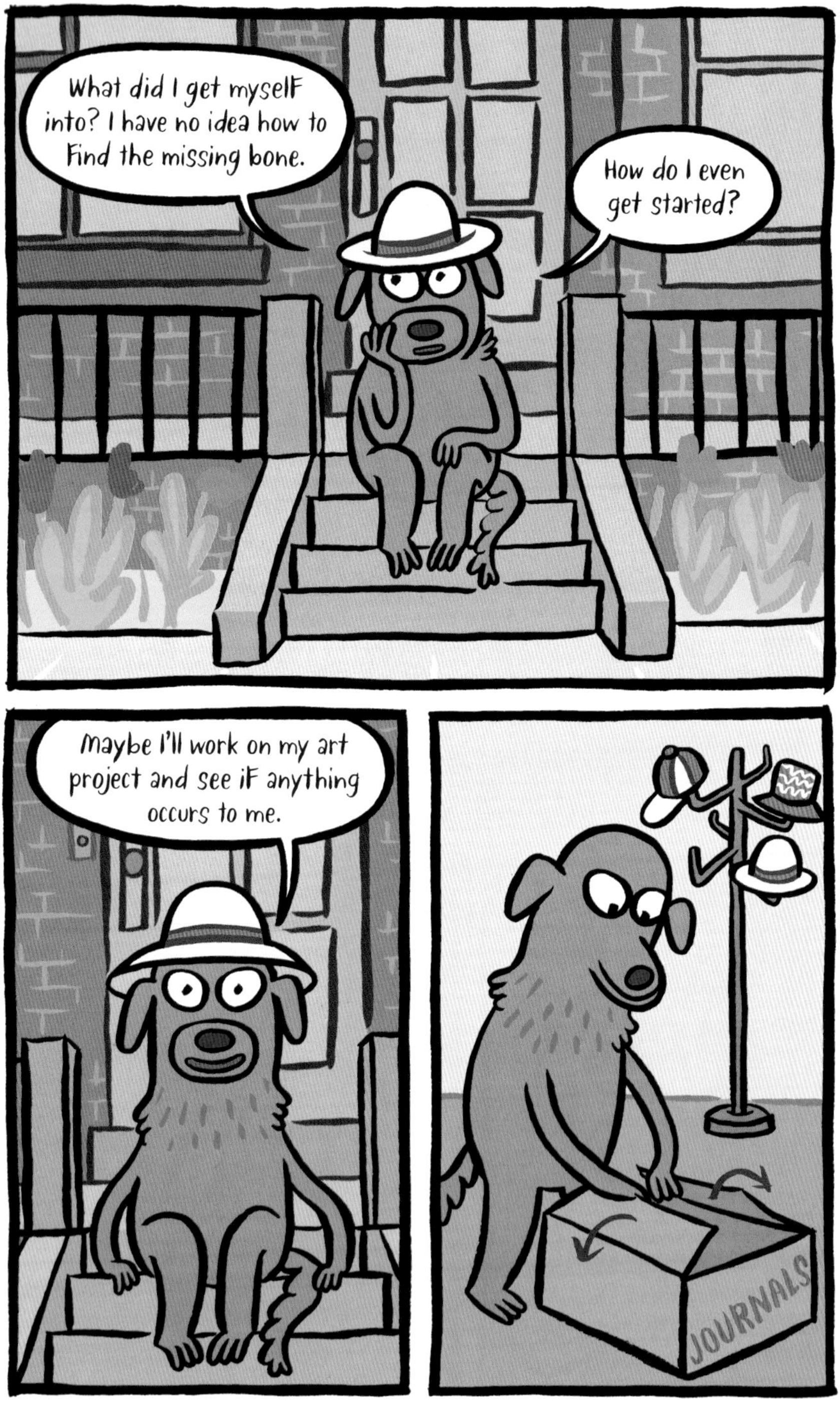
What did I get myself into? I have no idea how to find the missing bone.
How do I even get started?
Maybe I'll work on my art project and see if anything occurs to me.
JOURNALS

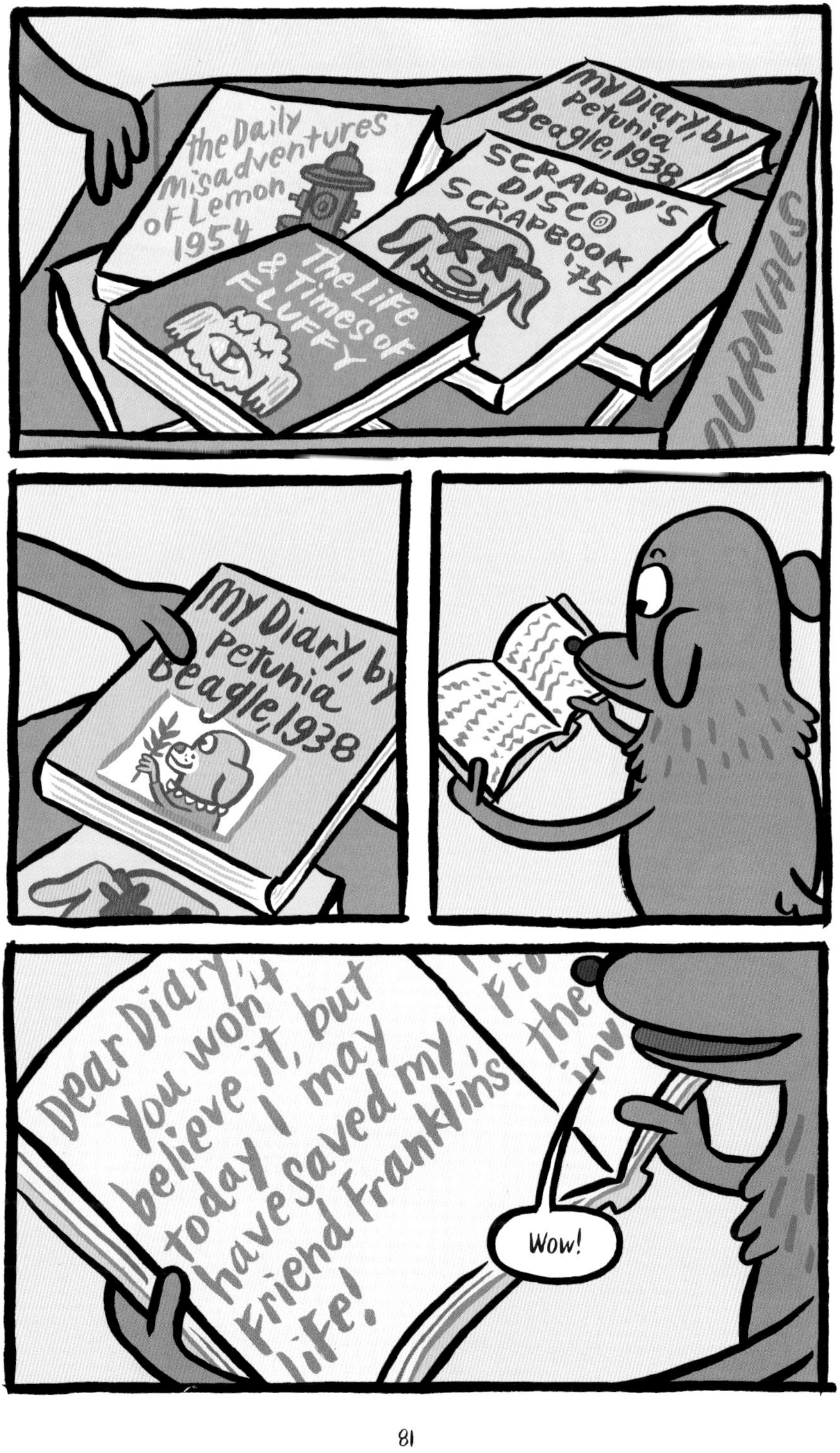

the Daily Misadventures of Lemon 1954
My Diary, by Petunia Beagle, 1938
SCRAPPY'S DISCO SCRAPBOOK '75
The Life & Times of FLUFFY
My Diary, by Petunia Beagle, 1938
Dear Diary, You won't believe it, but today I may have saved my friend Franklin's life!
Wow!

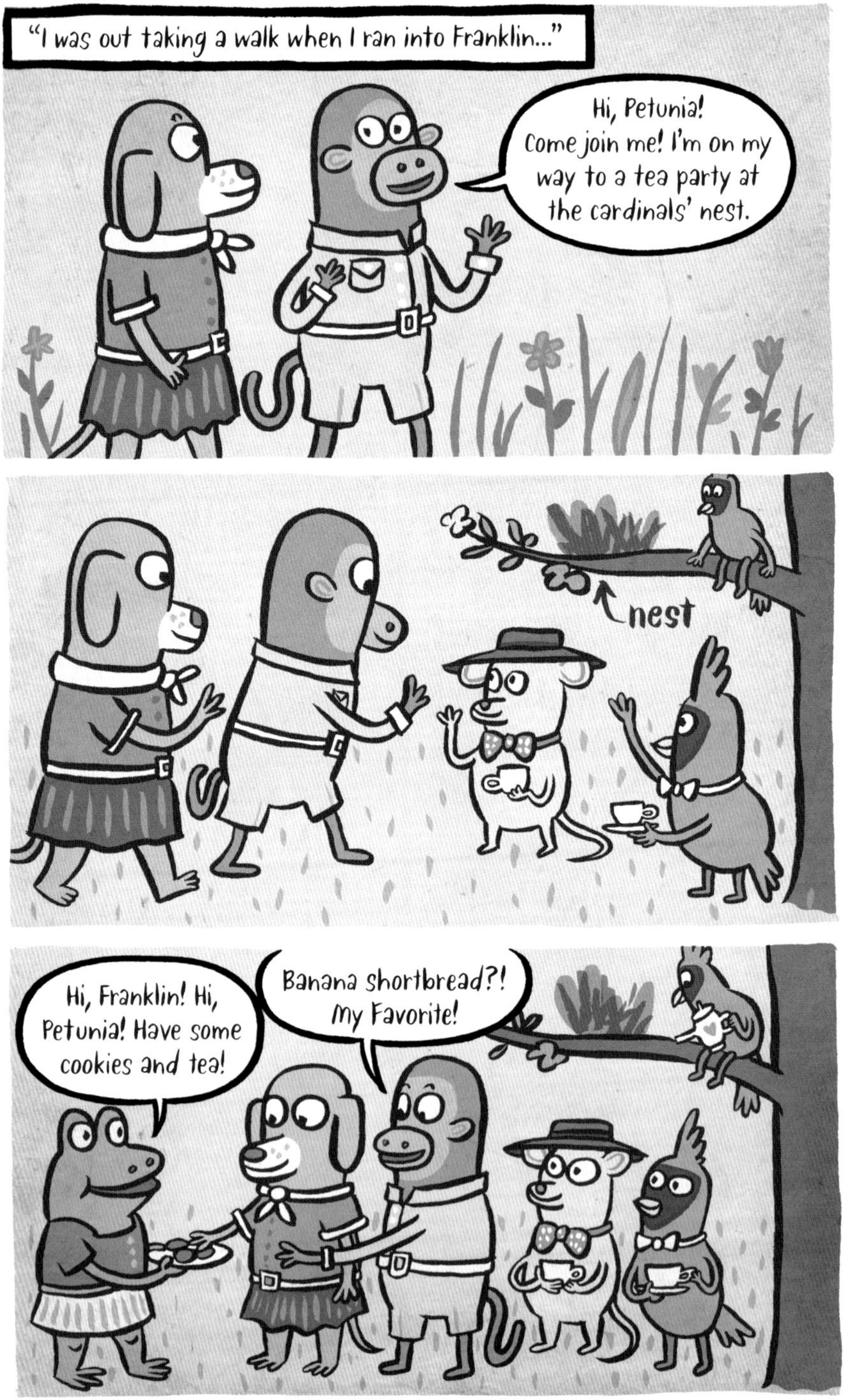
"I was out taking a walk when I ran into Franklin..."
Hi, Petunia! Come join me! I'm on my way to a tea party at the cardinals' nest.
nest
Hi, Franklin! Hi, Petunia! Have some cookies and tea!
Banana shortbread?! My Favorite!

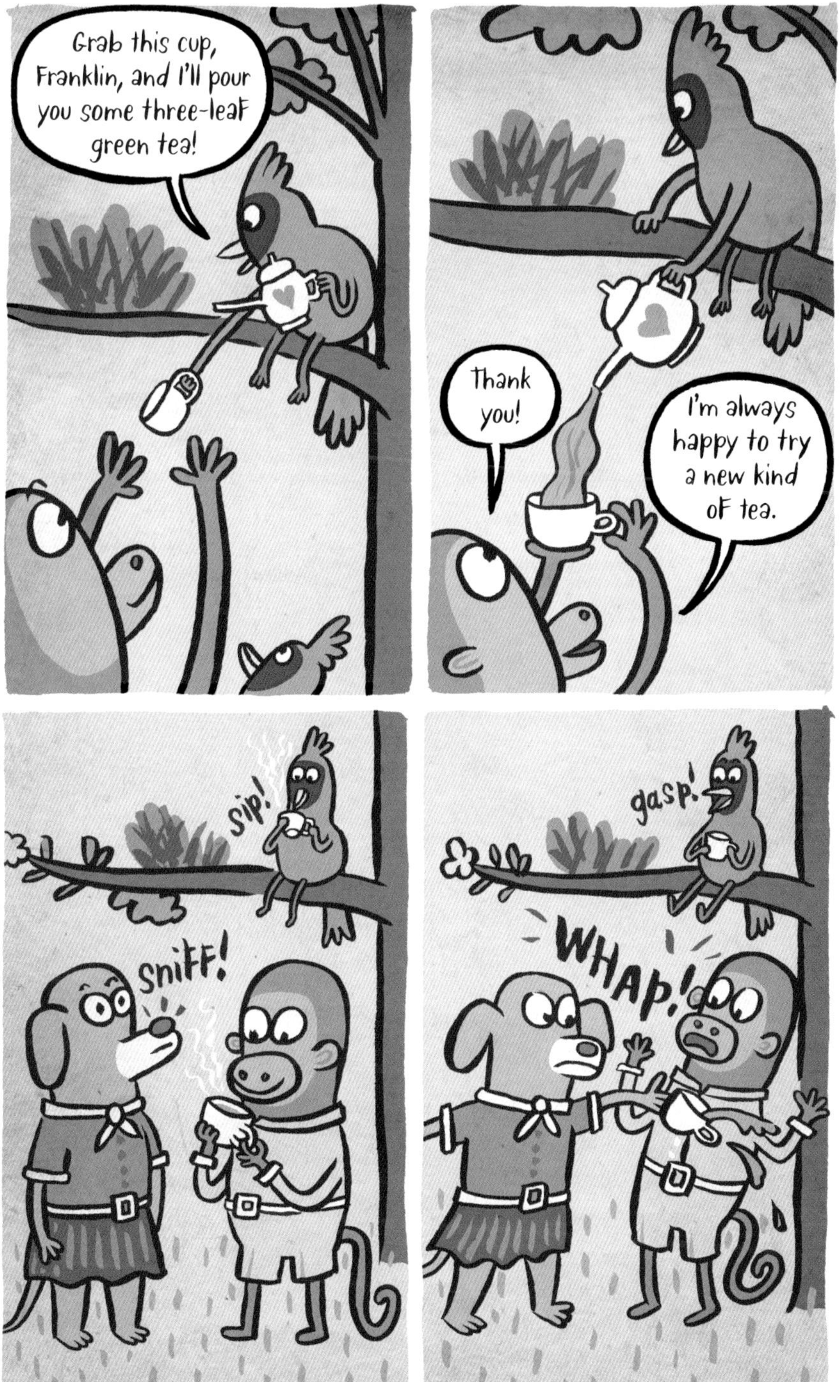
Grab this cup, Franklin, and I'll pour you some three-leaf green tea!
Thank you!
I'm always happy to try a new kind of tea.
sip!
SNIFF!
gasp!
WHAP!

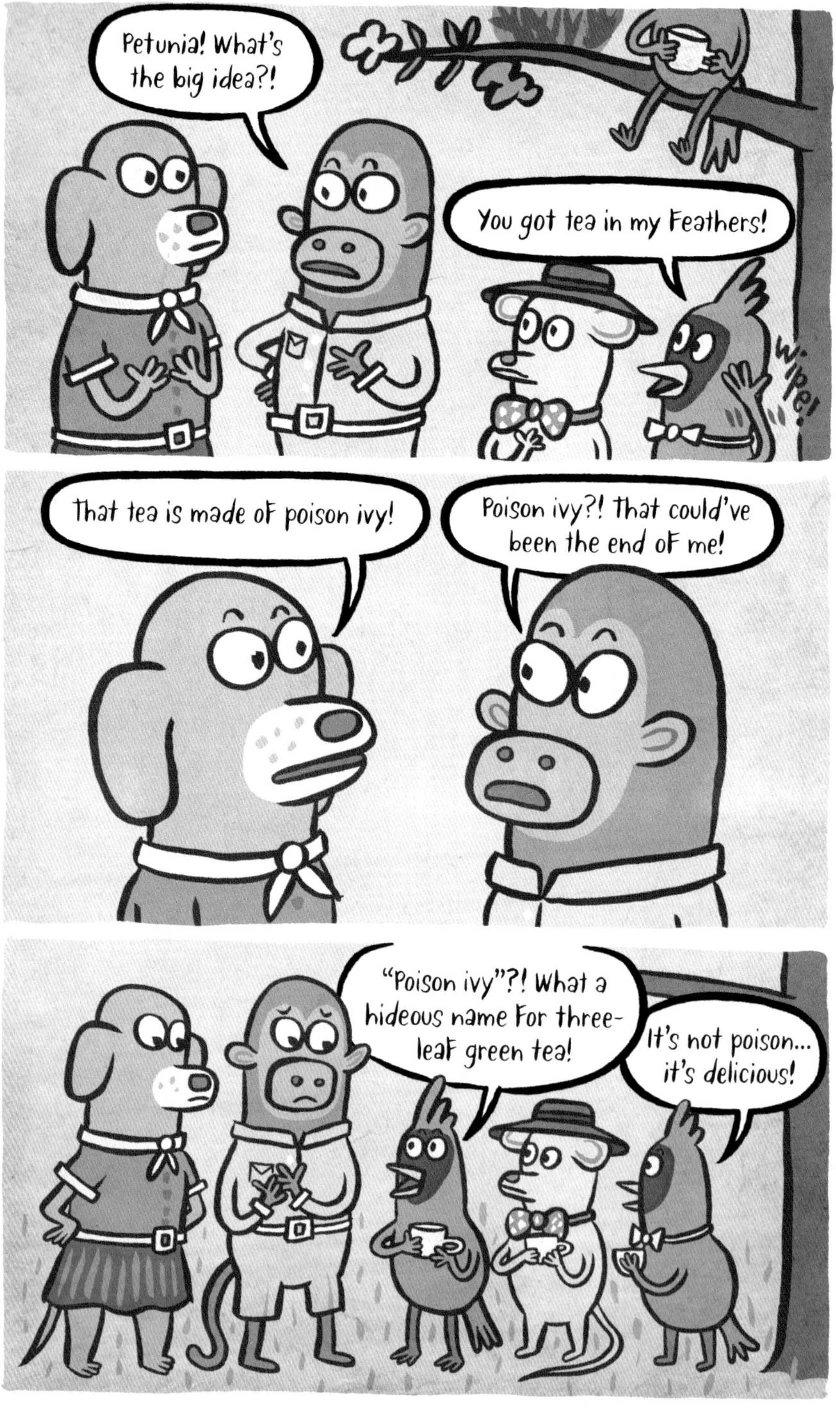
Petunia! What's the big idea?!
You got tea in my Feathers!
WIPE!
That tea is made of poison ivy!
Poison ivy?! That could've been the end of me!
"Poison ivy"?! What a hideous name for three-leaf green tea!
It's not poison... it's delicious!

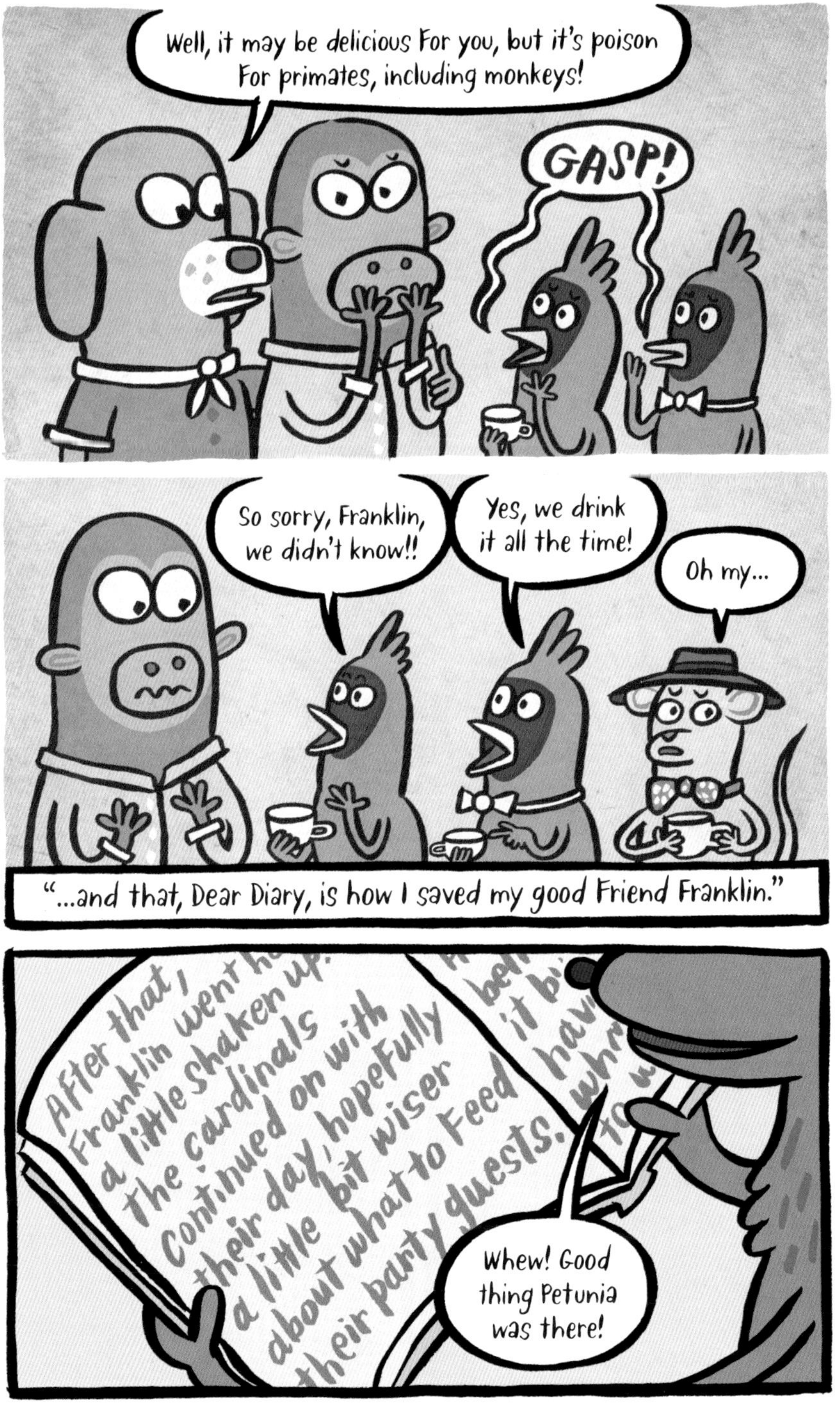
Well, it may be delicious for you, but it's poison for primates, including monkeys!
GASP!
So sorry, Franklin, we didn't know!!
Yes, we drink it all the time!
Oh my...
"...and that, Dear Diary, is how I saved my good friend Franklin."
Whew! Good thing Petunia was there!

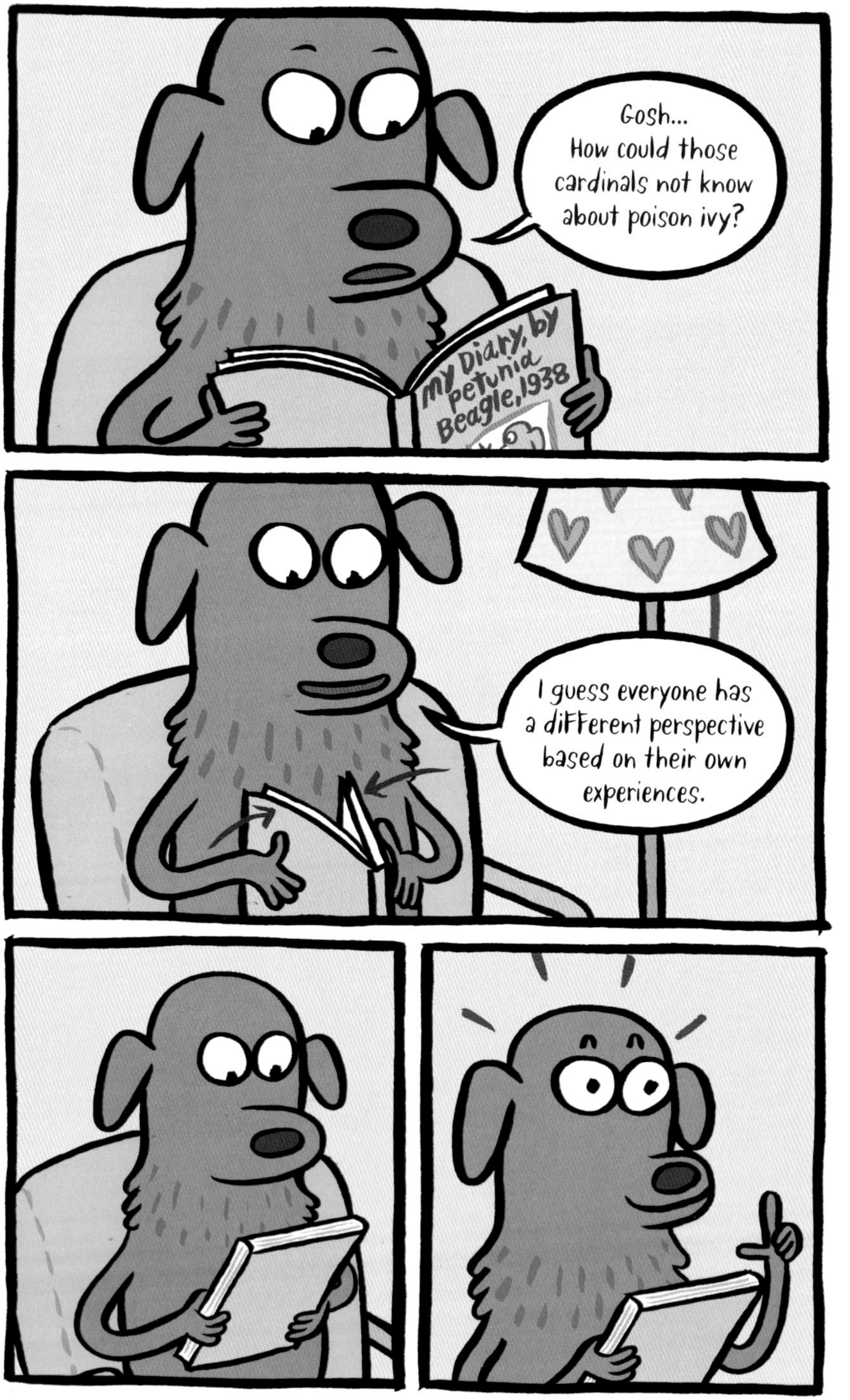
Gosh...
How could those cardinals not know about poison ivy?
My Diary, by Petunia Beagle, 1938
I guess everyone has a different perspective based on their own experiences.

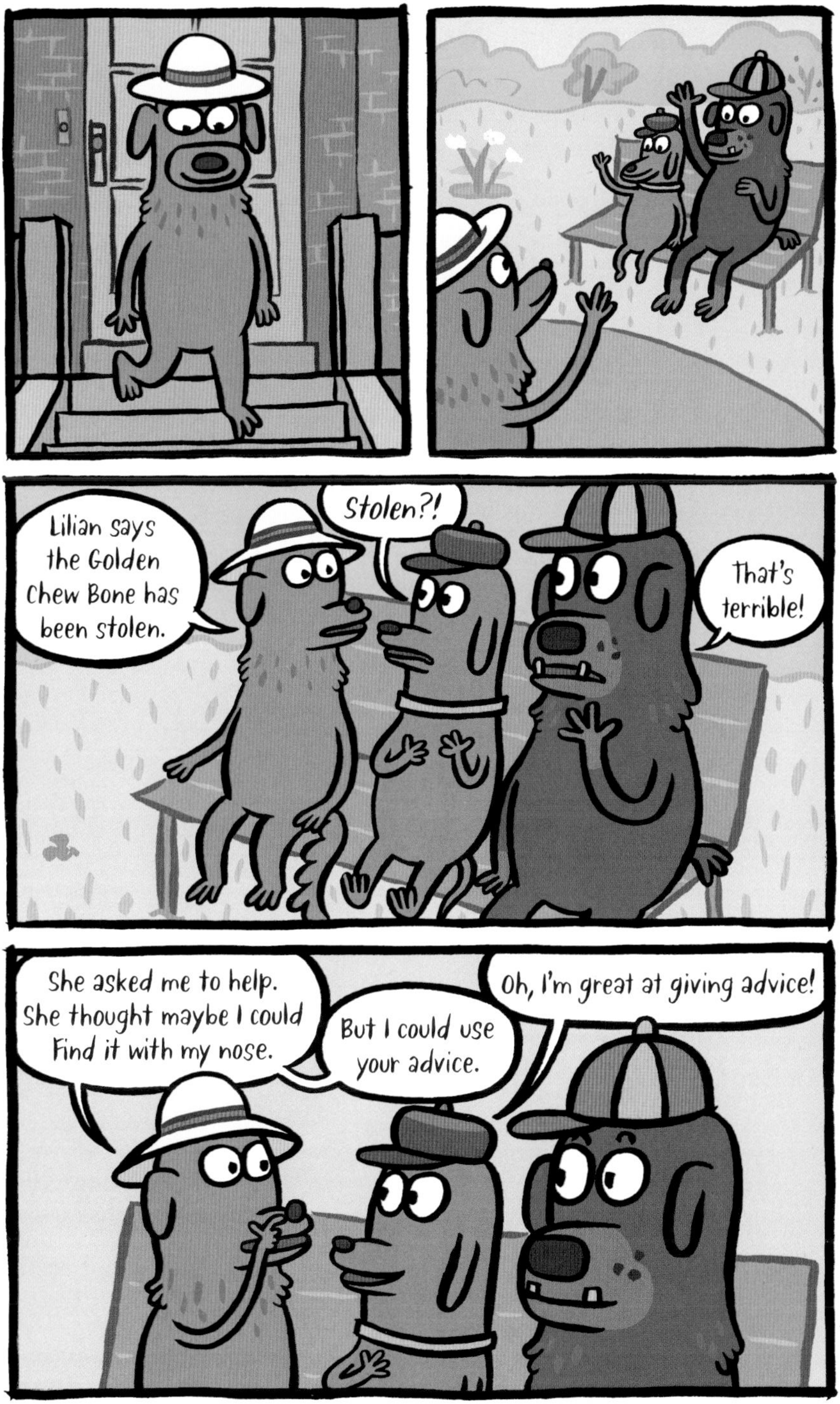
Lilian says the Golden Chew Bone has been stolen.
Stolen?!
That's terrible!
She asked me to help. She thought maybe I could Find it with my nose.
But I could use your advice.
Oh, I'm great at giving advice!

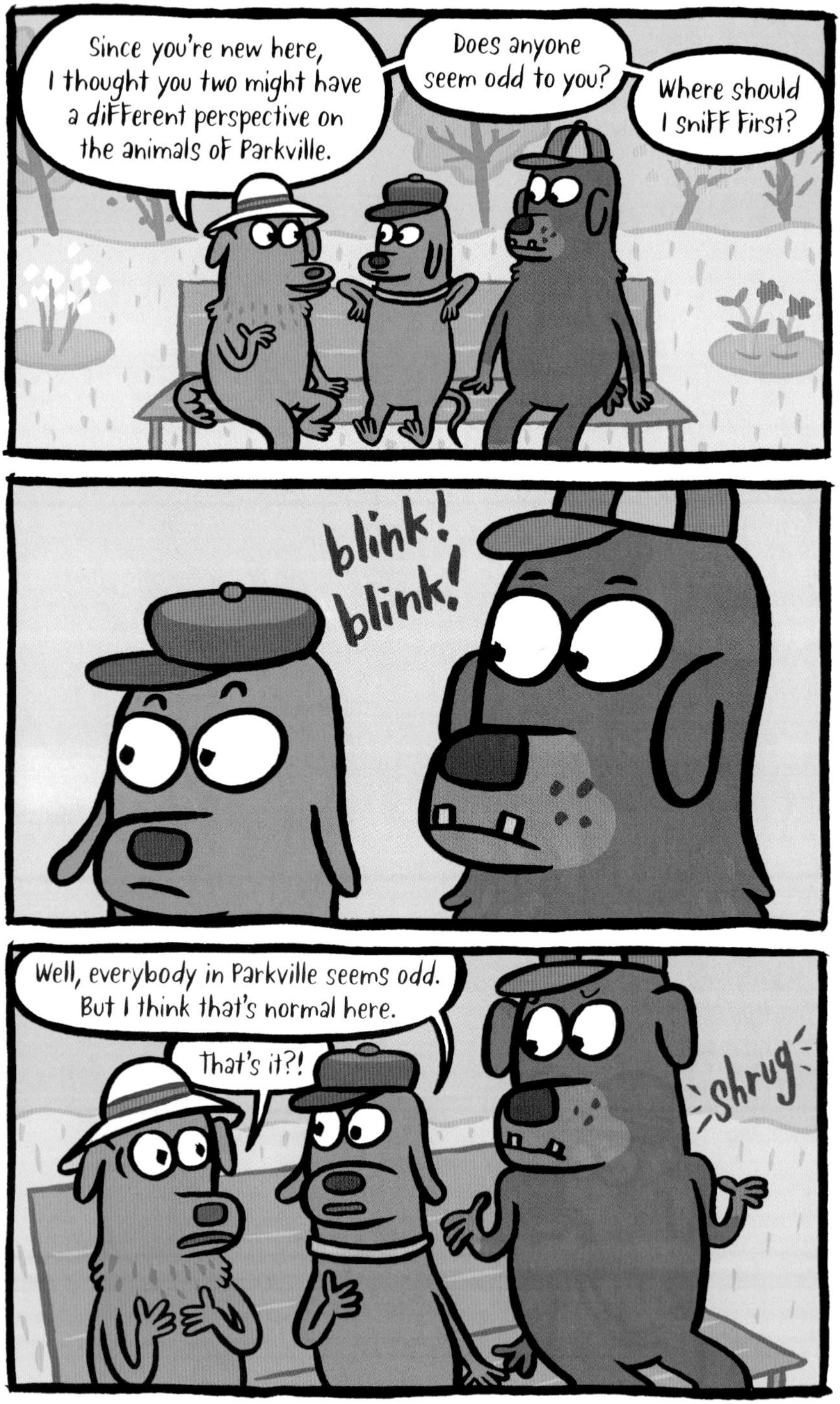
Since you're new here, I thought you two might have a diFFerent perspective on the animals oF Parkville.
Does anyone seem odd to you?
Where should I sniFF First?
blink! blink!
Well, everybody in Parkville seems odd. But I think that's normal here.
That's it?!
shrug

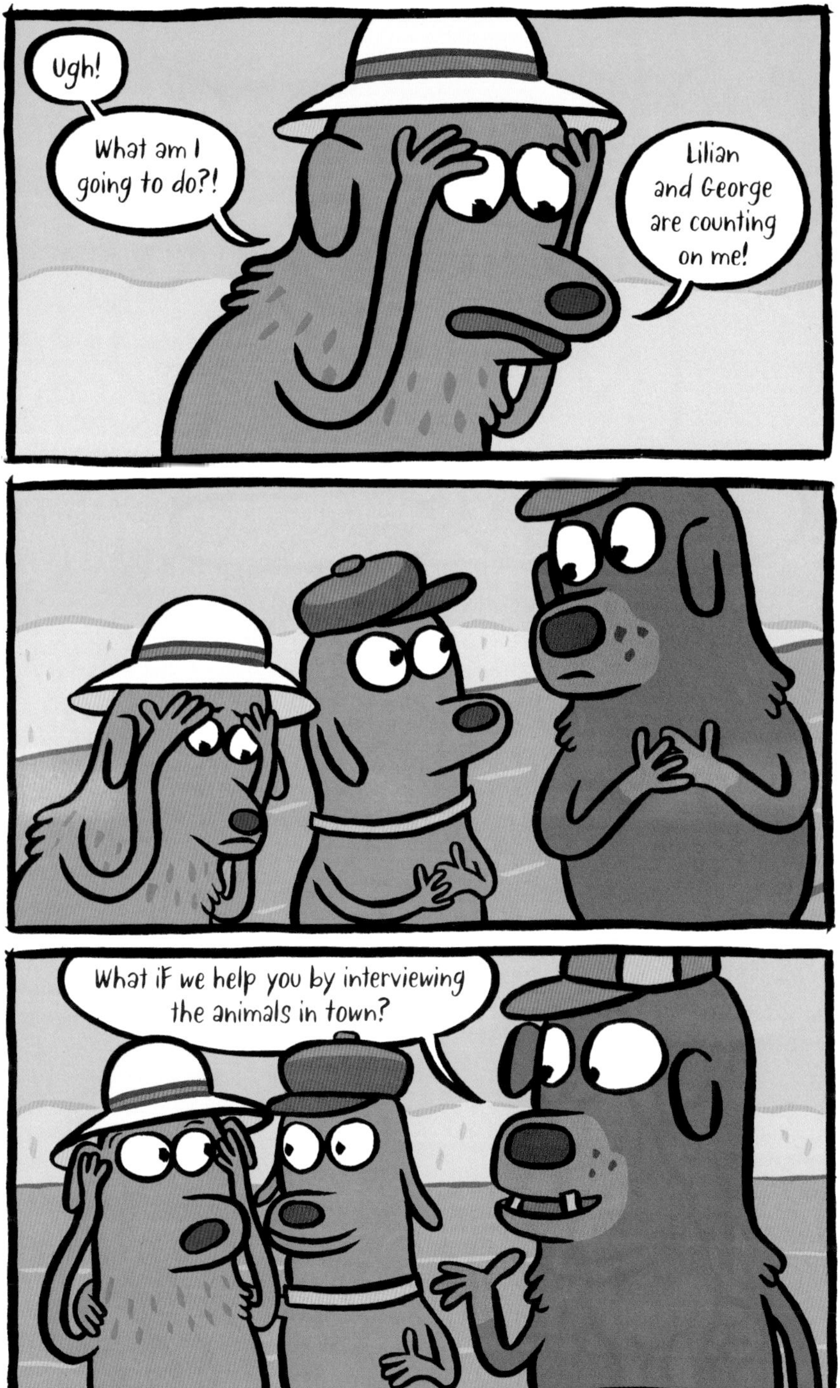
Ugh!
What am I going to do?!
Lilian and George are counting on me!
What if we help you by interviewing the animals in town?

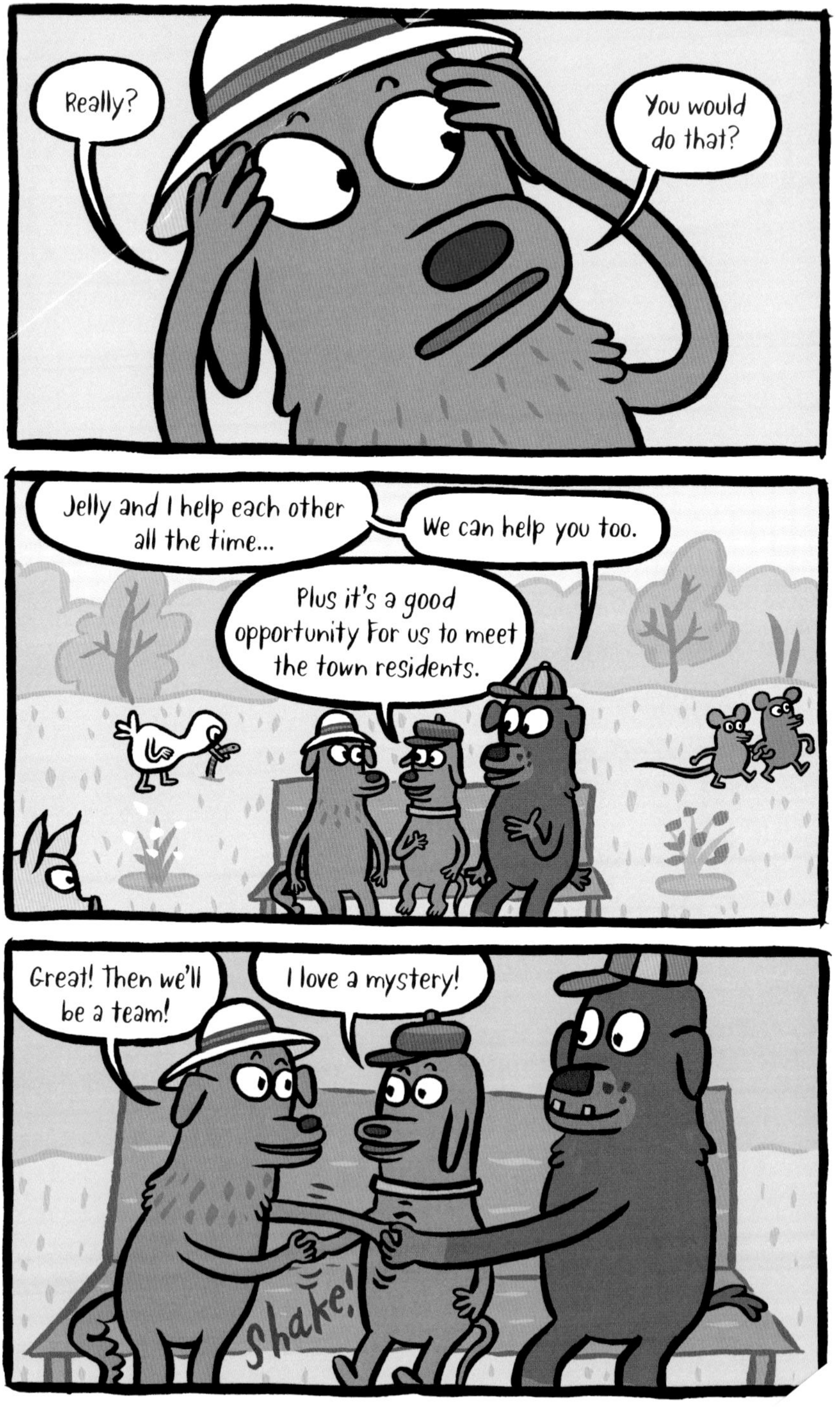
Really?
You would do that?
Jelly and I help each other all the time...
We can help you too.
Plus it's a good opportunity For us to meet the town residents.
Great! Then we'll be a team!
I love a mystery!
Shake!

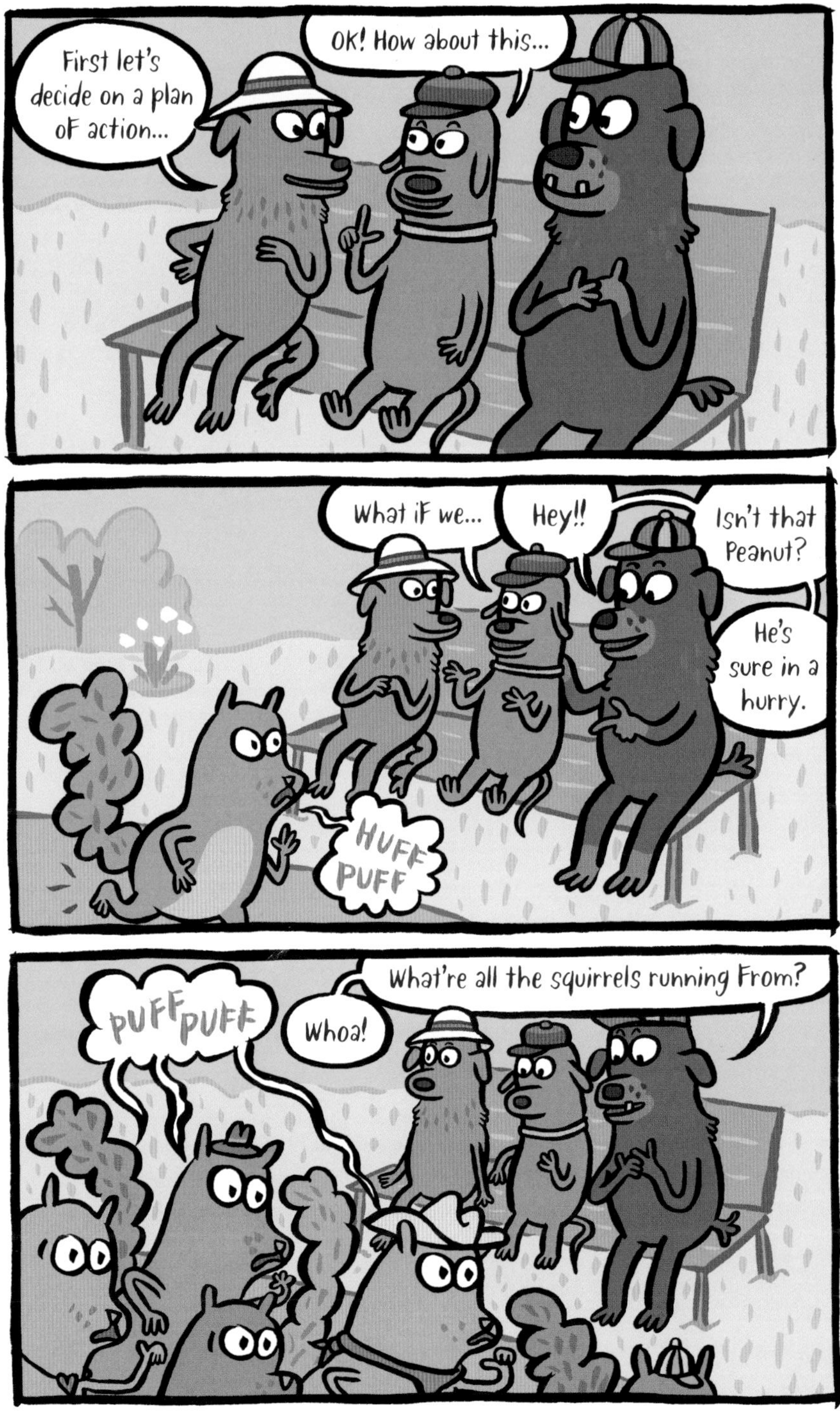
First let's decide on a plan oF action...
OK! How about this...
What iF we...
Hey!!
Isn't that Peanut?
He's sure in a hurry.
HUFF PUFF
PUFF PUFF
Whoa!
What're all the squirrels running From?

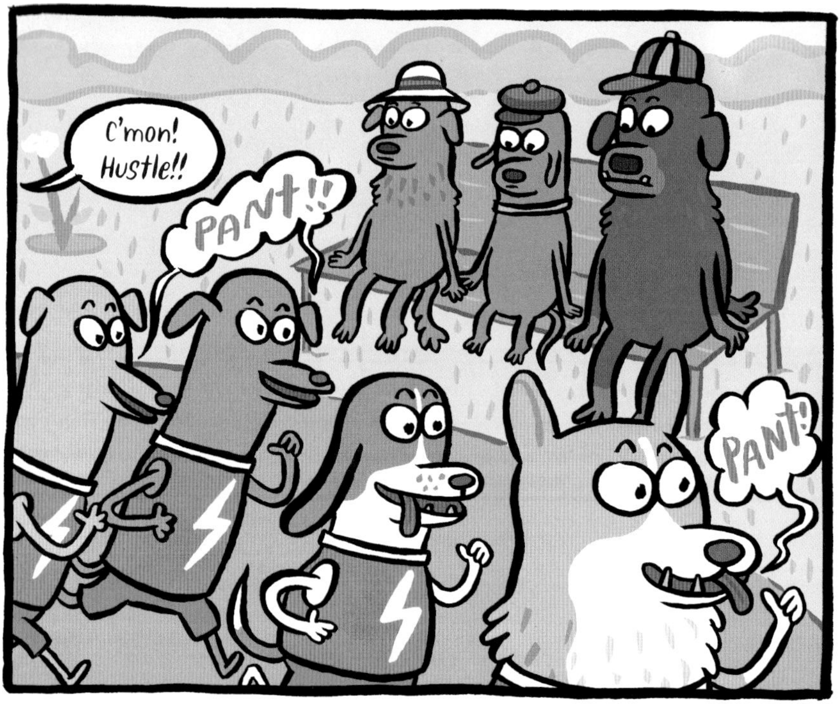
C'mon! Hustle!!
PANT!!
PANT!

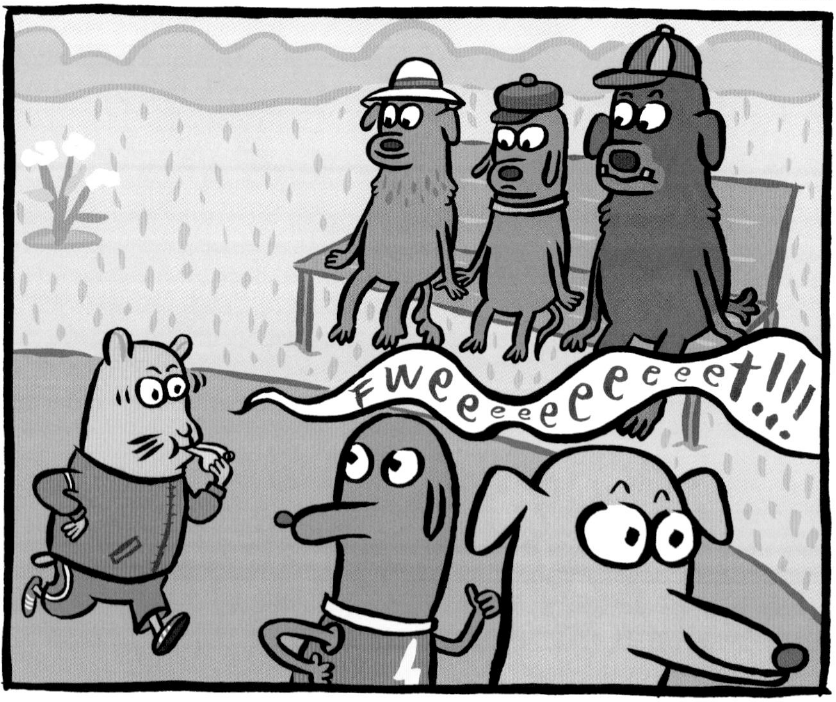
FWeeeeeeeeet!!!

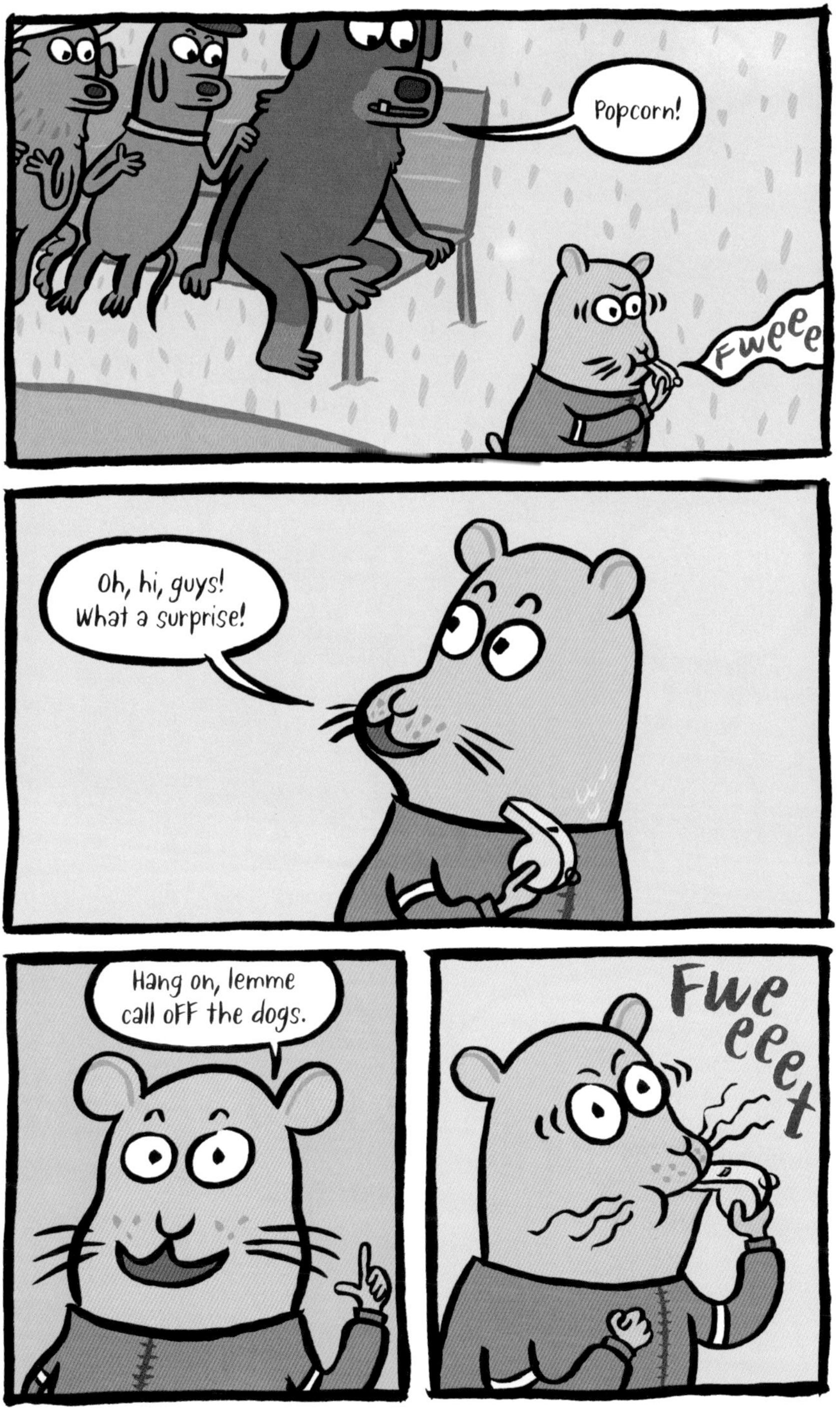
Popcorn!
Fweee
Oh, hi, guys! What a surprise!
Hang on, lemme call off the dogs.
Fweeeet

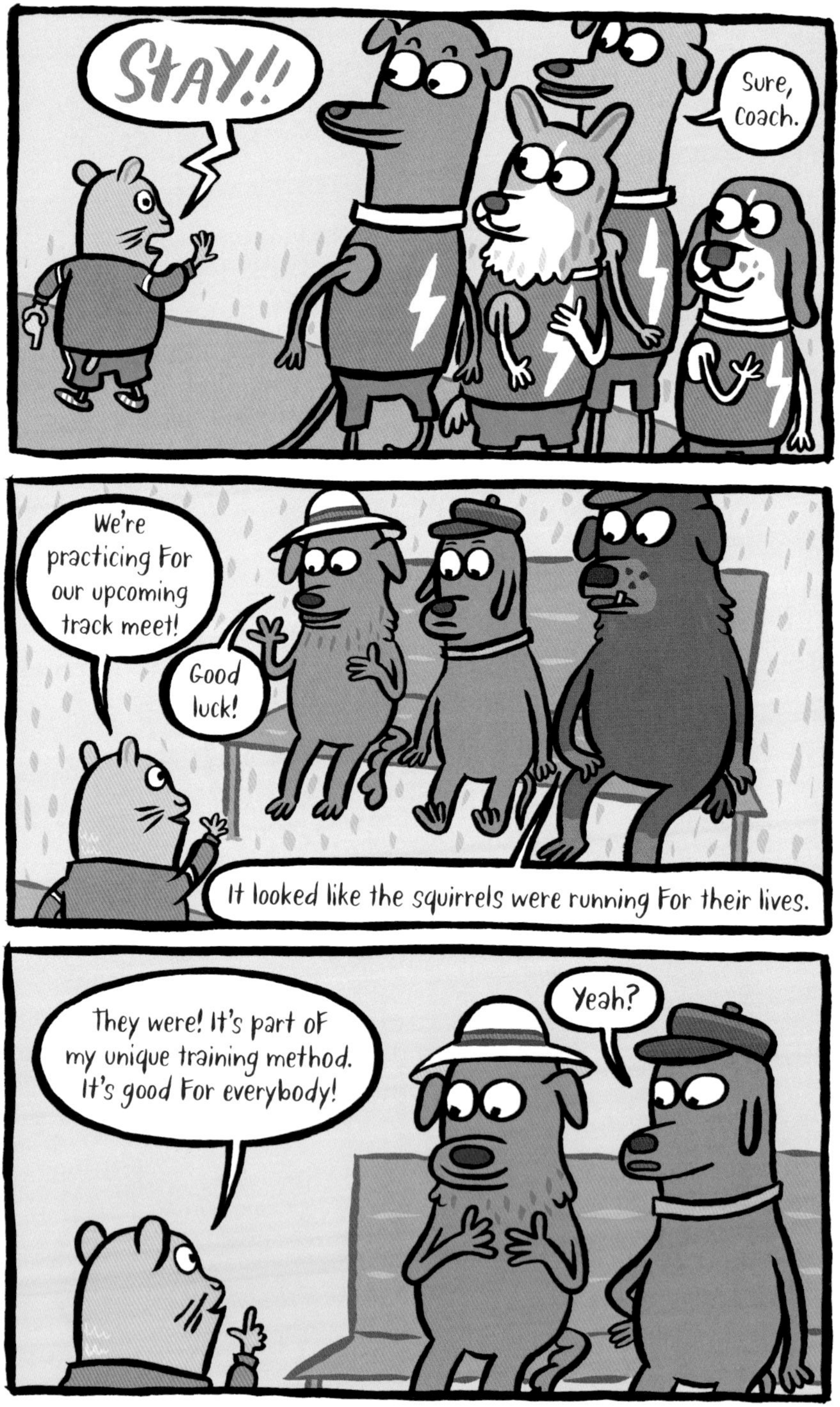
STAY!!
Sure, Coach.
We're practicing For our upcoming track meet!
Good luck!
It looked like the squirrels were running For their lives.
They were! It's part oF my unique training method. It's good For everybody!
Yeah?

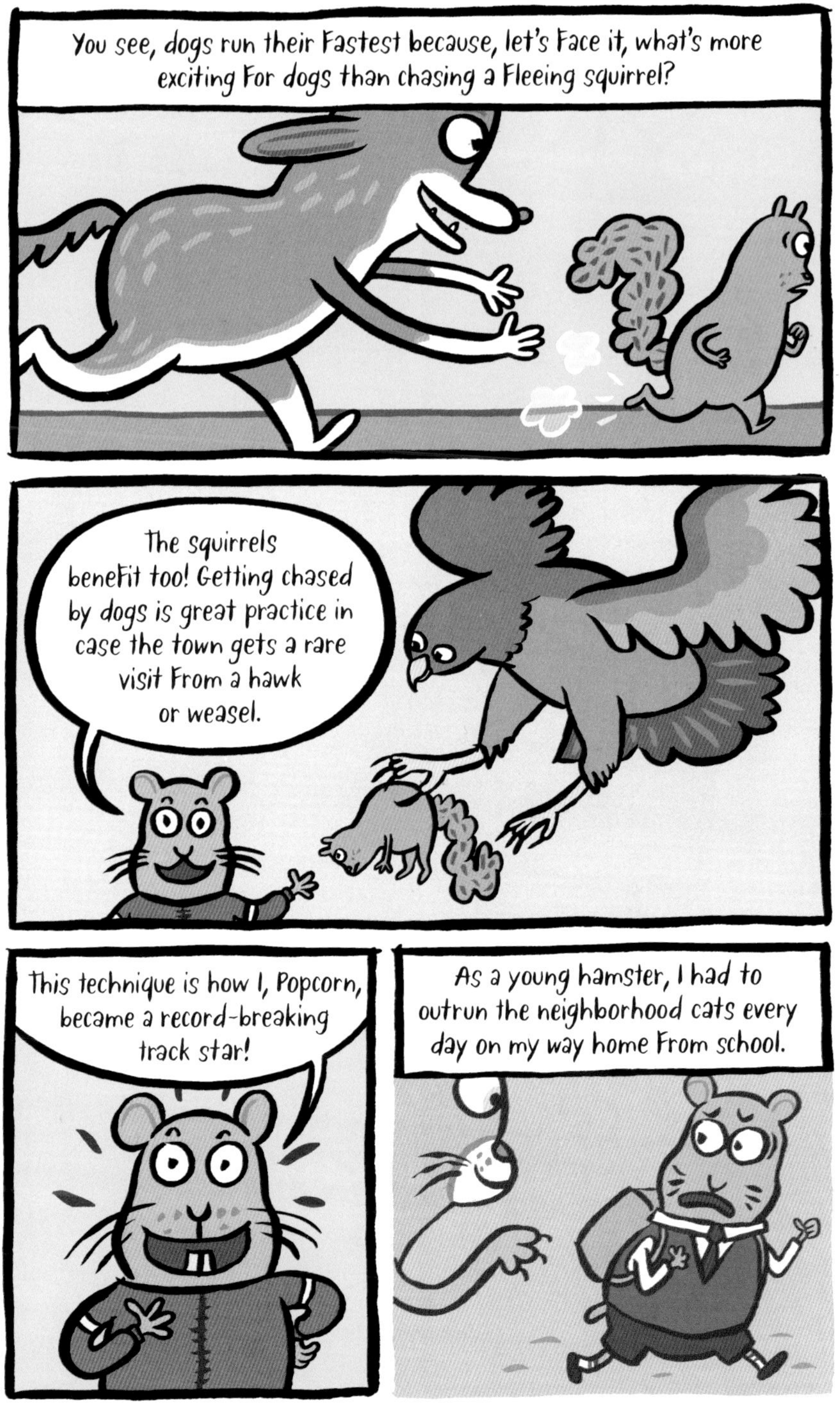
You see, dogs run their fastest because, let's face it, what's more exciting for dogs than chasing a fleeing squirrel?
The squirrels benefit too! Getting chased by dogs is great practice in case the town gets a rare visit from a hawk or weasel.
This technique is how I, Popcorn, became a record-breaking track star!
As a young hamster, I had to outrun the neighborhood cats every day on my way home from school.

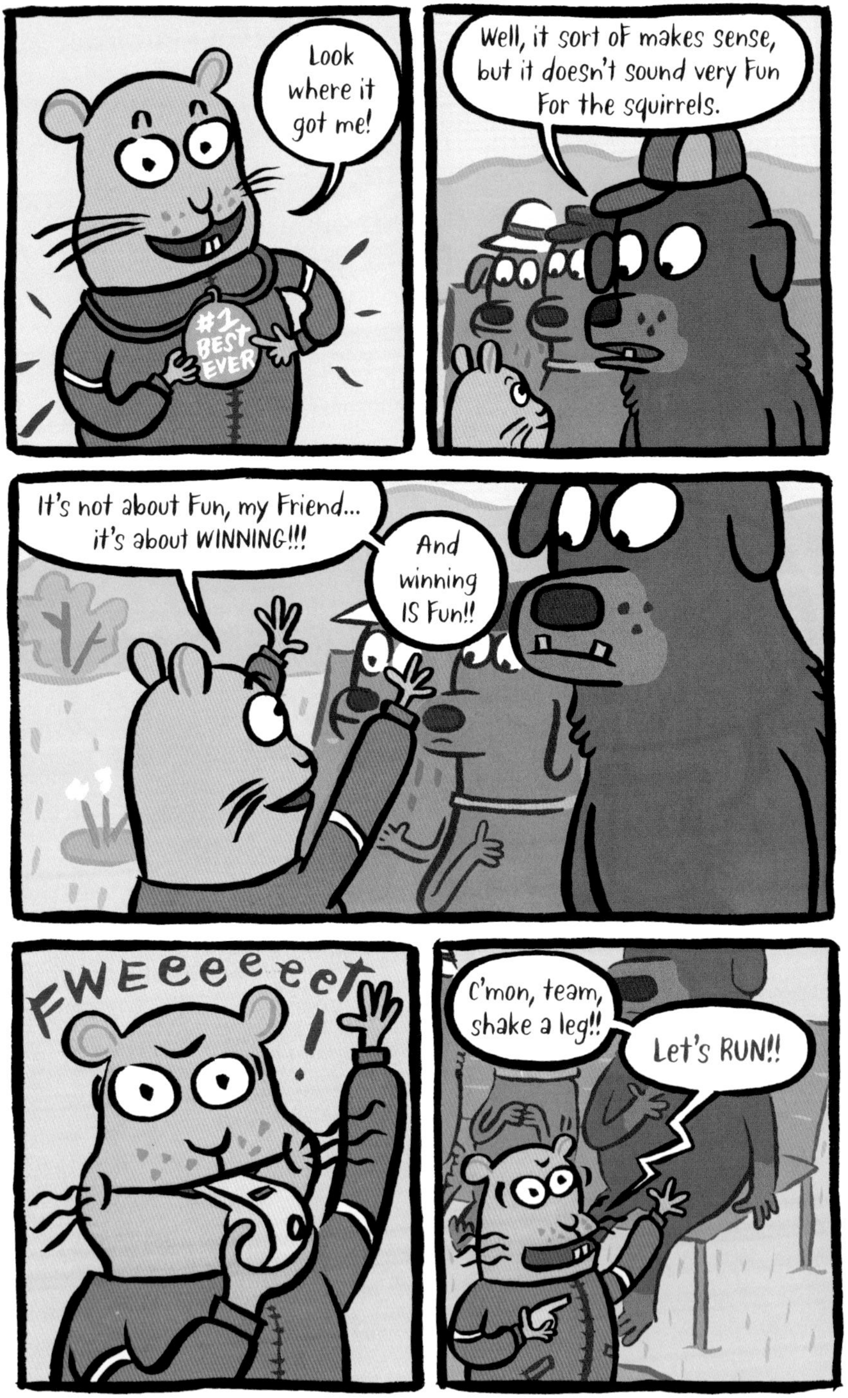
Look where it got me!
#1 BEST EVER
Well, it sort of makes sense, but it doesn't sound very fun for the squirrels.
It's not about fun, my friend... it's about WINNING!!!
And winning IS fun!!
FWEeeeeet!
C'mon, team, shake a leg!!
Let's RUN!!

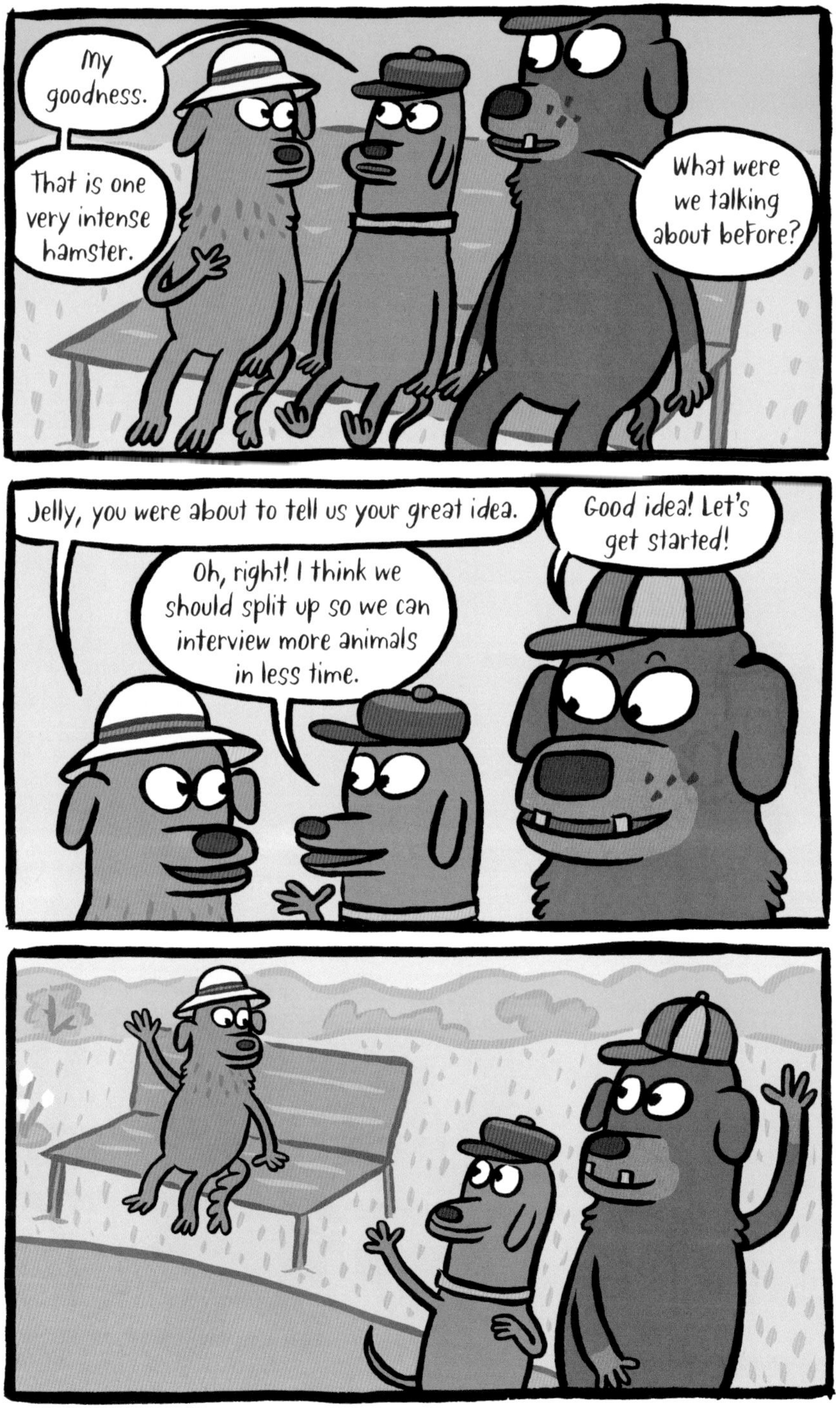
My goodness.
That is one very intense hamster.
What were we talking about before?
Jelly, you were about to tell us your great idea.
Oh, right! I think we should split up so we can interview more animals in less time.
Good idea! Let's get started!

Chapter 5

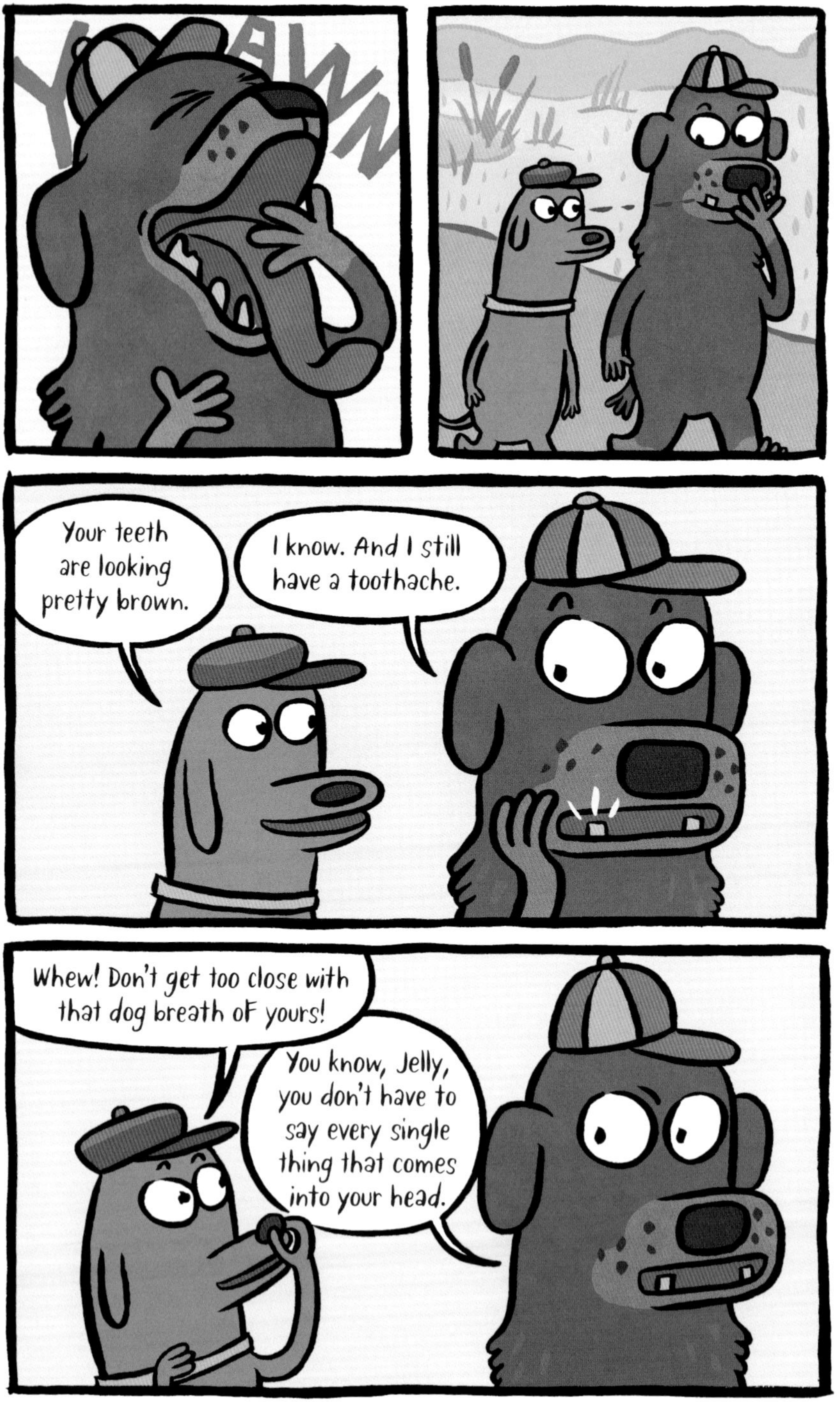
YAWN
Your teeth are looking pretty brown.
I know. And I still have a toothache.
Whew! Don't get too close with that dog breath of yours!
You know, Jelly, you don't have to say every single thing that comes into your head.

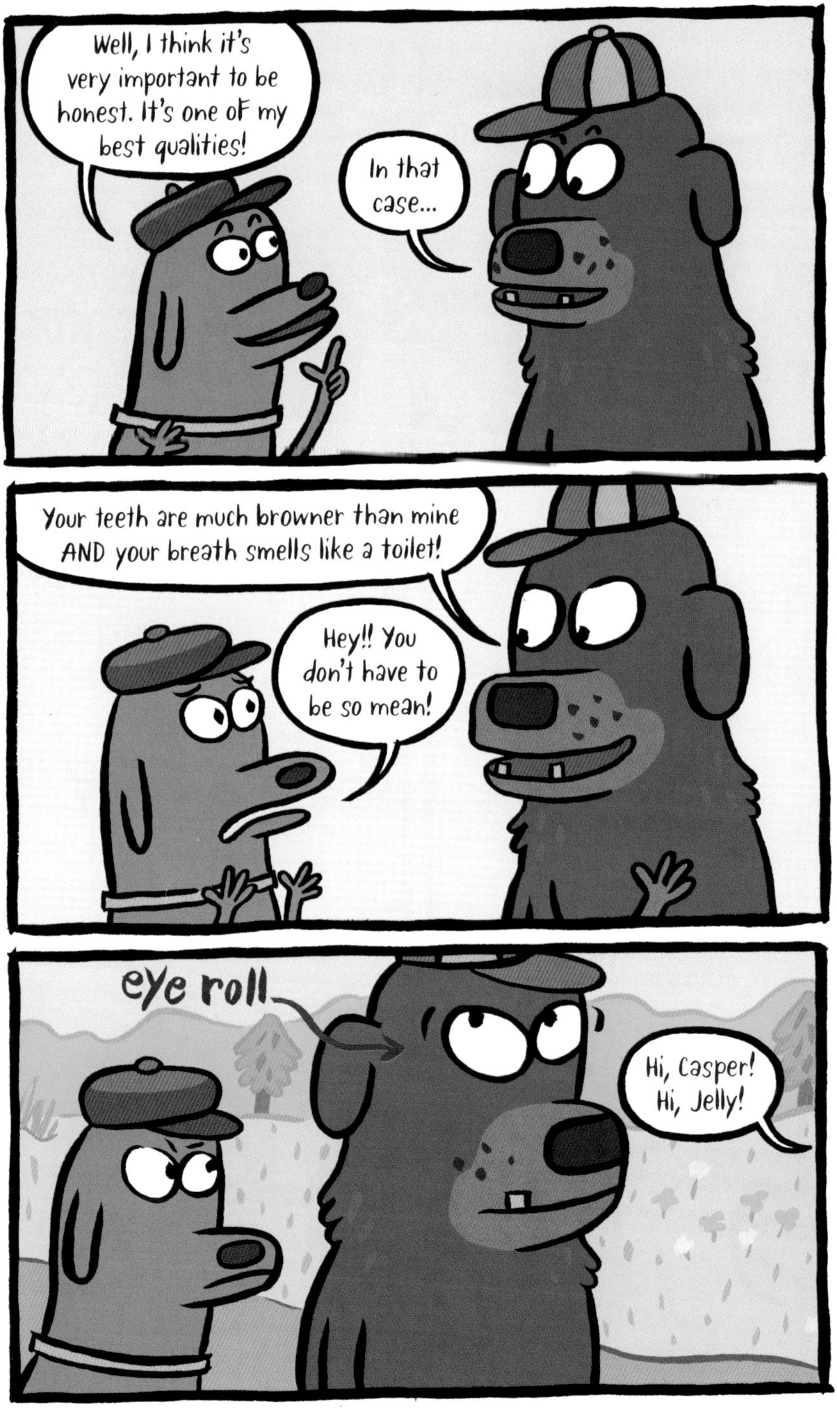
Well, I think it's very important to be honest. It's one of my best qualities!
In that case...
Your teeth are much browner than mine AND your breath smells like a toilet!
Hey!! You don't have to be so mean!
eye roll
Hi, Casper! Hi, Jelly!

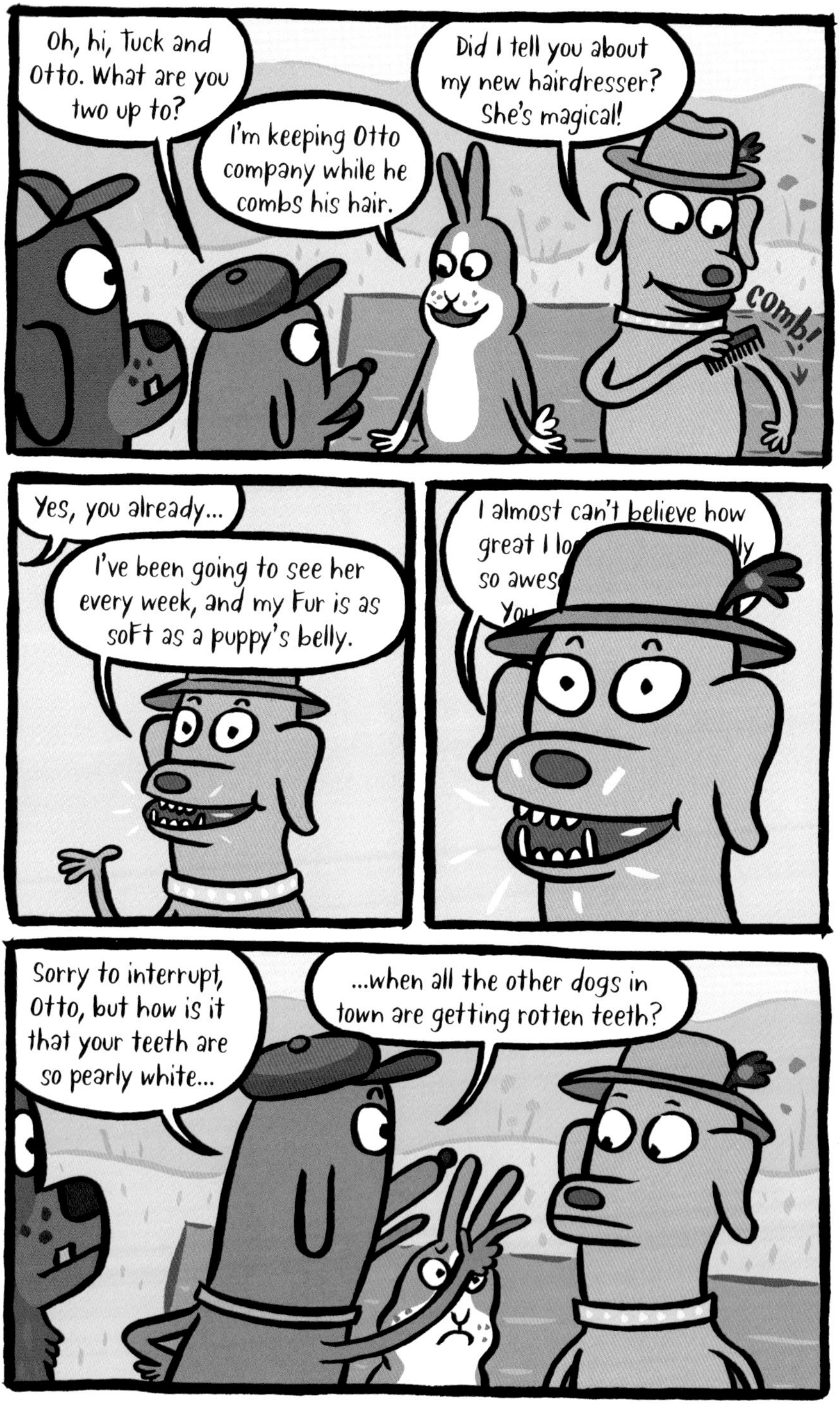
Oh, hi, Tuck and Otto. What are you two up to?
I'm keeping Otto company while he combs his hair.
Did I tell you about my new hairdresser? She's magical!
comb!
Yes, you already...
I've been going to see her every week, and my fur is as soft as a puppy's belly.
I almost can't believe how
Sorry to interrupt, Otto, but how is it that your teeth are so pearly white...
...when all the other dogs in town are getting rotten teeth?

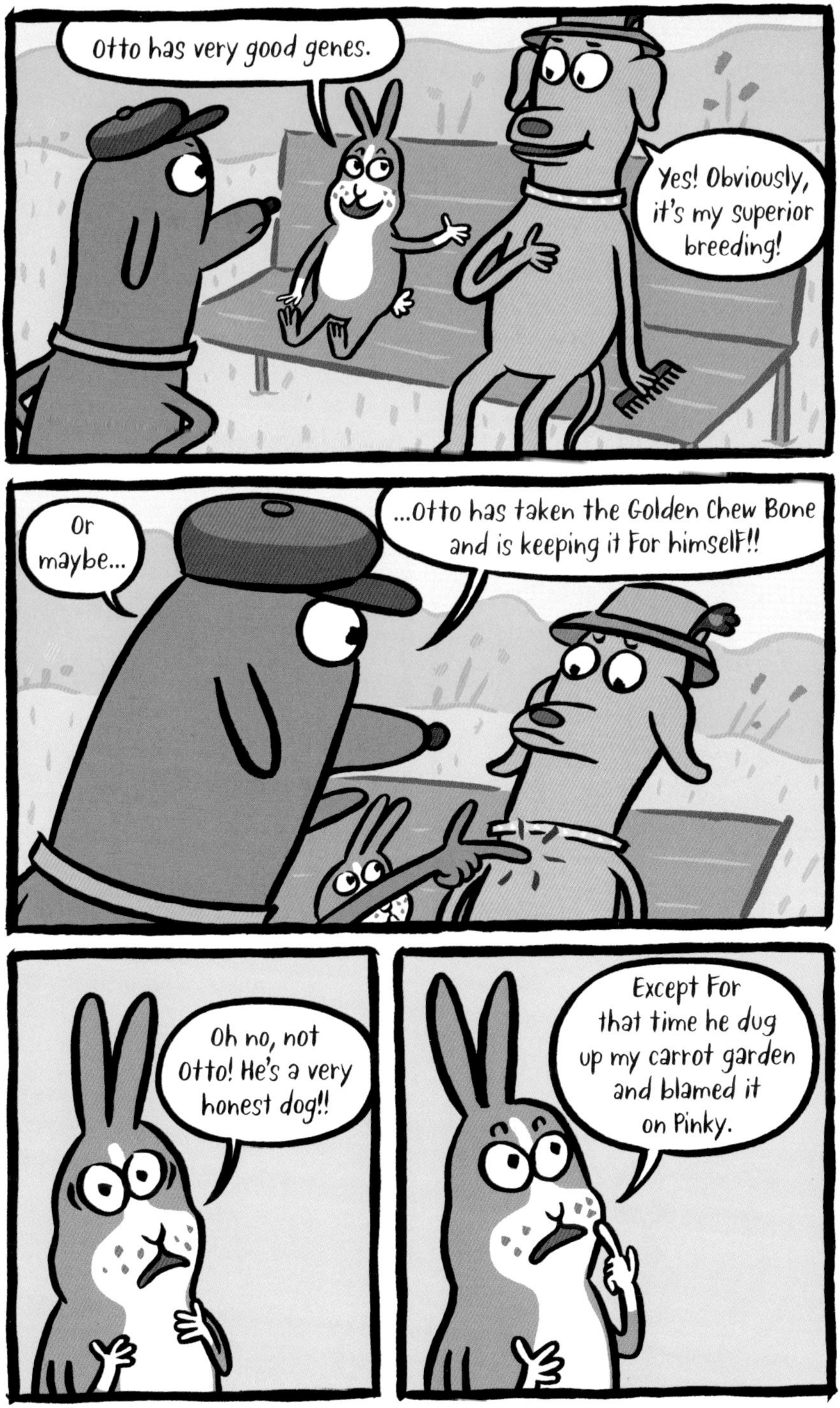
Otto has very good genes.
Yes! Obviously, it's my superior breeding!
Or maybe...
...Otto has taken the Golden Chew Bone and is keeping it For himselF!!
Oh no, not Otto! He's a very honest dog!!
Except For that time he dug up my carrot garden and blamed it on Pinky.

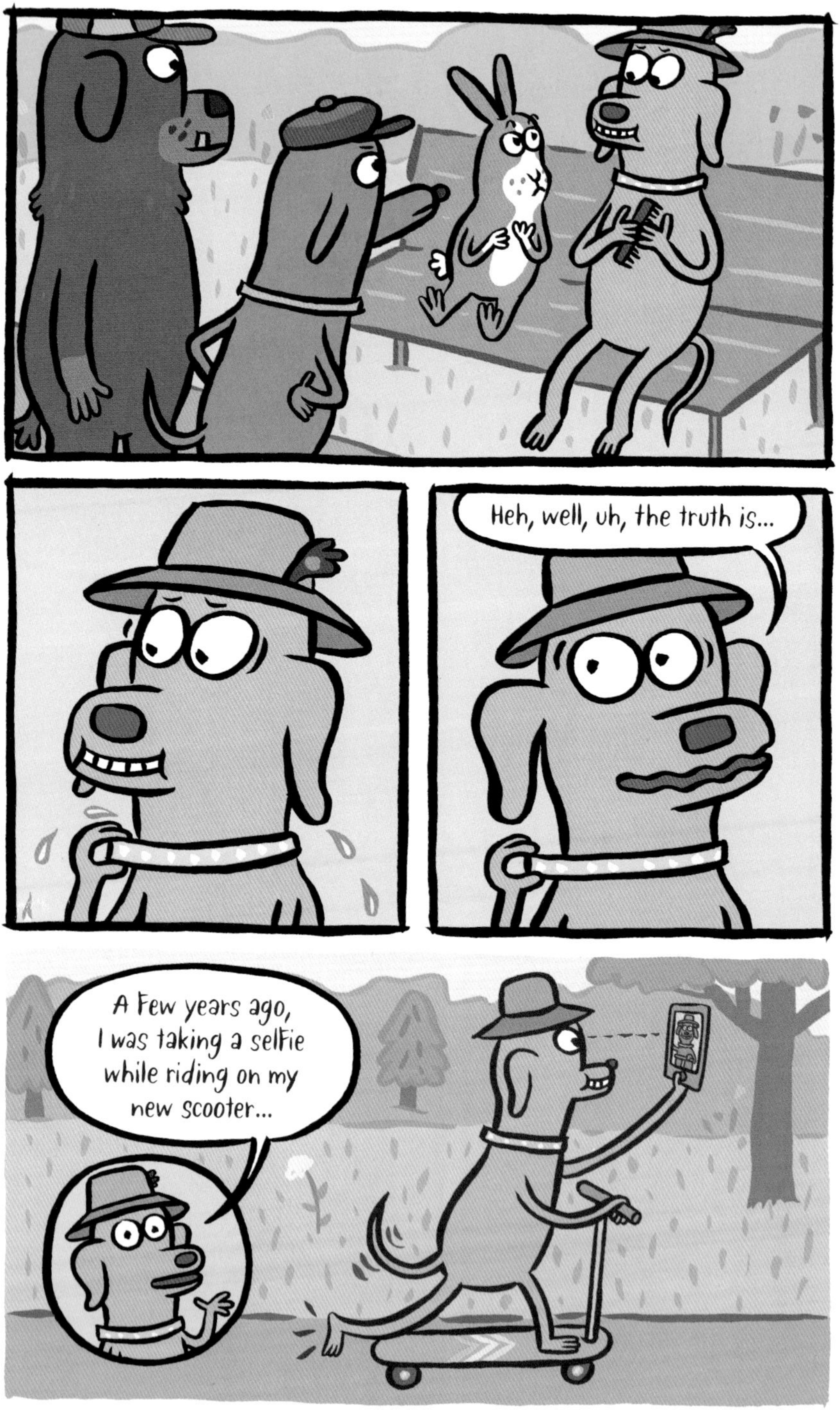
Heh, well, uh, the truth is...
A Few years ago, I was taking a selFie while riding on my new scooter...

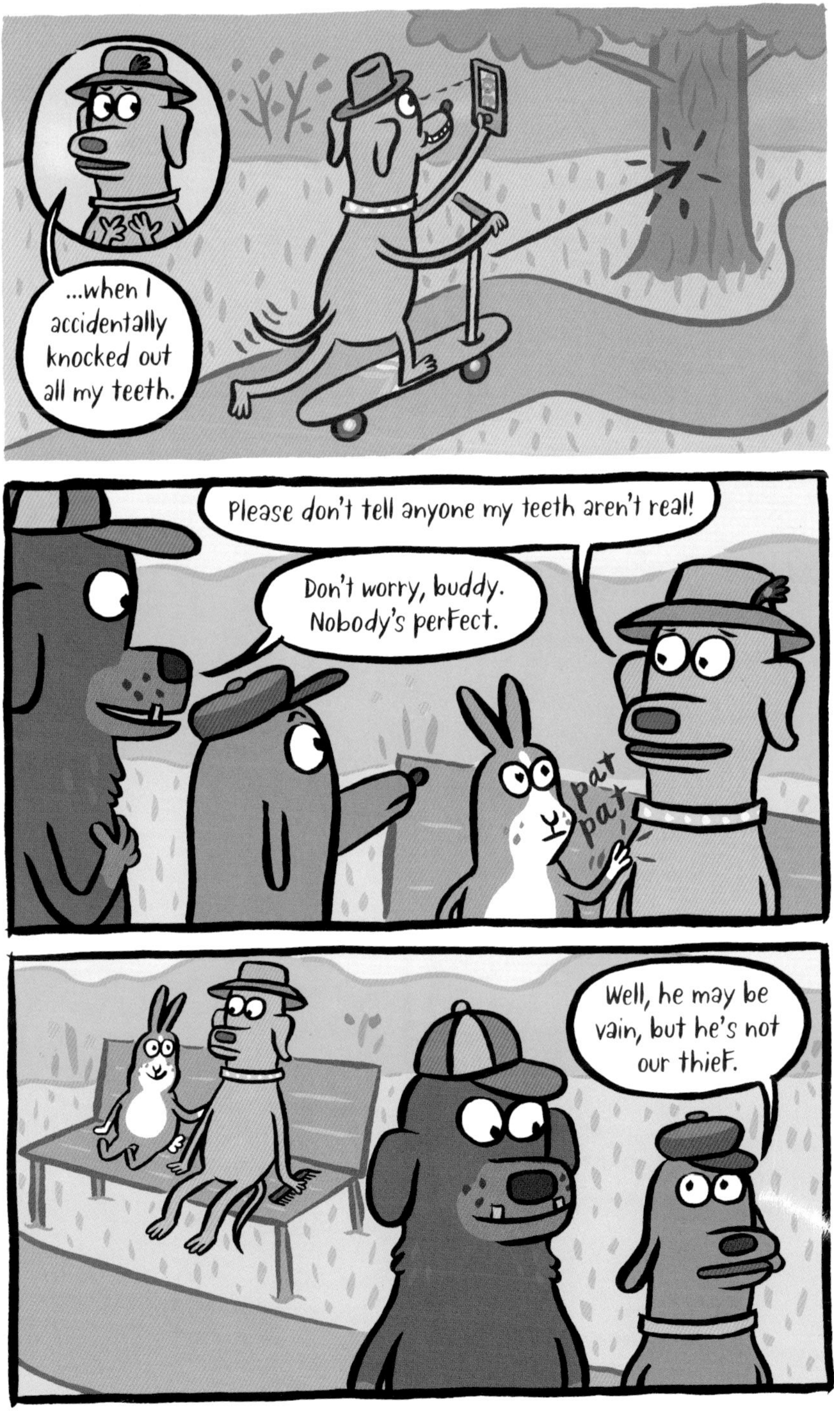
...when I accidentally knocked out all my teeth.
Please don't tell anyone my teeth aren't real!
Don't worry, buddy. Nobody's perFect.
pat pat
Well, he may be vain, but he's not our thieF.

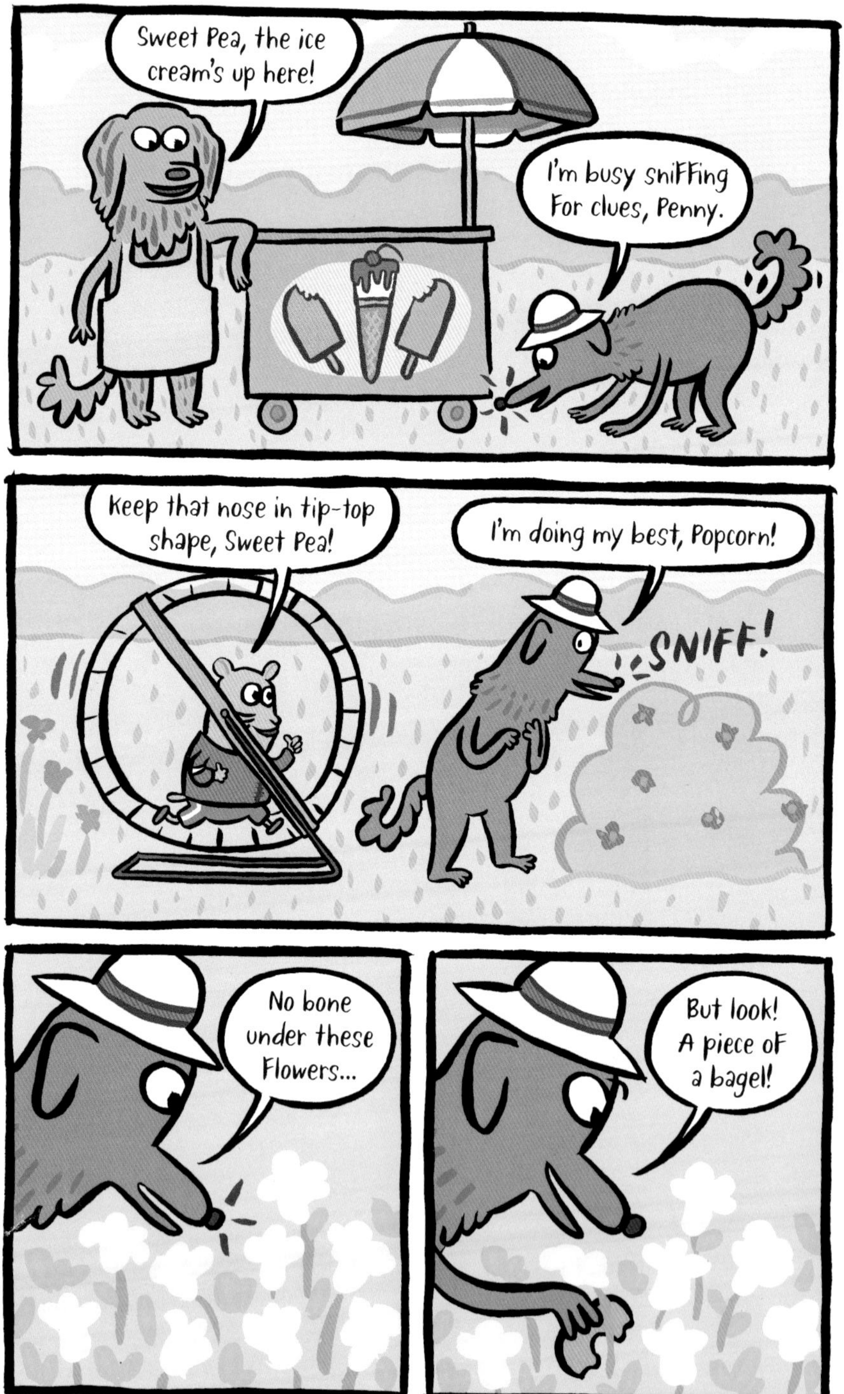
Sweet Pea, the ice cream's up here!
I'm busy sniFFing For clues, Penny.
Keep that nose in tip-top shape, Sweet Pea!
I'm doing my best, Popcorn!
SNIFF!
No bone under these Flowers...
But look! A piece oF a bagel!

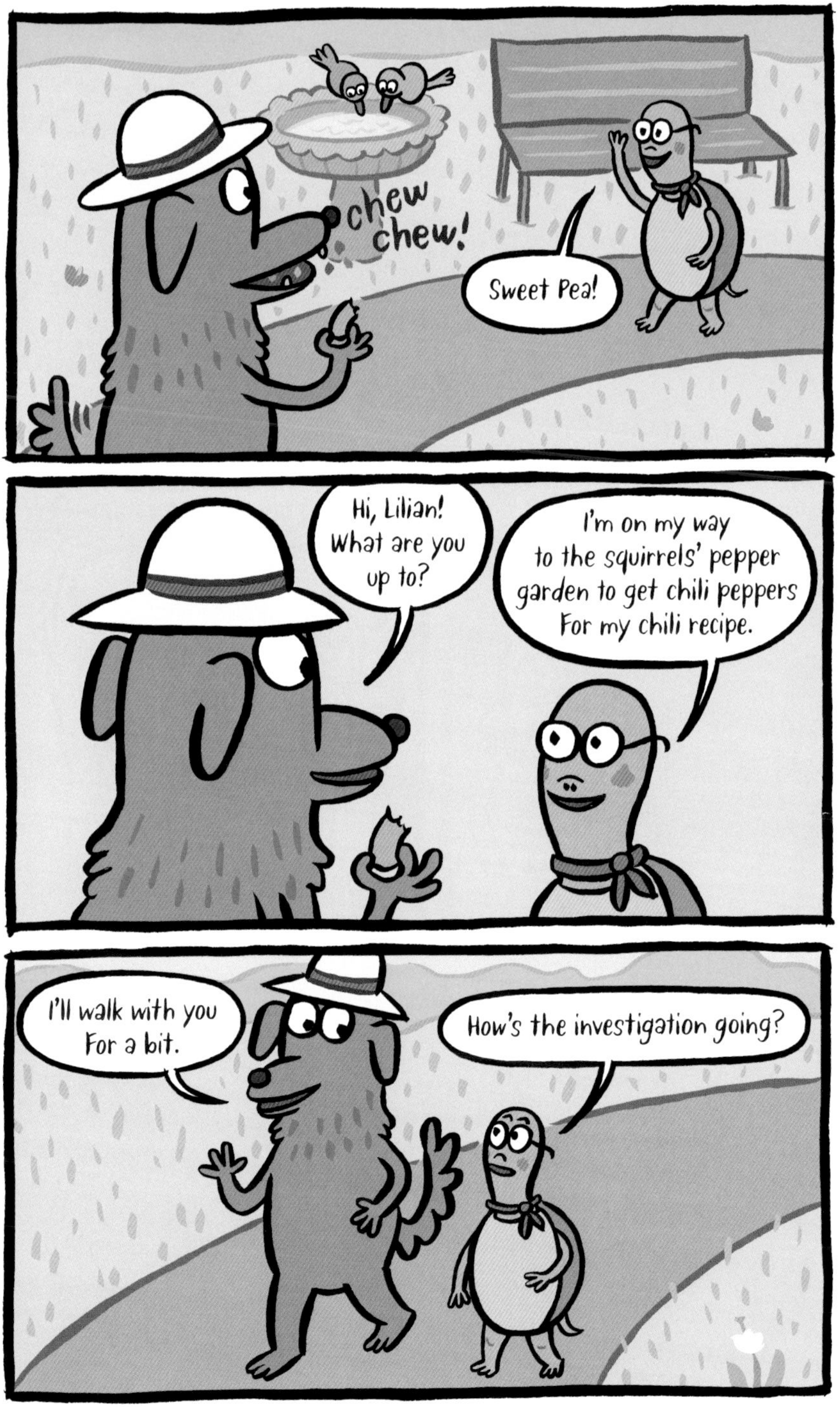
chew chew!
Sweet Pea!
Hi, Lilian! What are you up to?
I'm on my way to the squirrels' pepper garden to get chili peppers for my chili recipe.
I'll walk with you for a bit.
How's the investigation going?

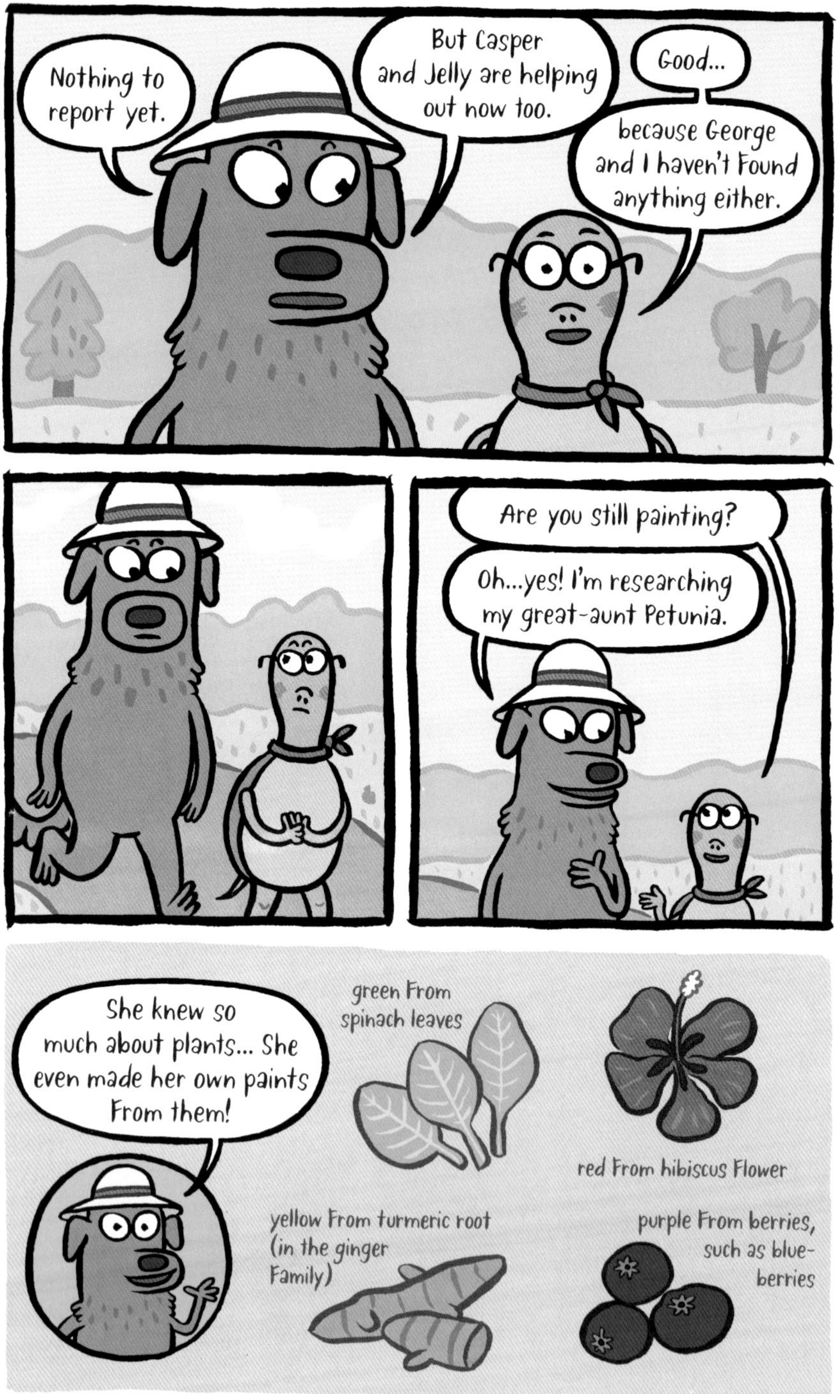
Nothing to report yet.
But Casper and Jelly are helping out now too.
Good...
because George and I haven't Found anything either.
Are you still painting?
Oh...yes! I'm researching my great-aunt Petunia.
She knew so much about plants... She even made her own paints From them!
green From spinach leaves
red From hibiscus Flower
yellow From turmeric root (in the ginger Family)
purple From berries, such as blue-berries

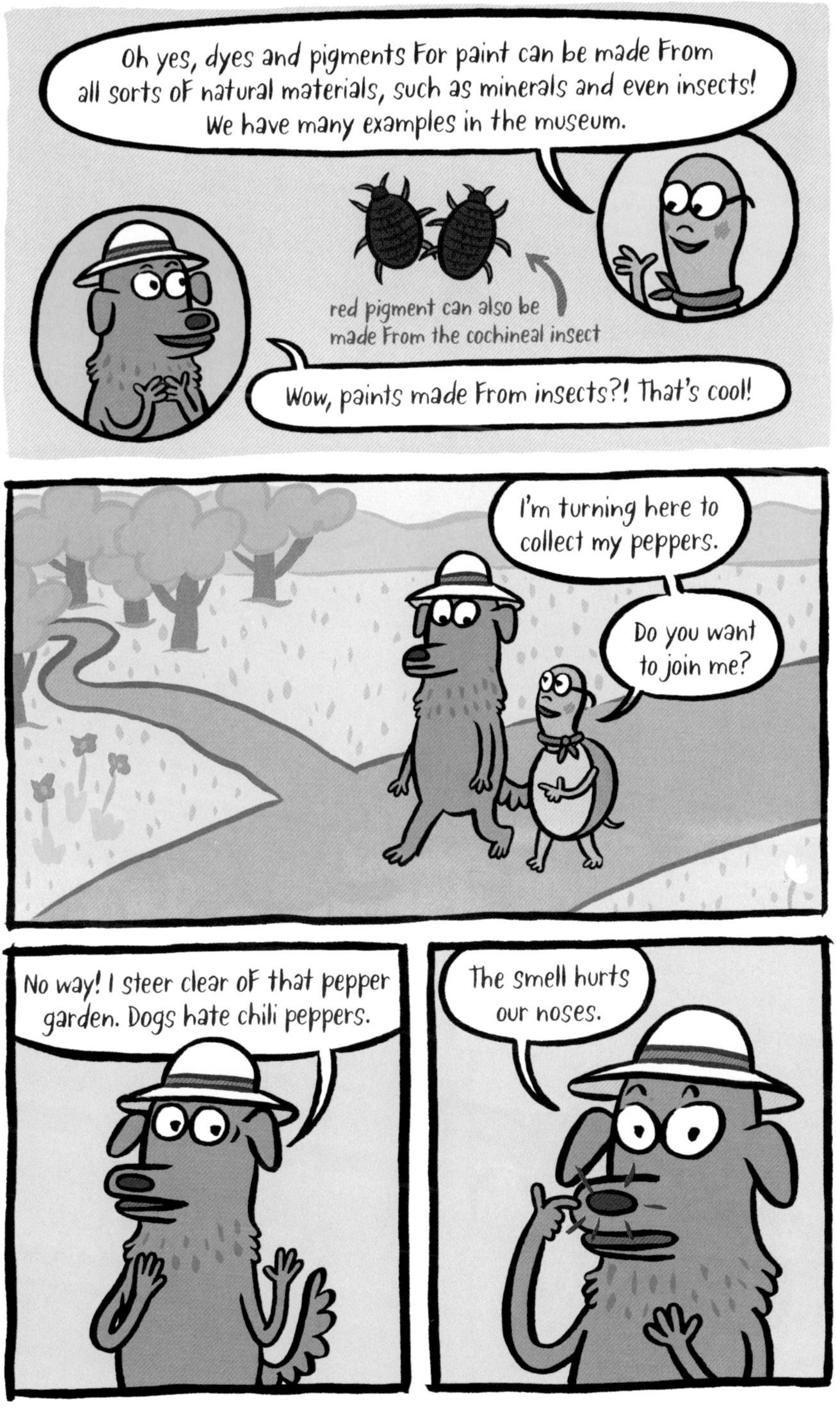
Oh yes, dyes and pigments for paint can be made from all sorts of natural materials, such as minerals and even insects! We have many examples in the museum.
red pigment can also be made from the cochineal insect
Wow, paints made from insects?! That's cool!
I'm turning here to collect my peppers.
Do you want to join me?
No way! I steer clear of that pepper garden. Dogs hate chili peppers.
The smell hurts our noses.

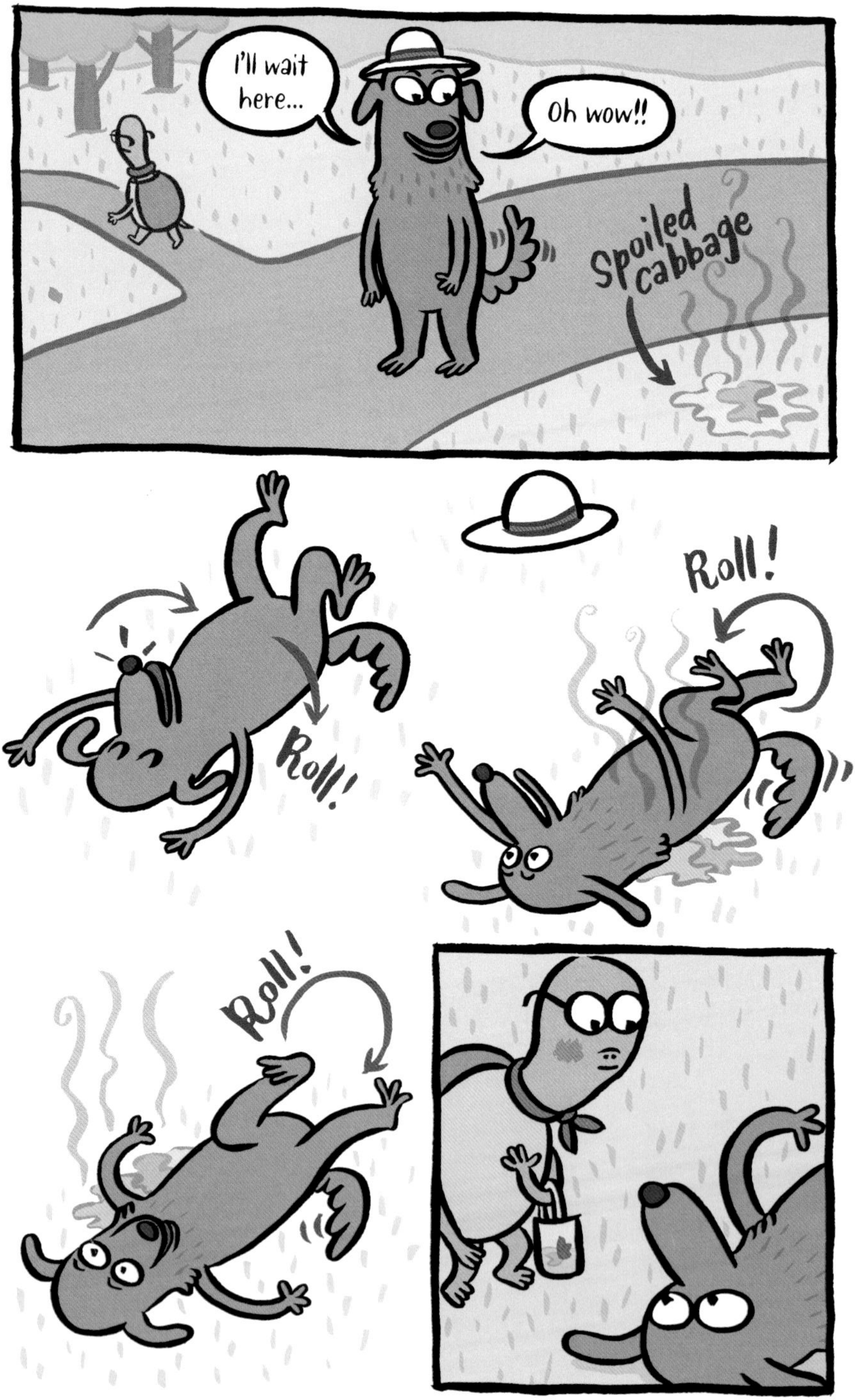
I'll wait here...
Oh wow!!
Spoiled cabbage
Roll!
Roll!
Roll!

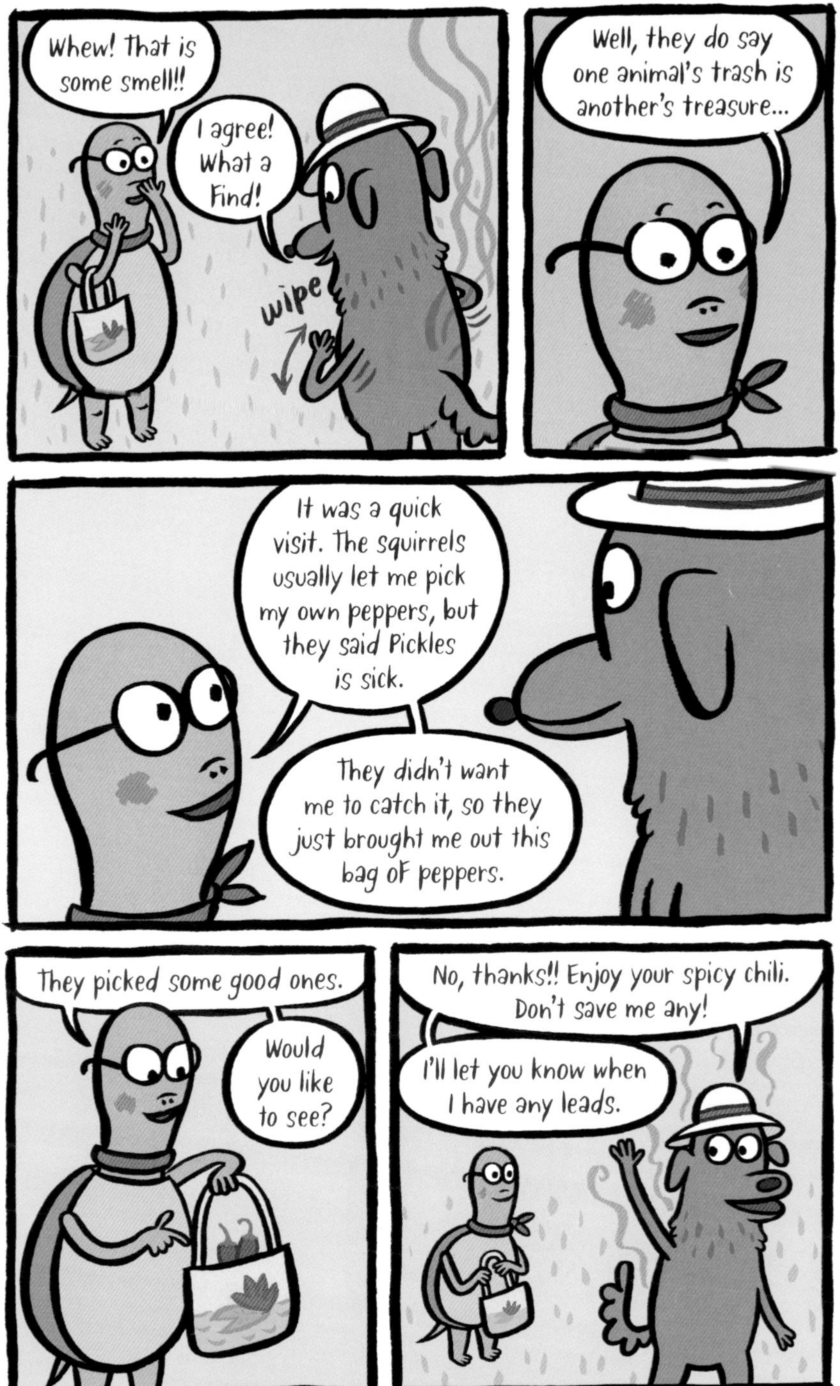

Whew! That is some smell!!
I agree! What a find!
wipe
Well, they do say one animal's trash is another's treasure...
It was a quick visit. The squirrels usually let me pick my own peppers, but they said Pickles is sick.
They didn't want me to catch it, so they just brought me out this bag of peppers.
They picked some good ones.
Would you like to see?
No, thanks!! Enjoy your spicy chili. Don't save me any!
I'll let you know when I have any leads.

Chapter 6

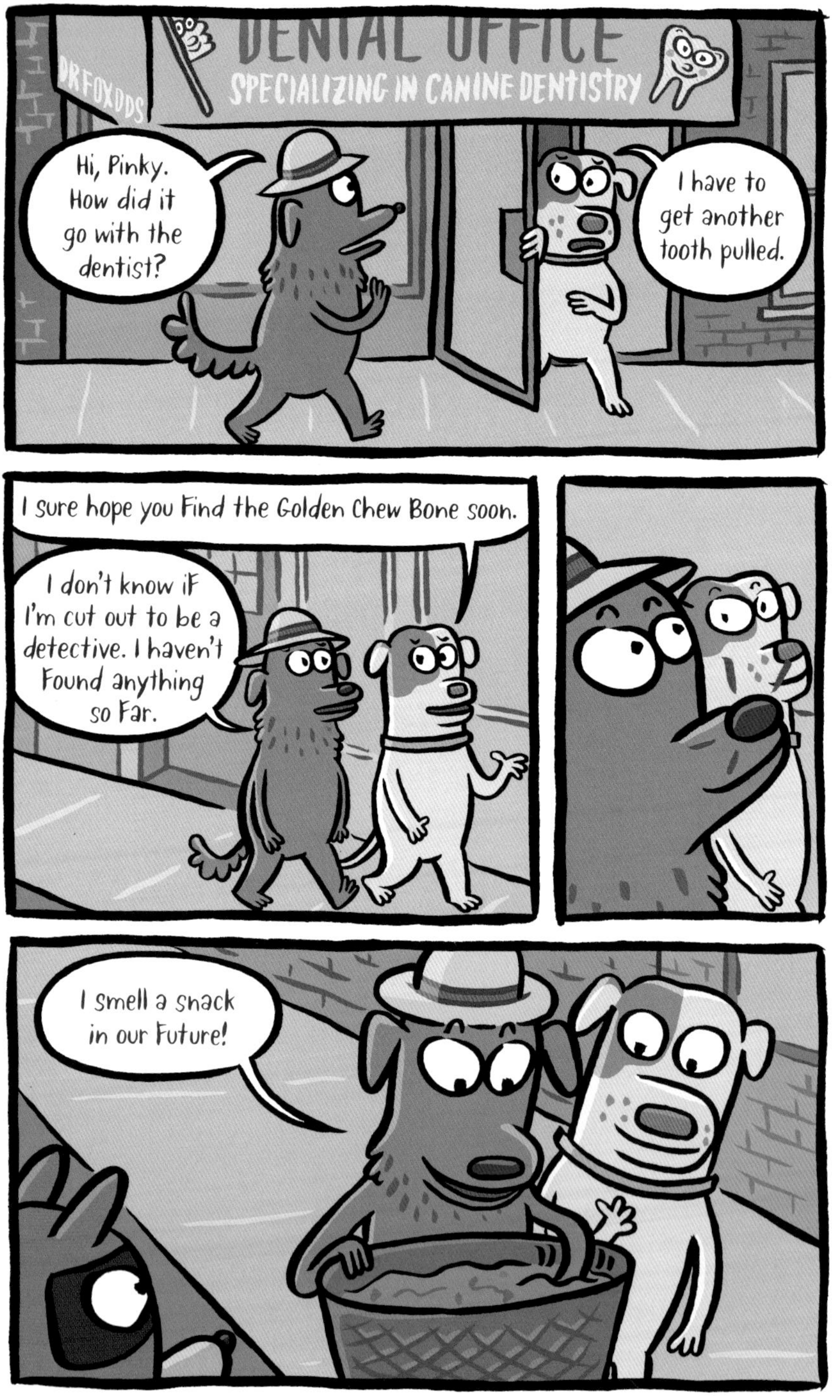
DENTAL OFFICE
SPECIALIZING IN CANINE DENTISTRY
DR FOX DDS
Hi, Pinky. How did it go with the dentist?
I have to get another tooth pulled.
I sure hope you find the Golden Chew Bone soon.
I don't know if I'm cut out to be a detective. I haven't found anything so far.
I smell a snack in our future!

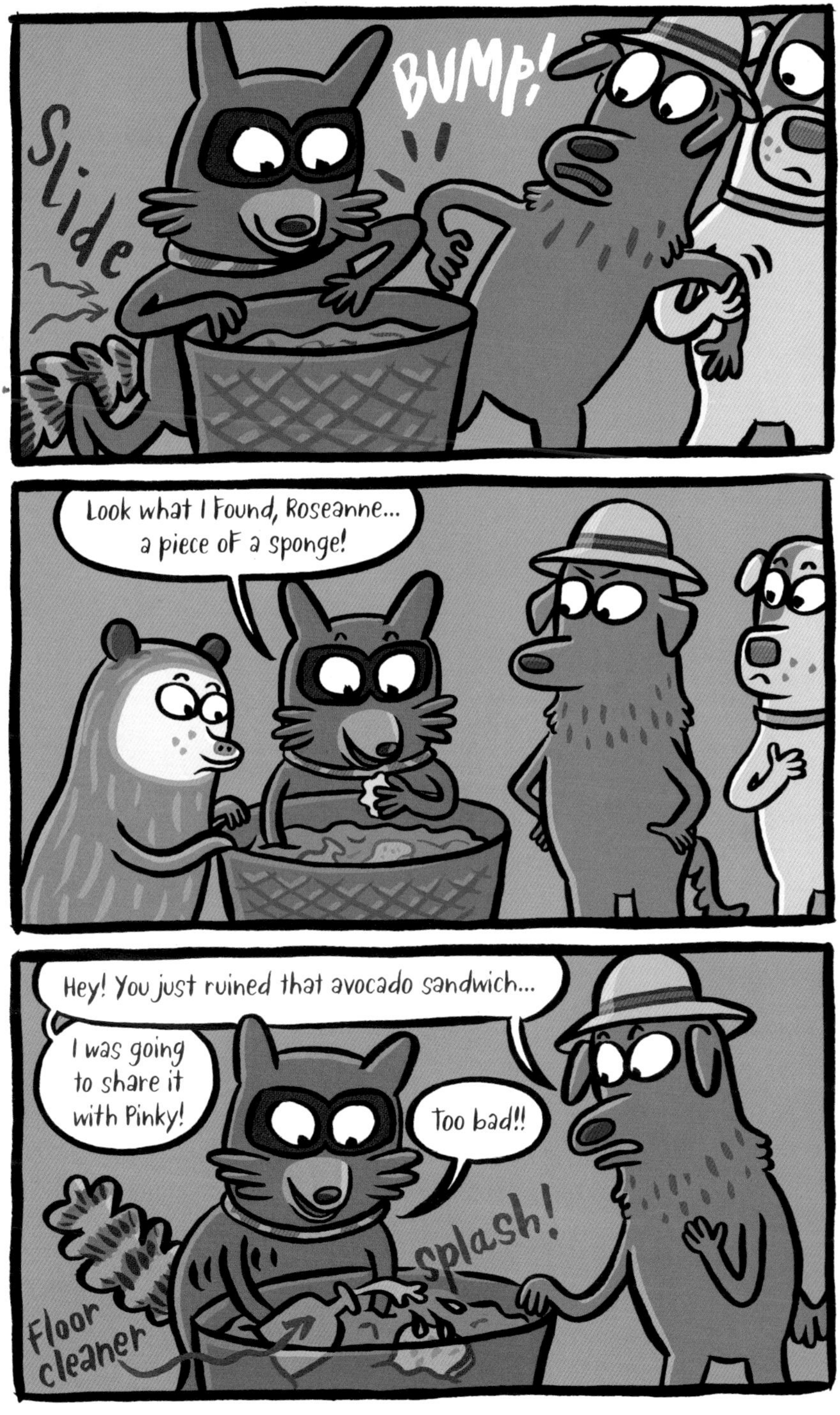

Slide
BUMP!
Look what I Found, Roseanne... a piece oF a sponge!
Hey! You just ruined that avocado sandwich...
I was going to share it with Pinky!
Too bad!!
Splash!
Floor cleaner

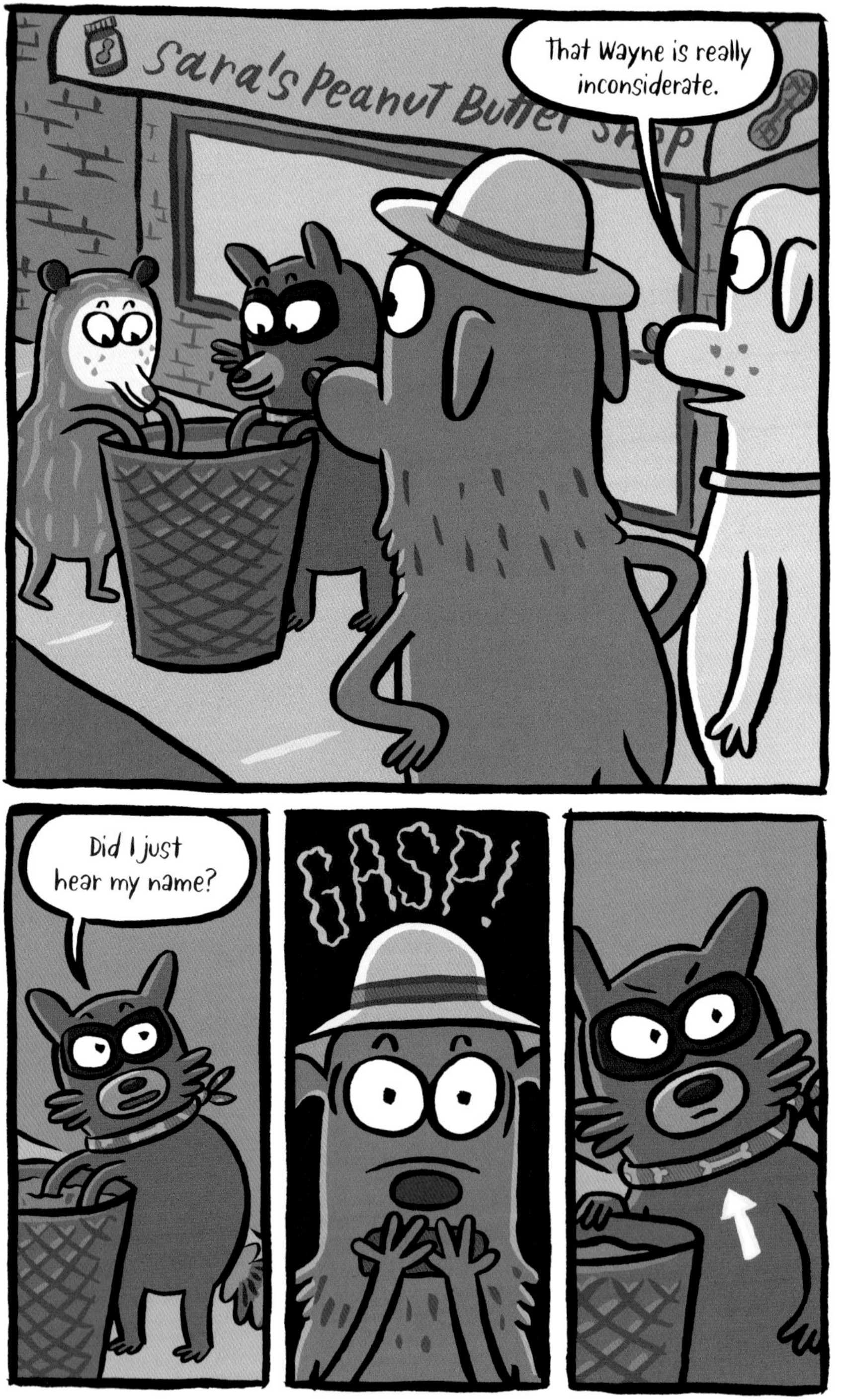
Sara's Peanut Butter Shop
That Wayne is really inconsiderate.
Did I just hear my name?
GASP!

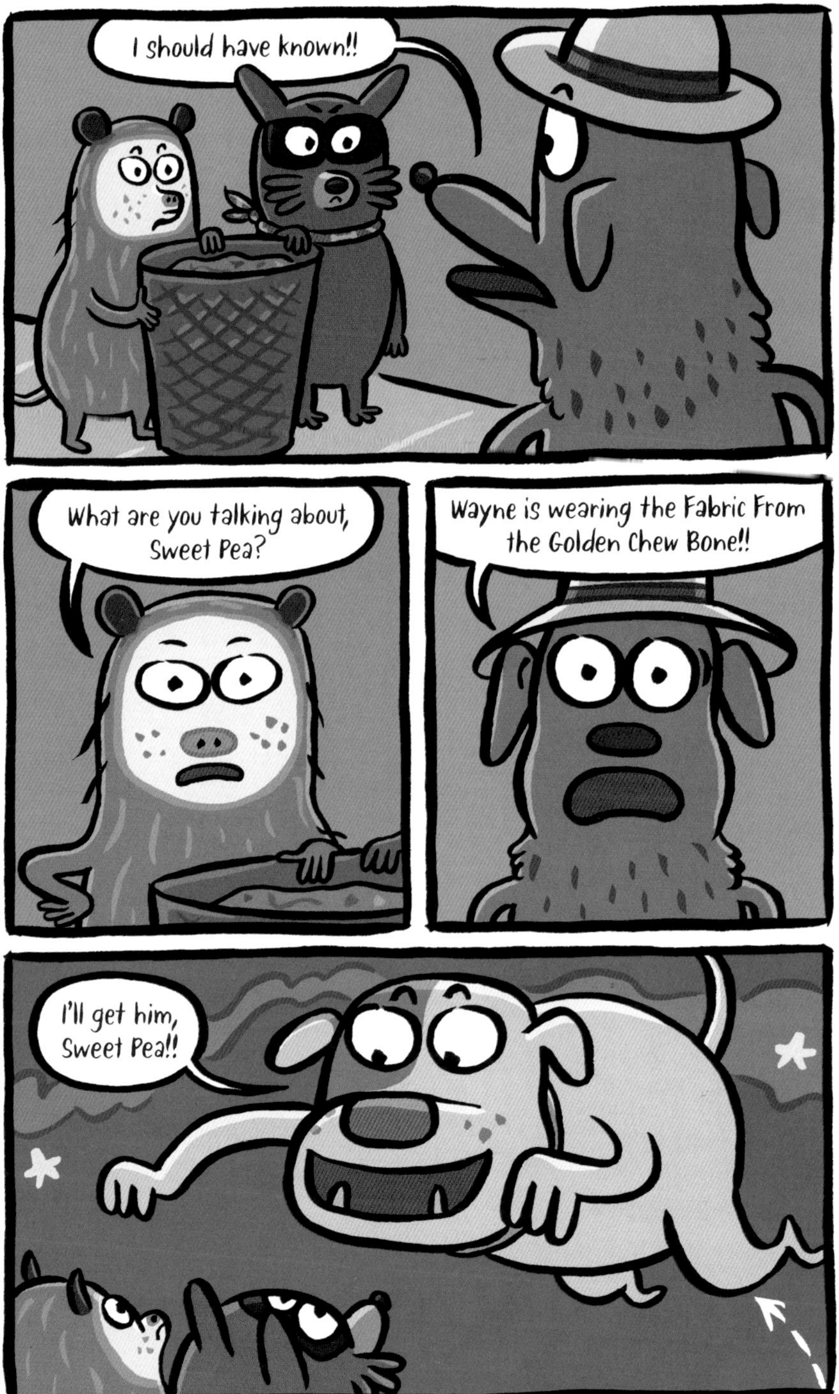
I should have known!!
What are you talking about, Sweet Pea?
Wayne is wearing the Fabric From the Golden Chew Bone!!
I'll get him, Sweet Pea!!

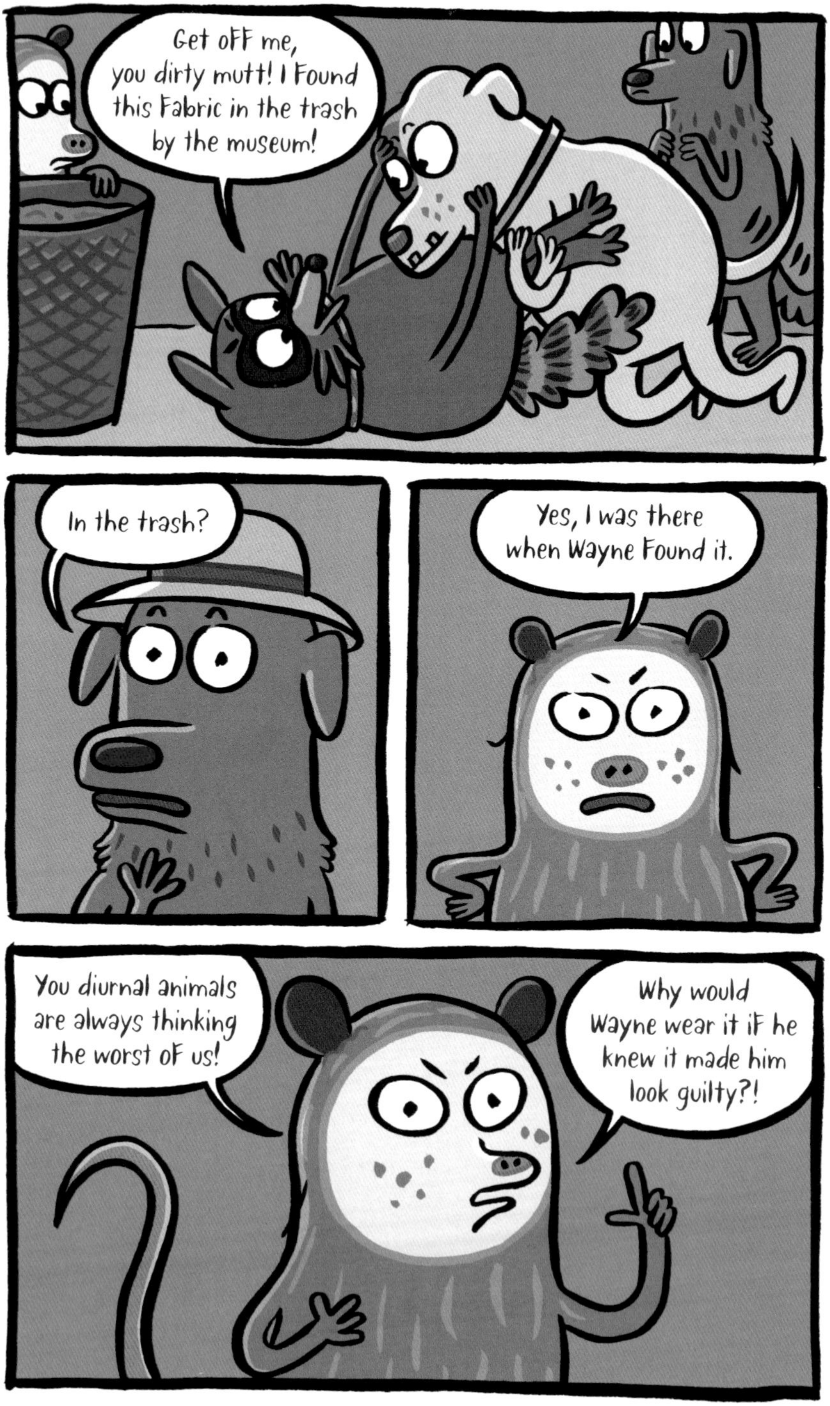
Get oFF me, you dirty mutt! I Found this Fabric in the trash by the museum!
In the trash?
Yes, I was there when Wayne Found it.
You diurnal animals are always thinking the worst oF us!
Why would Wayne wear it iF he knew it made him look guilty?!

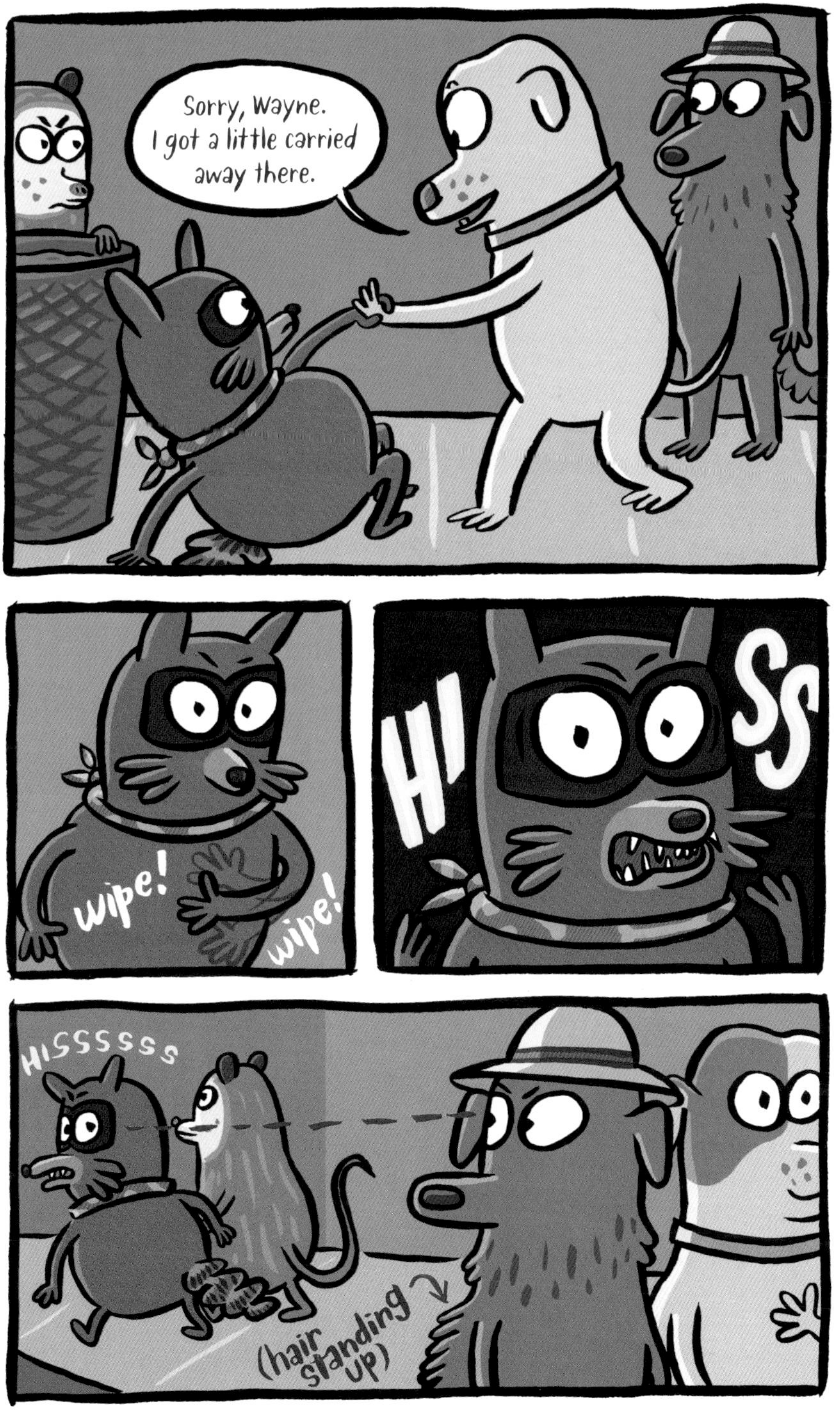
Sorry, Wayne. I got a little carried away there.
wipe!
wipe!
HISS
HISSSSSS
(hair standing up)

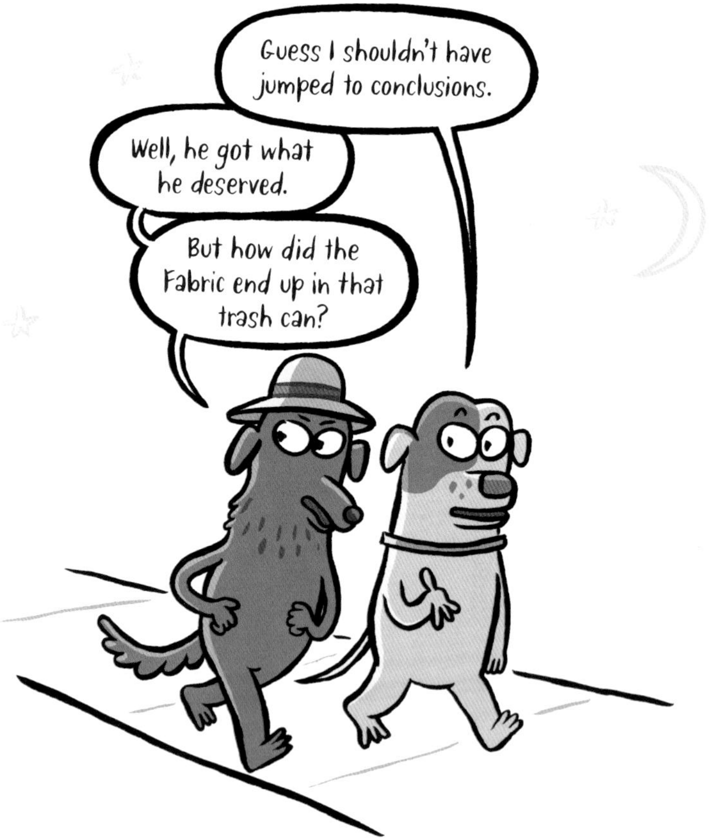
Guess I shouldn't have jumped to conclusions.
Well, he got what he deserved.
But how did the Fabric end up in that trash can?

Chapter 7

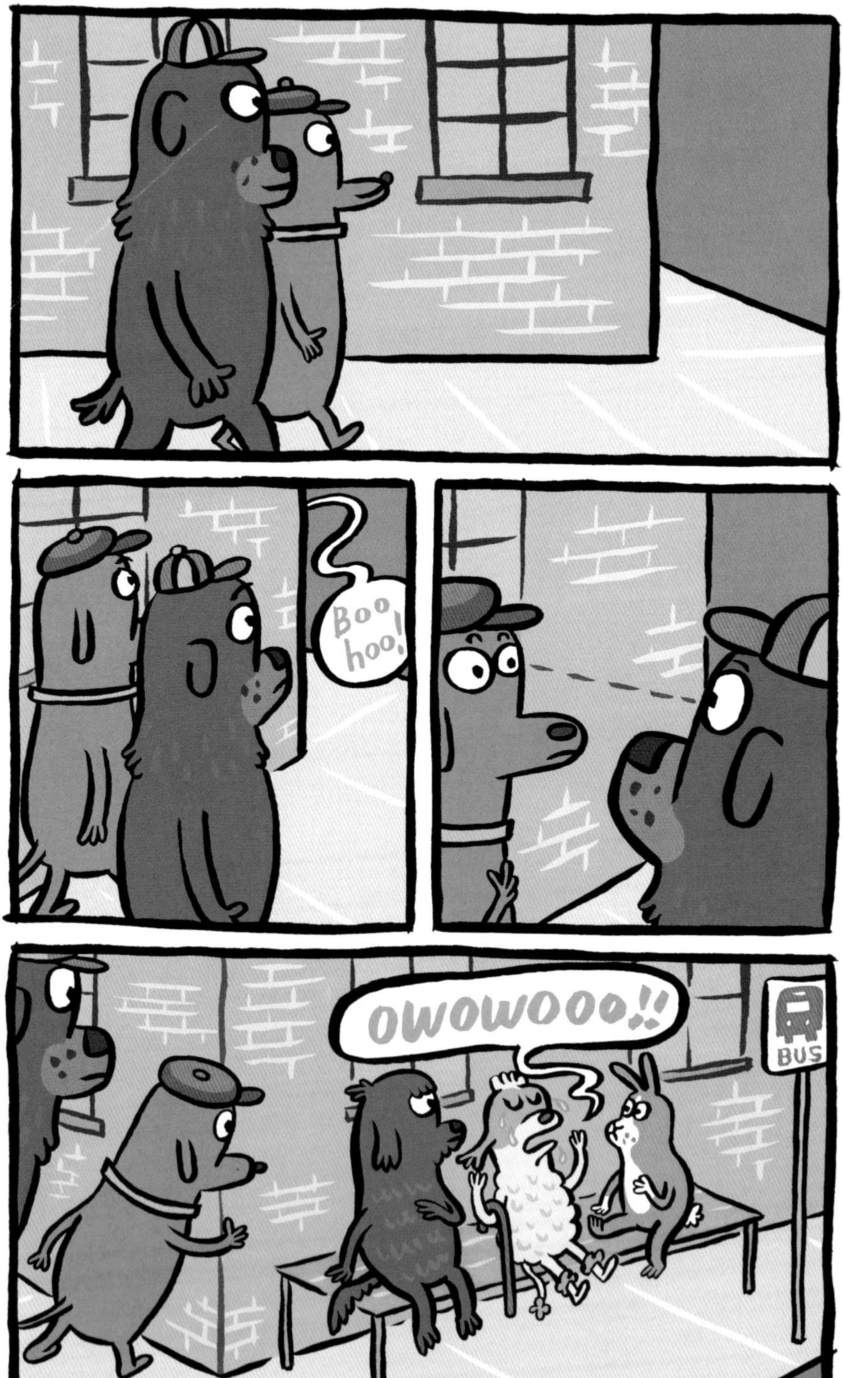
Boo hoo!
OWOWOOO!!
BUS

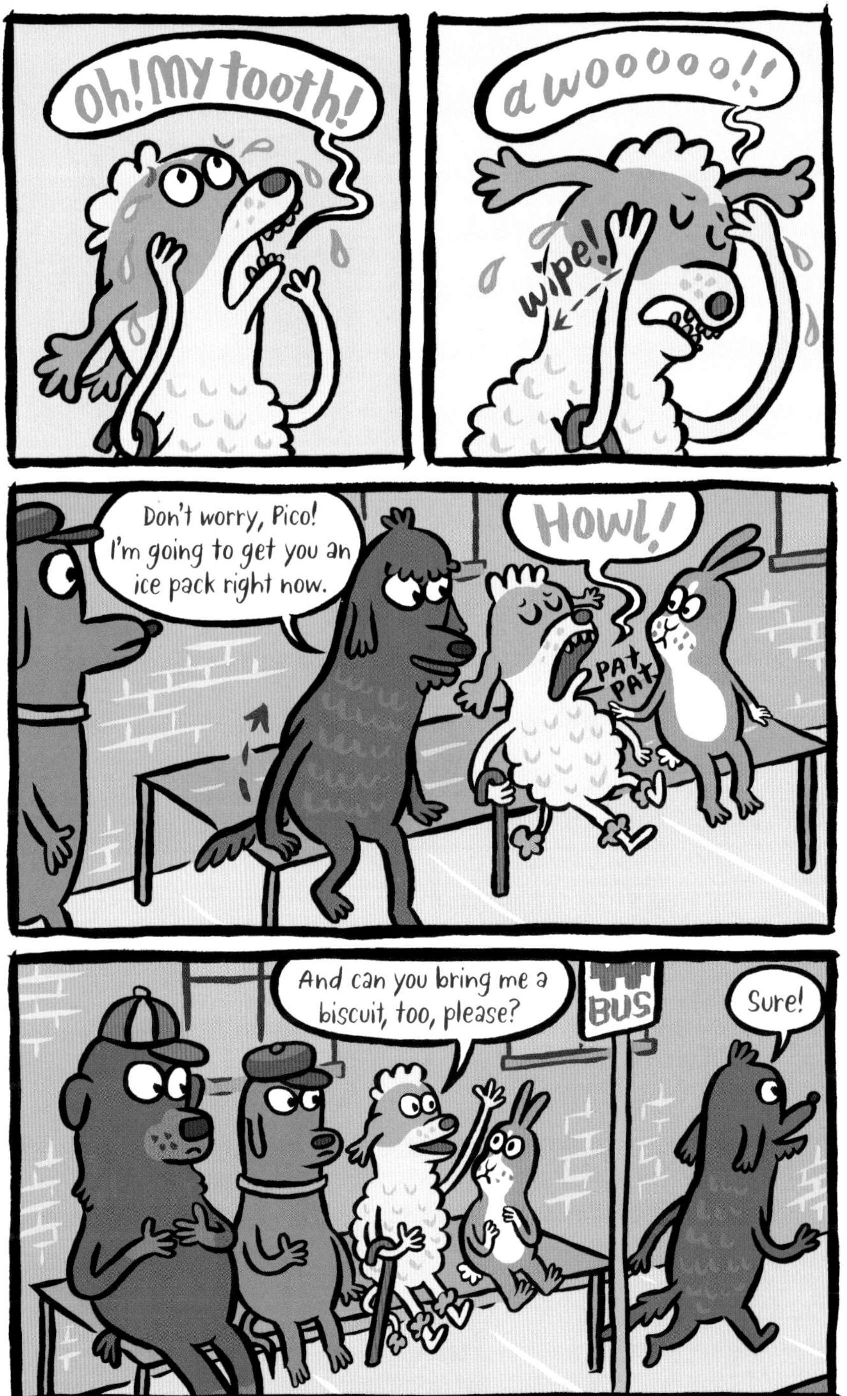

Oh! My tooth!
awooooo!!
wipe!
Don't worry, Pico!
I'm going to get you an
ice pack right now.
HOWL!
PAT PAT
And can you bring me a biscuit, too, please?
BUS
Sure!

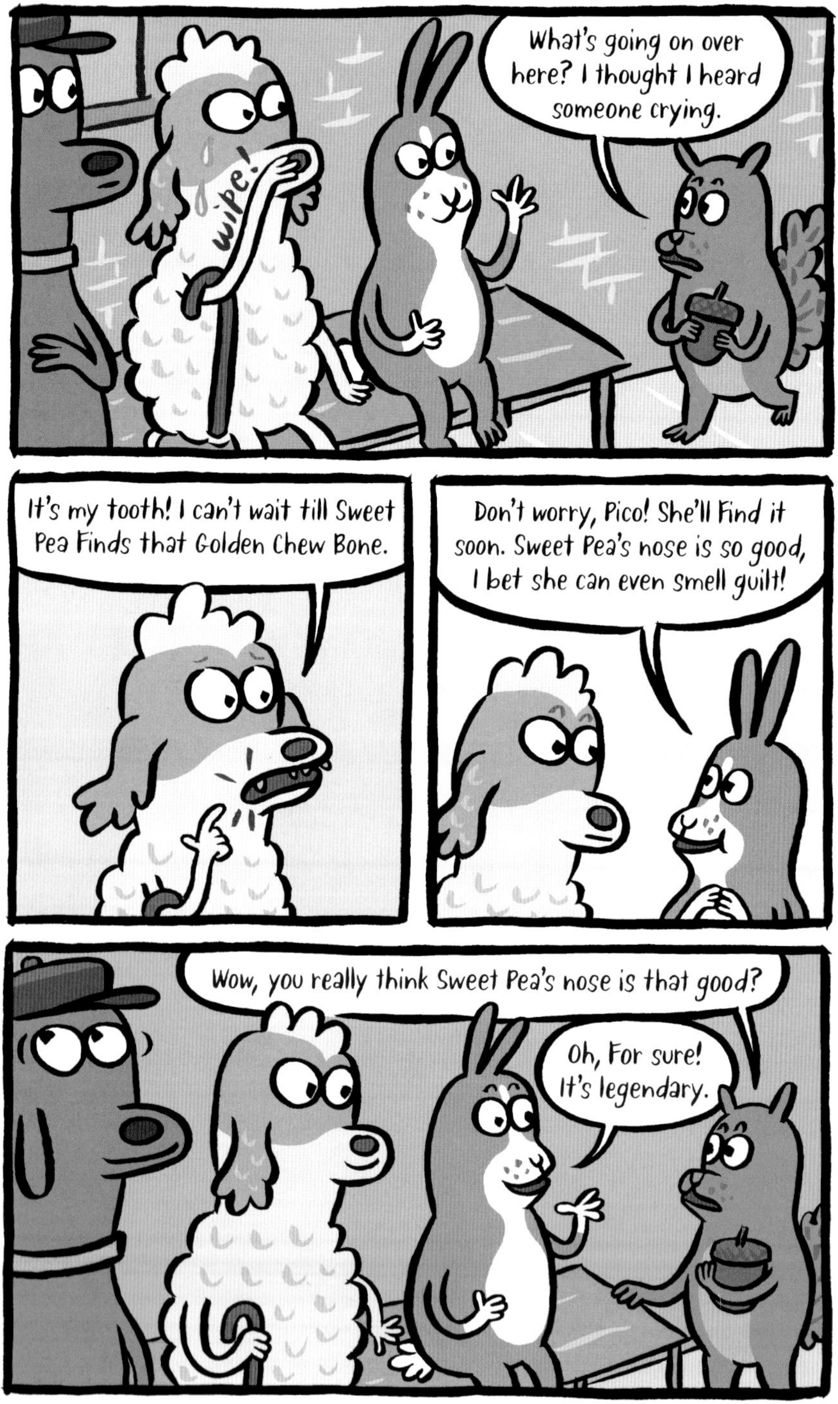
What's going on over here? I thought I heard someone crying.
wipe!
It's my tooth! I can't wait till Sweet Pea finds that Golden Chew Bone.
Don't worry, Pico! She'll find it soon. Sweet Pea's nose is so good, I bet she can even smell guilt!
Wow, you really think Sweet Pea's nose is that good?
Oh, for sure! It's legendary.

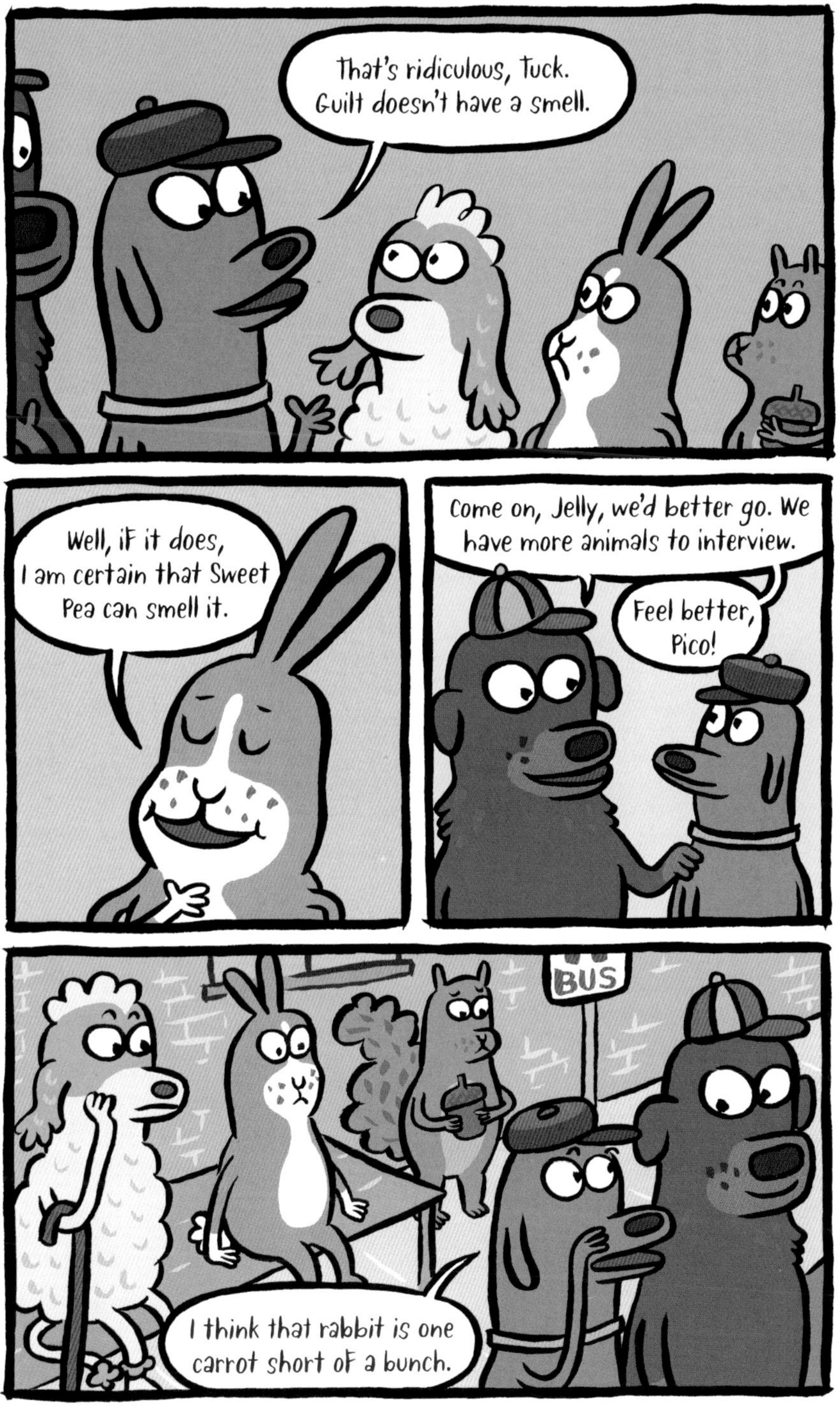
That's ridiculous, Tuck. Guilt doesn't have a smell.
Well, iF it does, I am certain that Sweet Pea can smell it.
Come on, Jelly, we'd better go. We have more animals to interview.
Feel better, Pico!
BUS
I think that rabbit is one carrot short oF a bunch.

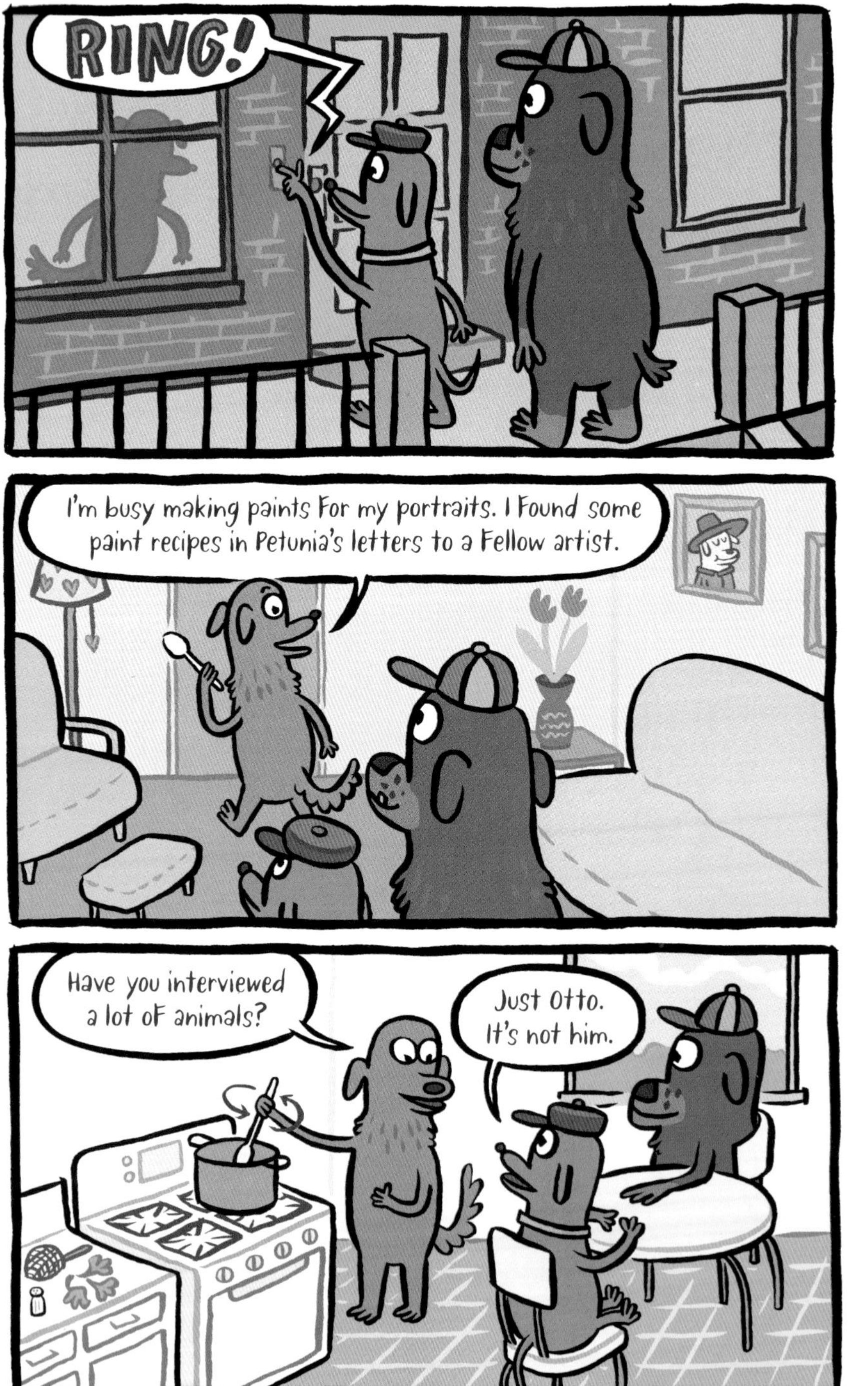
RING!
I'm busy making paints For my portraits. I Found some paint recipes in Petunia's letters to a Fellow artist.
Have you interviewed a lot oF animals?
Just Otto. It's not him.

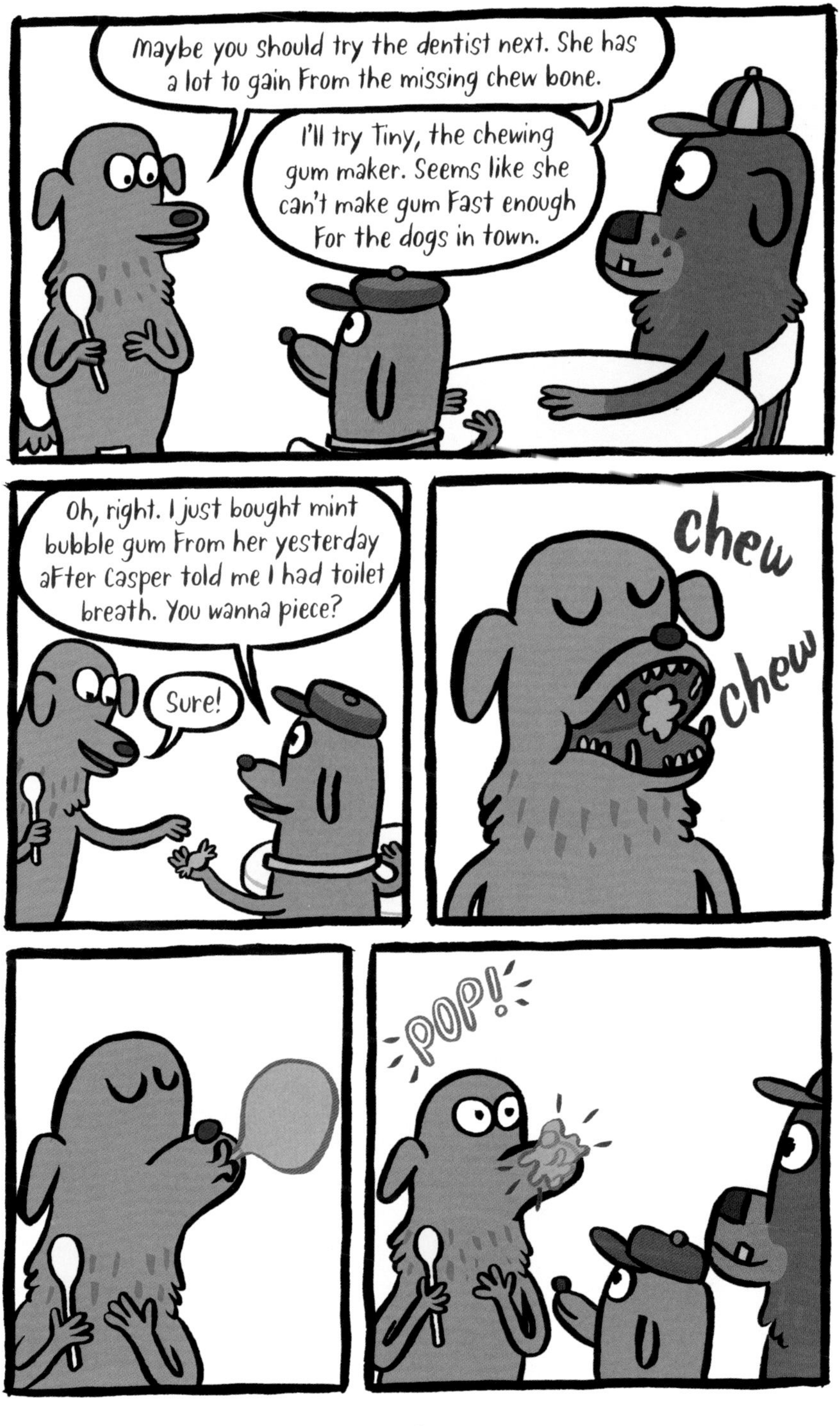
Maybe you should try the dentist next. She has a lot to gain from the missing chew bone.
I'll try Tiny, the chewing gum maker. Seems like she can't make gum fast enough for the dogs in town.
Oh, right. I just bought mint bubble gum from her yesterday after Casper told me I had toilet breath. You wanna piece?
Sure!
chew
chew
POP!

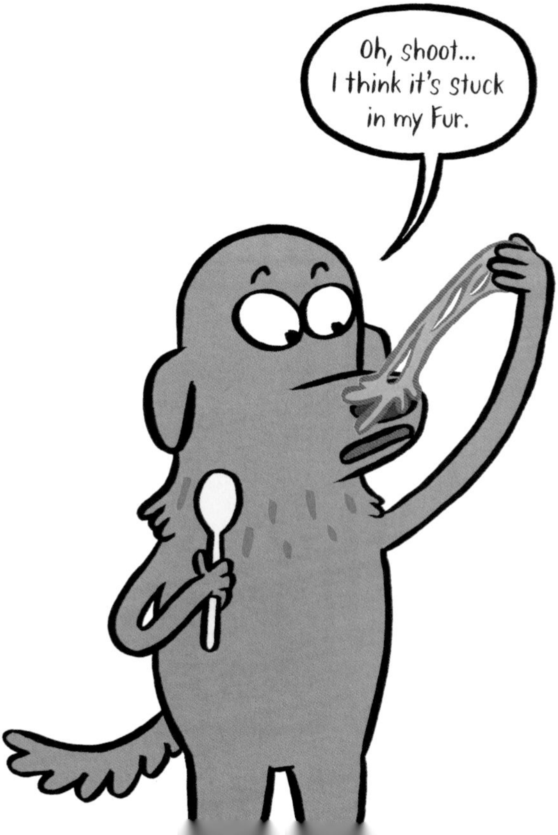
Oh, shoot... I think it's stuck in my Fur.

Chapter 8

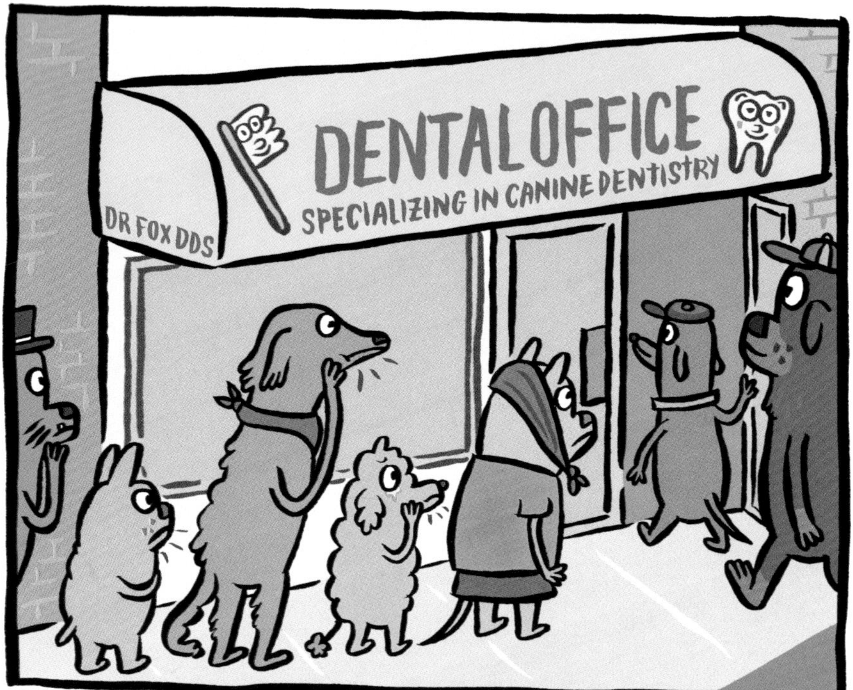
DENTAL OFFICE
SPECIALIZING IN CANINE DENTISTRY
DR FOX DDS

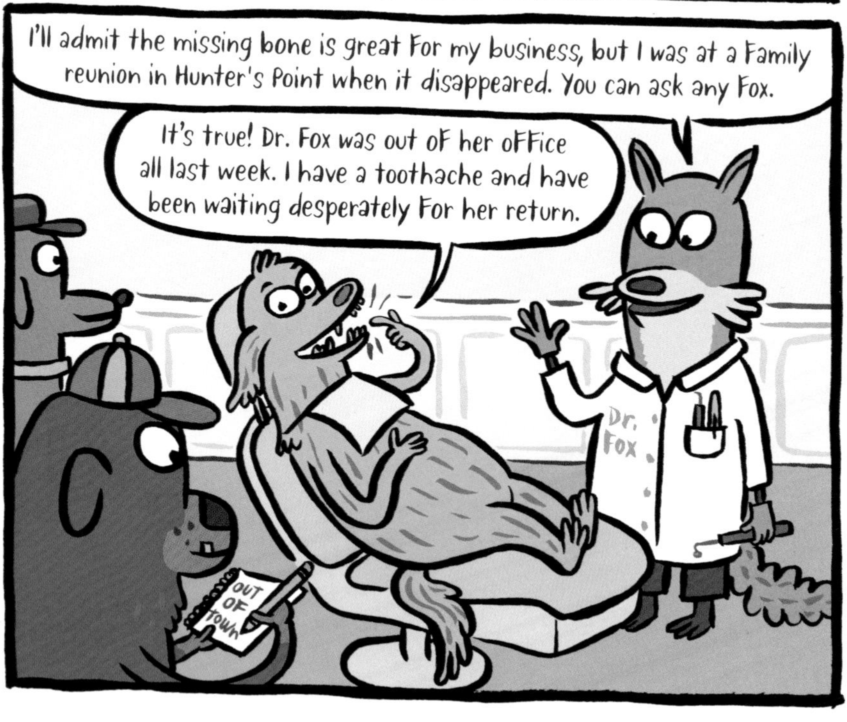
I'll admit the missing bone is great for my business, but I was at a family reunion in Hunter's Point when it disappeared. You can ask any fox.
It's true! Dr. Fox was out of her office all last week. I have a toothache and have been waiting desperately for her return.
Dr. Fox
OUT OF TOWN

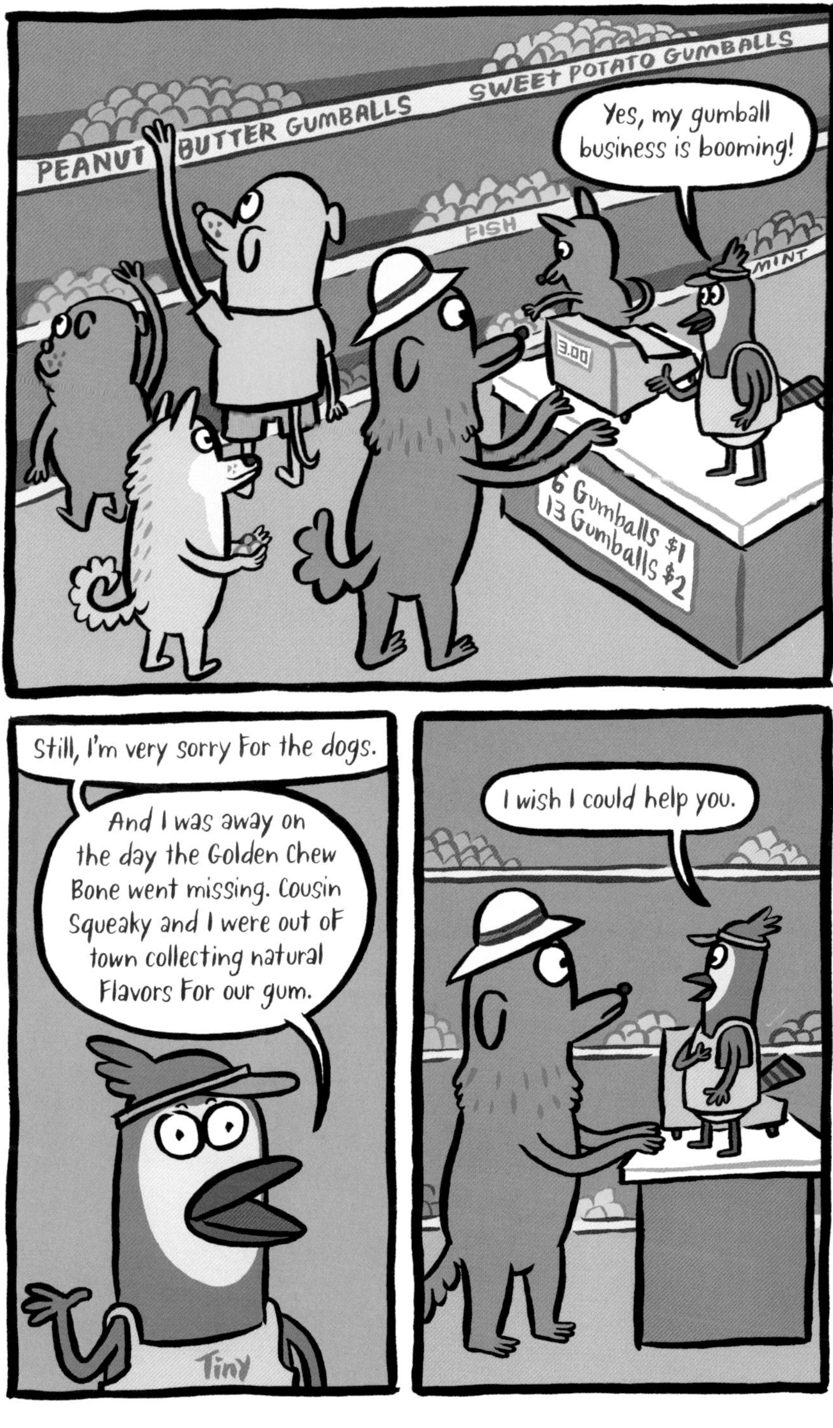
PEANUT BUTTER GUMBALLS
SWEET POTATO GUMBALLS
FISH
MINT
Yes, my gumball business is booming!
3.00
6 Gumballs $1
13 Gumballs $2
Still, I'm very sorry for the dogs.
And I was away on the day the Golden Chew Bone went missing. Cousin Squeaky and I were out of town collecting natural flavors for our gum.
TINY
I wish I could help you.

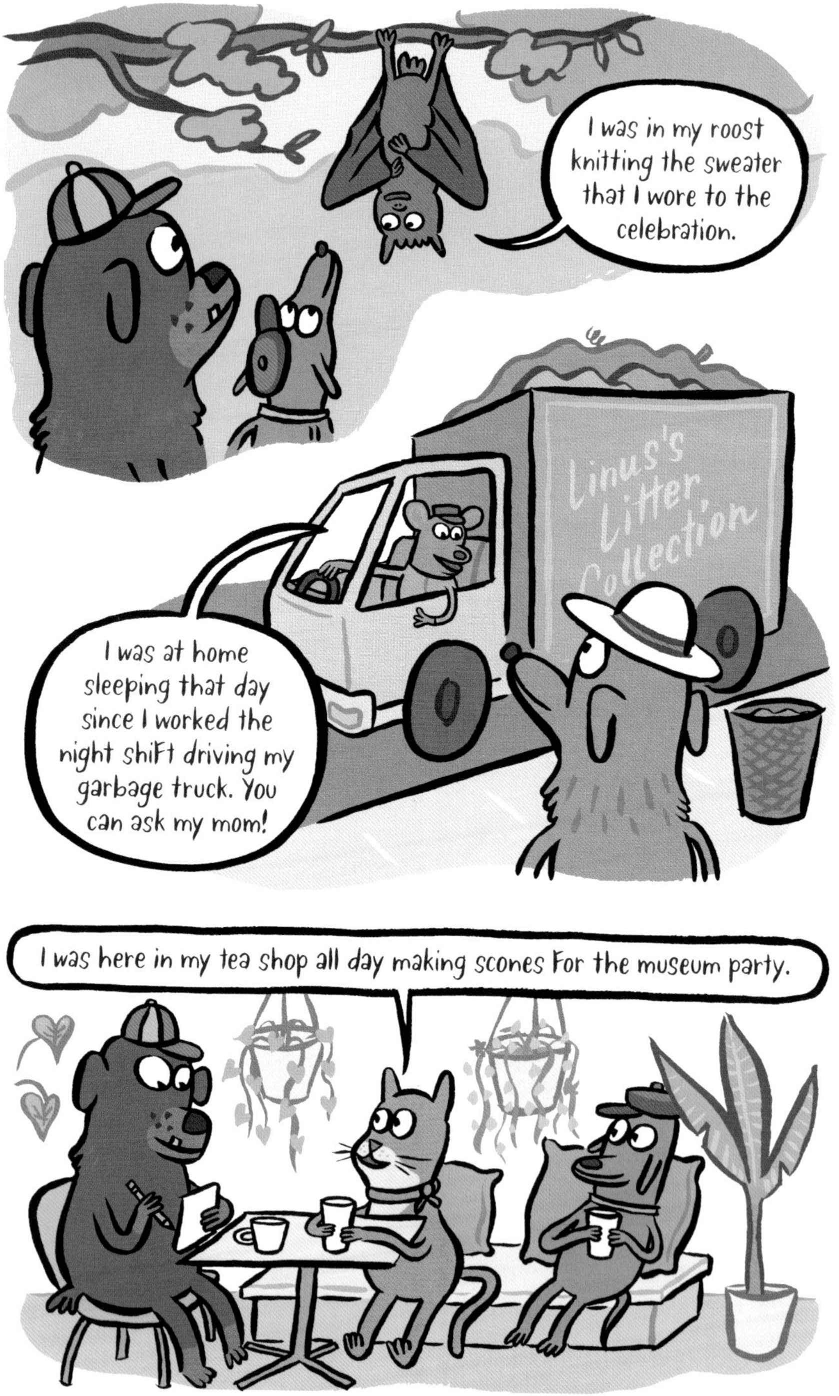
I was in my roost knitting the sweater that I wore to the celebration.
Linus's Litter Collection
I was at home sleeping that day since I worked the night shift driving my garbage truck. You can ask my mom!
I was here in my tea shop all day making scones for the museum party.

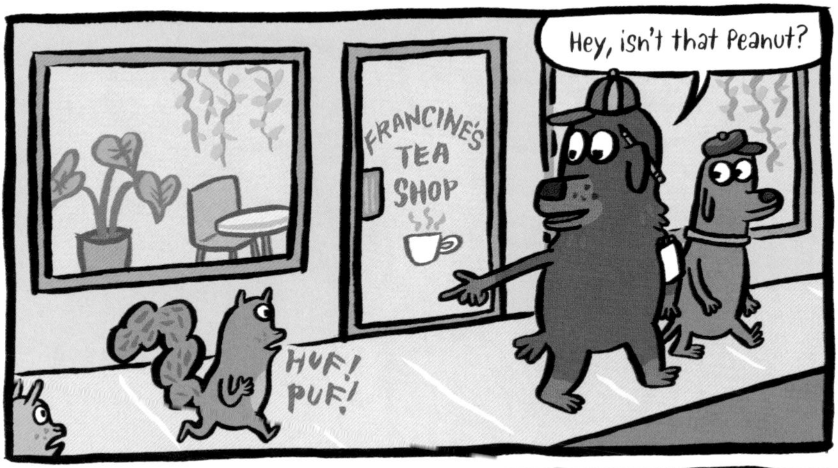

FRANCINE'S TEA SHOP
Hey, isn't that Peanut?
HUF! PUF!

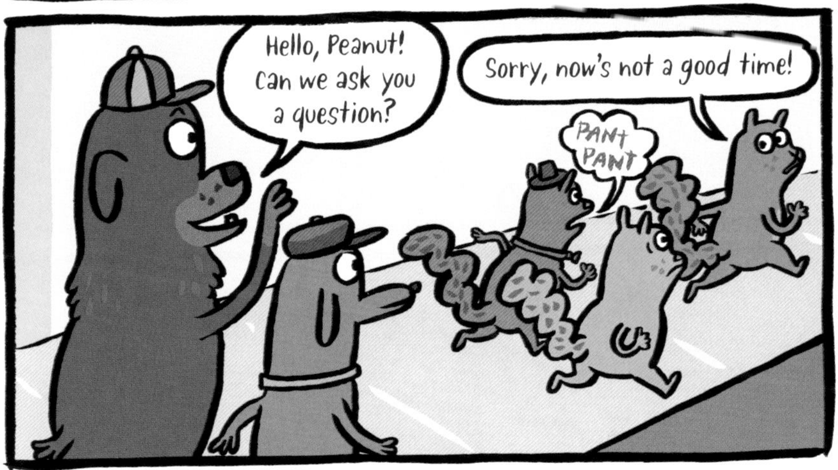

Hello, Peanut! Can we ask you a question?
Sorry, now's not a good time!
PANT PANT

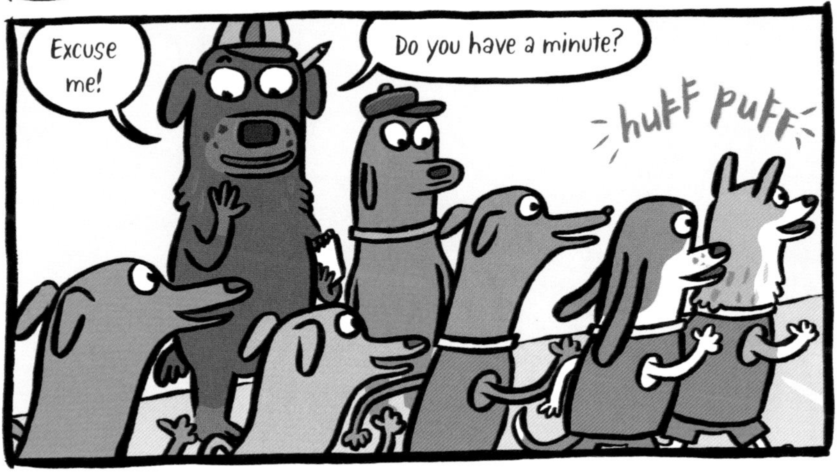

Excuse me!
Do you have a minute?
huff puff

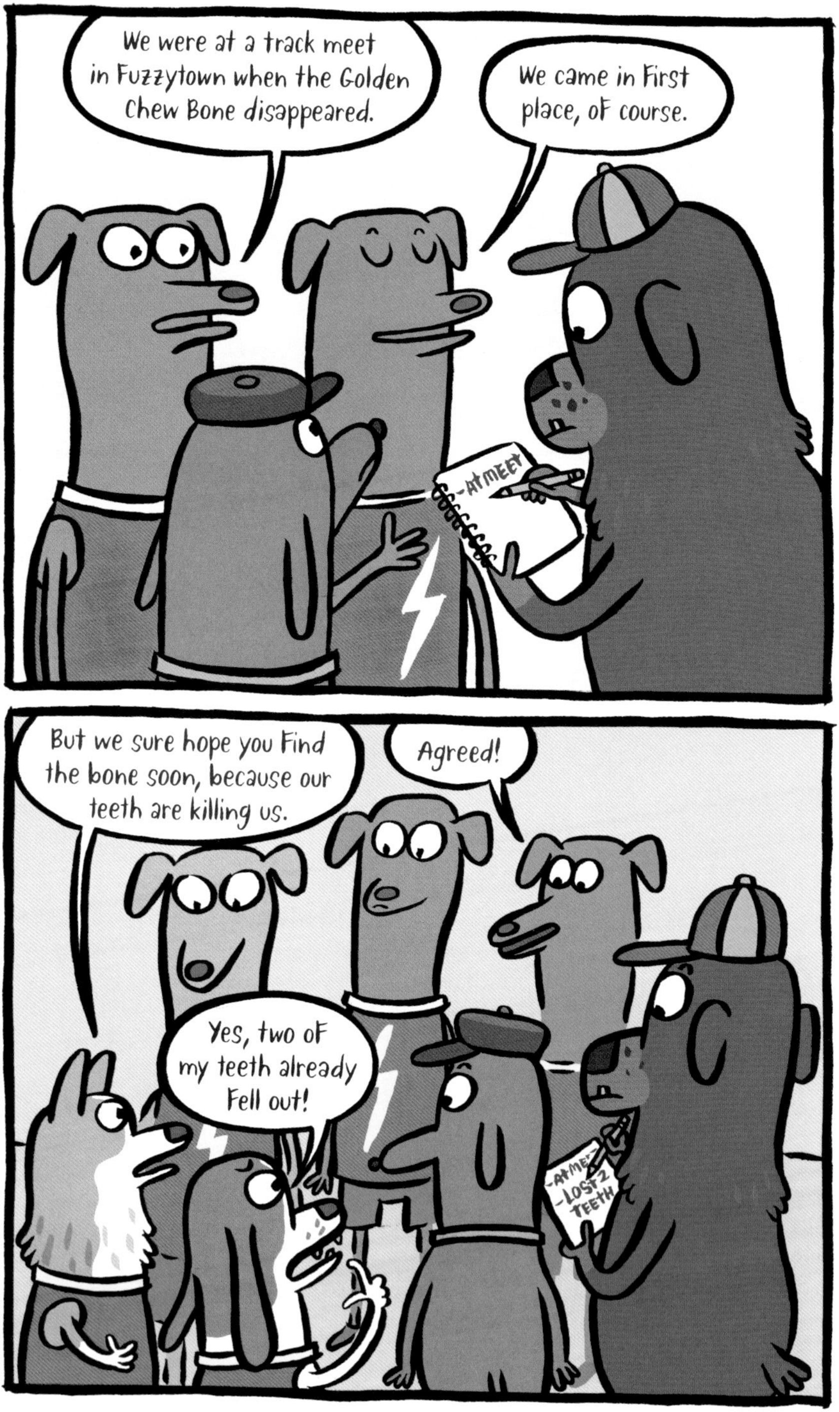
We were at a track meet in Fuzzytown when the Golden Chew Bone disappeared.
We came in First place, oF course.
-AT MEET
But we sure hope you Find the bone soon, because our teeth are killing us.
Agreed!
Yes, two oF my teeth already Fell out!
-LOST 2 TEETH

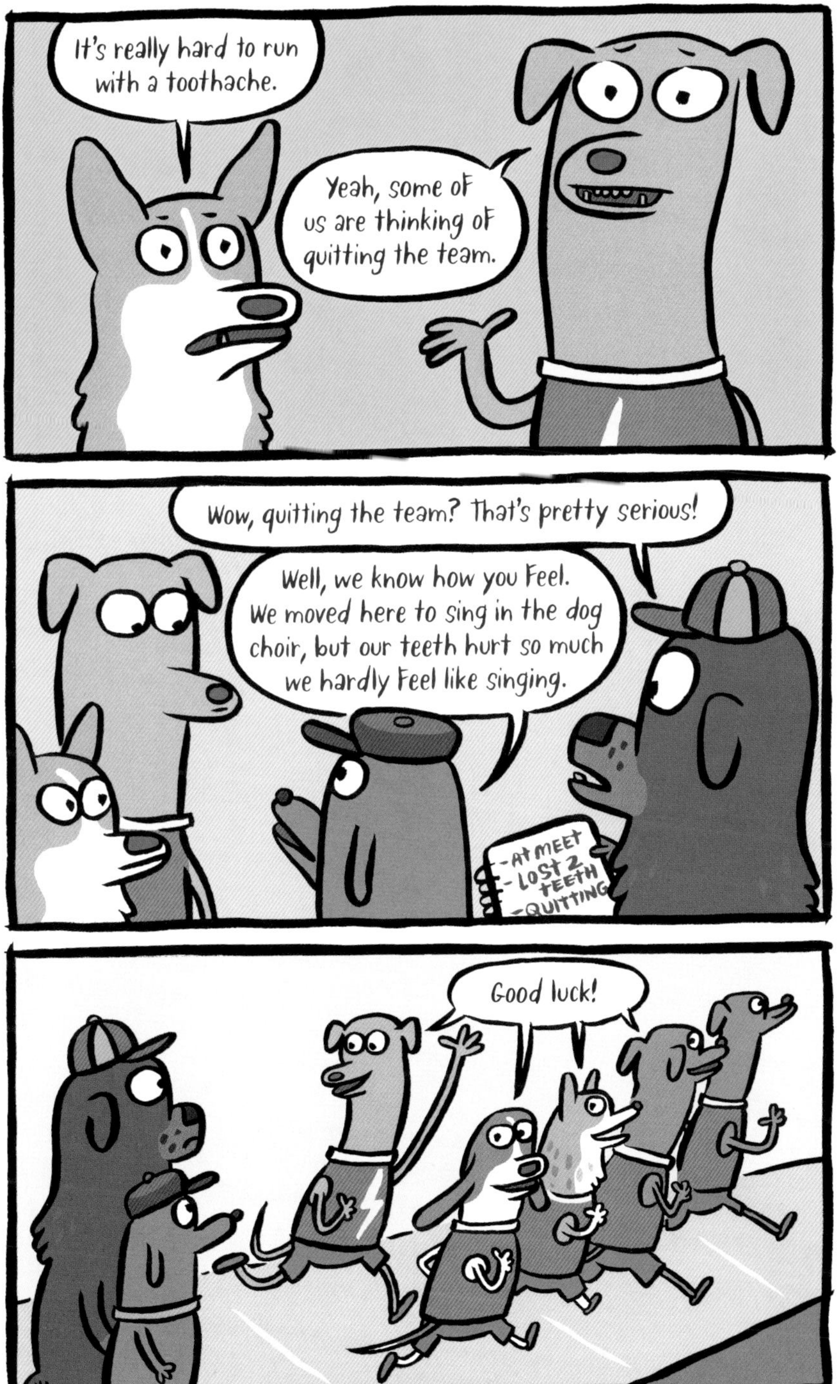
It's really hard to run with a toothache.
Yeah, some of us are thinking of quitting the team.
Wow, quitting the team? That's pretty serious!
Well, we know how you feel. We moved here to sing in the dog choir, but our teeth hurt so much we hardly feel like singing.
-AT MEET
-LOST 2 TEETH
-QUITTING
Good luck!

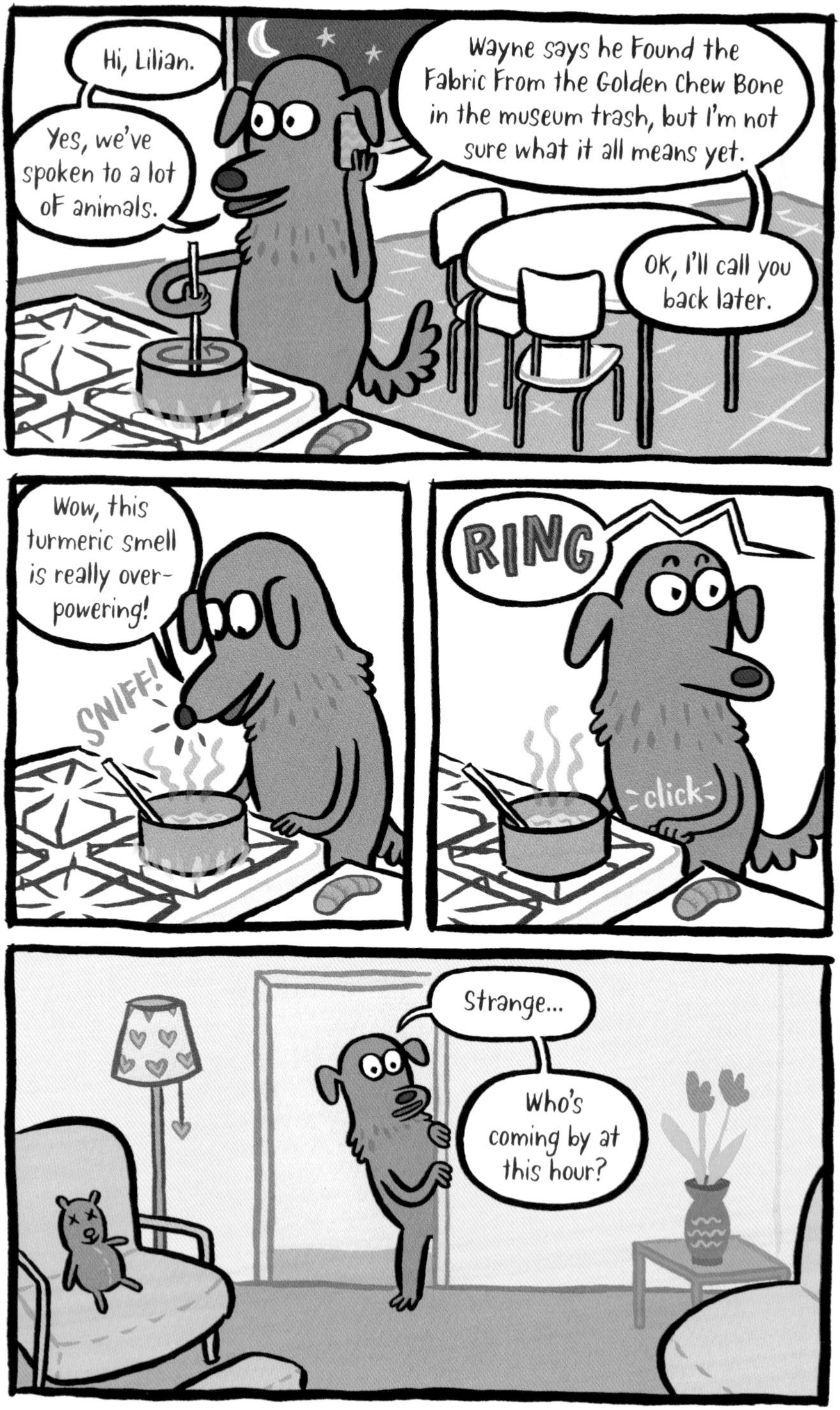
Hi, Lilian.
Yes, we've spoken to a lot of animals.
Wayne says he found the fabric from the Golden Chew Bone in the museum trash, but I'm not sure what it all means yet.
OK, I'll call you back later.
Wow, this turmeric smell is really over-powering!
SNIFF!
RING
click
Strange...
Who's coming by at this hour?

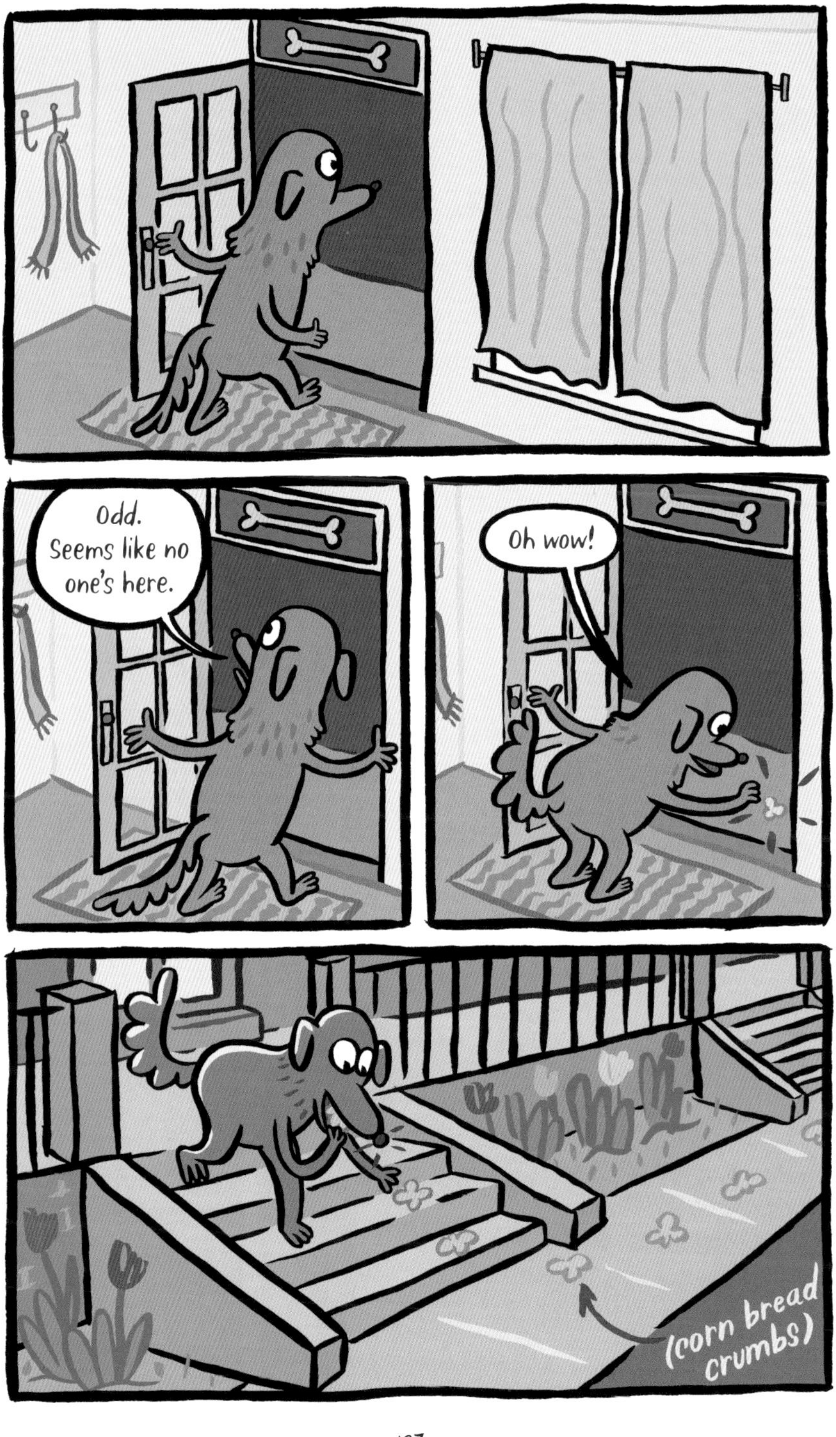
Odd. Seems like no one's here.
Oh wow!
(corn bread crumbs)

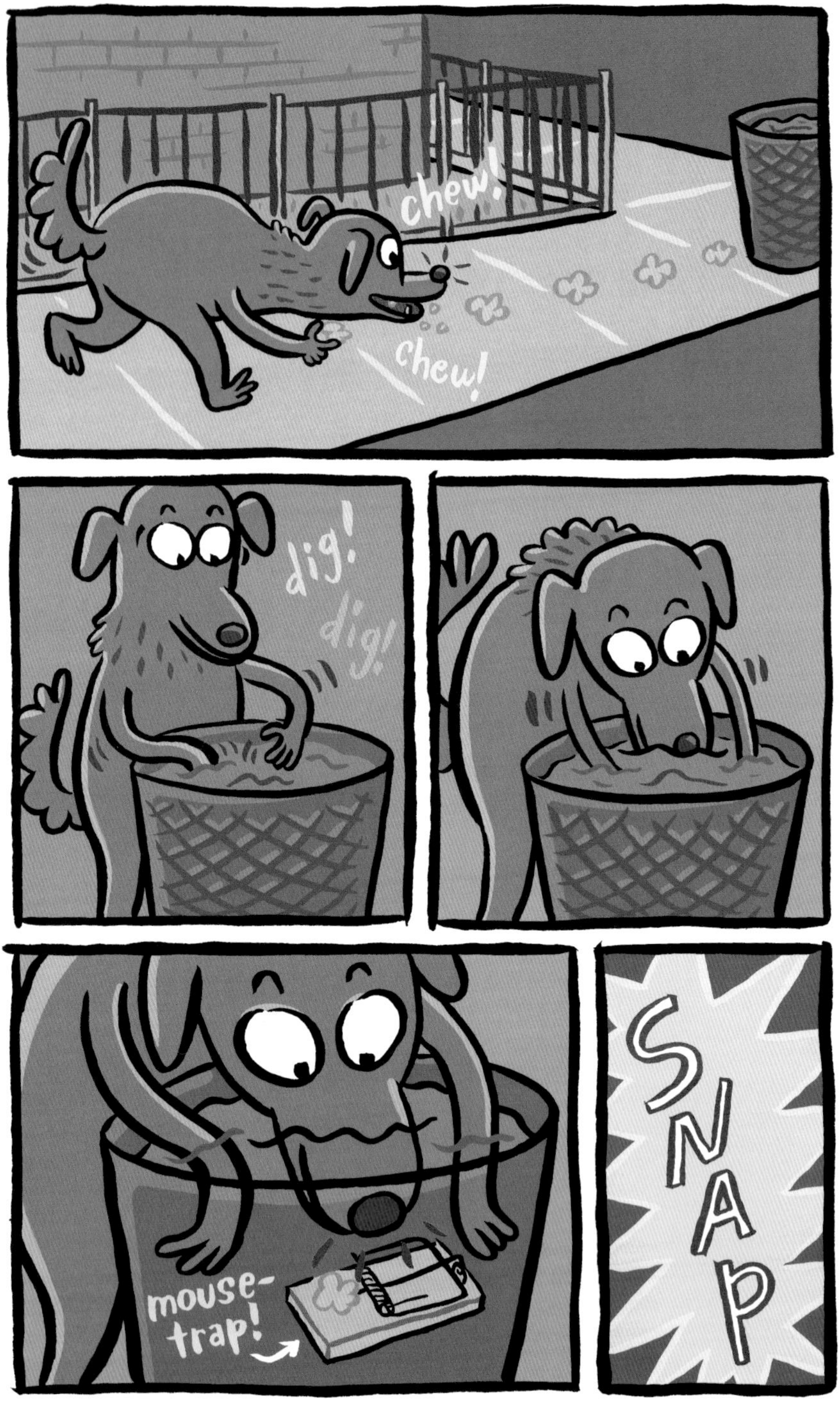
chew!
chew!
dig!
dig!
mouse-
trap!
SNAP

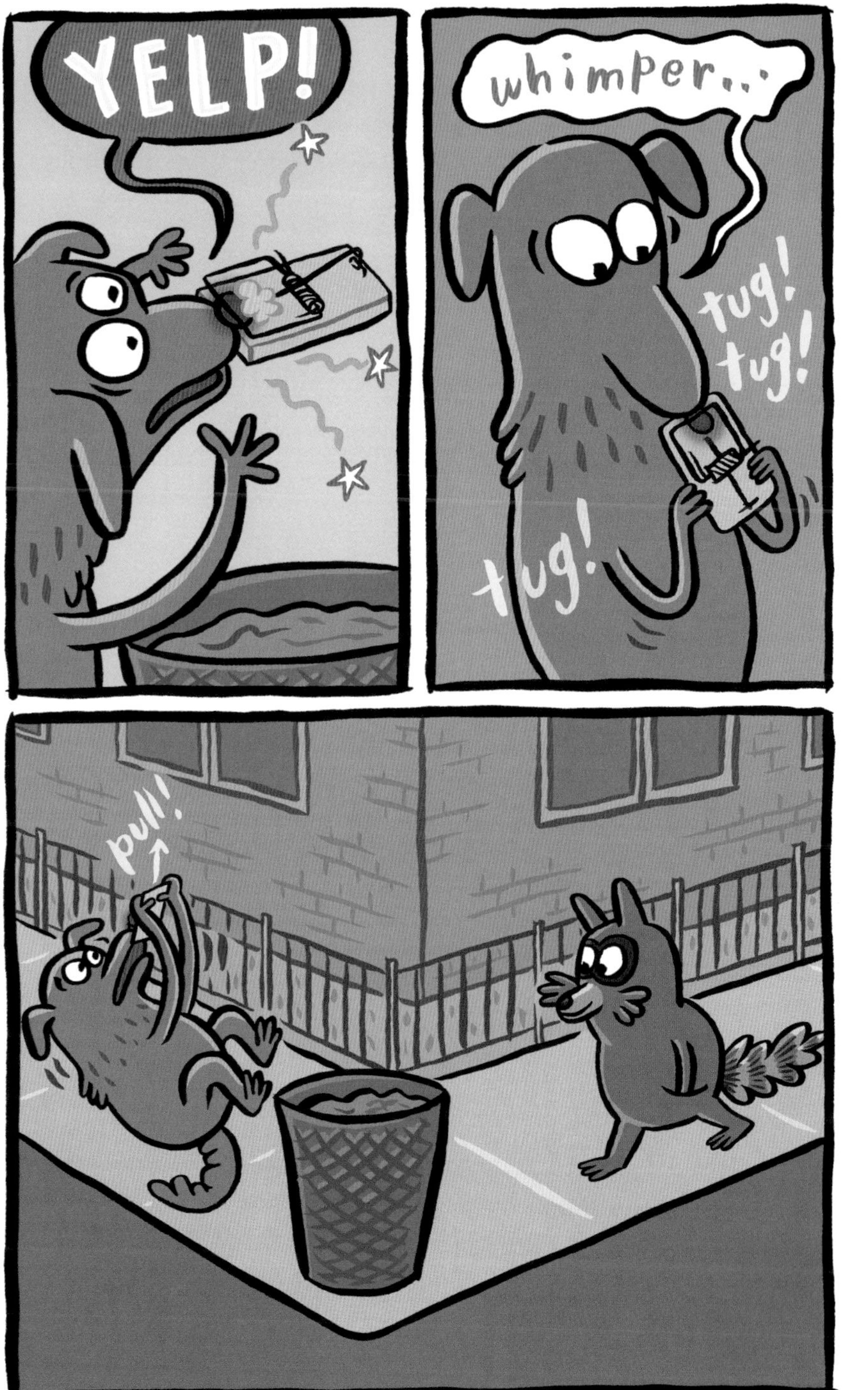
YELP!
whimper...
tug!
tug!
tug!
pull!

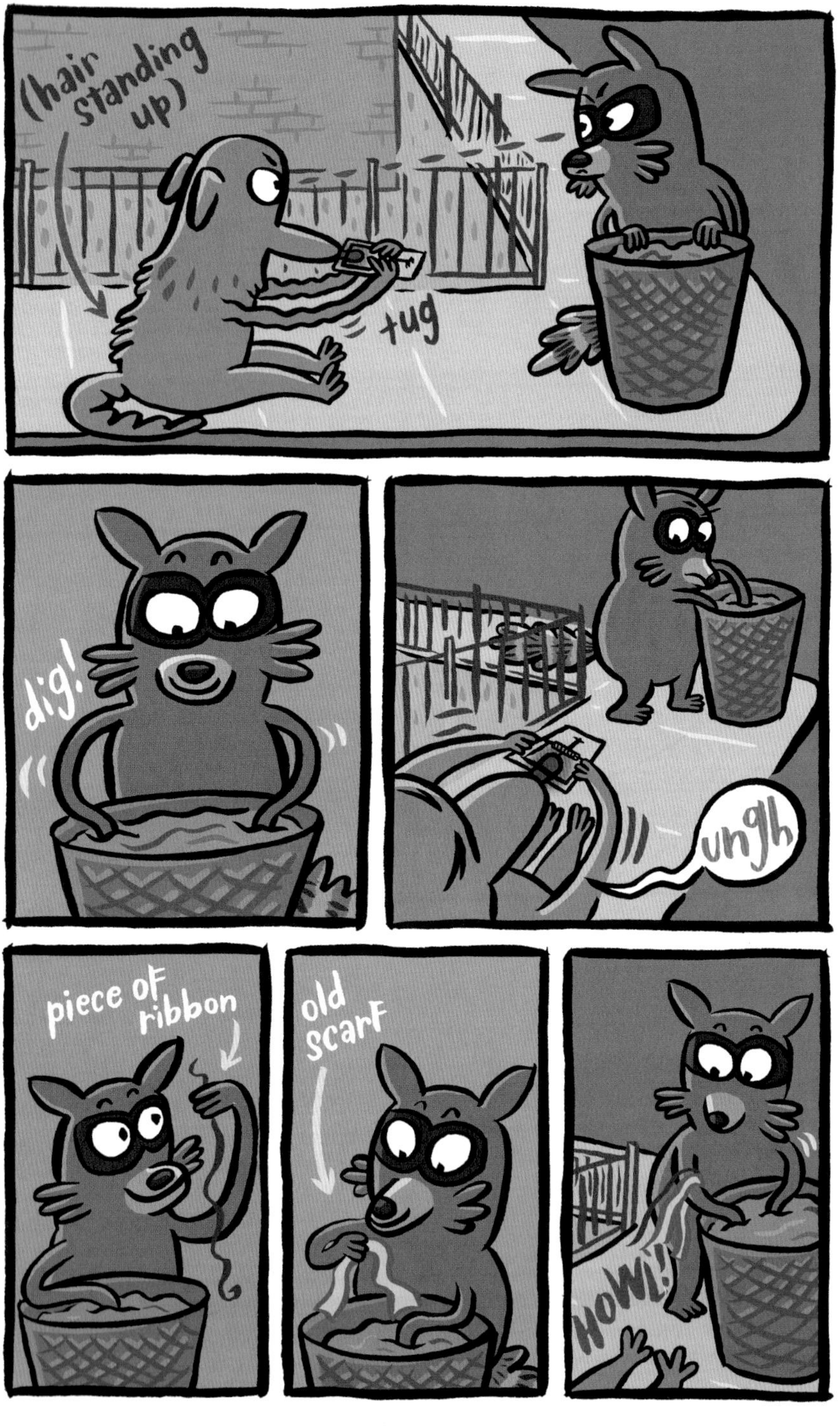
(hair standing up)
tug
dig!
ungh
piece of ribbon
old scarf
HOWL!

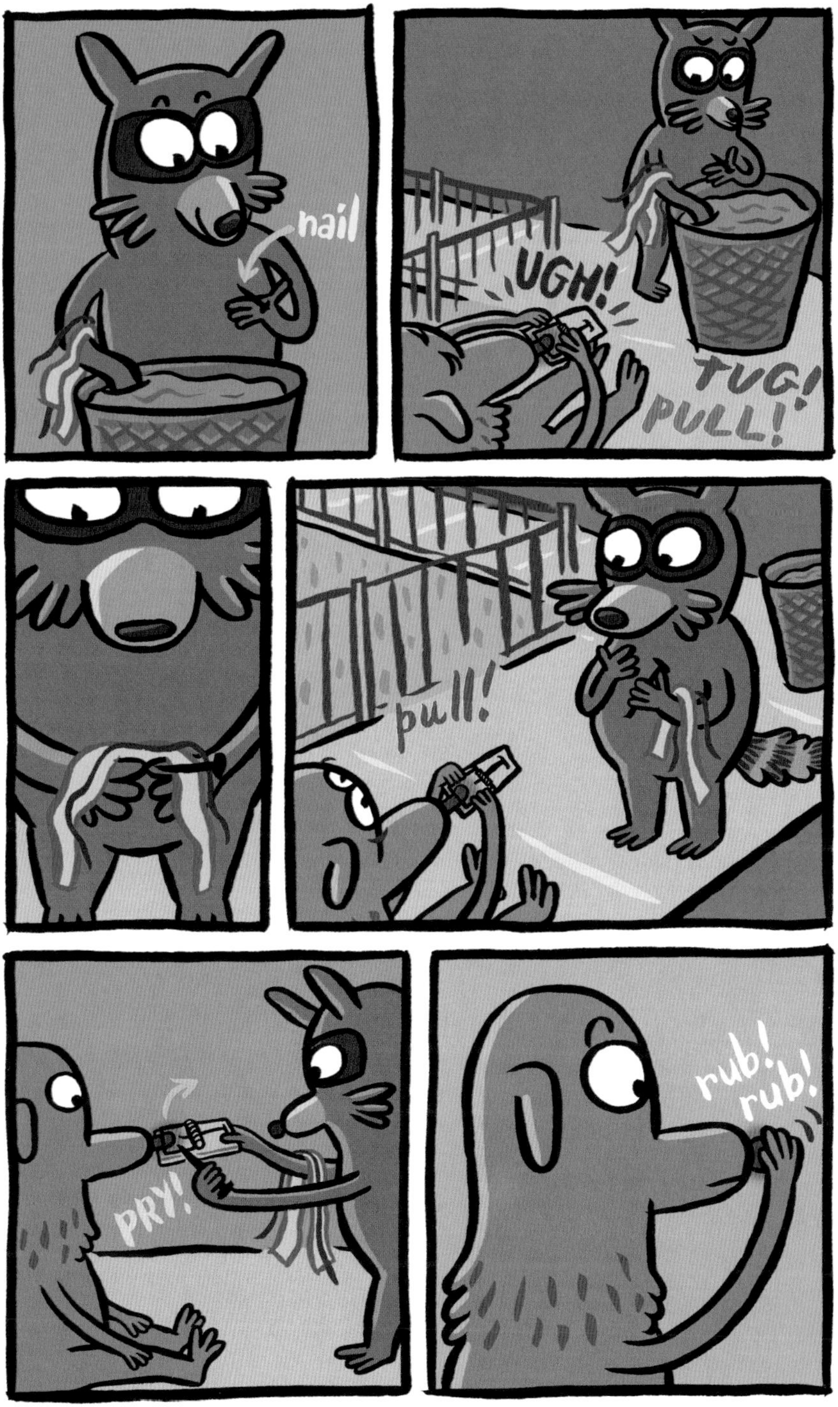
nail
UGH!
TUG!
PULL!
pull!
PRY!
rub!
rub!

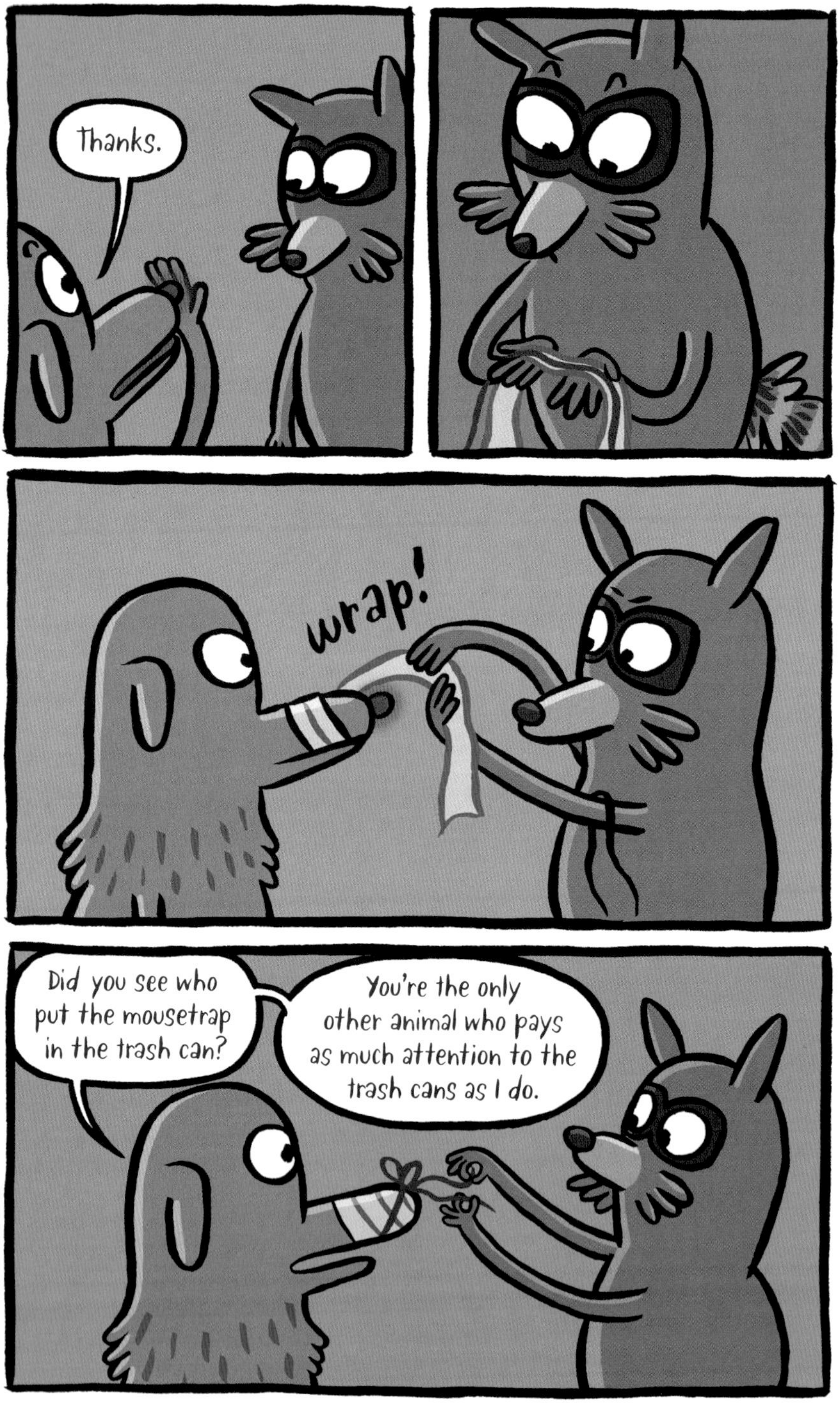
Thanks.
wrap!
Did you see who put the mousetrap in the trash can?
You're the only other animal who pays as much attention to the trash cans as I do.

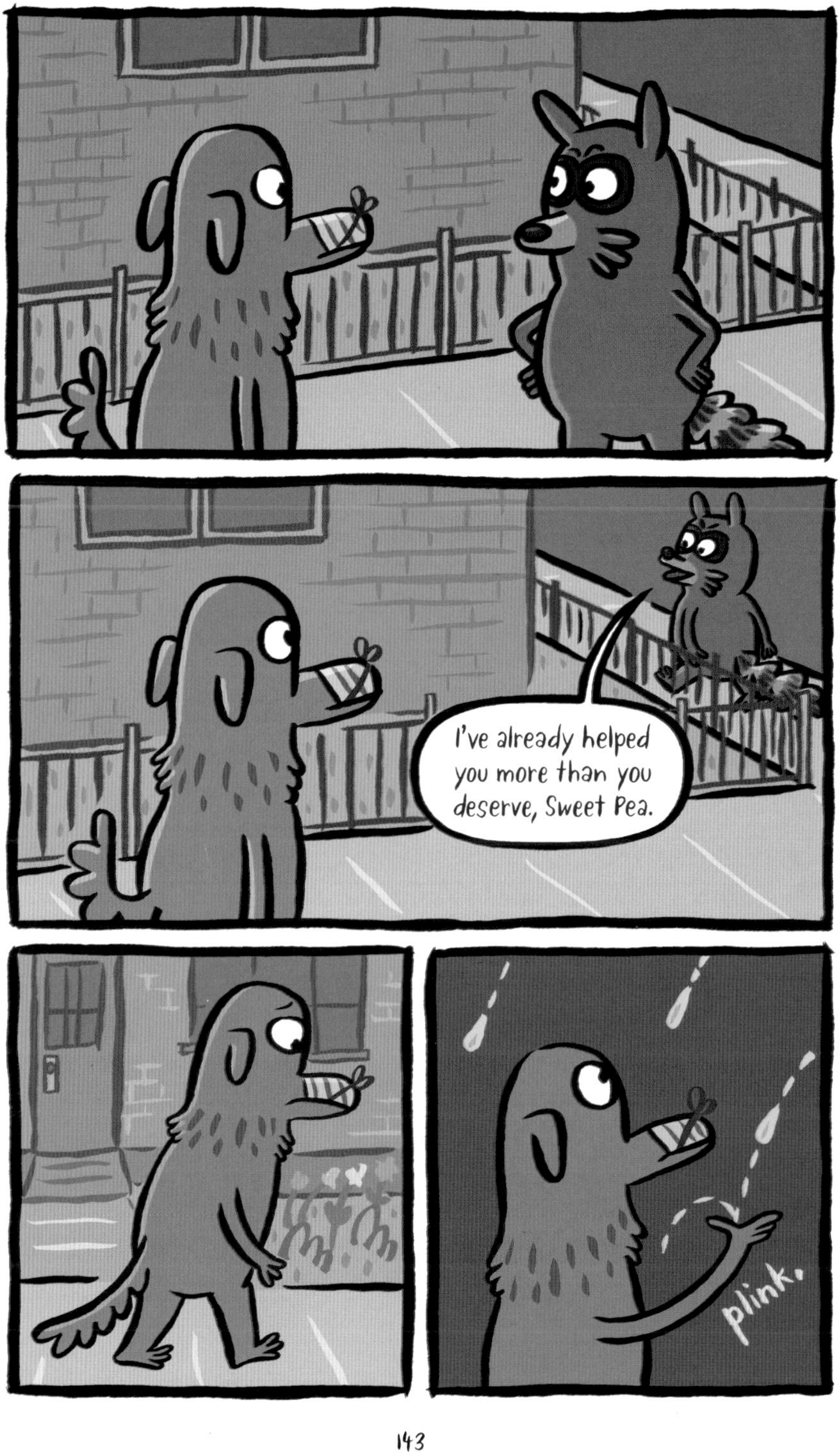
I've already helped you more than you deserve, Sweet Pea.
plink.

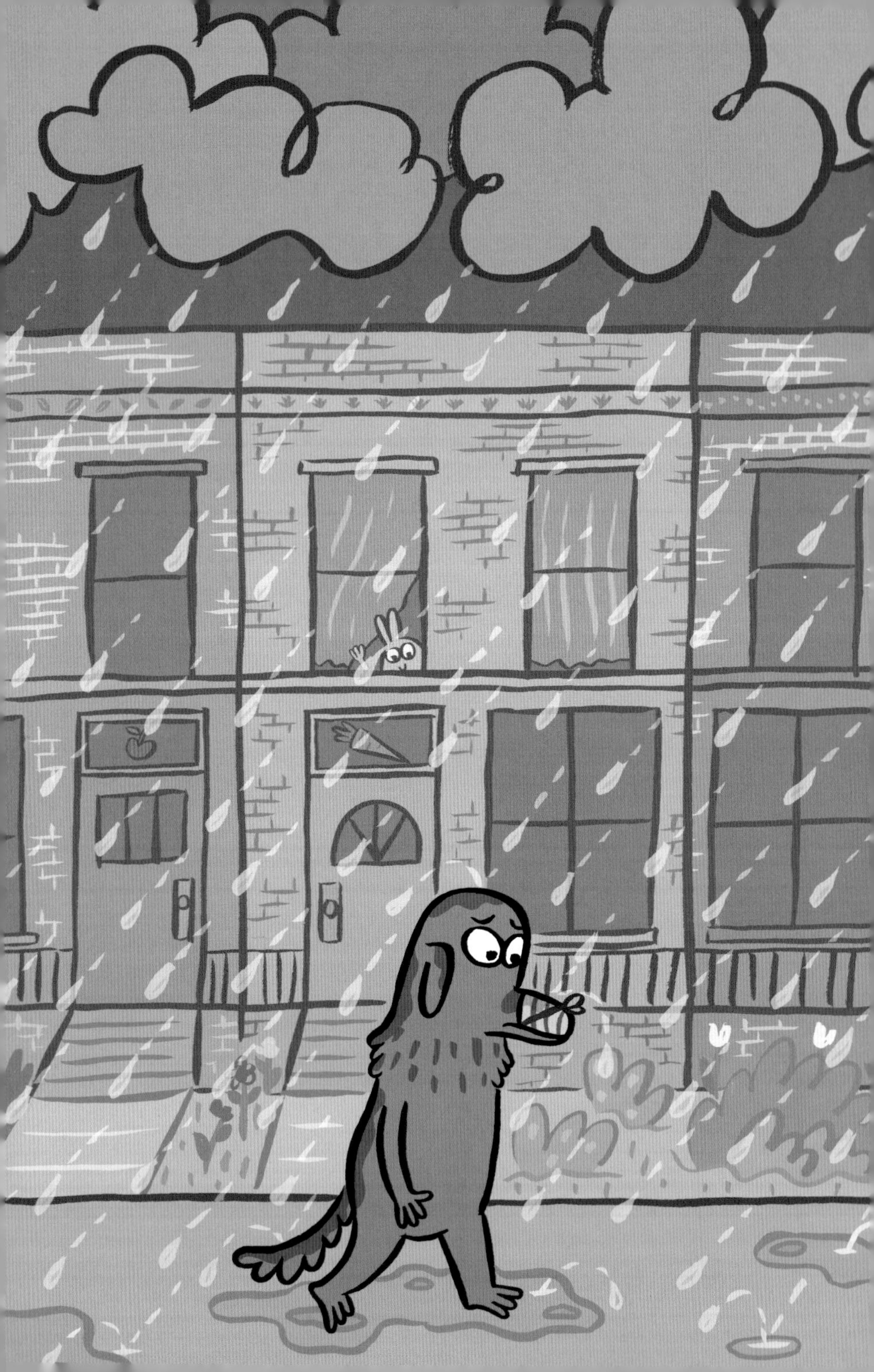

Chapter 9

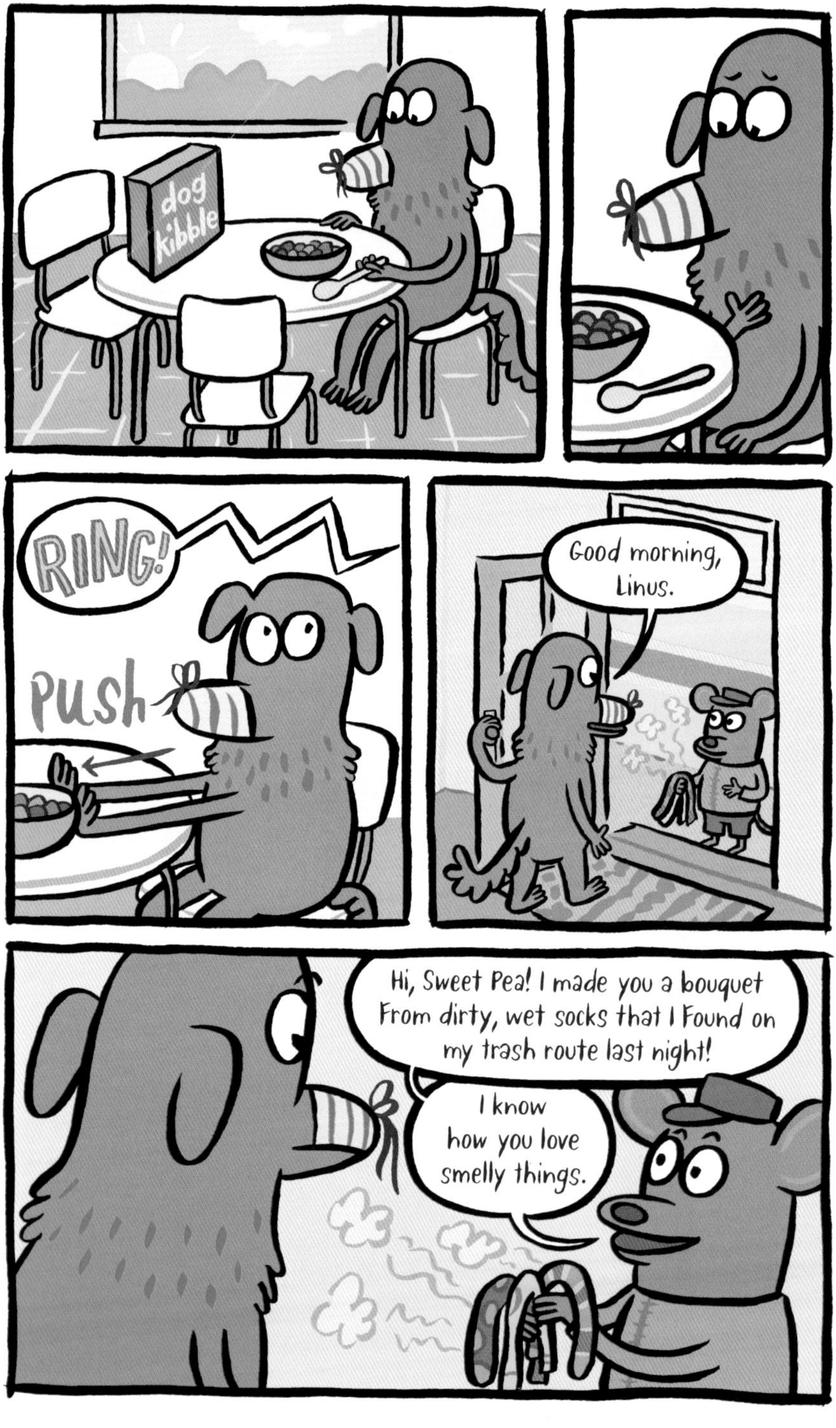
dog kibble
RING!
PUSH
Good morning, Linus.
Hi, Sweet Pea! I made you a bouquet from dirty, wet socks that I found on my trash route last night!
I know how you love smelly things.

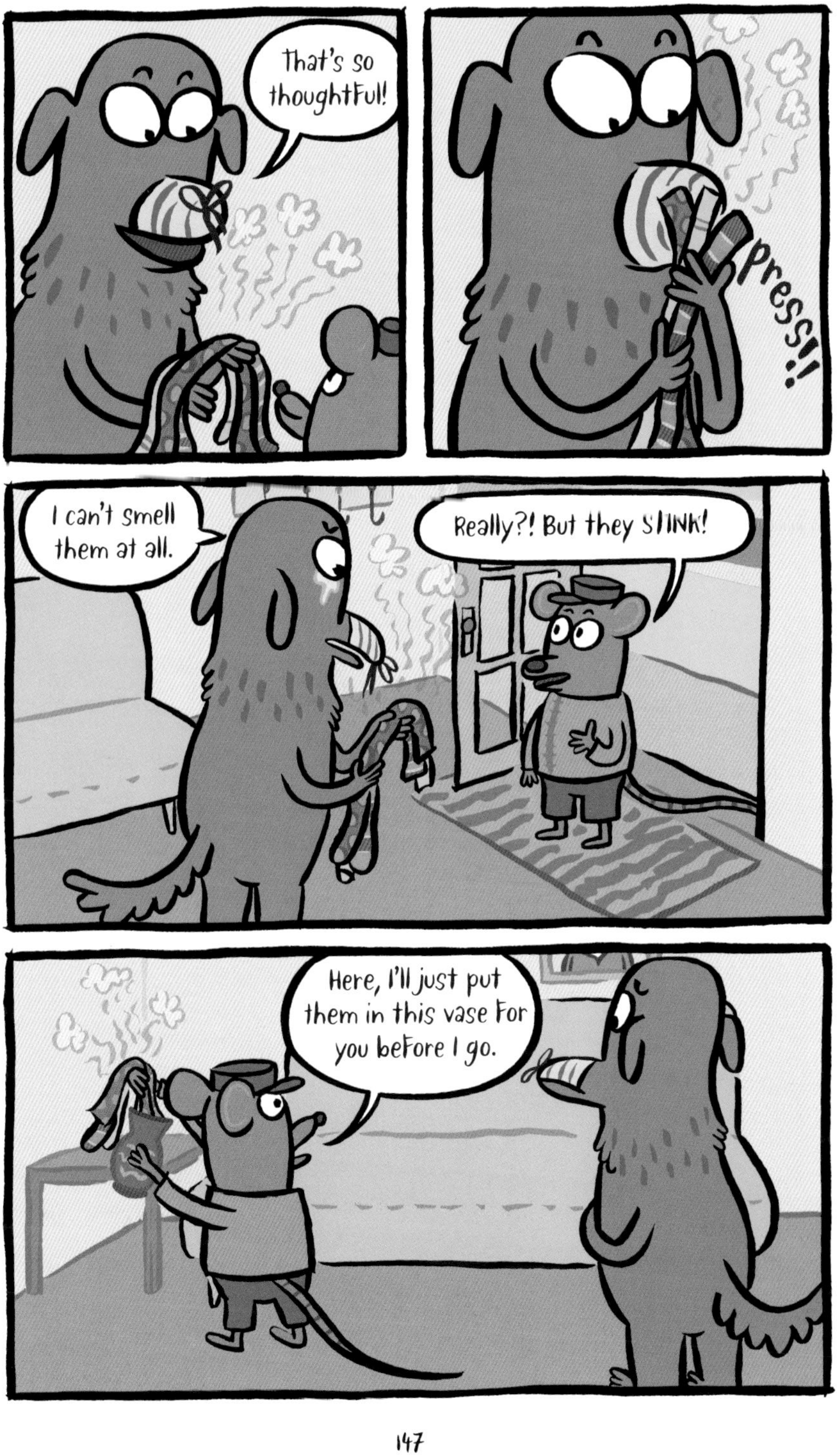
That's so thoughtful!
PRESS!!
I can't smell them at all.
Really?! But they STINK!
Here, I'll just put them in this vase for you before I go.

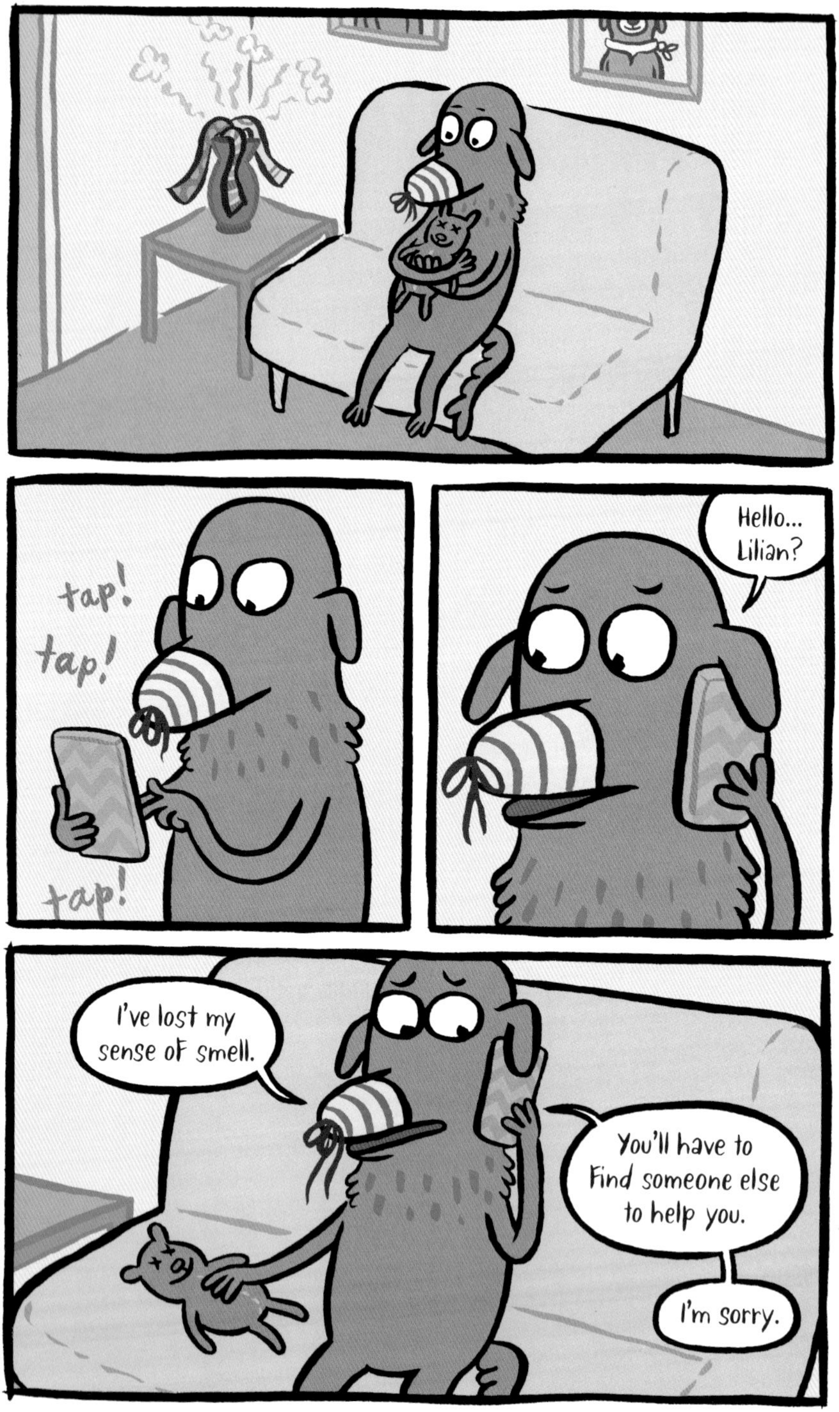
tap!
tap!
tap!
Hello... Lilian?
I've lost my sense oF smell.
You'll have to Find someone else to help you.
I'm sorry.

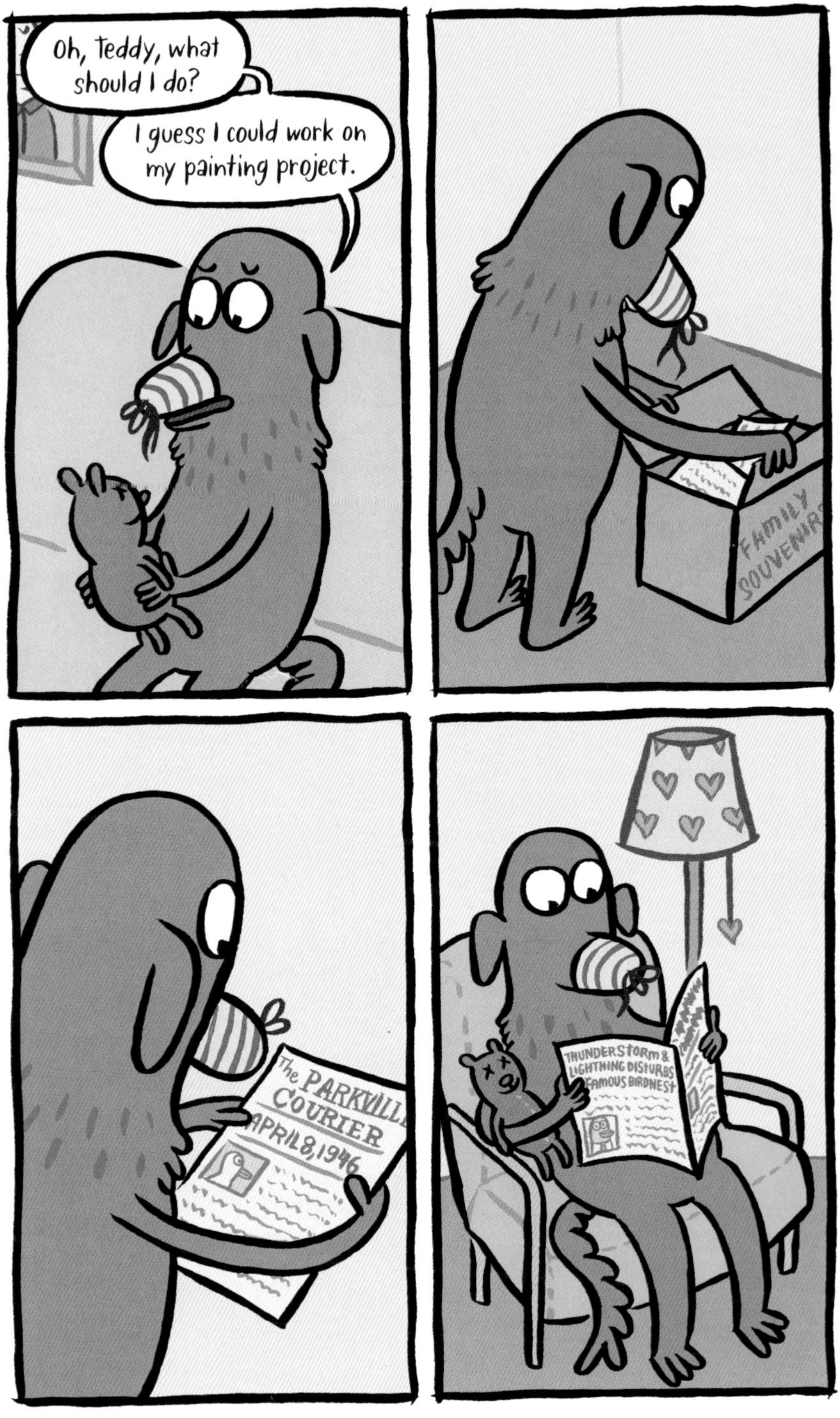
Oh, teddy, what should I do?
I guess I could work on my painting project.
FAMILY SOUVENIR
The PARKVILL
COURIER
APRIL 8, 1946
THUNDERSTORM & LIGHTNING DISTURBS FAMOUS BIRDNEST

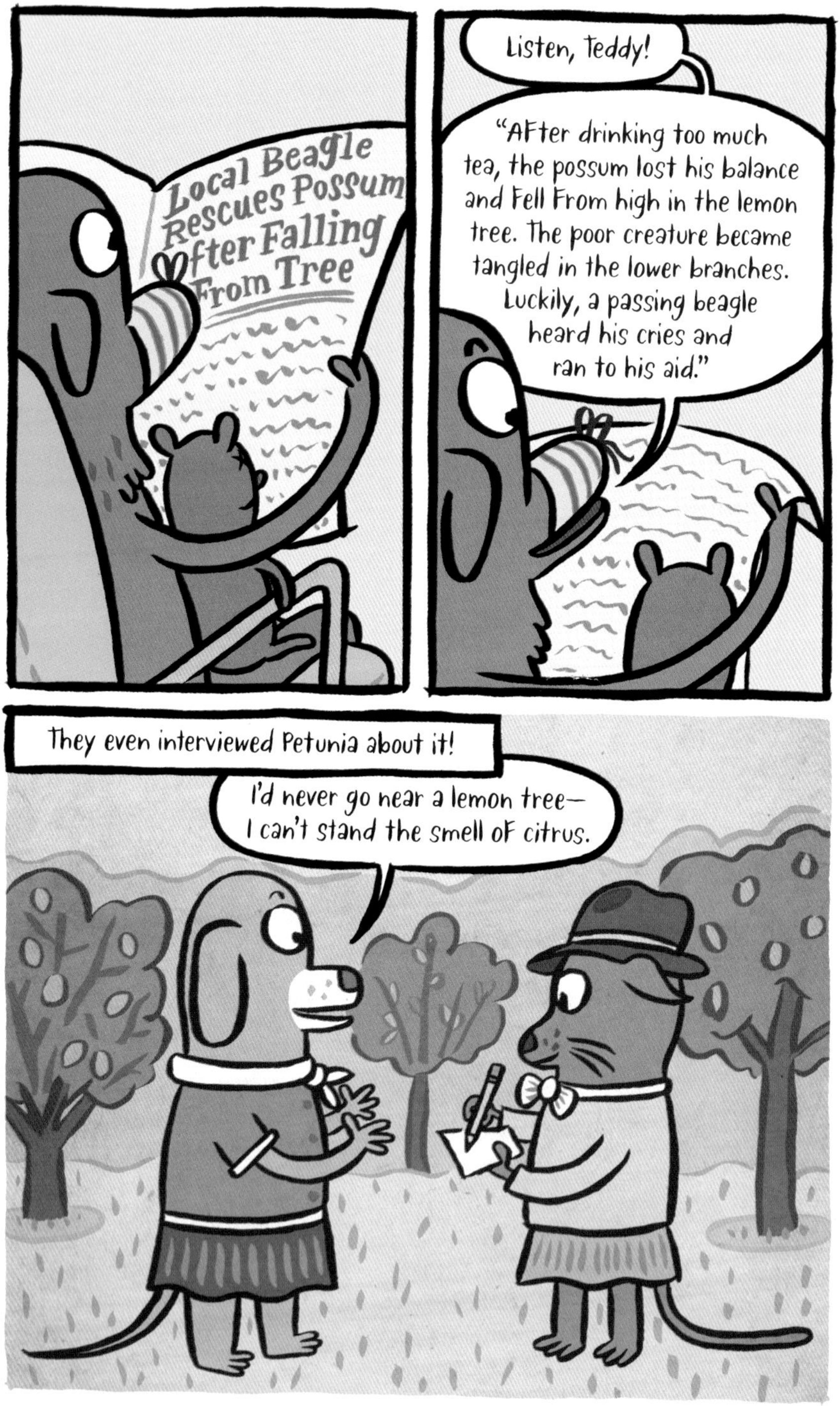
Local Beagle Rescues Possum After Falling From Tree
Listen, Teddy!
"After drinking too much tea, the possum lost his balance and fell from high in the lemon tree. The poor creature became tangled in the lower branches. Luckily, a passing beagle heard his cries and ran to his aid."
They even interviewed Petunia about it!
I'd never go near a lemon tree—I can't stand the smell of citrus.

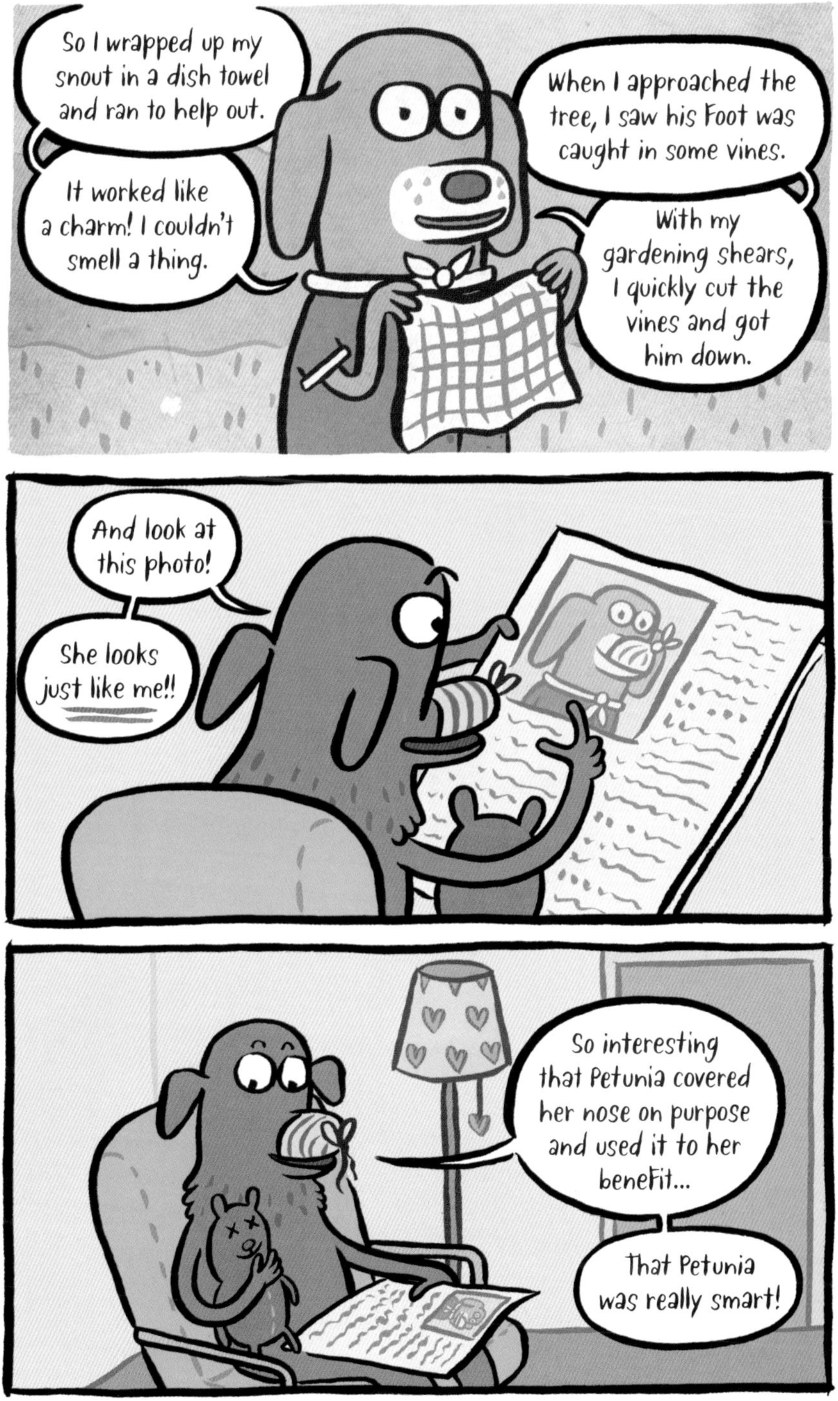
So I wrapped up my snout in a dish towel and ran to help out.
It worked like a charm! I couldn't smell a thing.
When I approached the tree, I saw his foot was caught in some vines.
With my gardening shears, I quickly cut the vines and got him down.
And look at this photo!
She looks just like me!!
So interesting that Petunia covered her nose on purpose and used it to her benefit...
That Petunia was really smart!

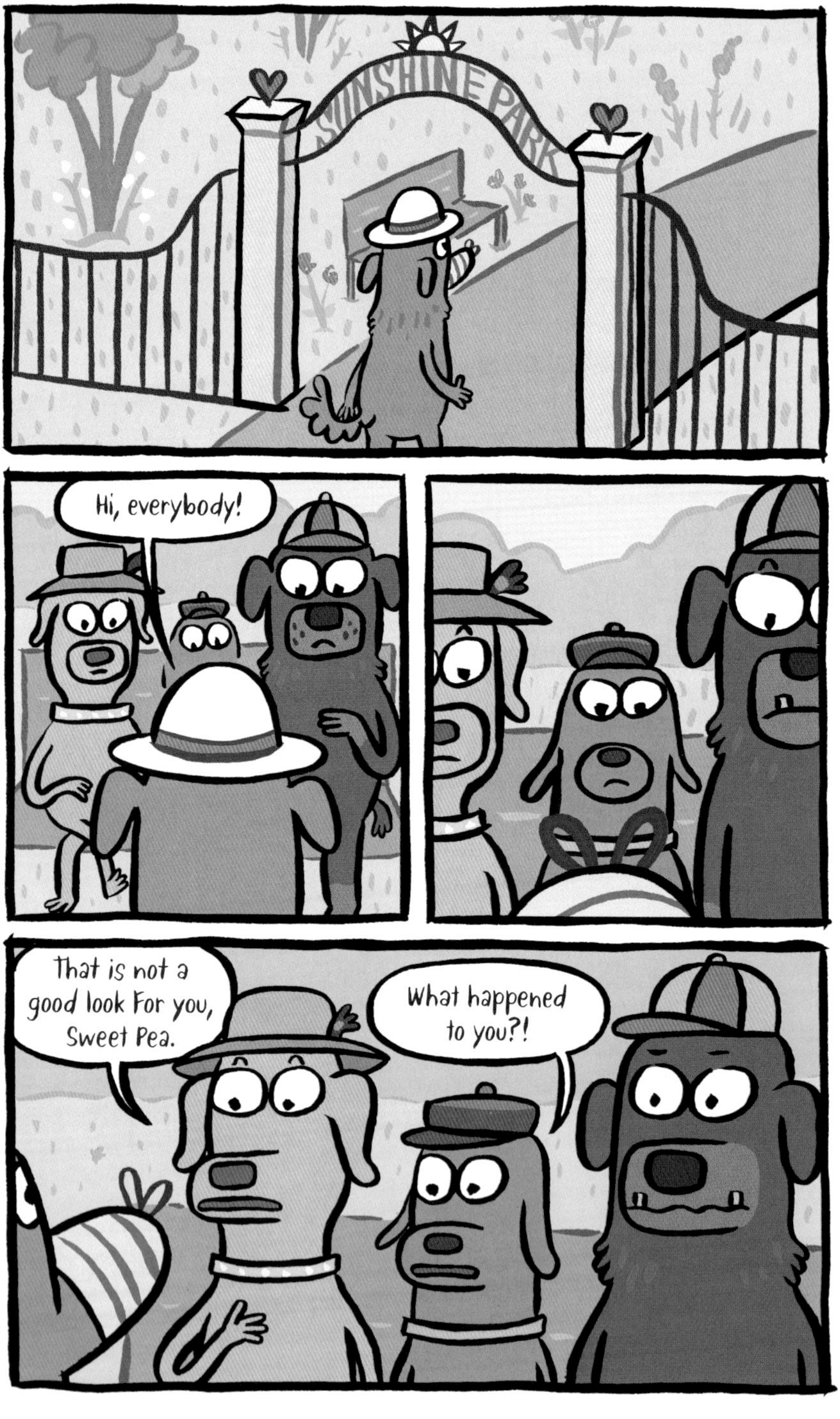
SUNSHINE PARK
Hi, everybody!
That is not a good look For you, Sweet Pea.
What happened to you?!

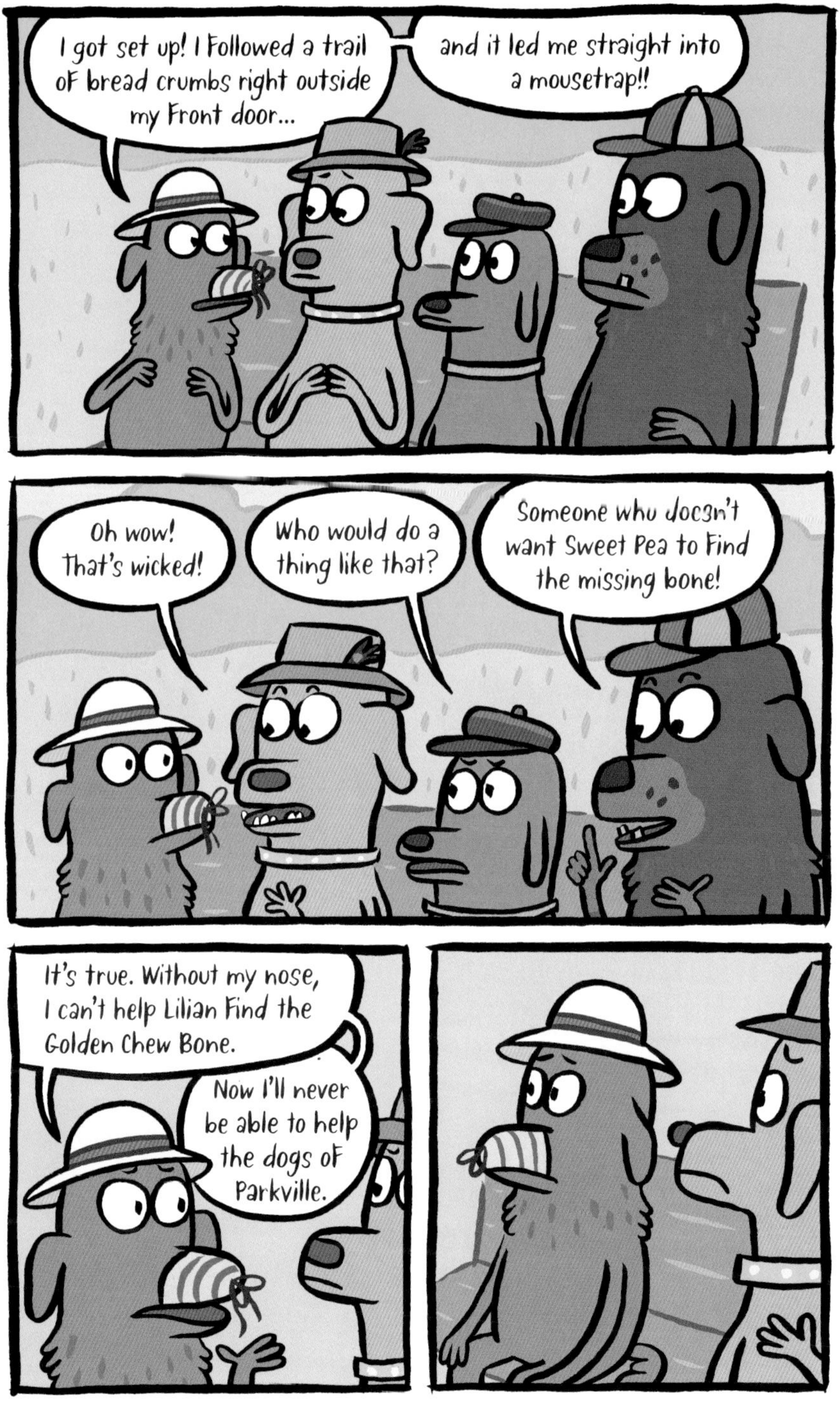

I got set up! I Followed a trail oF bread crumbs right outside my Front door...
and it led me straight into a mousetrap!!
Oh wow! That's wicked!
Who would do a thing like that?
Someone who doesn't want Sweet Pea to Find the missing bone!
It's true. Without my nose, I can't help Lilian Find the Golden Chew Bone.
Now I'll never be able to help the dogs oF Parkville.

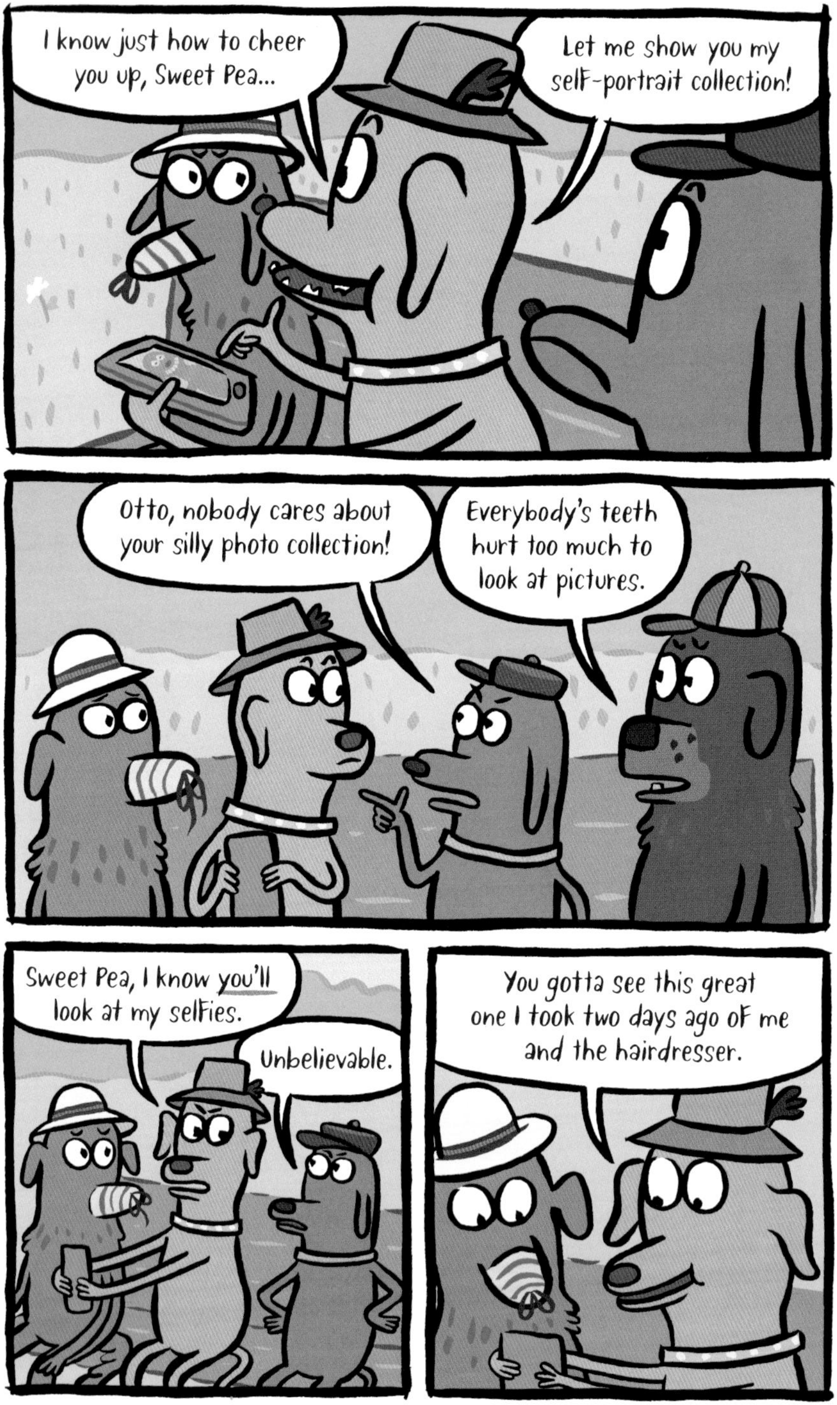
I know just how to cheer you up, Sweet Pea...
Let me show you my self-portrait collection!
Otto, nobody cares about your silly photo collection!
Everybody's teeth hurt too much to look at pictures.
Sweet Pea, I know you'll look at my selfies.
Unbelievable.
You gotta see this great one I took two days ago of me and the hairdresser.

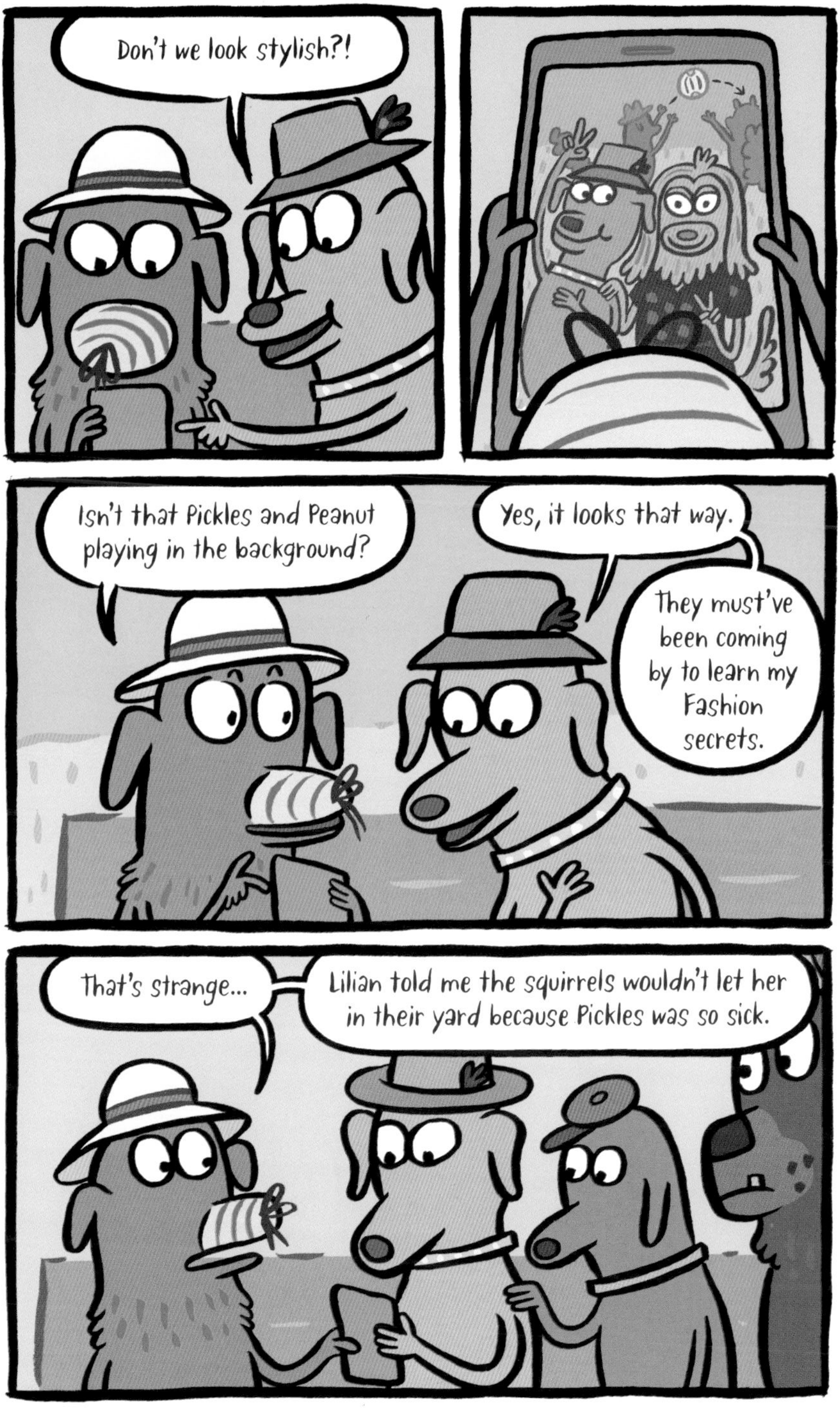
Don't we look stylish?!
Isn't that Pickles and Peanut playing in the background?
Yes, it looks that way.
They must've been coming by to learn my Fashion secrets.
That's strange...
Lilian told me the squirrels wouldn't let her in their yard because Pickles was so sick.

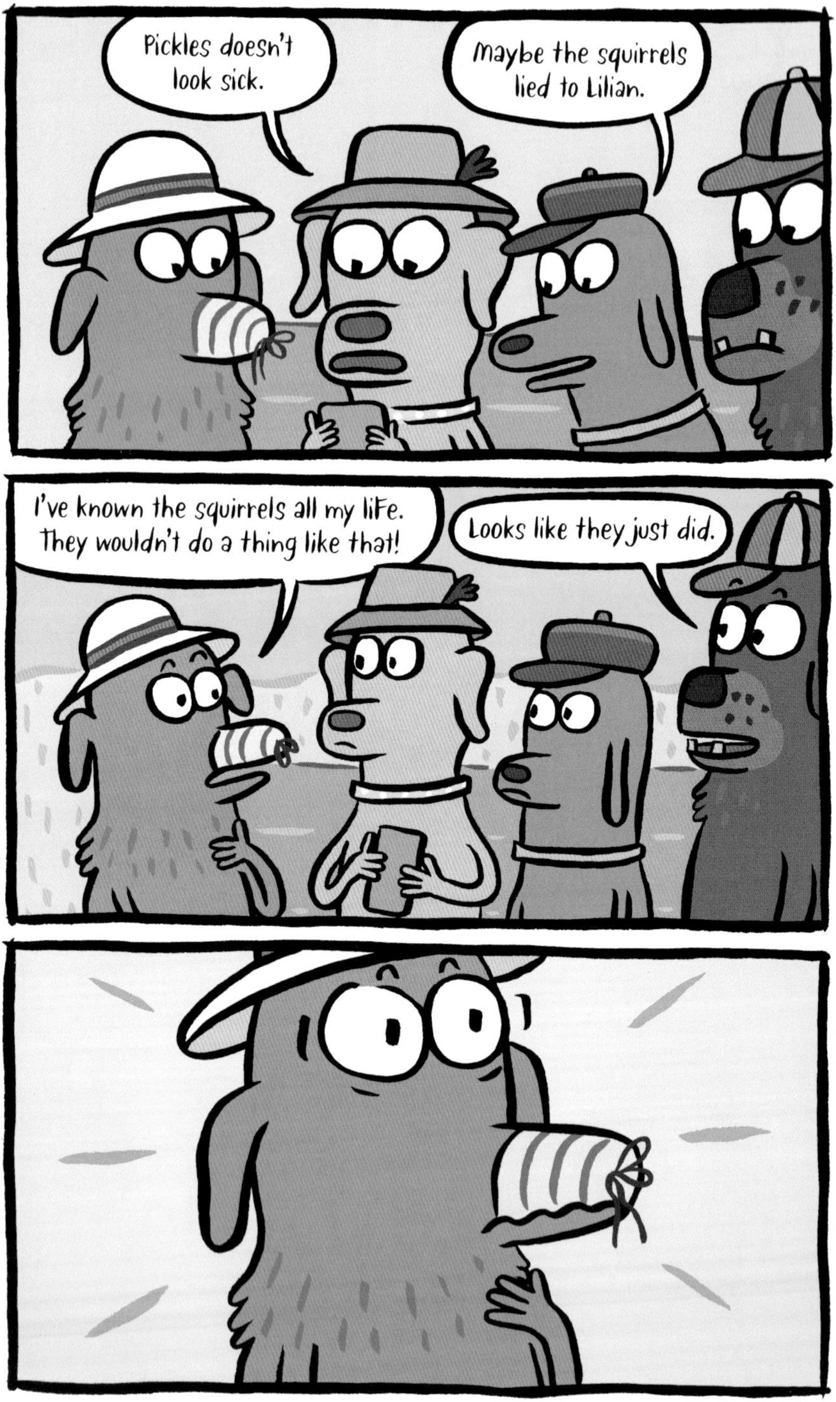
Pickles doesn't look sick.
Maybe the squirrels lied to Lilian.
I've known the squirrels all my liFe. They wouldn't do a thing like that!
Looks like they just did.

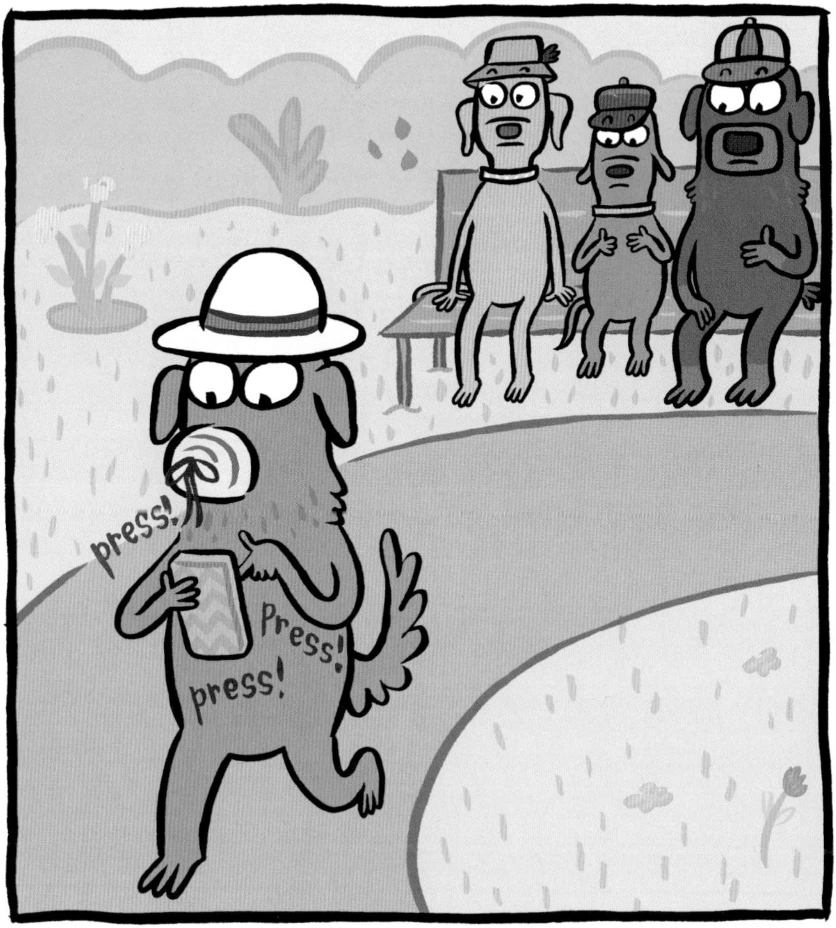
press!
Press!
press!

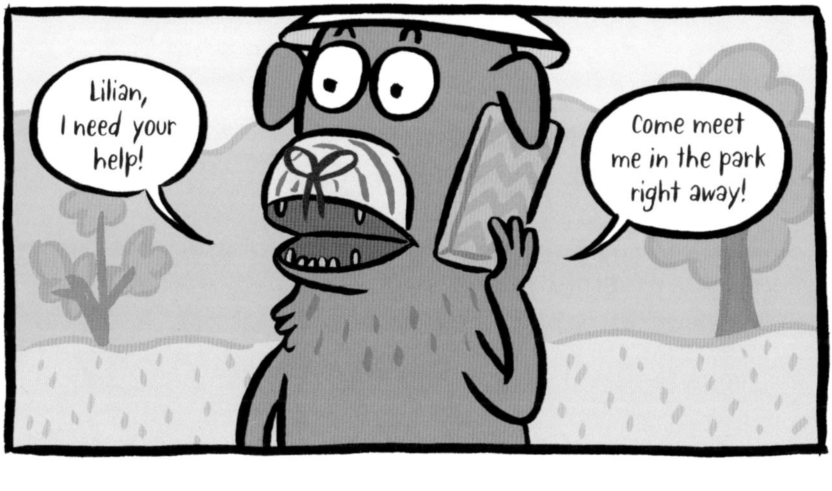
Lilian, I need your help!
Come meet me in the park right away!

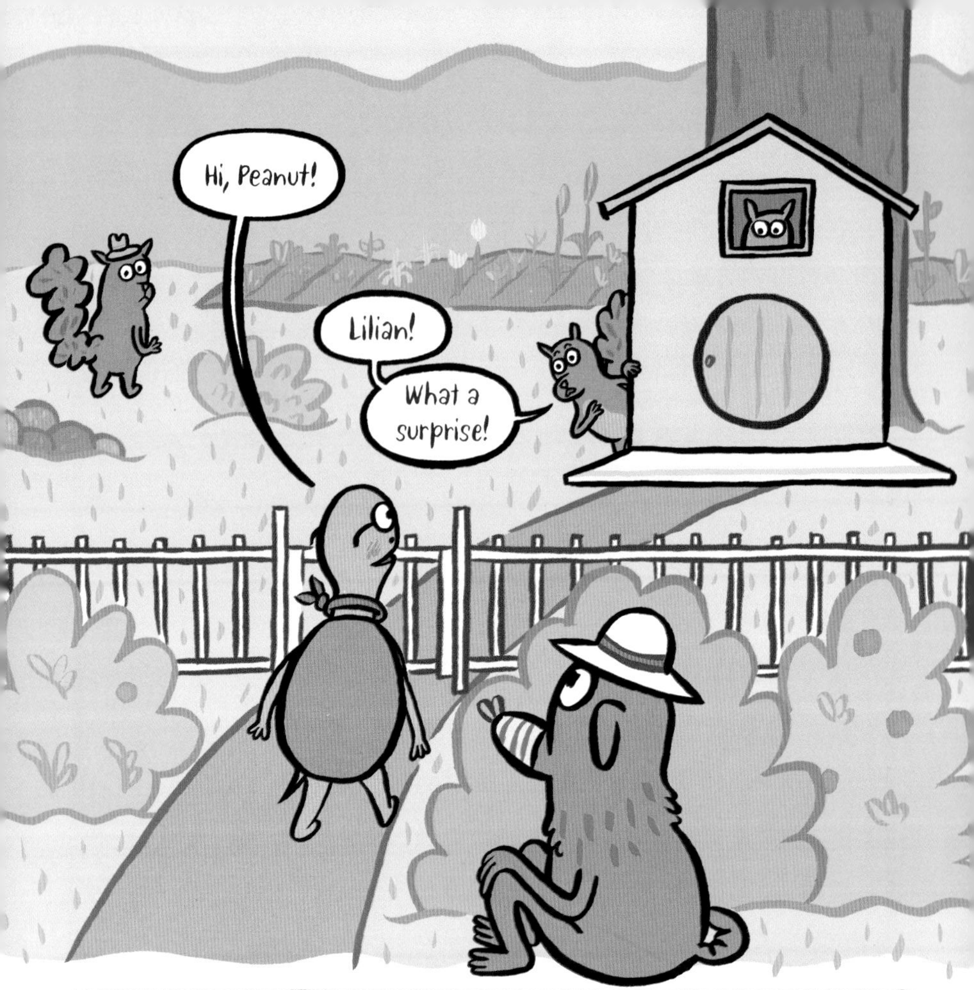
Hi, Peanut!
Lilian!
What a surprise!

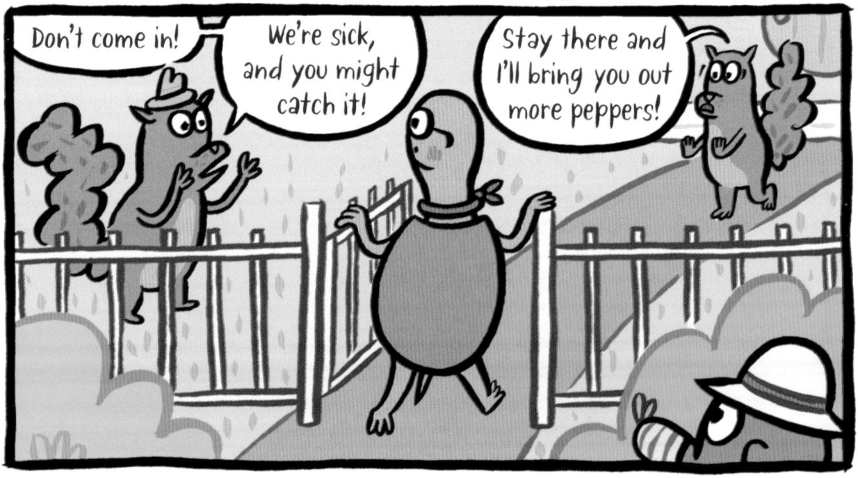
Don't come in!
We're sick, and you might catch it!
Stay there and I'll bring you out more peppers!

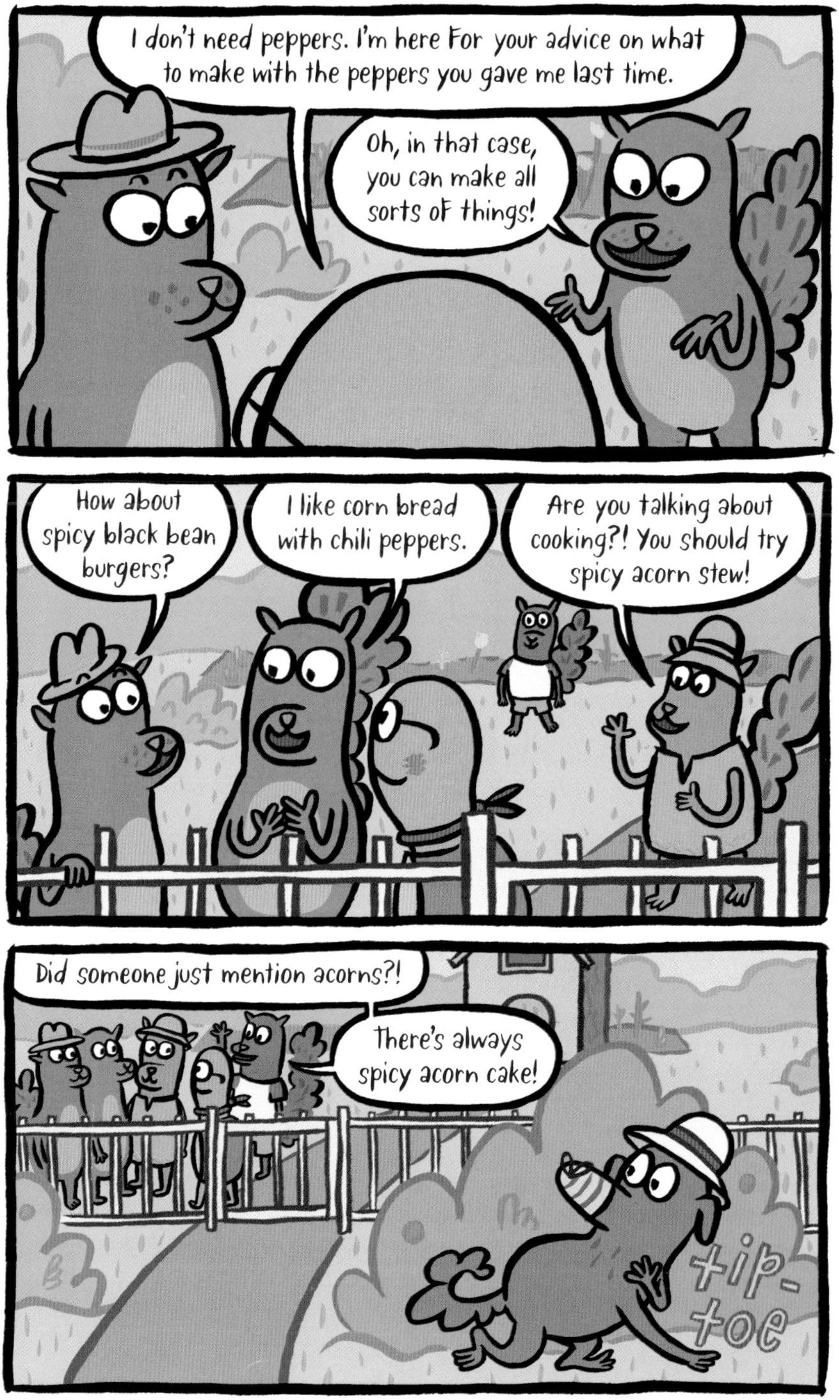
I don't need peppers. I'm here for your advice on what to make with the peppers you gave me last time.
Oh, in that case, you can make all sorts of things!
How about spicy black bean burgers?
I like corn bread with chili peppers.
Are you talking about cooking?! You should try spicy acorn stew!
Did someone just mention acorns?!
There's always spicy acorn cake!
tip-toe

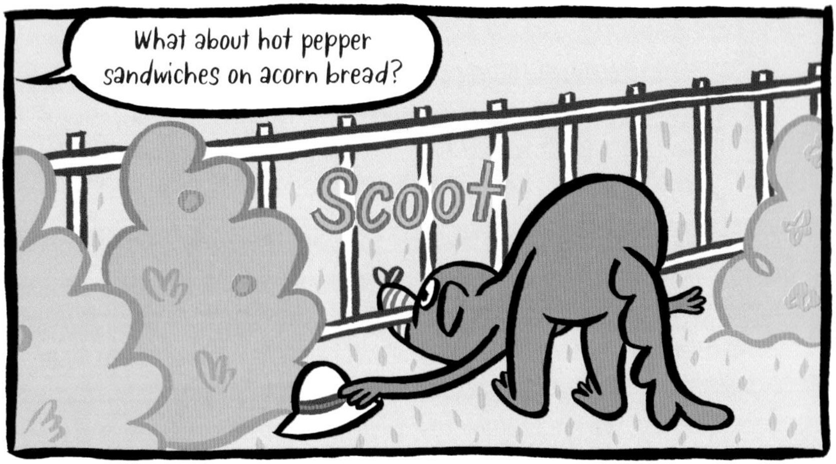
What about hot pepper sandwiches on acorn bread?
Scoot

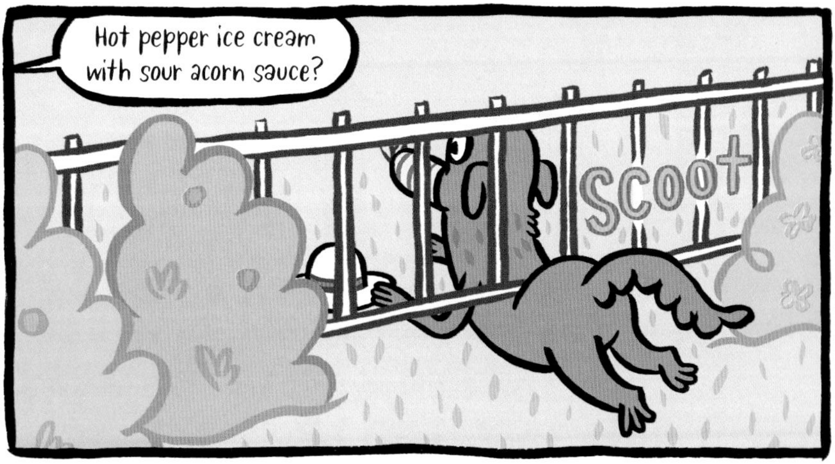
Hot pepper ice cream with sour acorn sauce?
Scoot

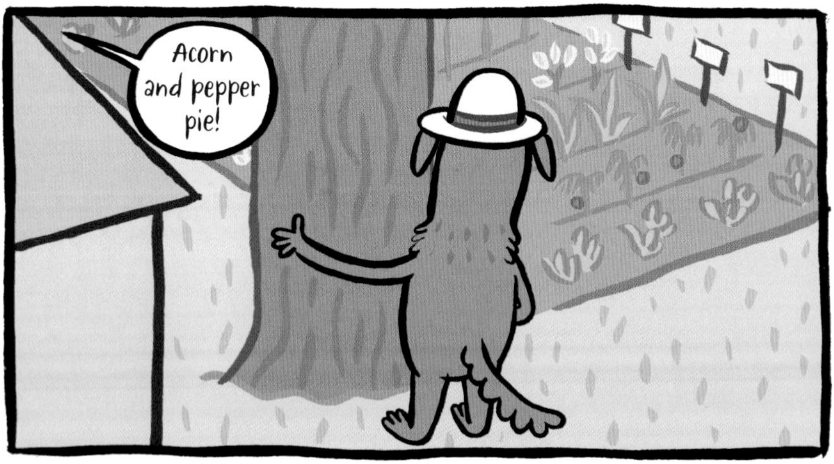
Acorn and pepper pie!

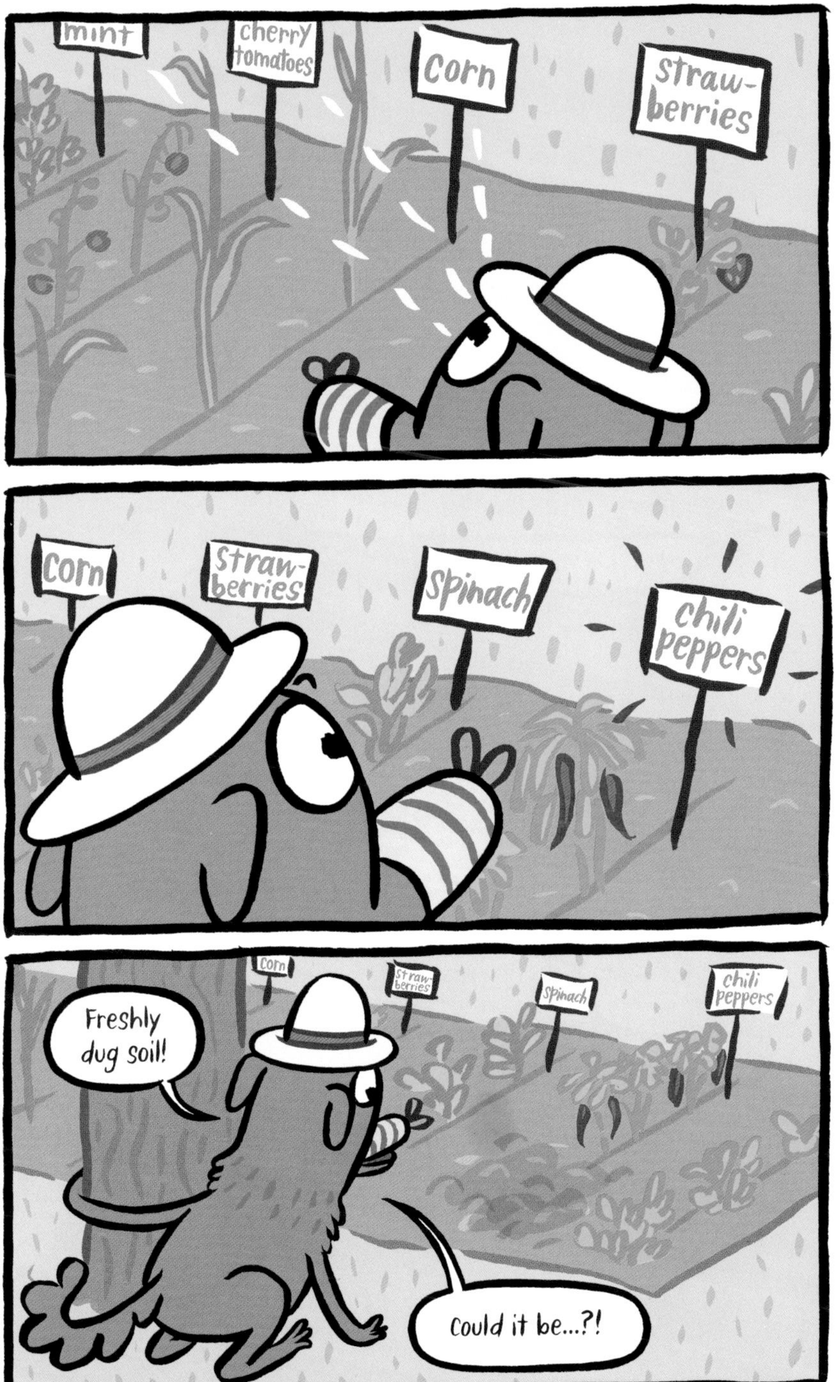
mint
cherry tomatoes
corn
straw-berries
corn
straw-berries
spinach
chili peppers
corn
straw-berries
spinach
chili peppers
Freshly dug soil!
Could it be...?!

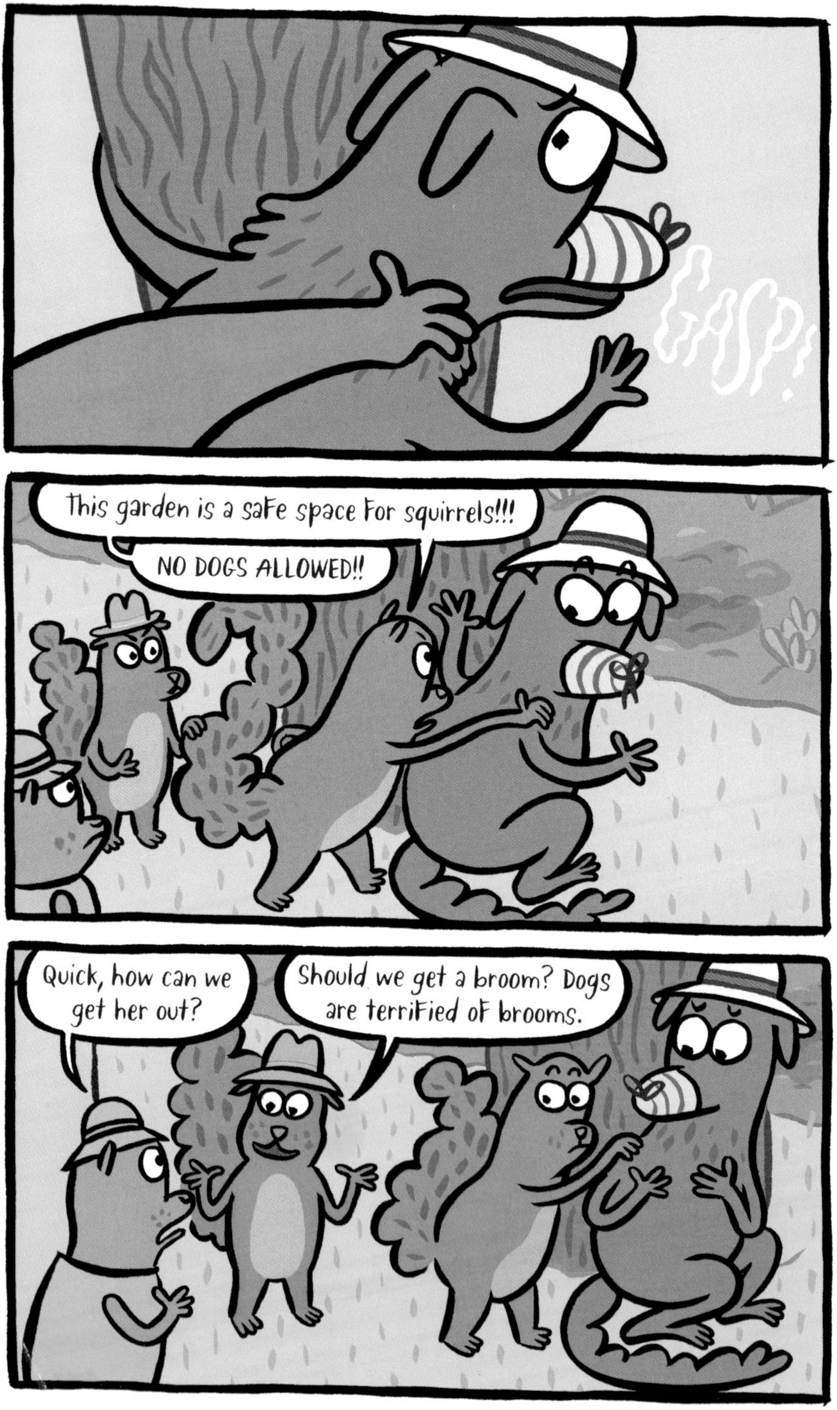
GASP!
This garden is a safe space for squirrels!!!
NO DOGS ALLOWED!!
Quick, how can we get her out?
Should we get a broom? Dogs are terrified of brooms.

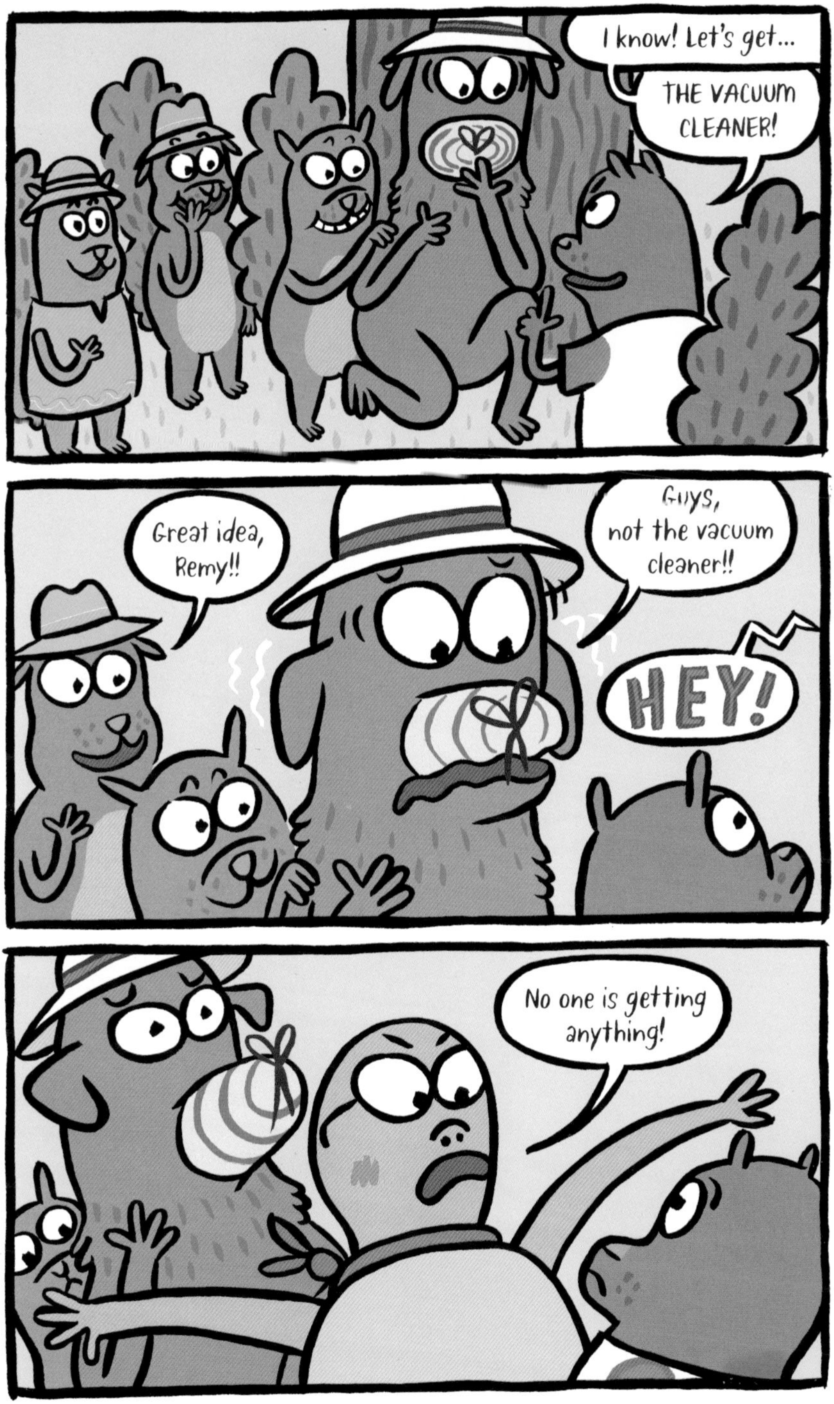
I know! Let's get...
THE VACUUM CLEANER!
Great idea, Remy!!
Guys, not the vacuum cleaner!!
HEY!
No one is getting anything!

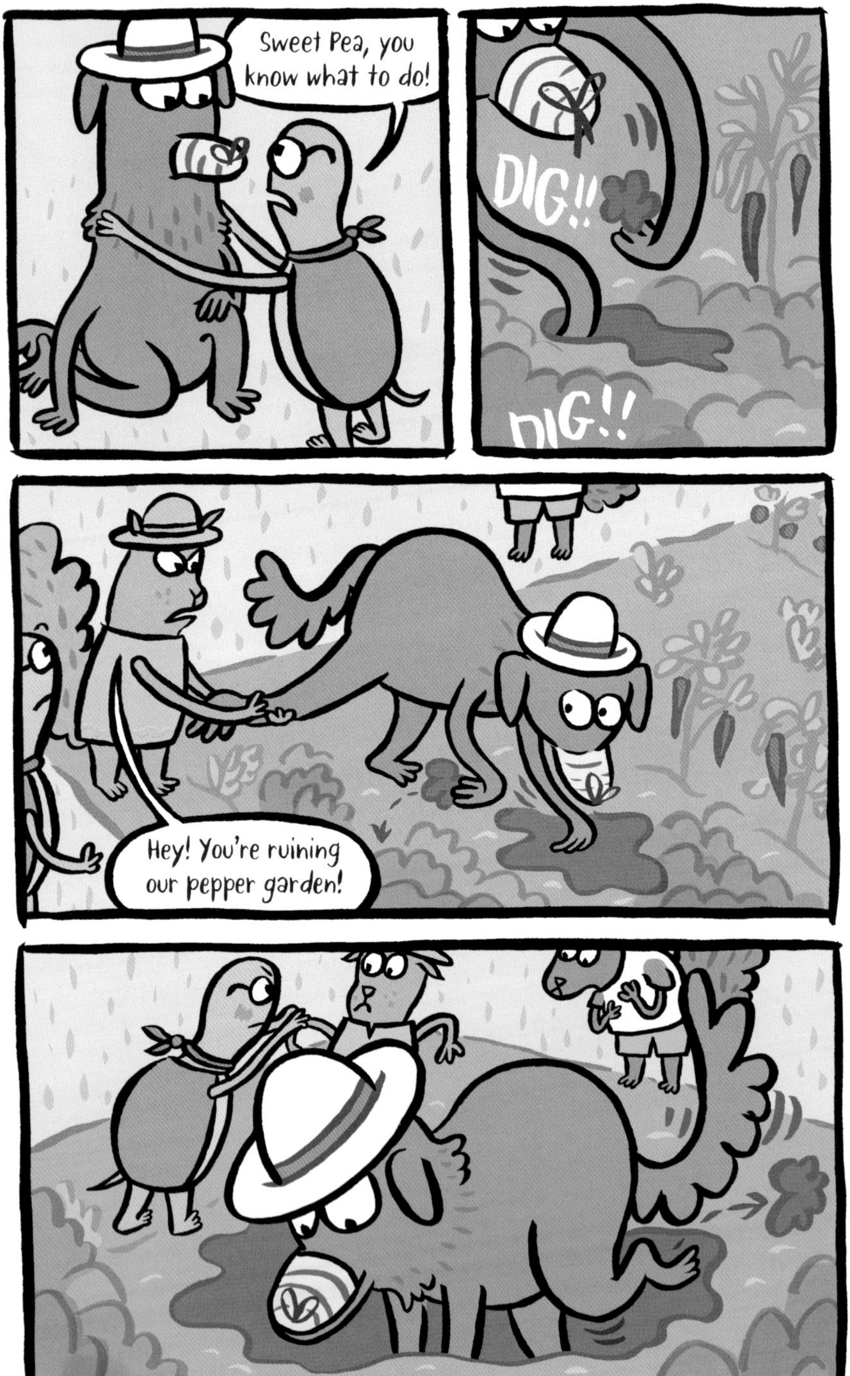
Sweet Pea, you know what to do!
DIG!!
DIG!!
Hey! You're ruining our pepper garden!

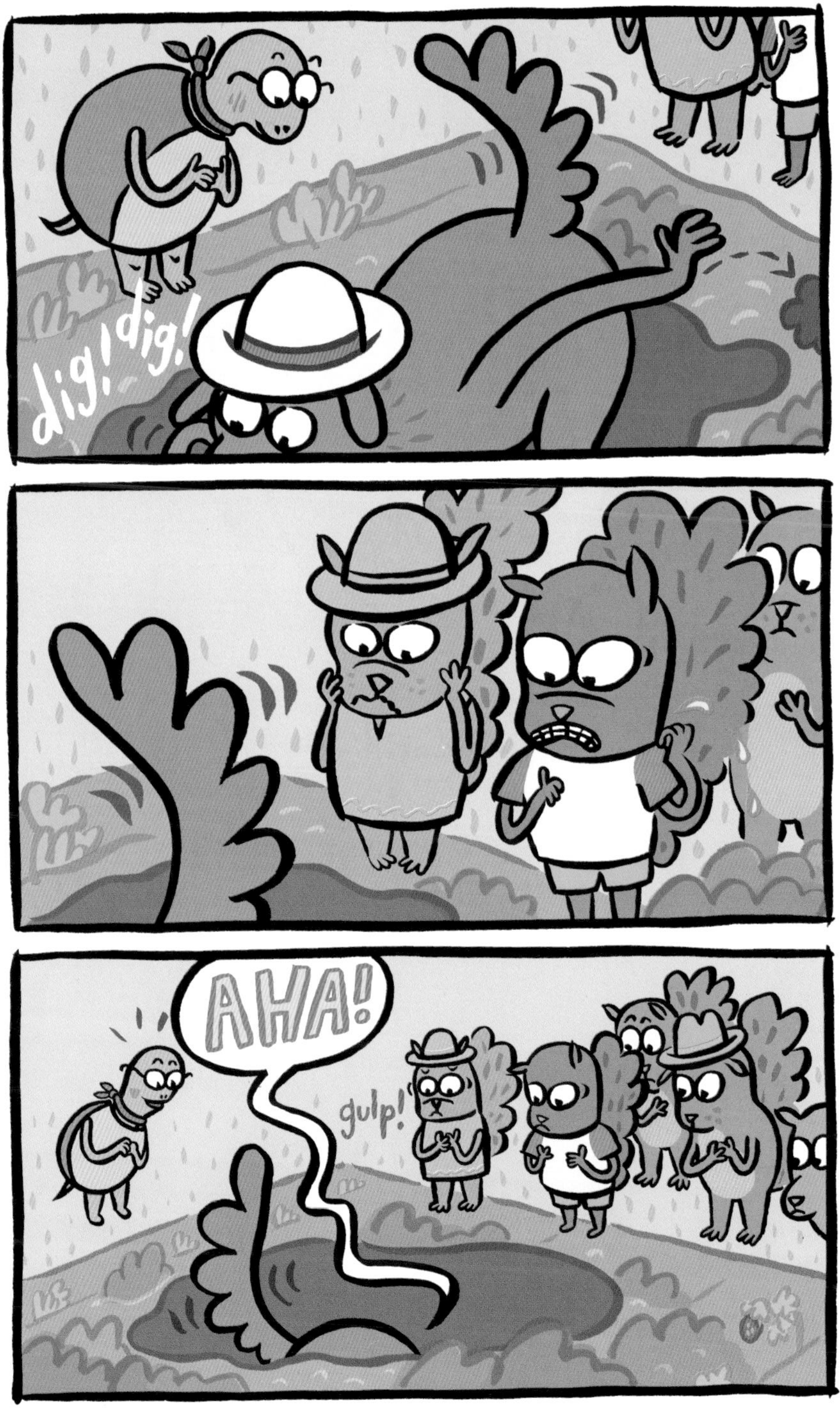
dig! dig!
AHA!
gulp!

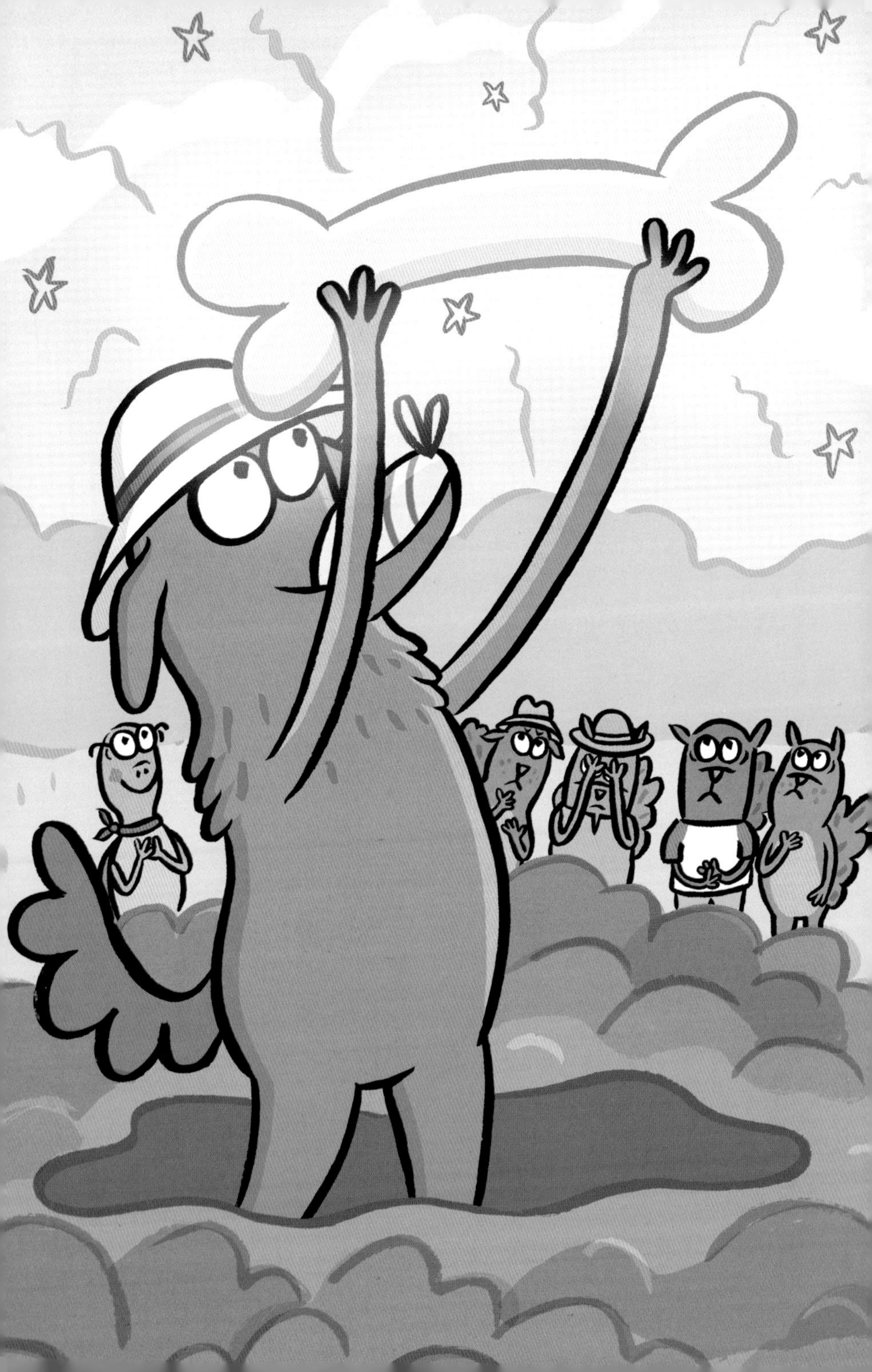

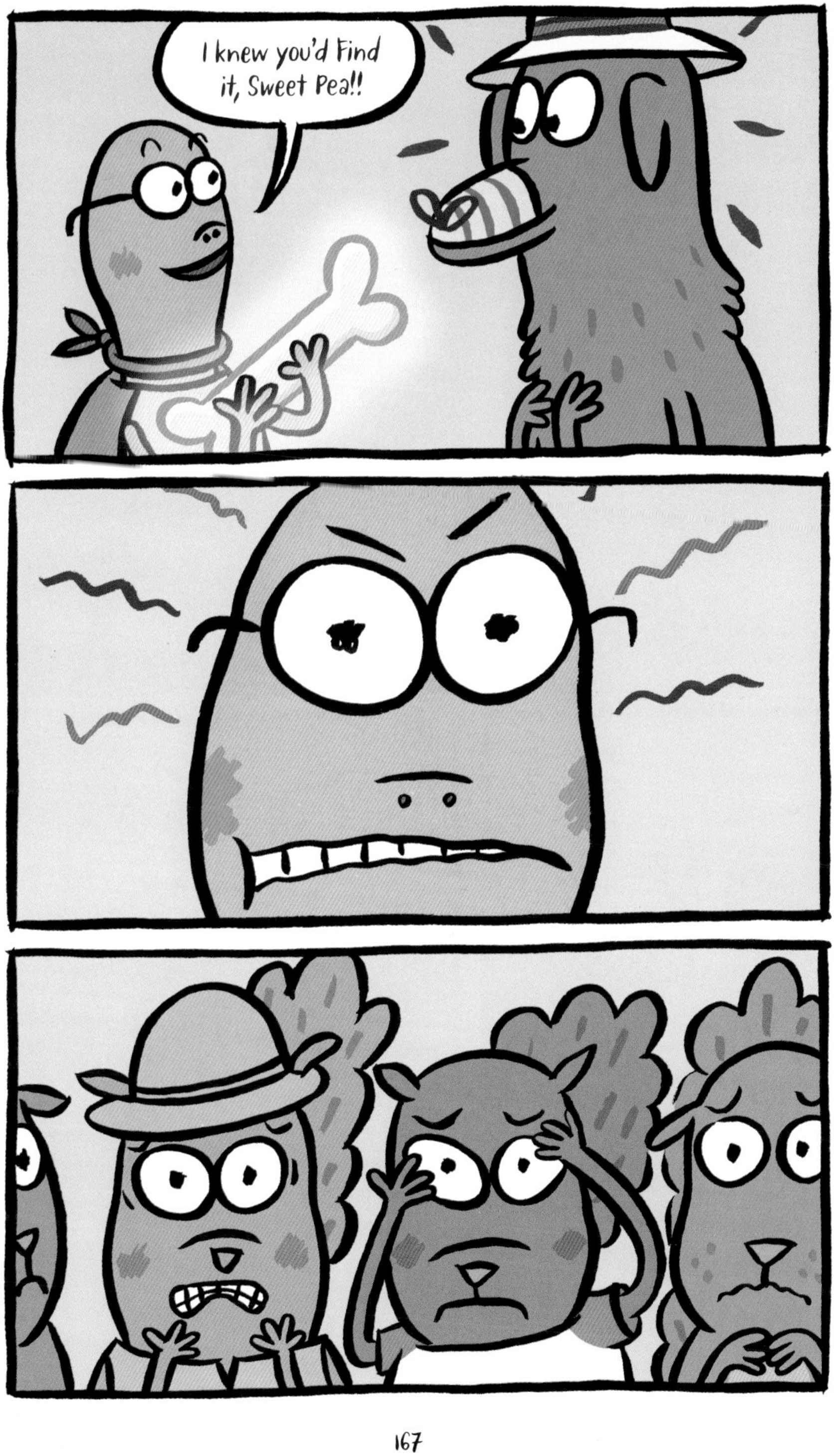
I knew you'd Find it, Sweet Pea!!

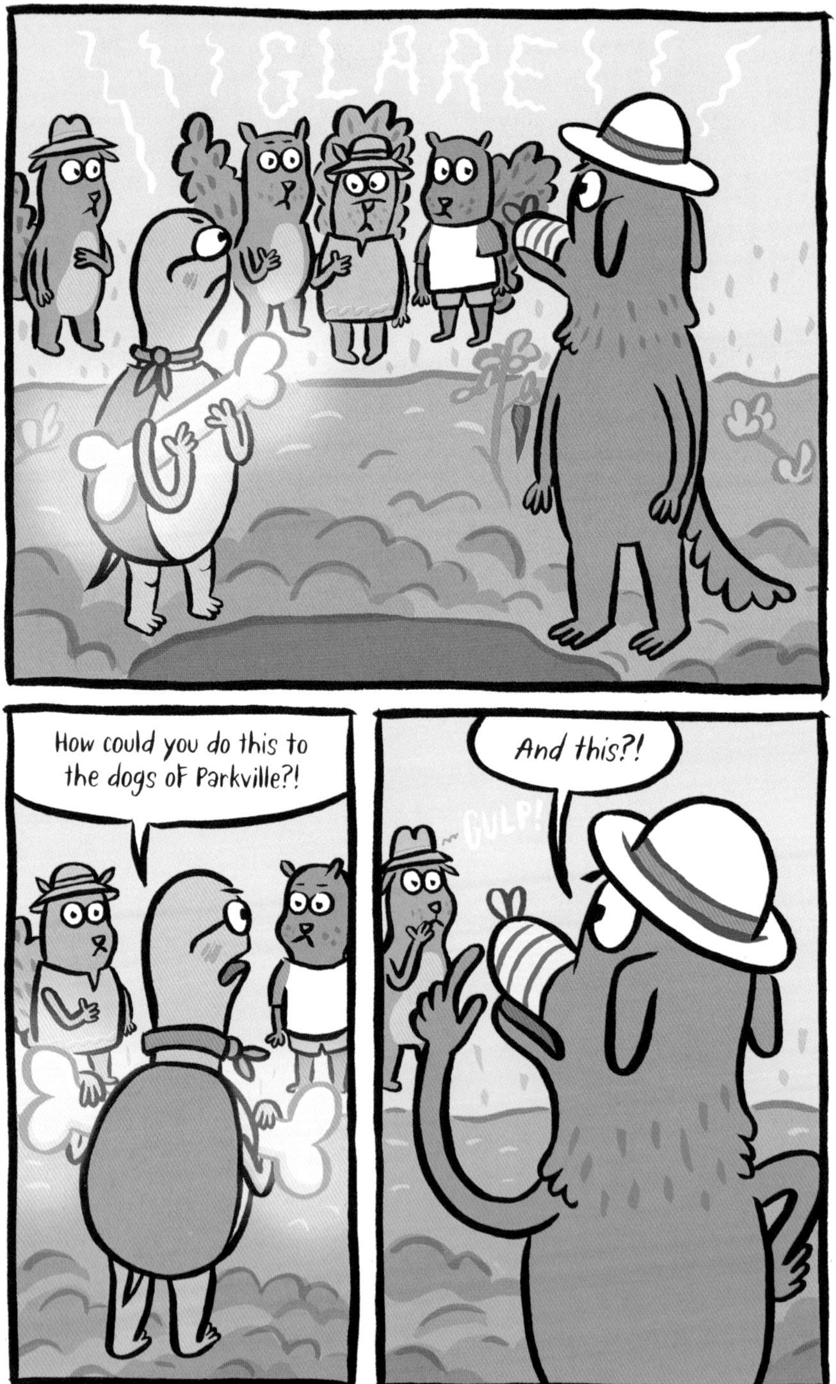
GLARE
How could you do this to the dogs of Parkville?!
GULP!
And this?!

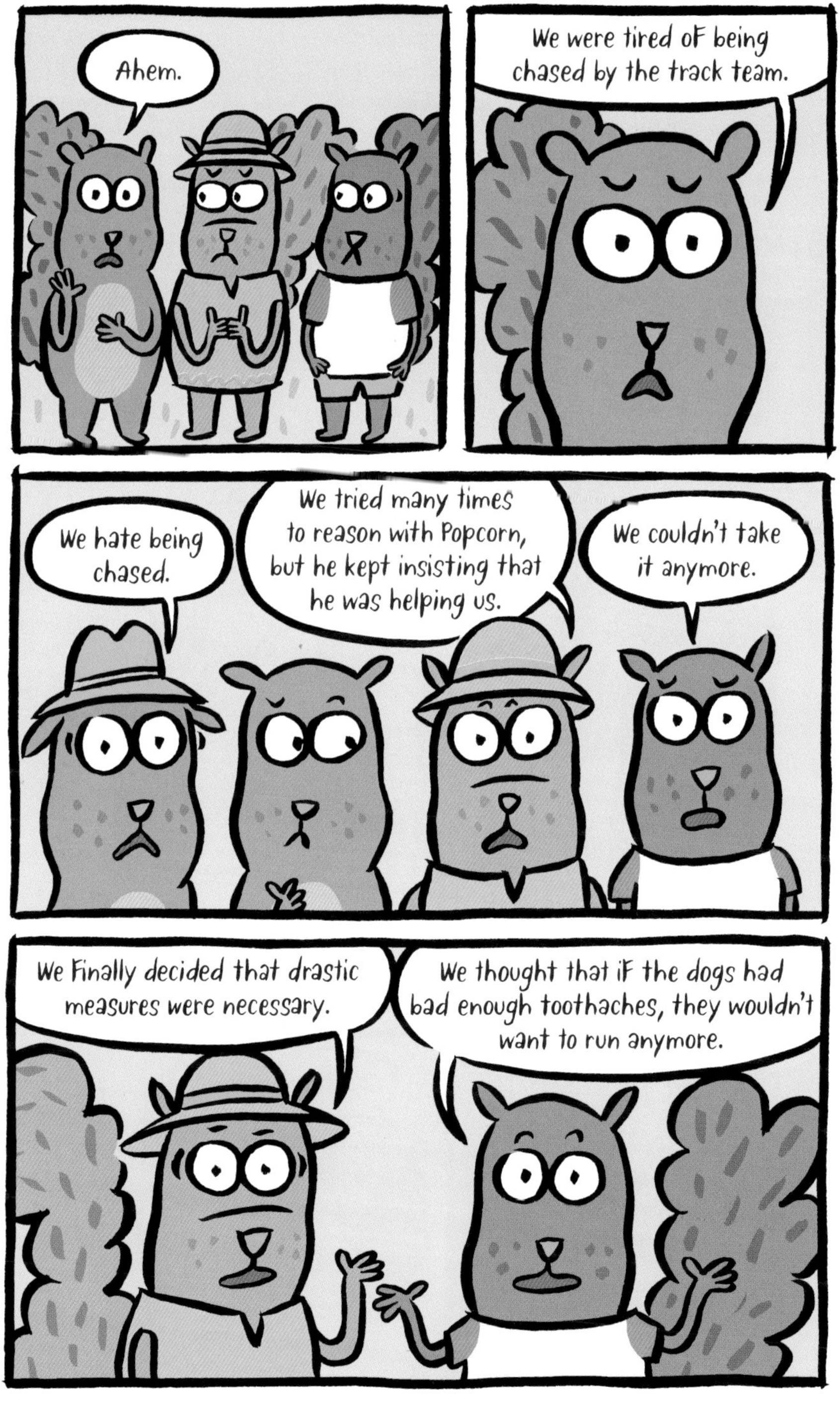

Ahem.
We were tired of being chased by the track team.
We hate being chased.
We tried many times to reason with Popcorn, but he kept insisting that he was helping us.
We couldn't take it anymore.
We finally decided that drastic measures were necessary.
We thought that if the dogs had bad enough toothaches, they wouldn't want to run anymore.

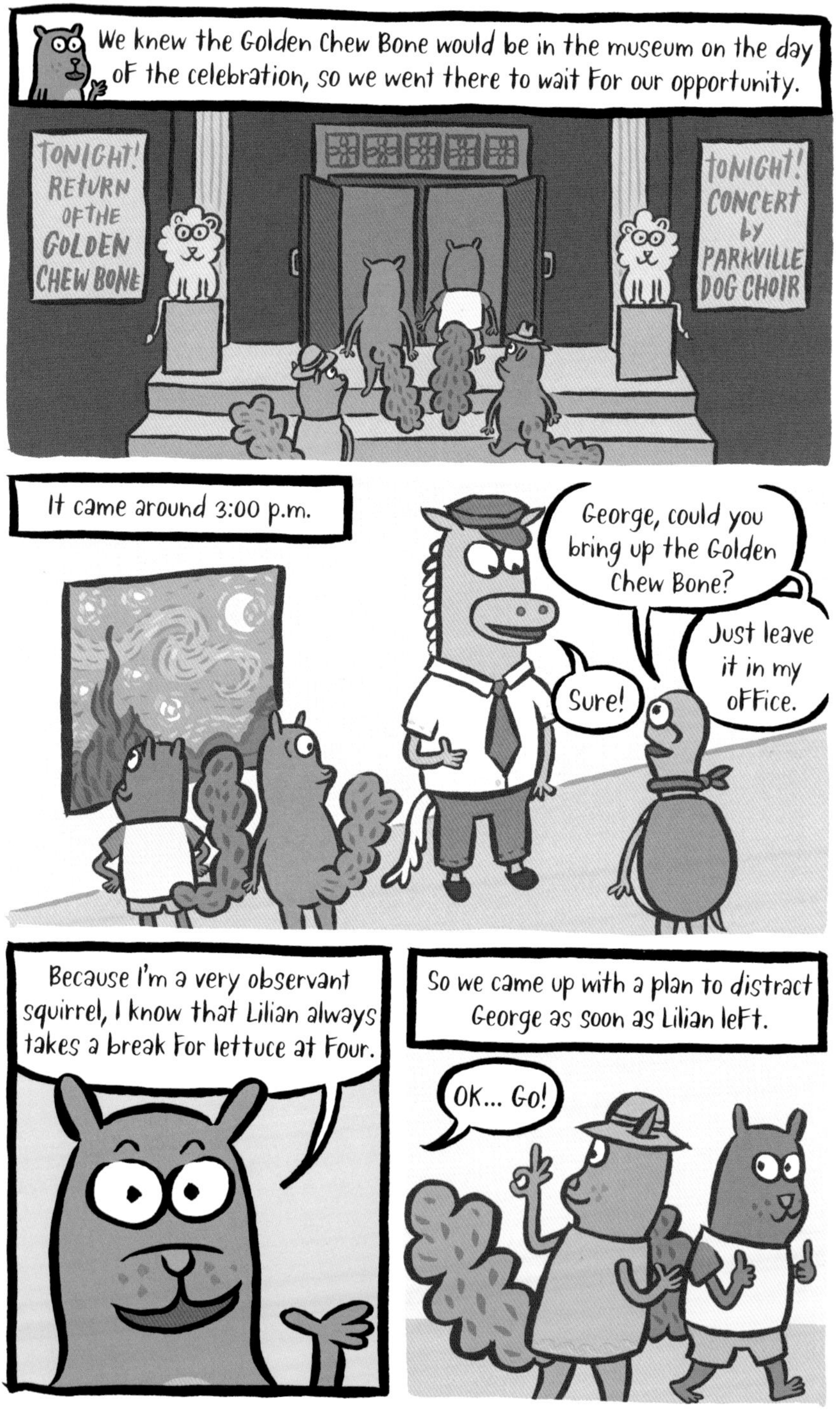
We knew the Golden Chew Bone would be in the museum on the day of the celebration, so we went there to wait for our opportunity.
TONIGHT! RETURN OF THE GOLDEN CHEW BONE
TONIGHT! CONCERT by PARKVILLE DOG CHOIR
It came around 3:00 p.m.
George, could you bring up the Golden Chew Bone?
Sure!
Just leave it in my office.
Because I'm a very observant squirrel, I know that Lilian always takes a break for lettuce at four.
So we came up with a plan to distract George as soon as Lilian left.
OK... Go!

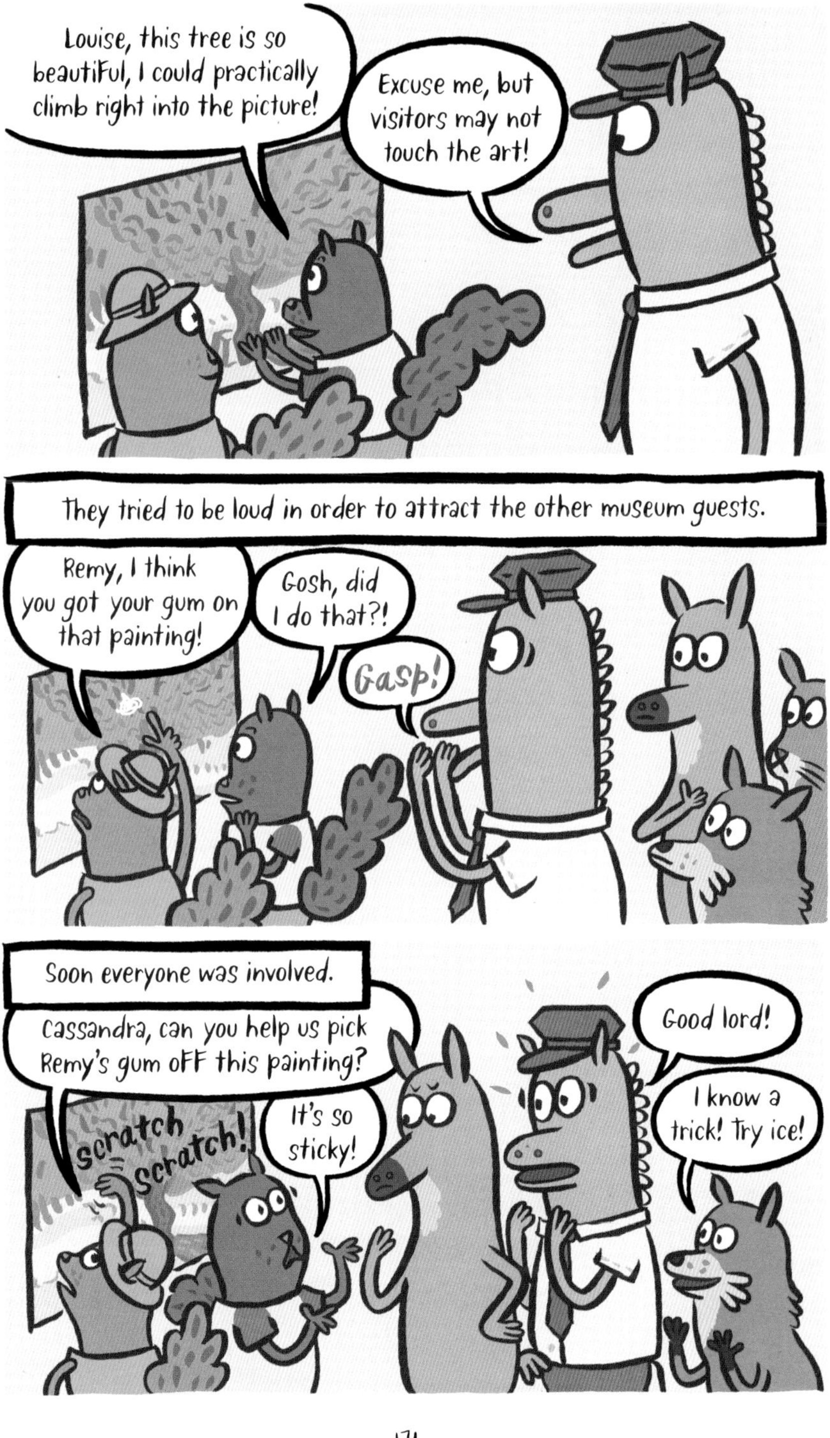
Louise, this tree is so beautiful, I could practically climb right into the picture!
Excuse me, but visitors may not touch the art!
They tried to be loud in order to attract the other museum guests.
Remy, I think you got your gum on that painting!
Gosh, did I do that?!
Gasp!
Soon everyone was involved.
Cassandra, can you help us pick Remy's gum off this painting?
scratch scratch!
It's so sticky!
Good lord!
I know a trick! Try ice!

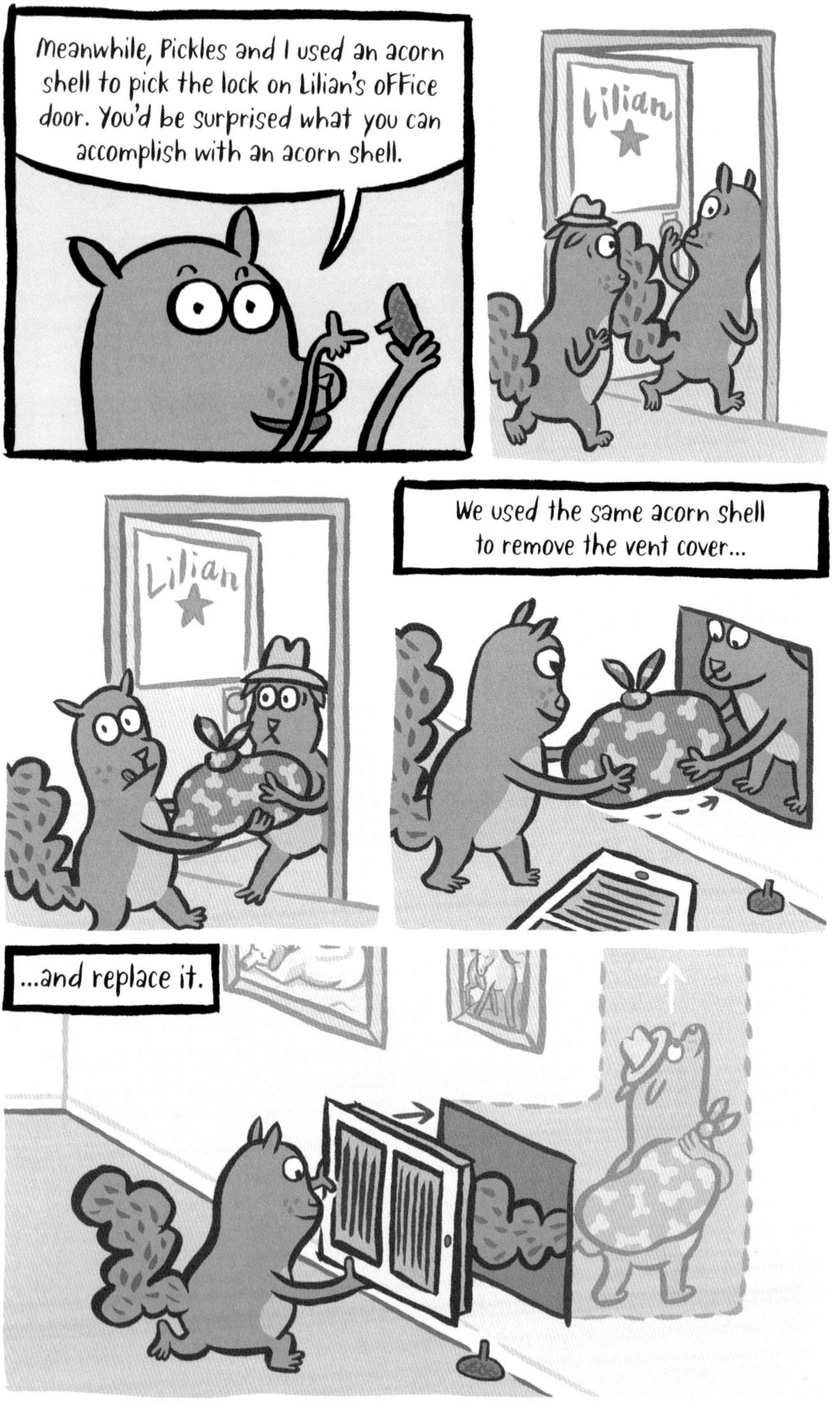
Meanwhile, Pickles and I used an acorn shell to pick the lock on Lilian's office door. You'd be surprised what you can accomplish with an acorn shell.
Lilian
Lilian
We used the same acorn shell to remove the vent cover...
...and replace it.

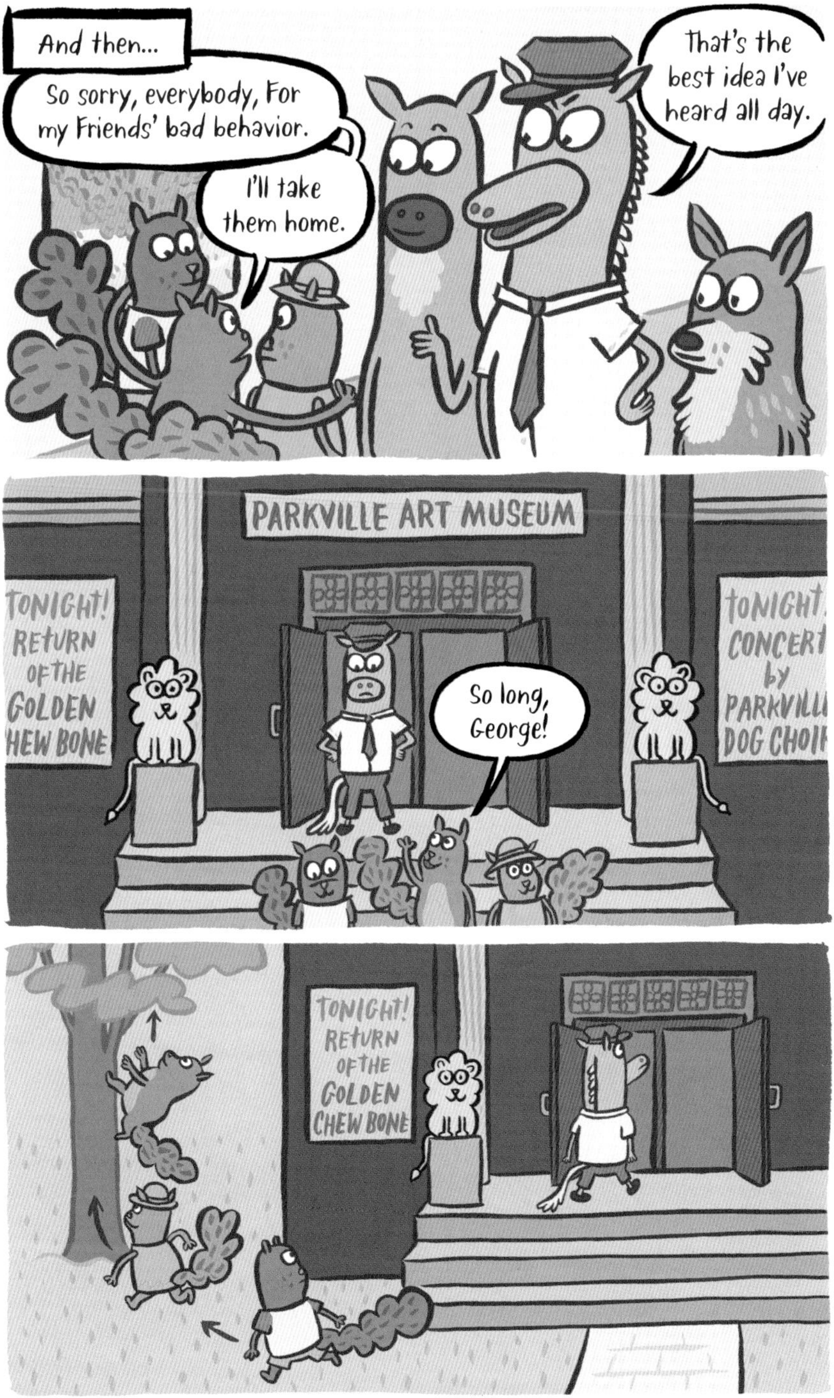
And then...
So sorry, everybody, for my friends' bad behavior.
I'll take them home.
That's the best idea I've heard all day.
PARKVILLE ART MUSEUM
TONIGHT! RETURN OF THE GOLDEN CHEW BONE
TONIGHT! CONCERT by PARKVILLE DOG CHOIR
So long, George!
TONIGHT! RETURN OF THE GOLDEN CHEW BONE

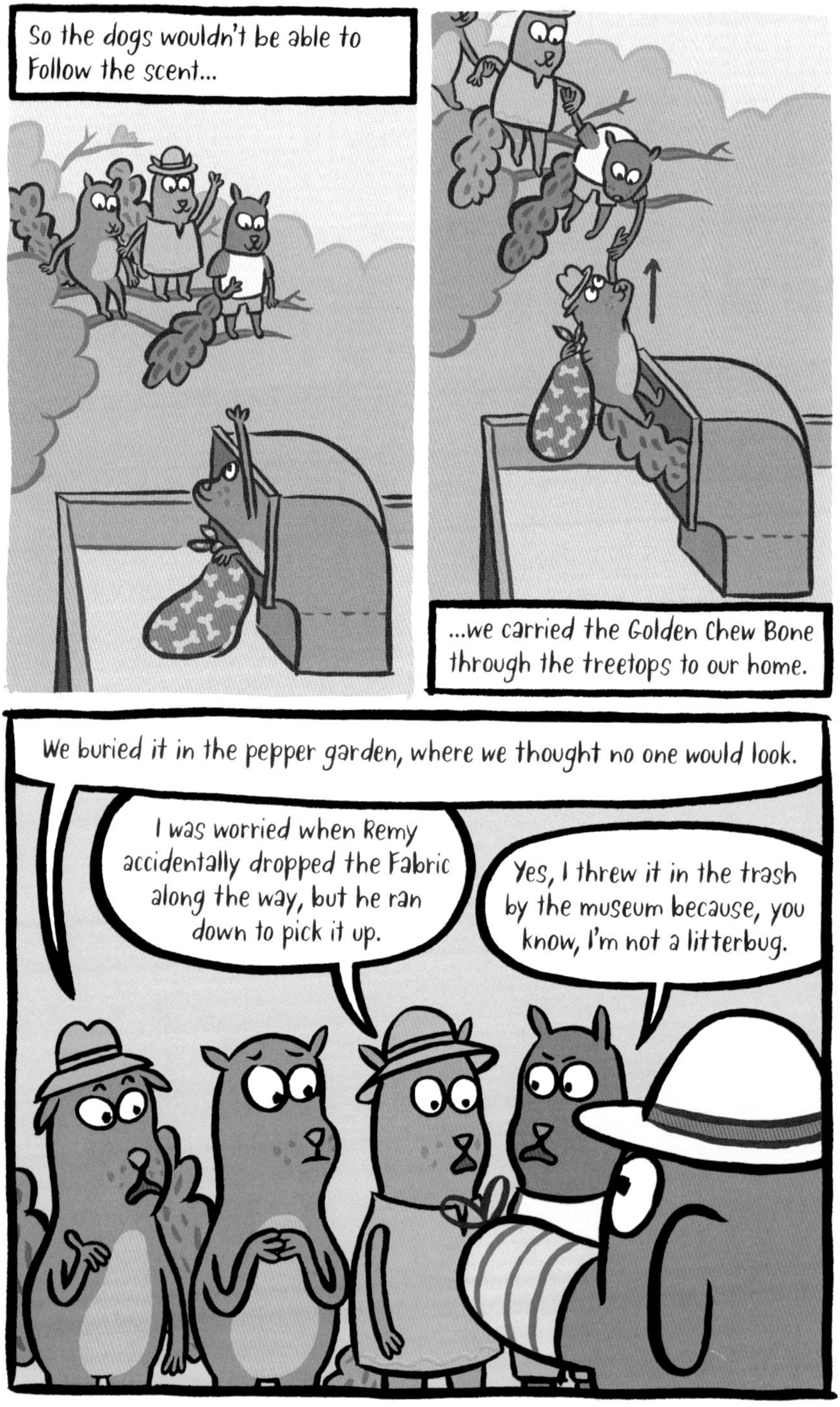
So the dogs wouldn't be able to Follow the scent...
...we carried the Golden Chew Bone through the treetops to our home.
We buried it in the pepper garden, where we thought no one would look.
I was worried when Remy accidentally dropped the Fabric along the way, but he ran down to pick it up.
Yes, I threw it in the trash by the museum because, you know, I'm not a litterbug.

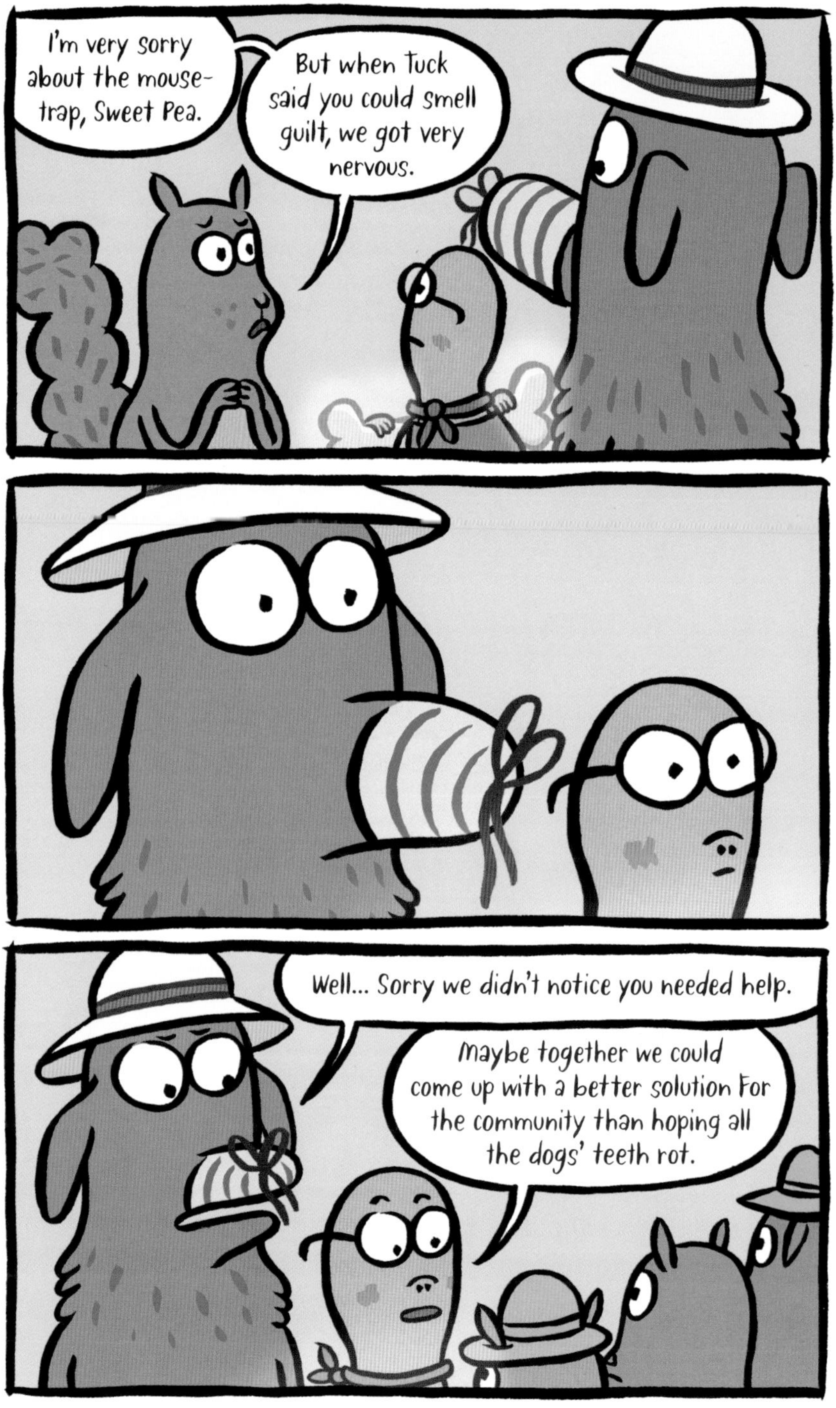
I'm very sorry about the mouse-trap, Sweet Pea.
But when Tuck said you could smell guilt, we got very nervous.
Well... Sorry we didn't notice you needed help.
Maybe together we could come up with a better solution for the community than hoping all the dogs' teeth rot.

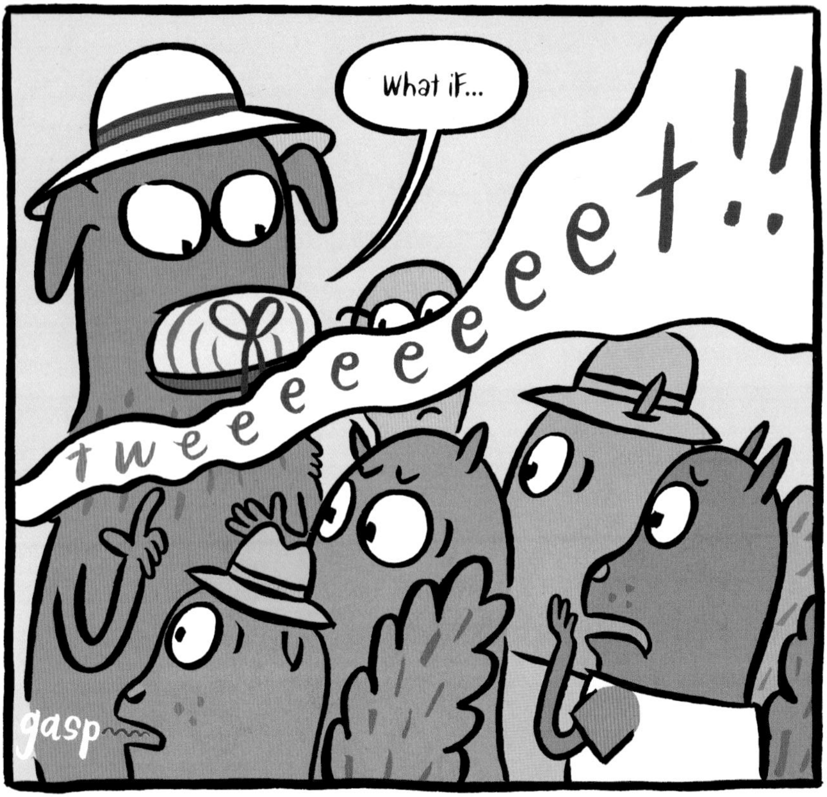
What if...
tweeeeeeeeet!!
gasp

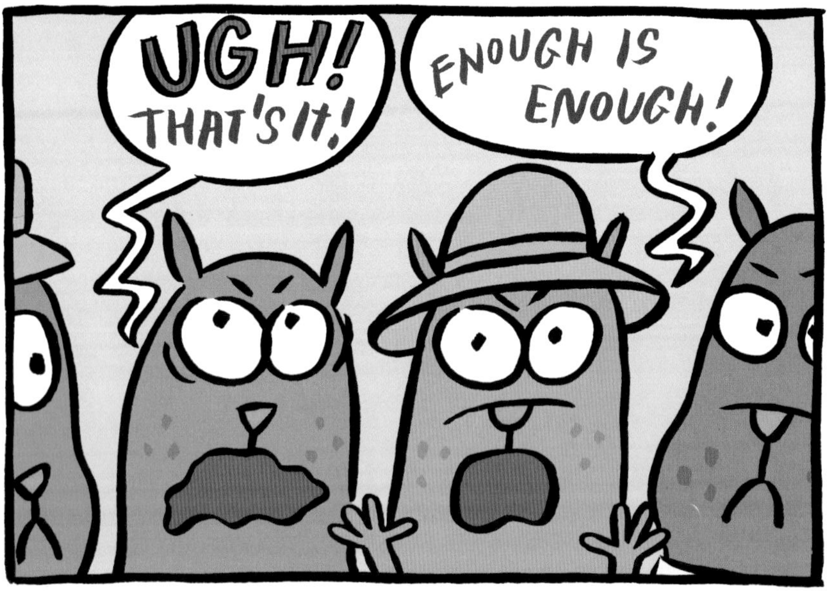
UGH! THAT'S IT!
ENOUGH IS ENOUGH!

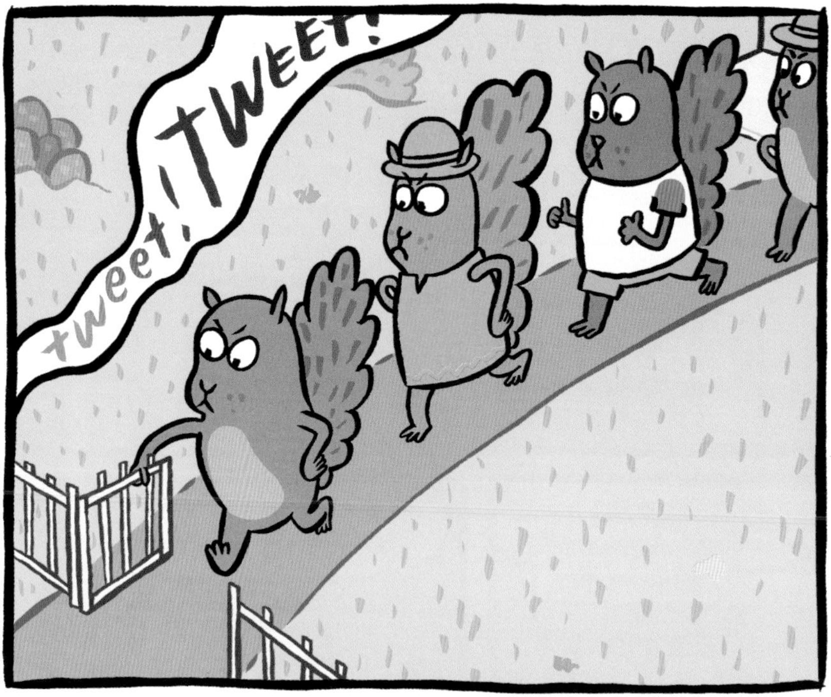
tweet! TWEET!

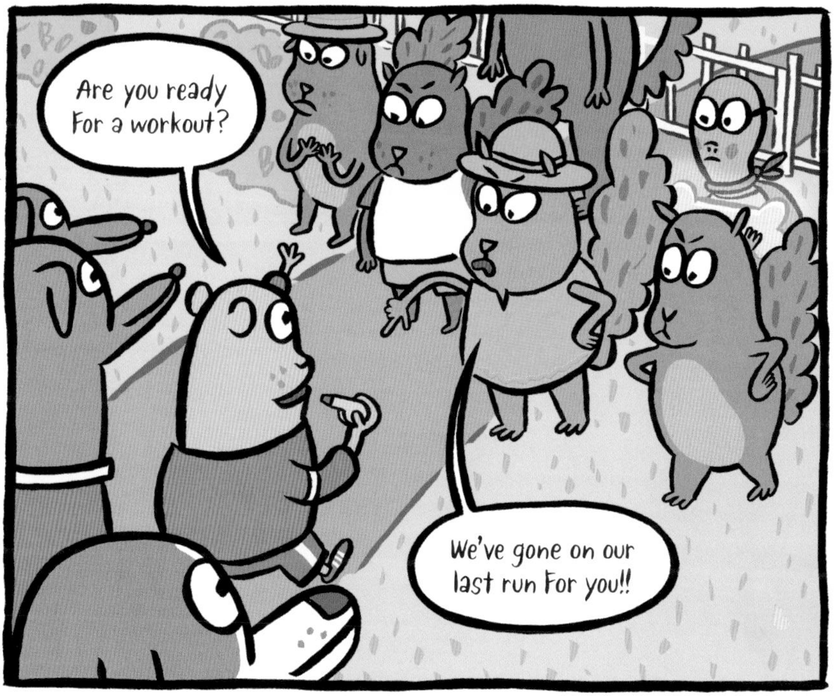
Are you ready For a workout?
We've gone on our last run For you!!

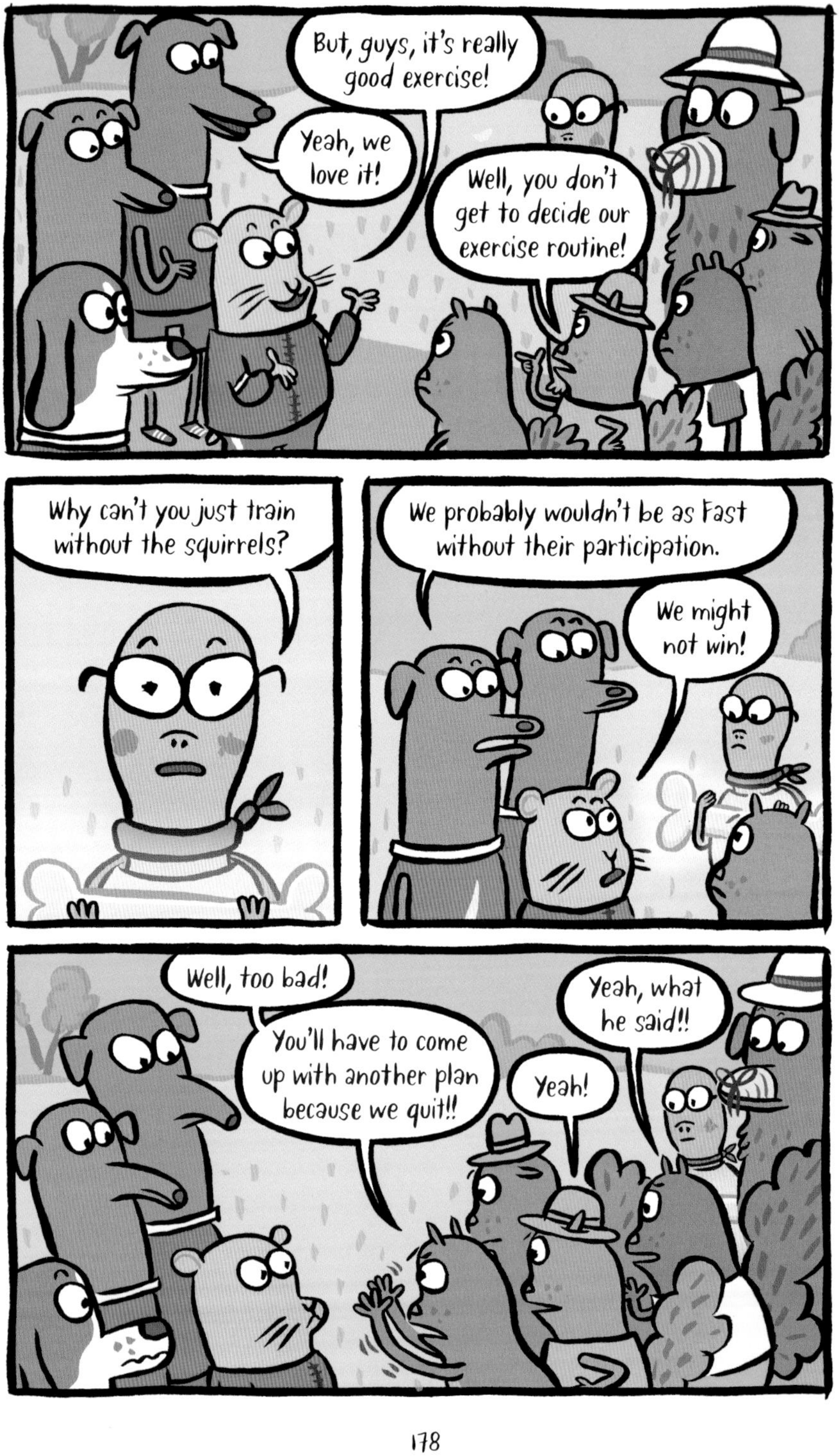
But, guys, it's really good exercise!
Yeah, we love it!
Well, you don't get to decide our exercise routine!
Why can't you just train without the squirrels?
We probably wouldn't be as fast without their participation.
We might not win!
Well, too bad!
You'll have to come up with another plan because we quit!!
Yeah!
Yeah, what he said!!

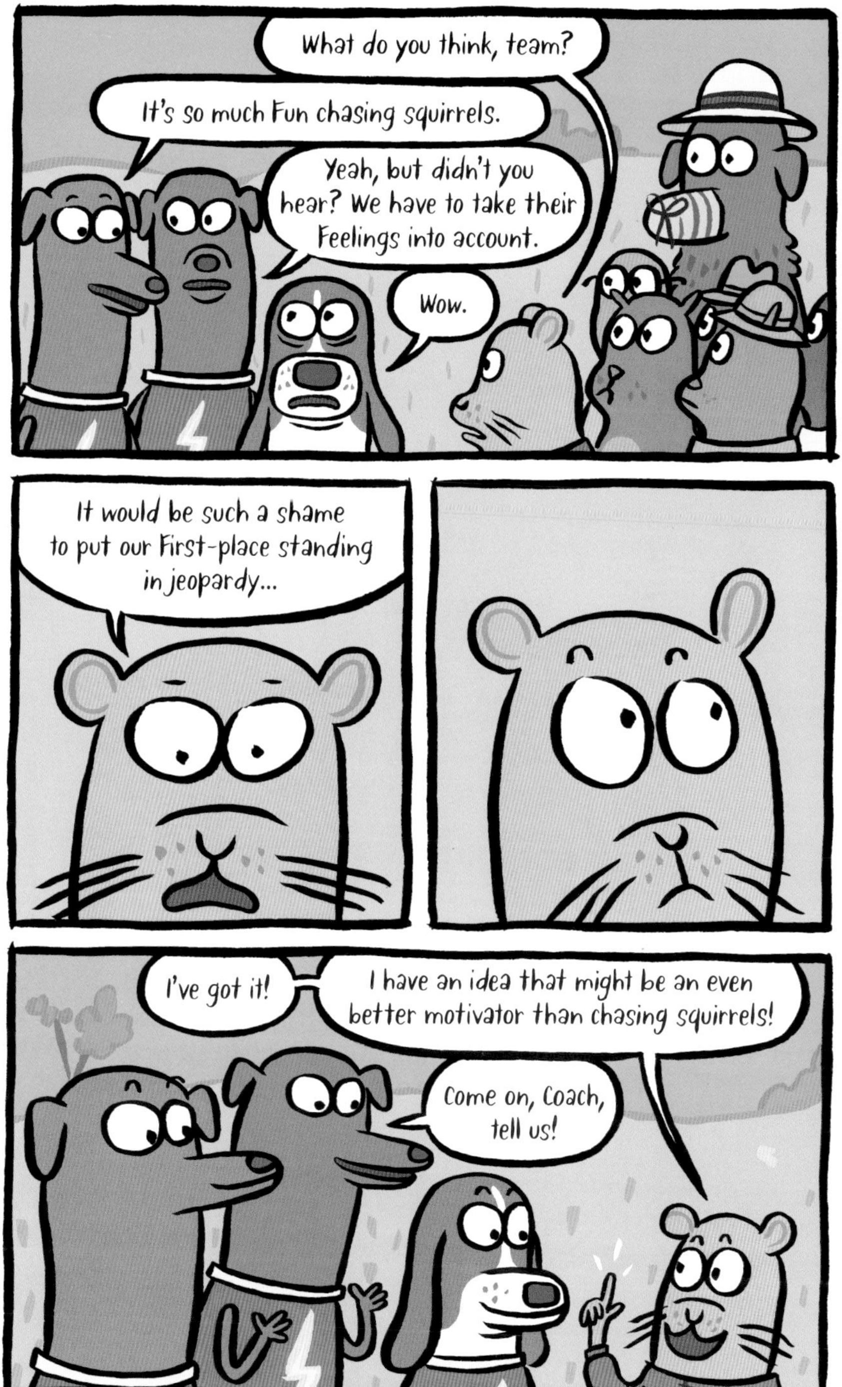
What do you think, team?
It's so much fun chasing squirrels.
Yeah, but didn't you hear? We have to take their feelings into account.
Wow.
It would be such a shame to put our first-place standing in jeopardy...
I've got it!
I have an idea that might be an even better motivator than chasing squirrels!
Come on, Coach, tell us!

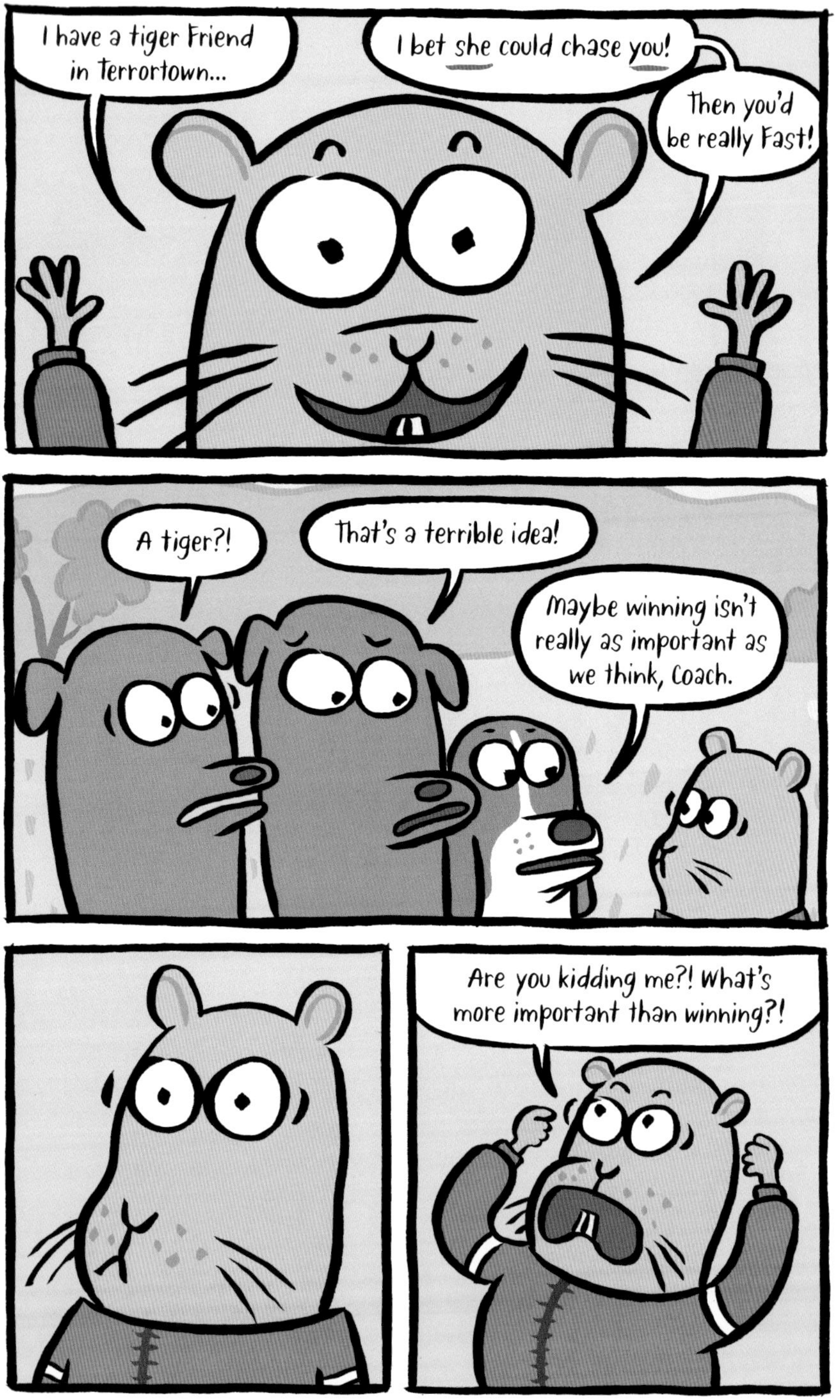
I have a tiger friend in Terrortown...
I bet she could chase you!
Then you'd be really fast!
A tiger?!
That's a terrible idea!
Maybe winning isn't really as important as we think, Coach.
Are you kidding me?! What's more important than winning?!

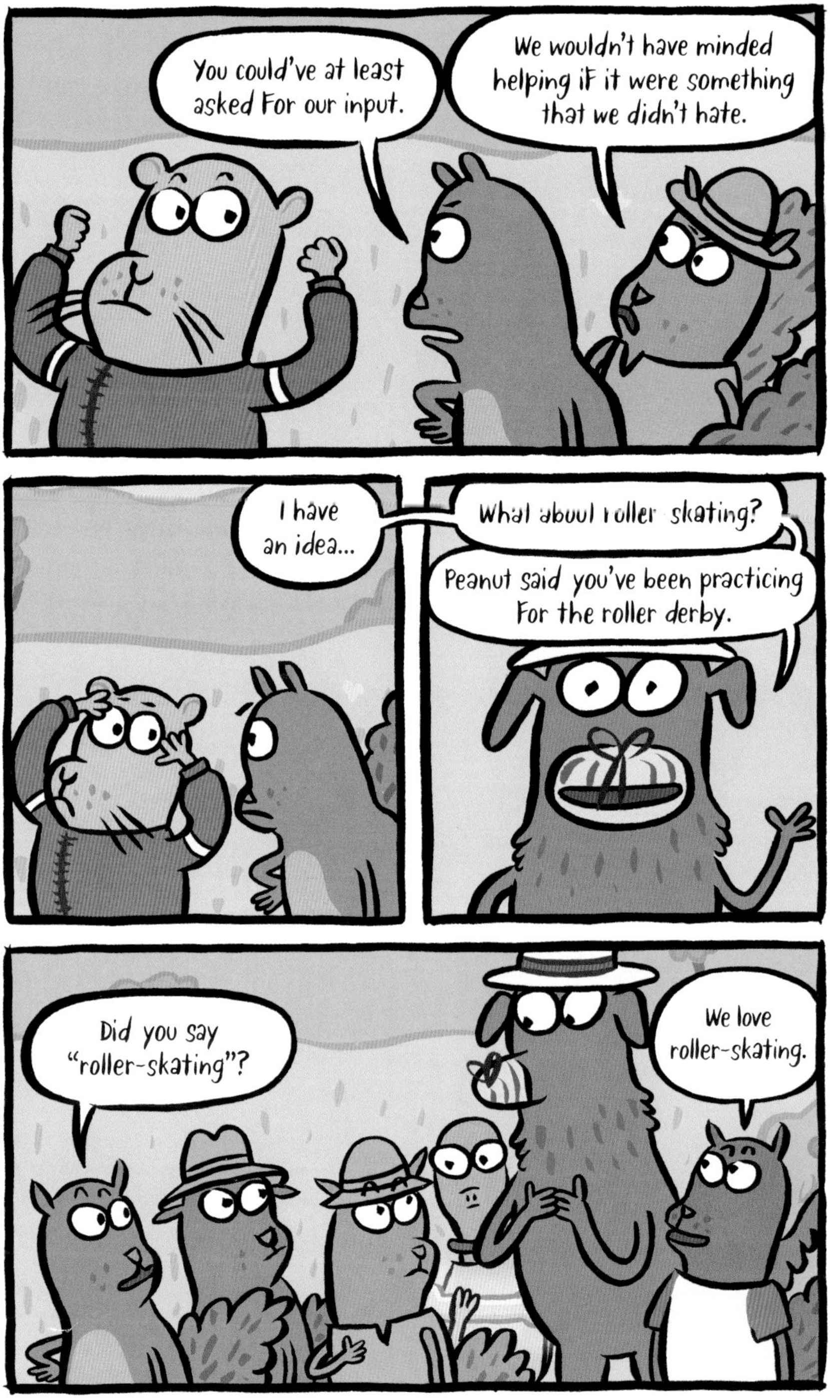
You could've at least asked For our input.
We wouldn't have minded helping iF it were something that we didn't hate.
I have an idea...
What about roller skating?
Peanut said you've been practicing For the roller derby.
Did you say "roller-skating"?
We love roller-skating.

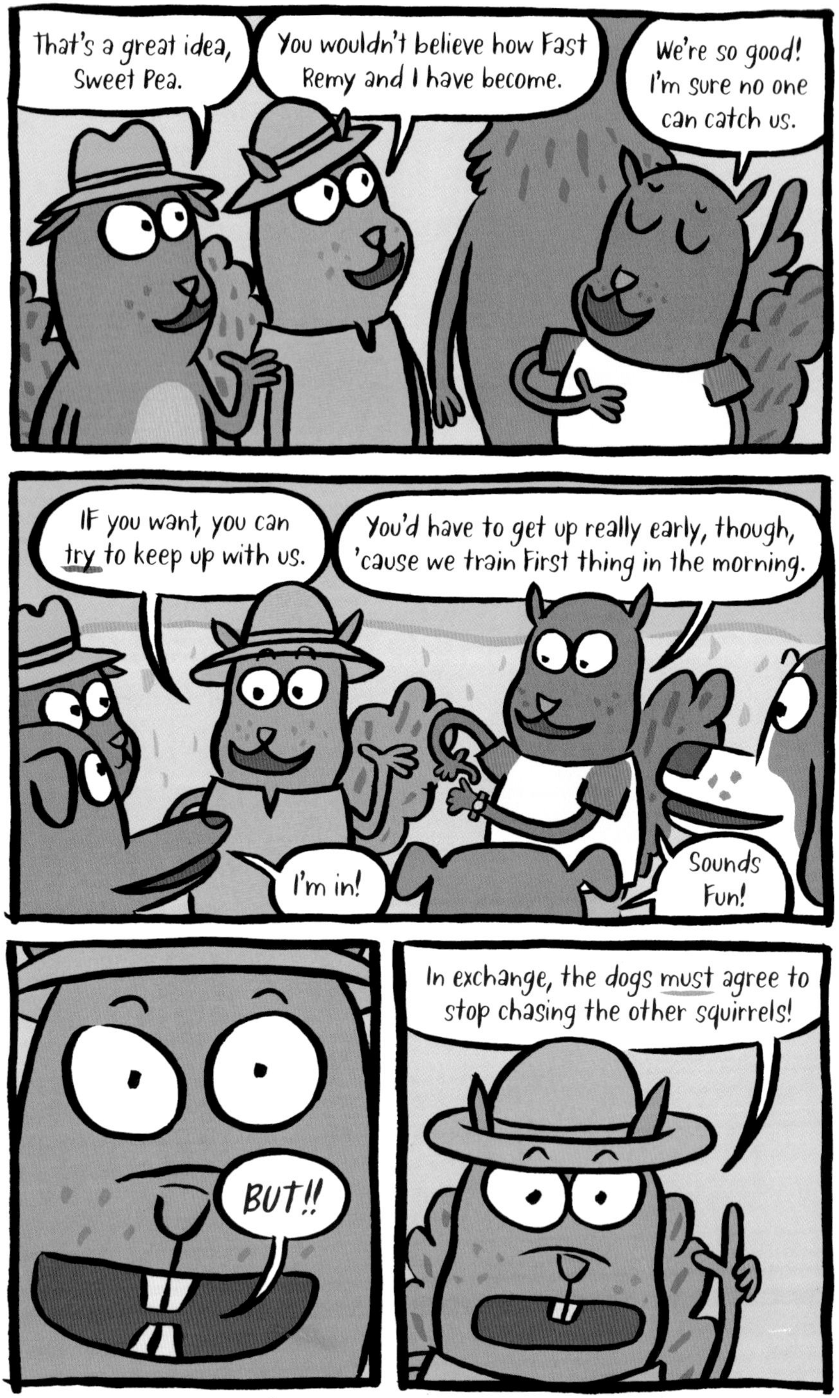
That's a great idea, Sweet Pea.
You wouldn't believe how fast Remy and I have become.
We're so good! I'm sure no one can catch us.
If you want, you can try to keep up with us.
You'd have to get up really early, though, 'cause we train first thing in the morning.
I'm in!
Sounds fun!
BUT!!
In exchange, the dogs must agree to stop chasing the other squirrels!

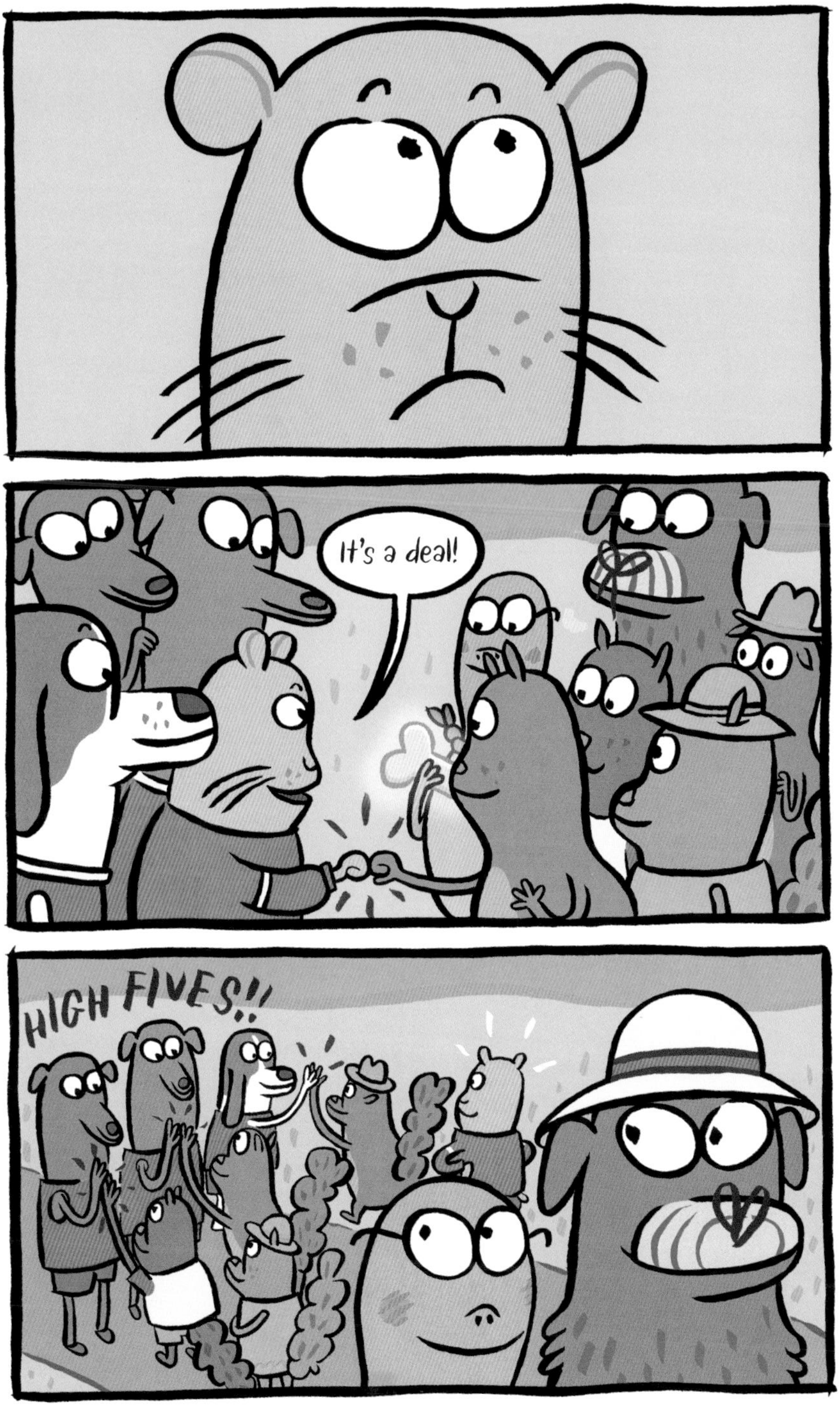
It's a deal!
HIGH FIVES!!

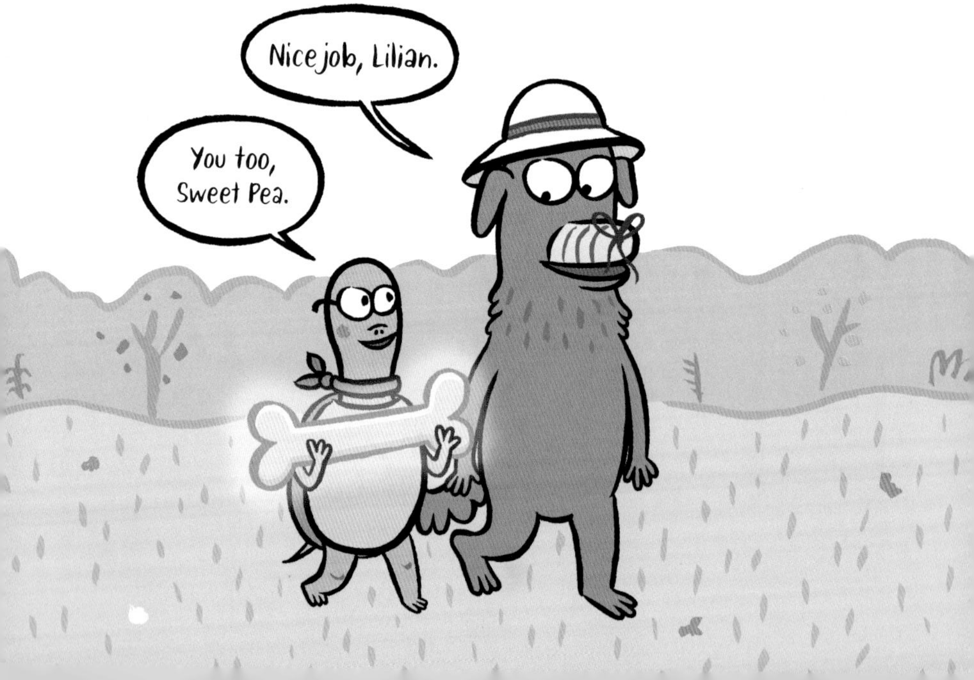
Nice job, Lilian.
You too, Sweet Pea.

Chapter 10

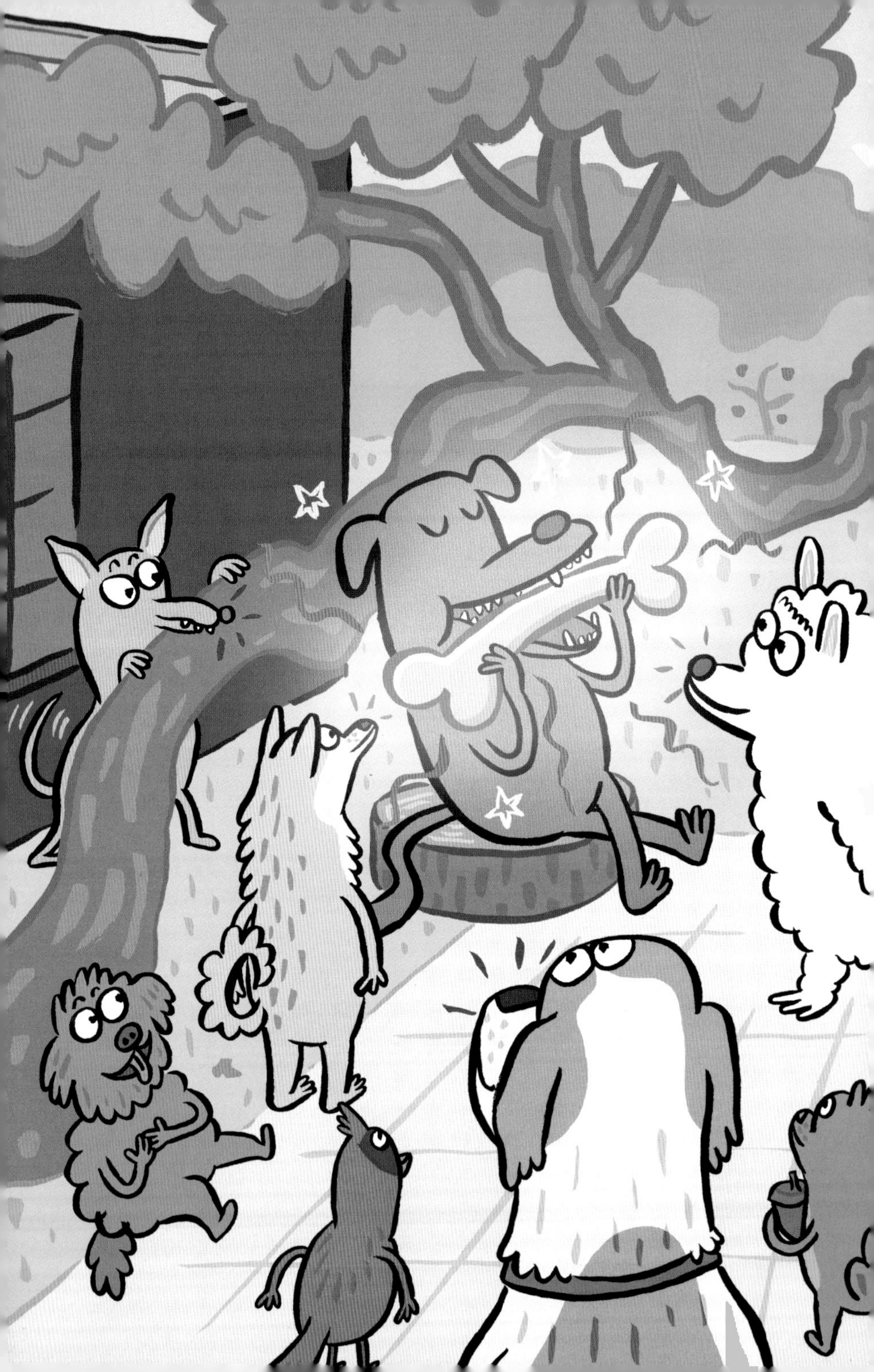

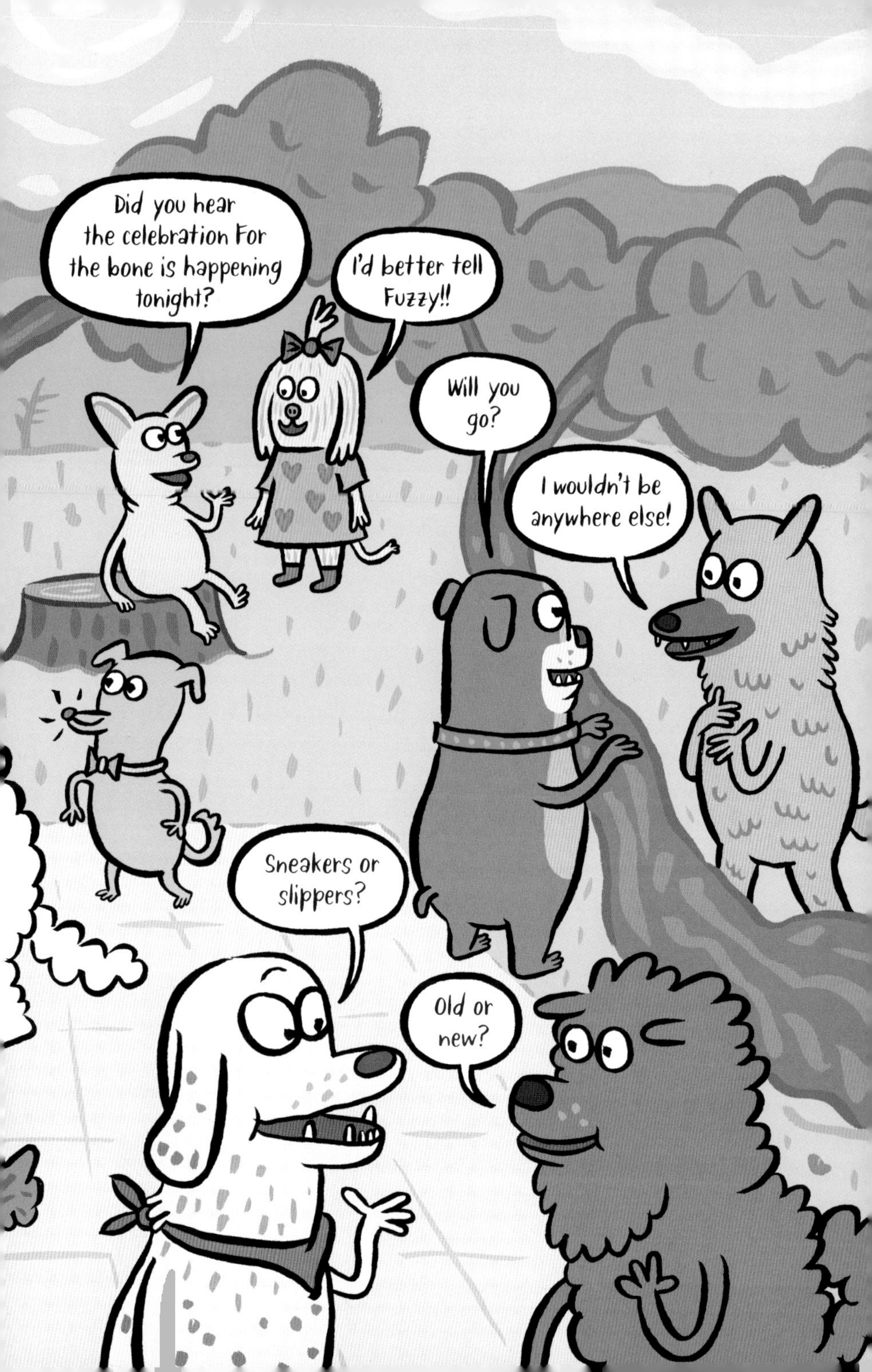
Did you hear the celebration For the bone is happening tonight?
I'd better tell Fuzzy!!
Will you go?
I wouldn't be anywhere else!
Sneakers or slippers?
Old or new?

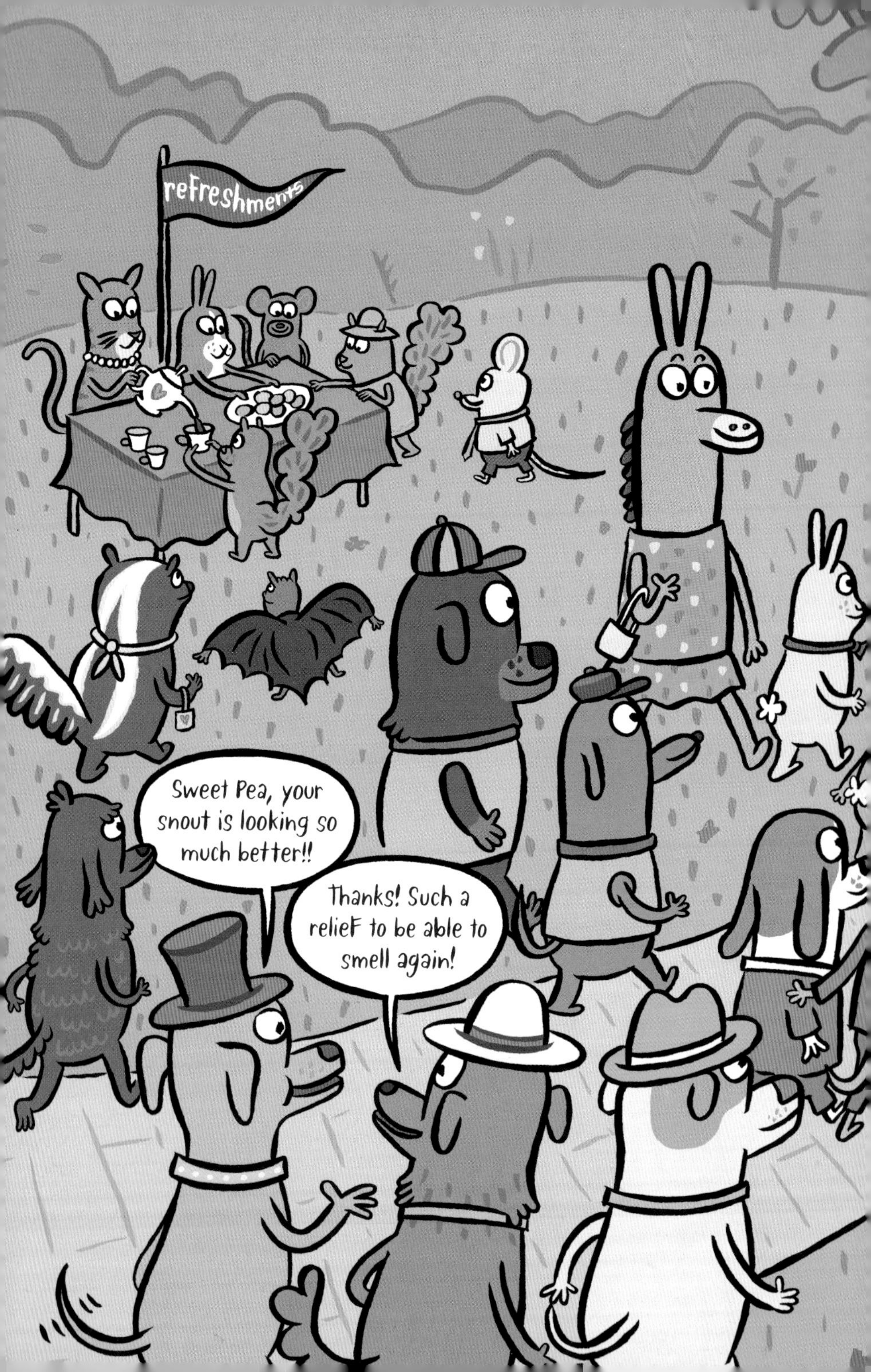
refreshments
Sweet Pea, your snout is looking so much better!!
Thanks! Such a relief to be able to smell again!

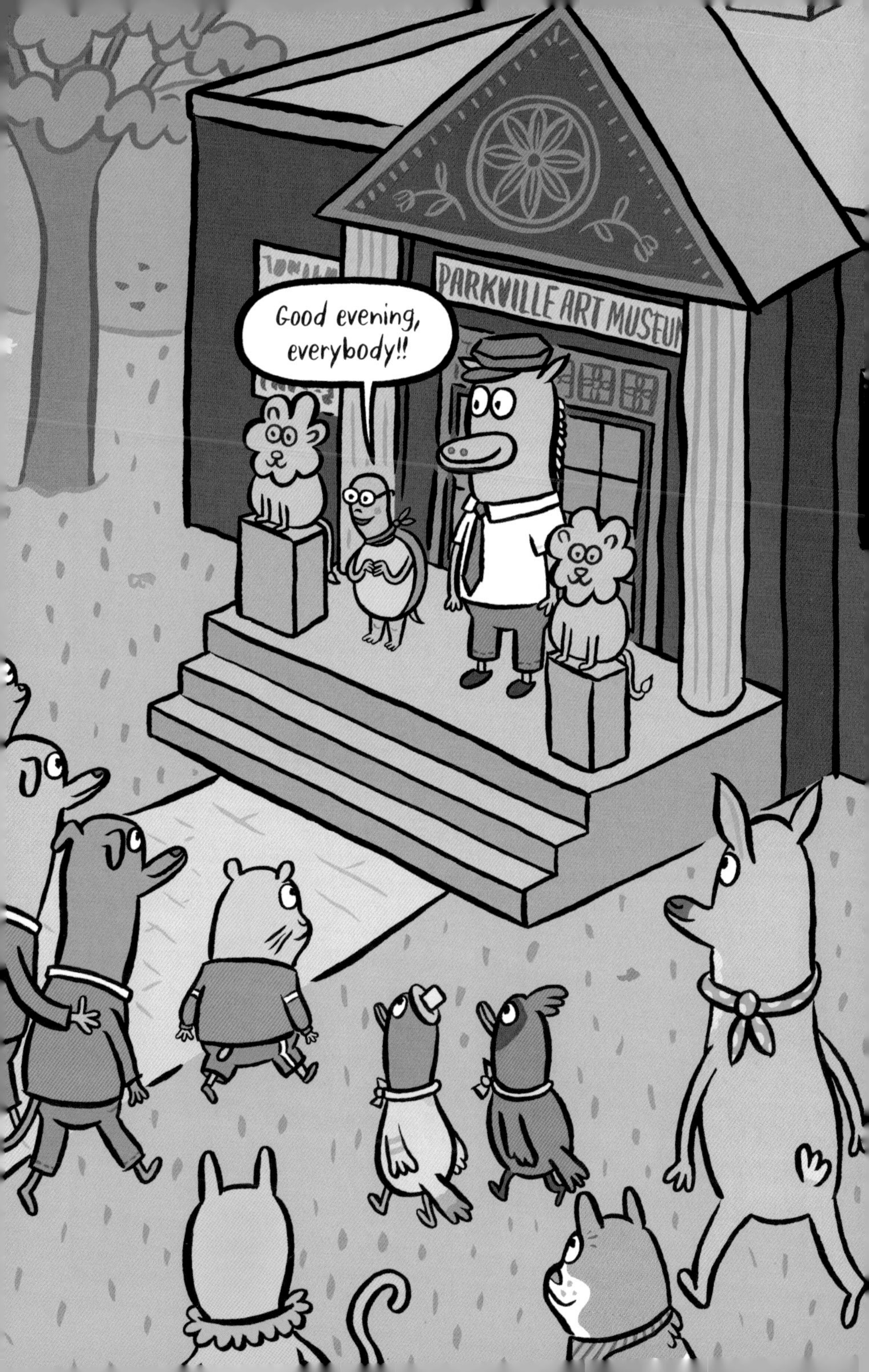
Good evening, everybody!!
PARKVILLE ART MUSEUM

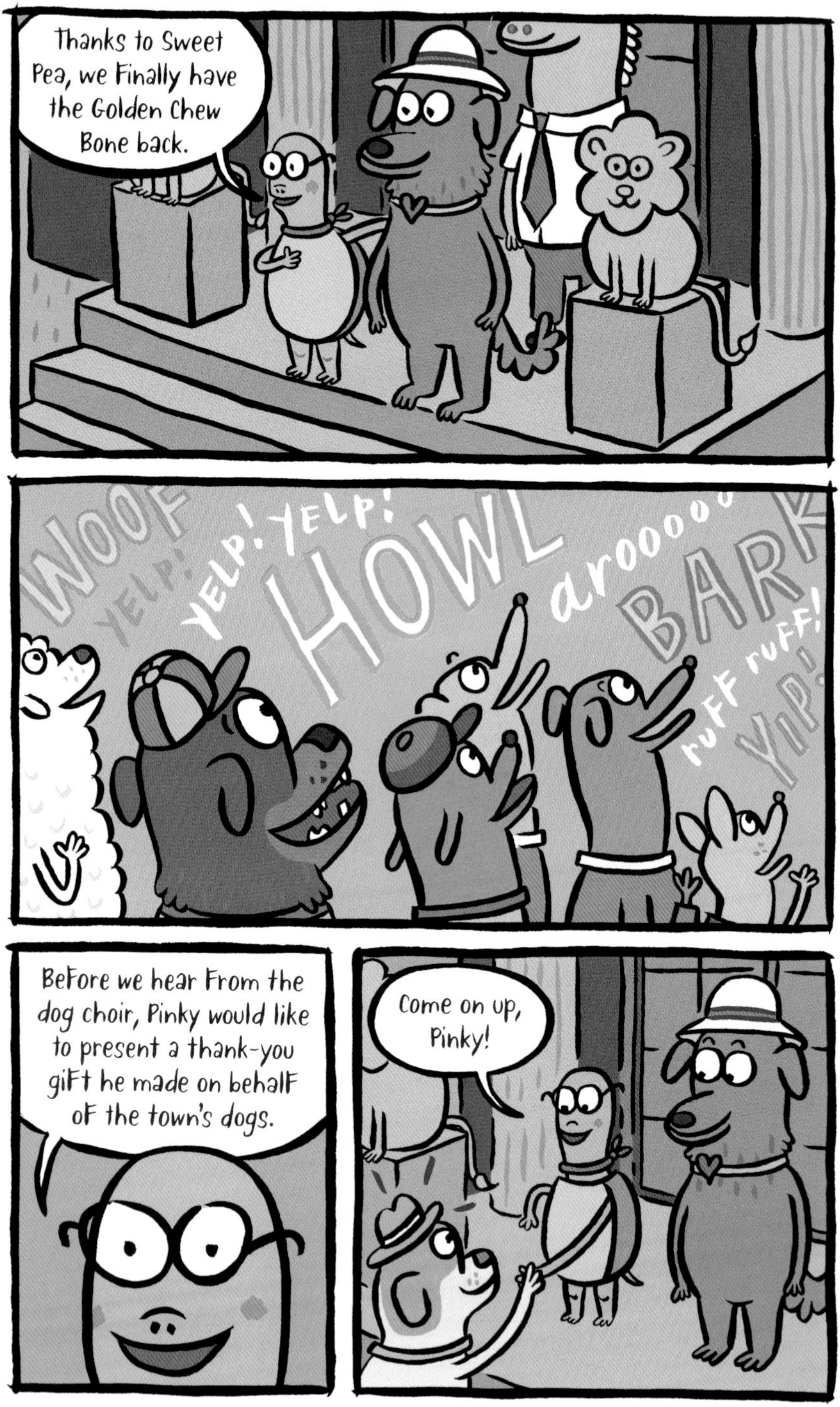
Thanks to Sweet Pea, we finally have the Golden Chew Bone back.
WOOF
YELP!
YELP! YELP!
HOWL
arooooo
BARK
ruff ruff!
YIP!
Before we hear from the dog choir, Pinky would like to present a thank-you gift he made on behalf of the town's dogs.
Come on up, Pinky!

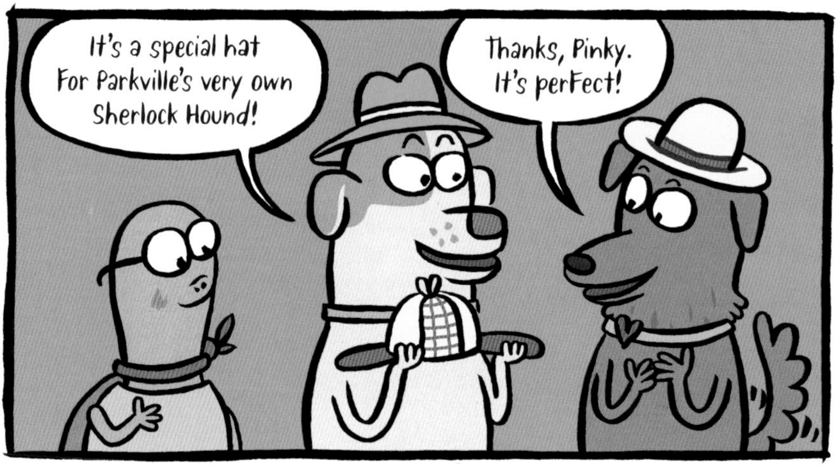
It's a special hat For Parkville's very own Sherlock Hound!
Thanks, Pinky. It's perFect!

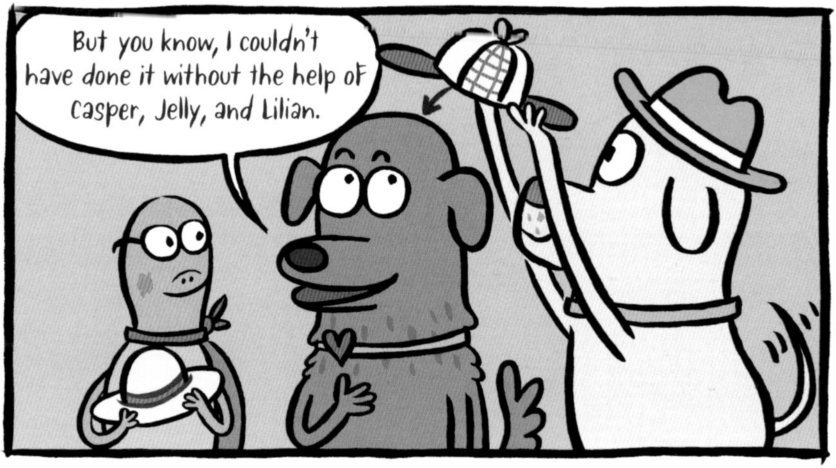
But you know, I couldn't have done it without the help oF Casper, Jelly, and Lilian.

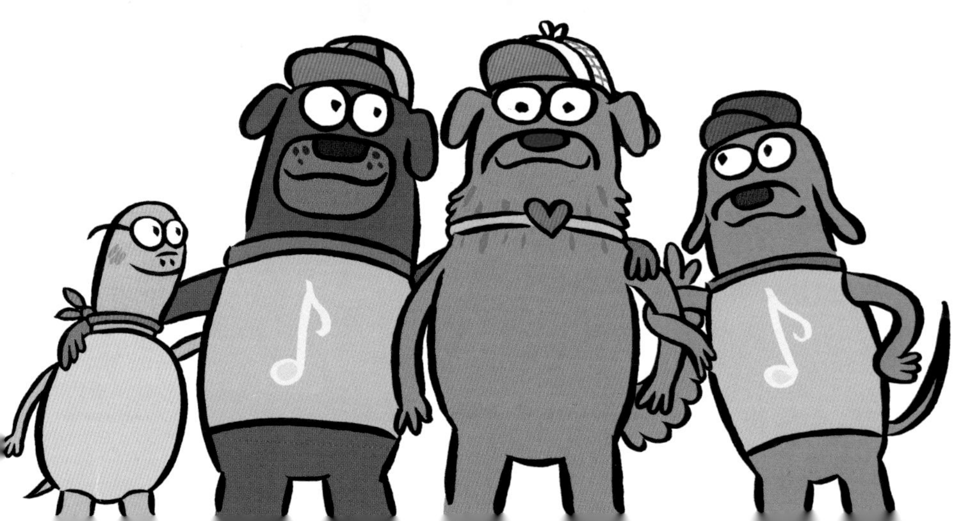

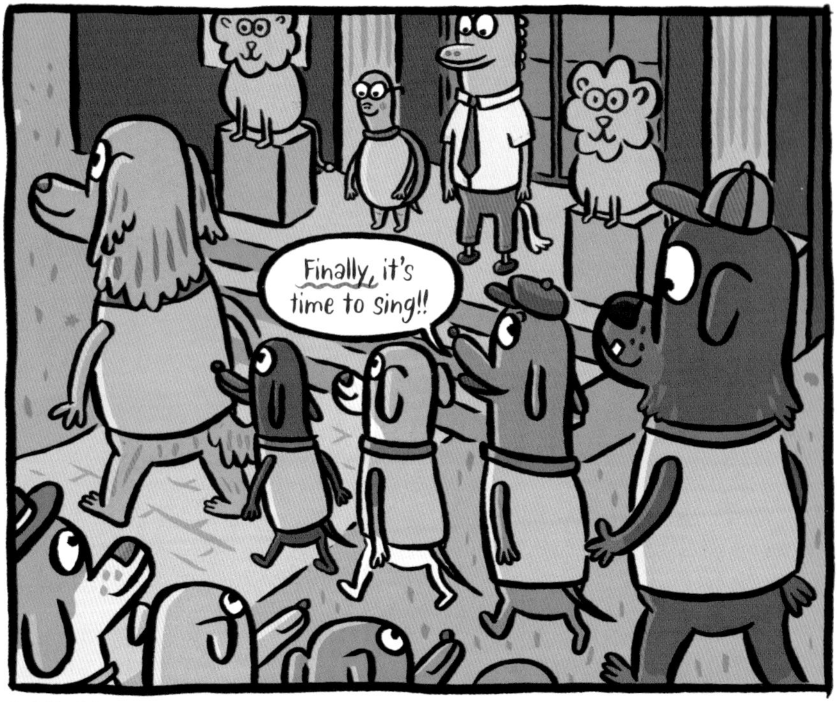
Finally, it's time to sing!!

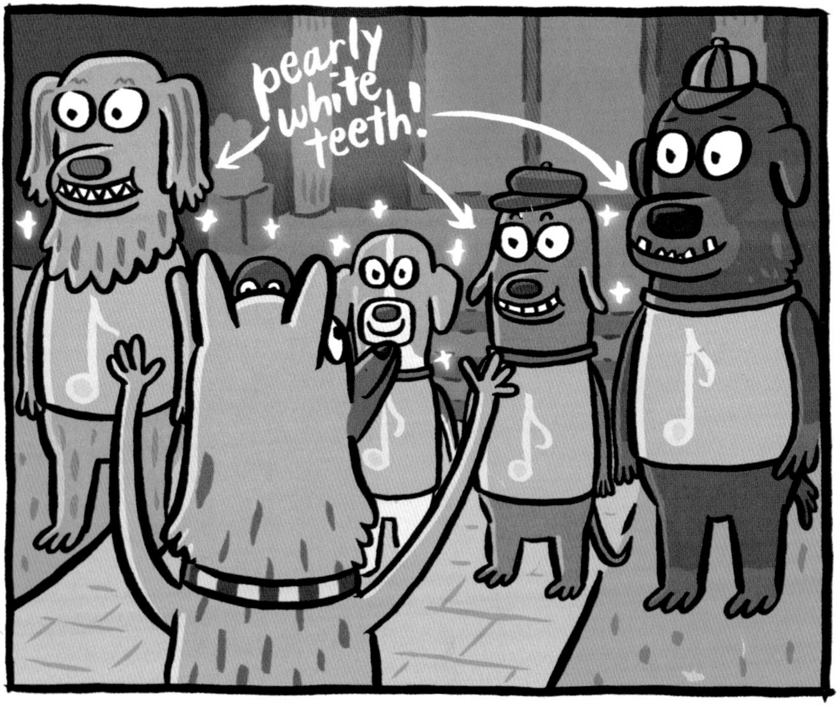
pearly white teeth!

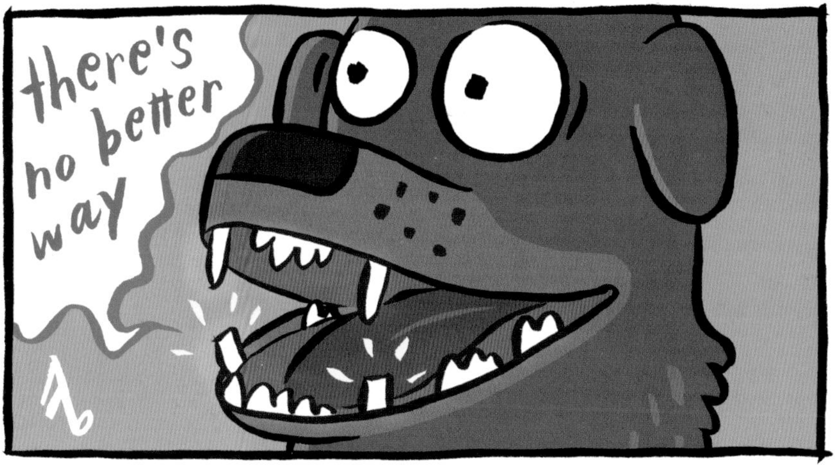
there's no better way

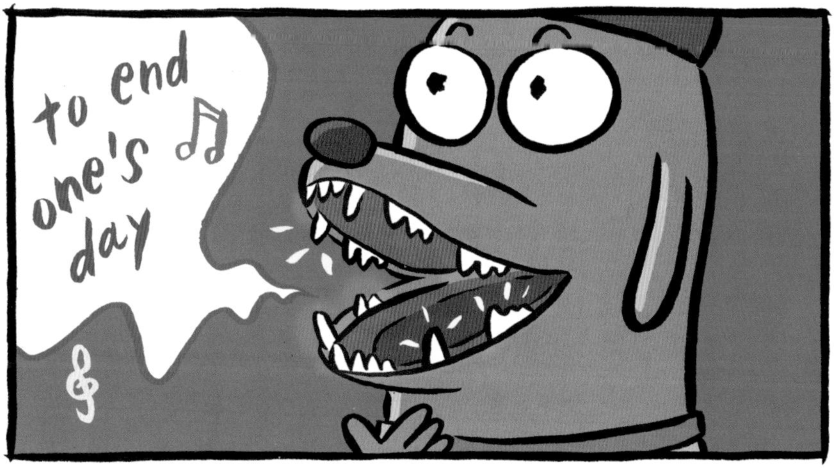
to end one's day

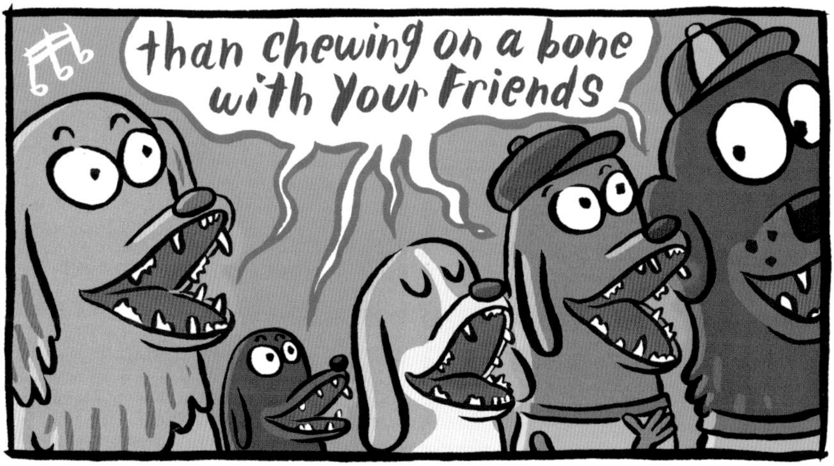
than chewing on a bone with Your Friends

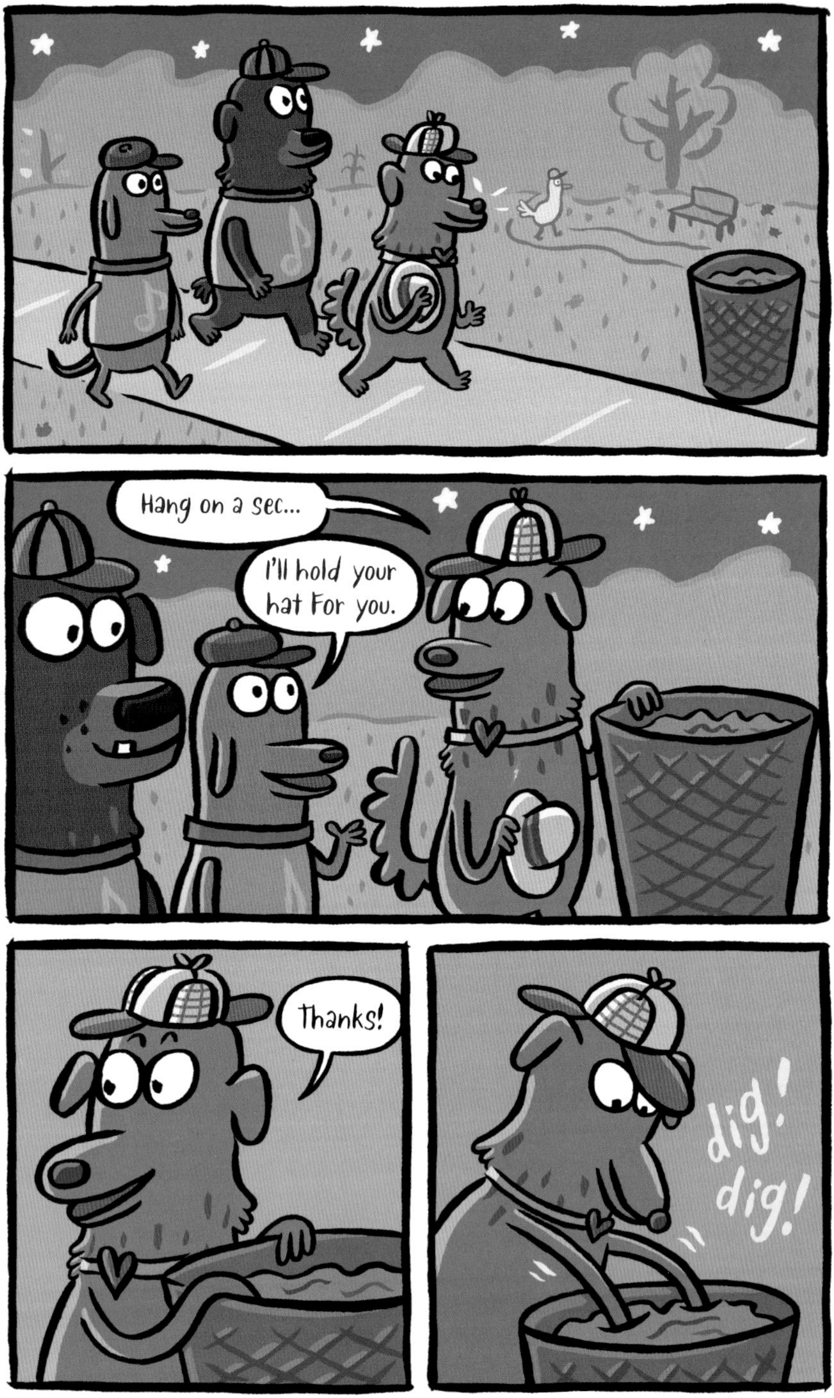
Hang on a sec...
I'll hold your hat For you.
Thanks!
dig! dig!

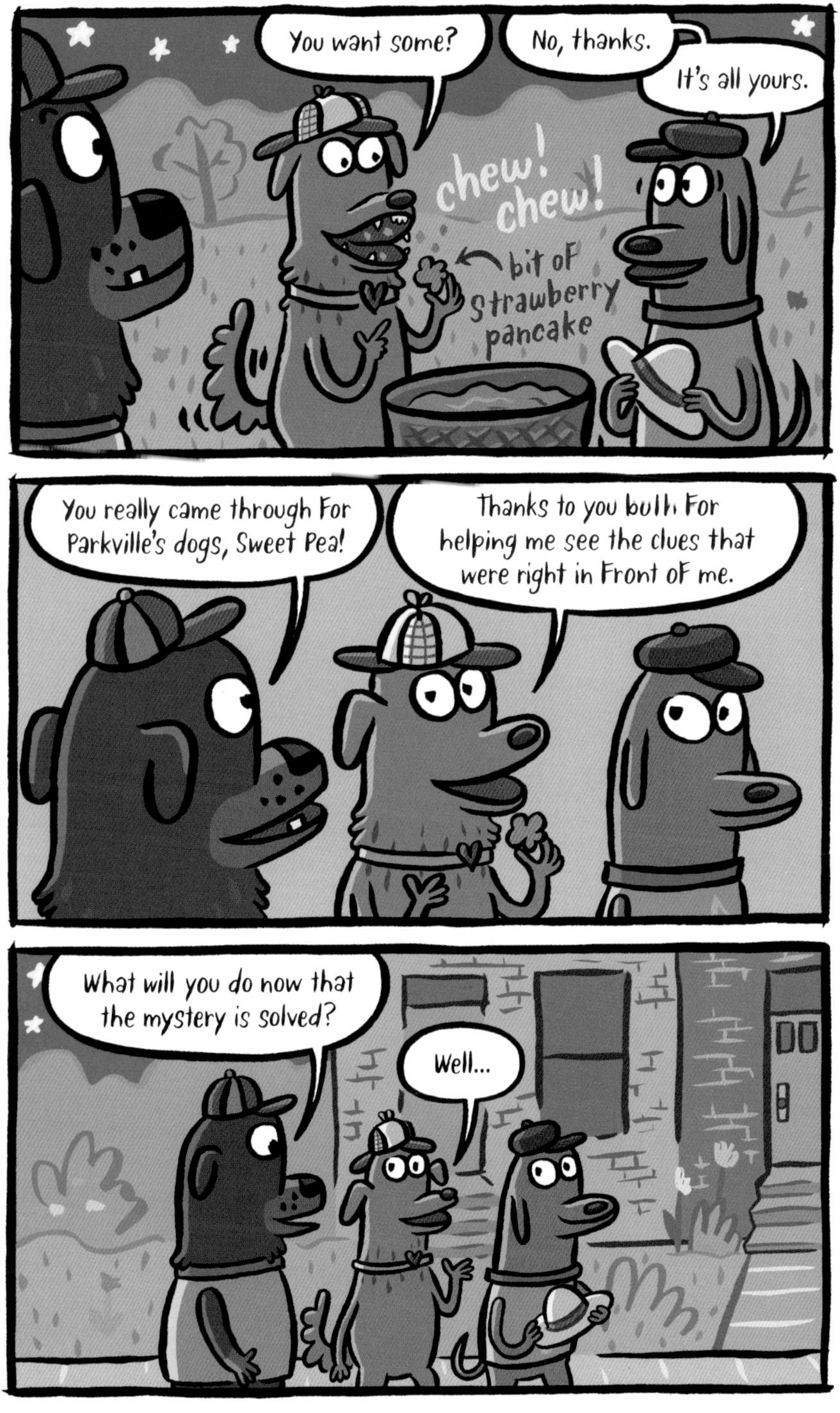
You want some?
No, thanks.
It's all yours.
chew! chew!
bit of strawberry pancake
You really came through for Parkville's dogs, Sweet Pea!
Thanks to you both for helping me see the clues that were right in front of me.
What will you do now that the mystery is solved?
Well...

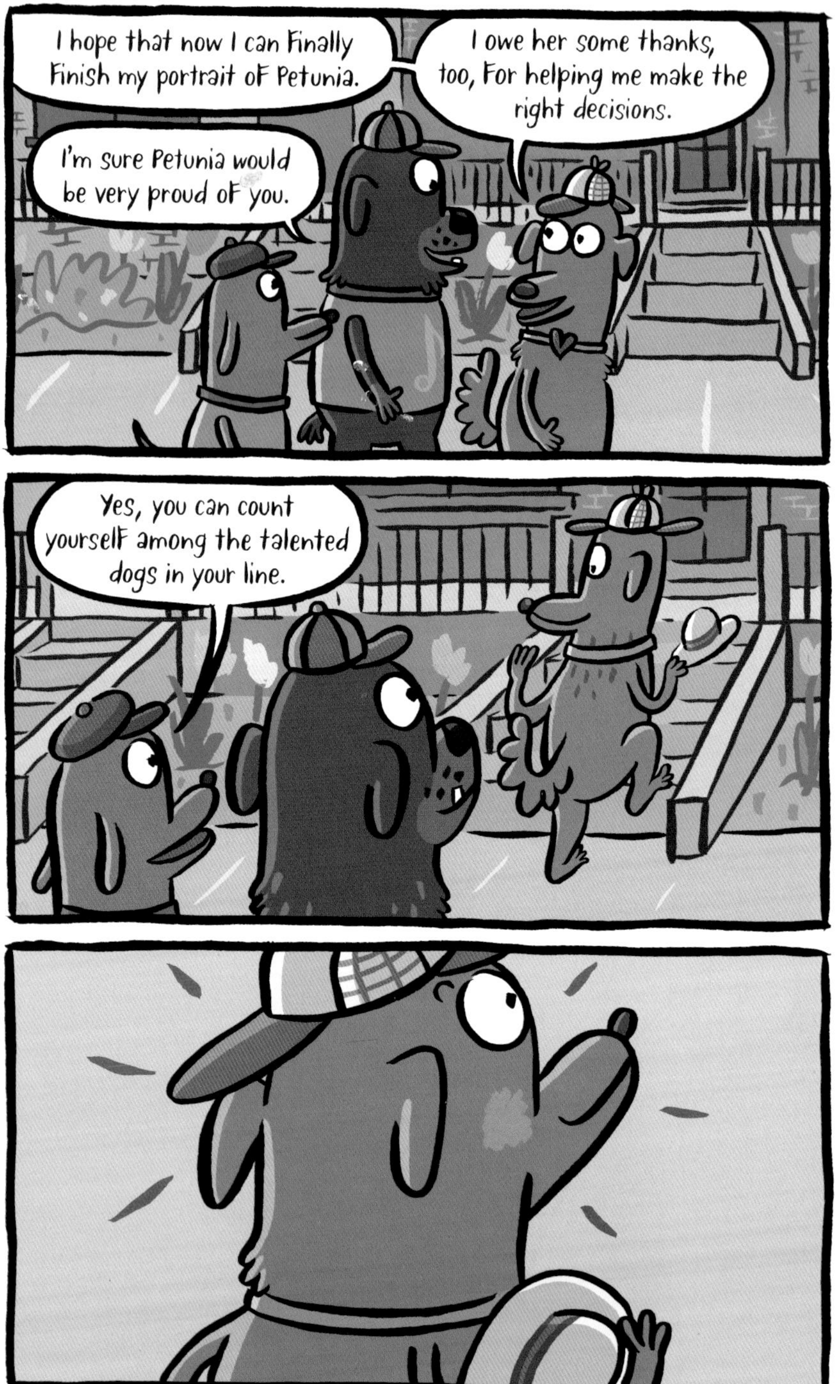
I hope that now I can Finally Finish my portrait oF Petunia.
I owe her some thanks, too, For helping me make the right decisions.
I'm sure Petunia would be very proud oF you.
Yes, you can count yourselF among the talented dogs in your line.

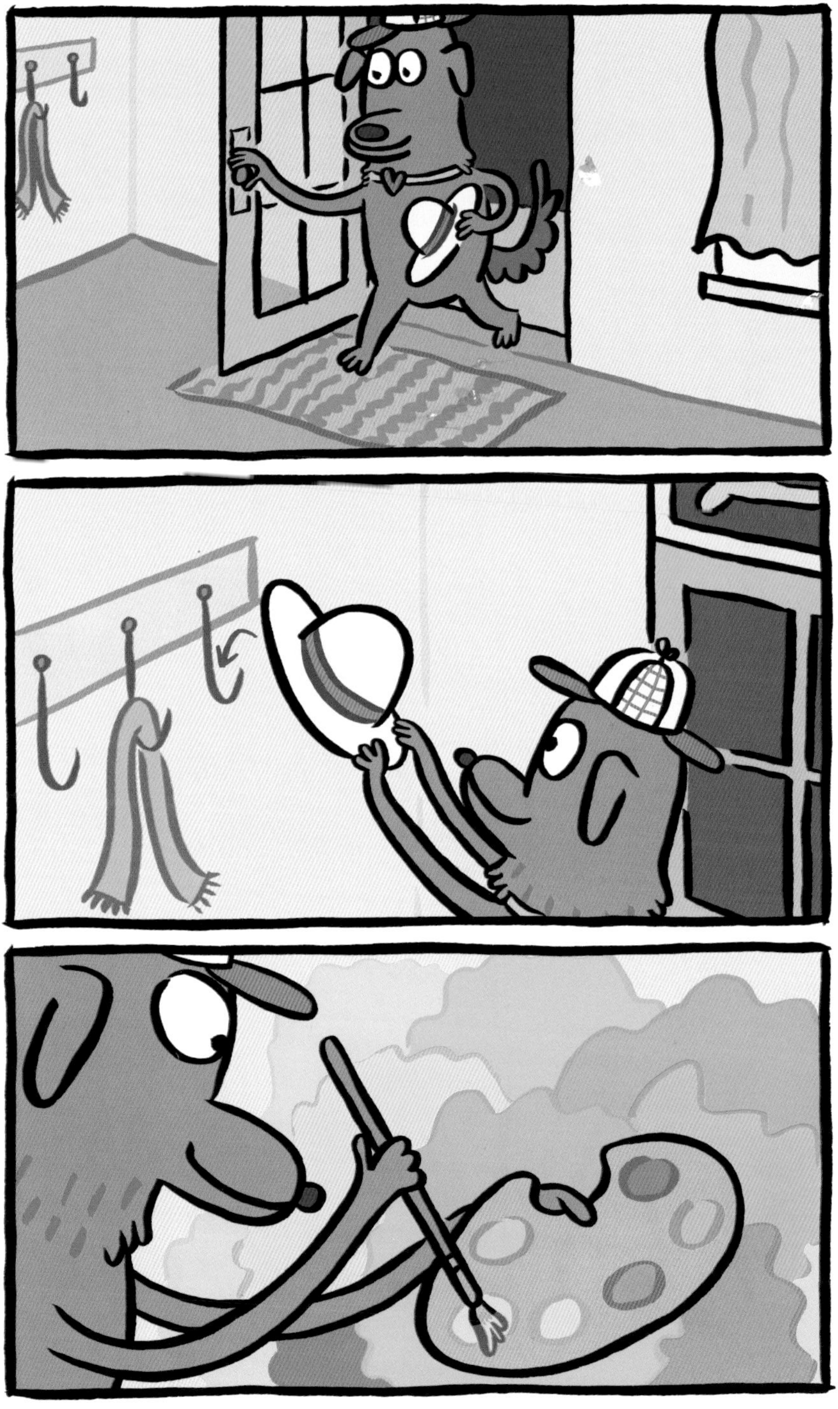

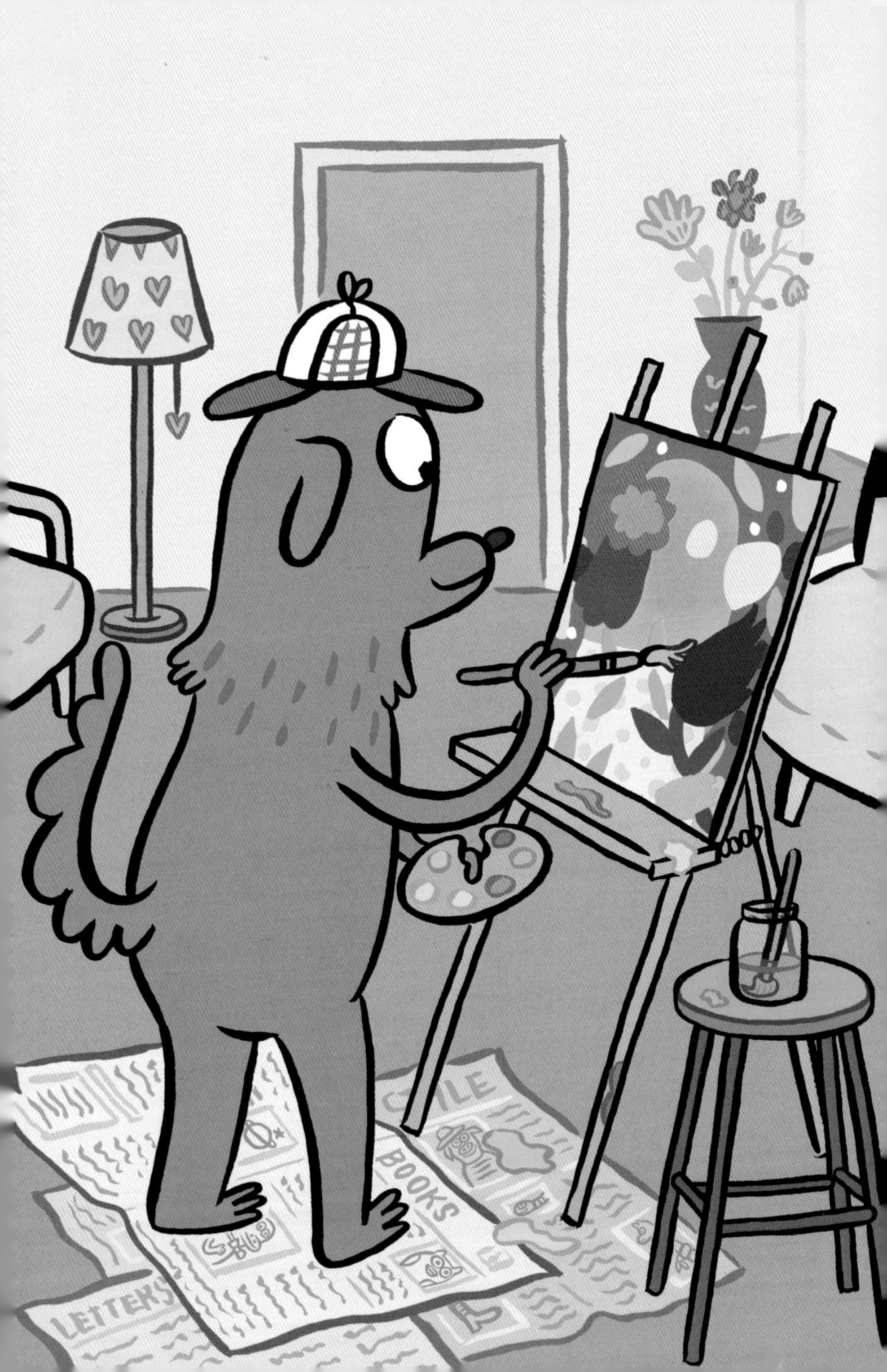
BOOKS
LETTERS

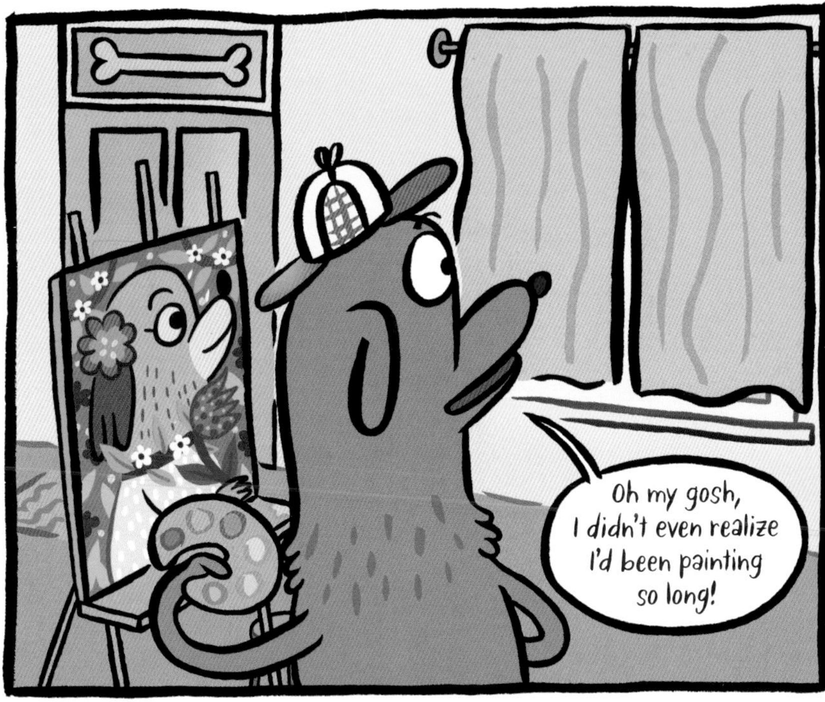
Oh my gosh,
I didn't even realize
I'd been painting
so long!

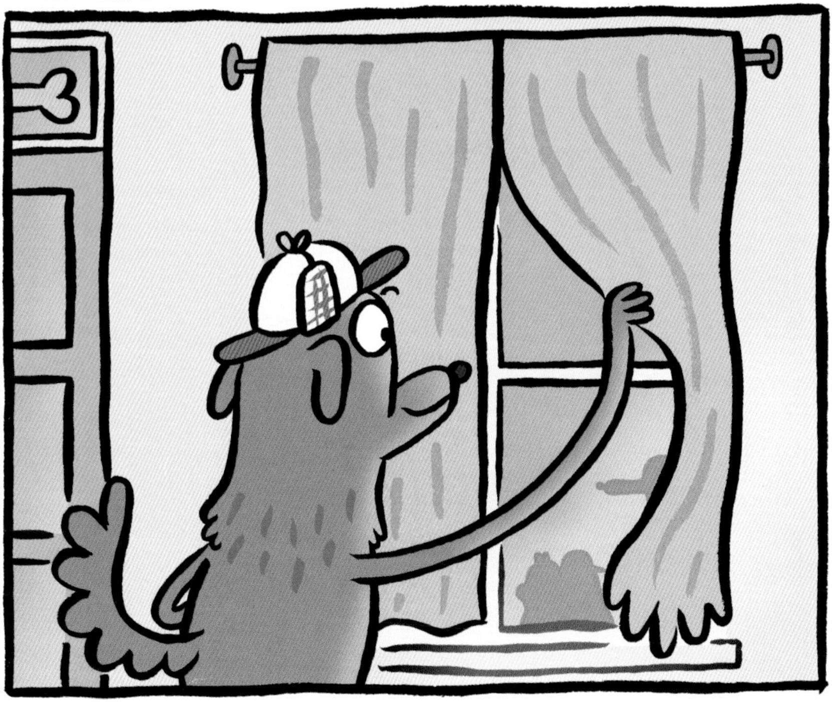

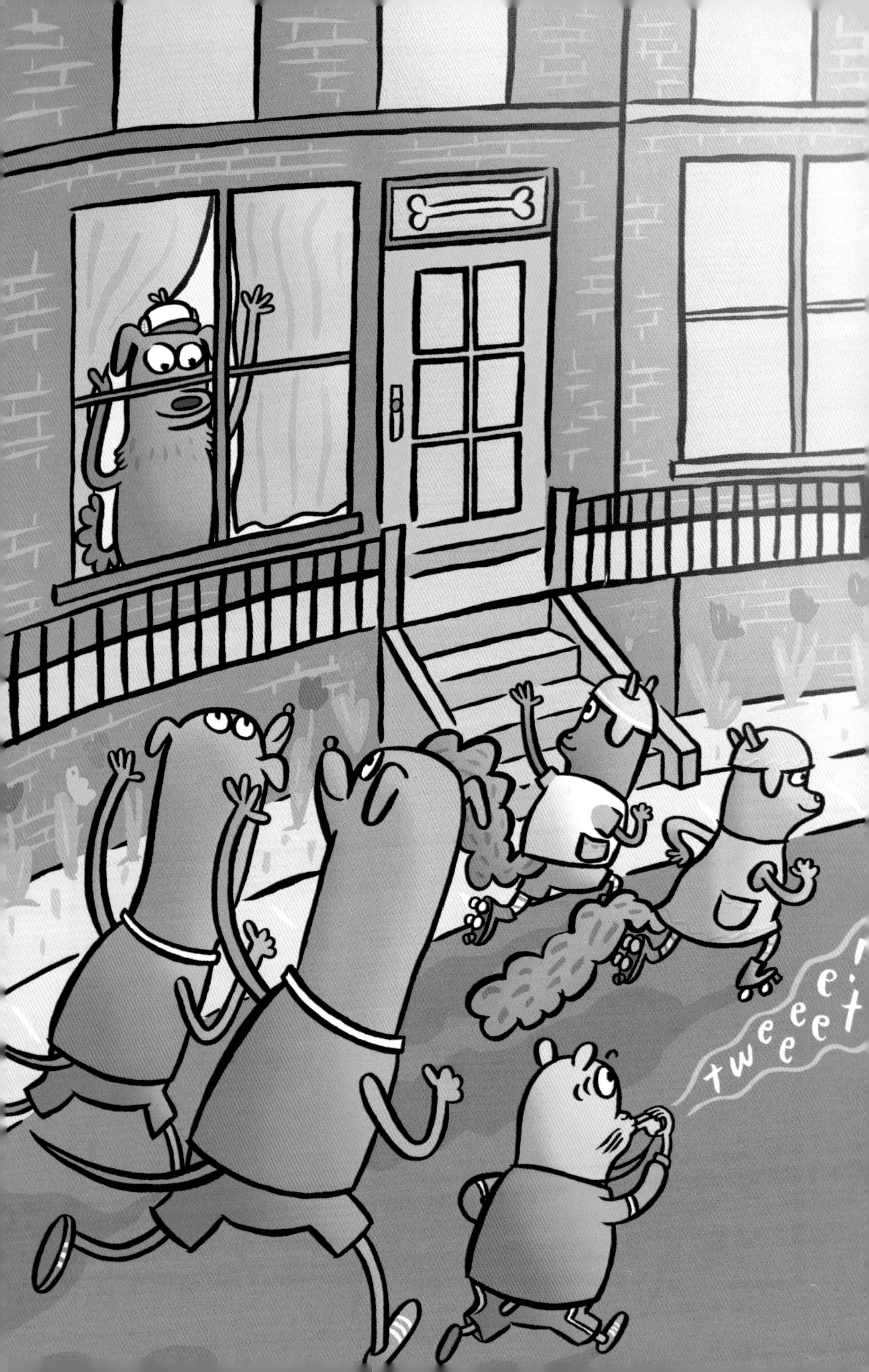
tweeeeet!

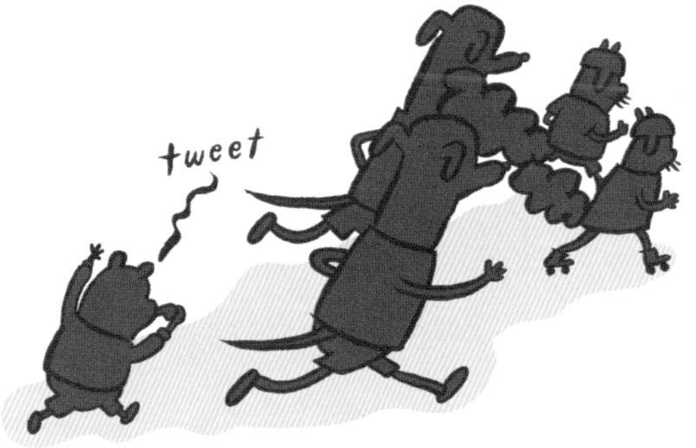
tweet

the end.

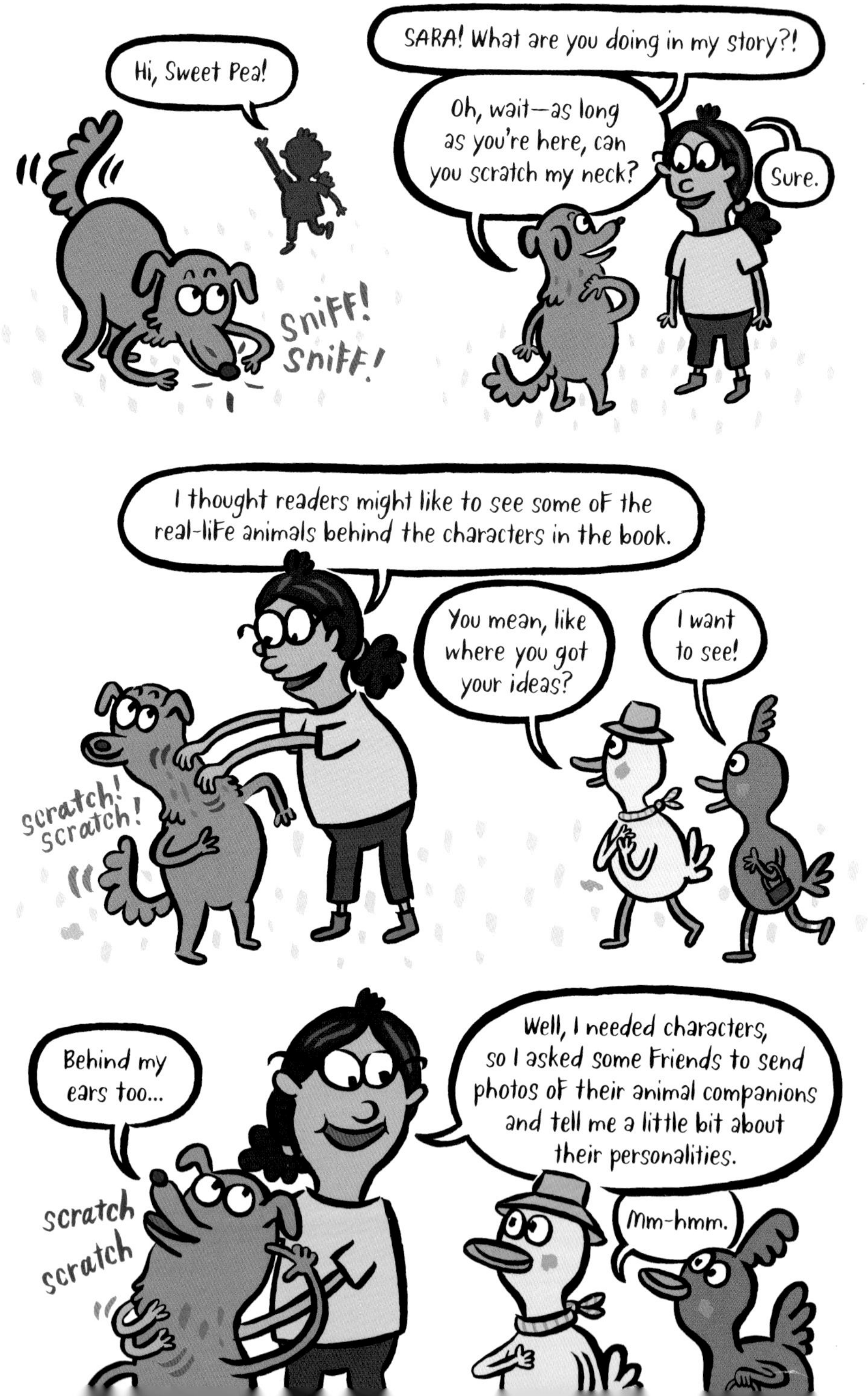
Hi, Sweet Pea!
SNIFF! SNIFF!
SARA! What are you doing in my story?!
Oh, wait—as long as you're here, can you scratch my neck?
Sure.
I thought readers might like to see some of the real-life animals behind the characters in the book.
You mean, like where you got your ideas?
I want to see!
scratch! scratch!
Behind my ears too...
scratch scratch
Well, I needed characters, so I asked some friends to send photos of their animal companions and tell me a little bit about their personalities.
Mm-hmm.

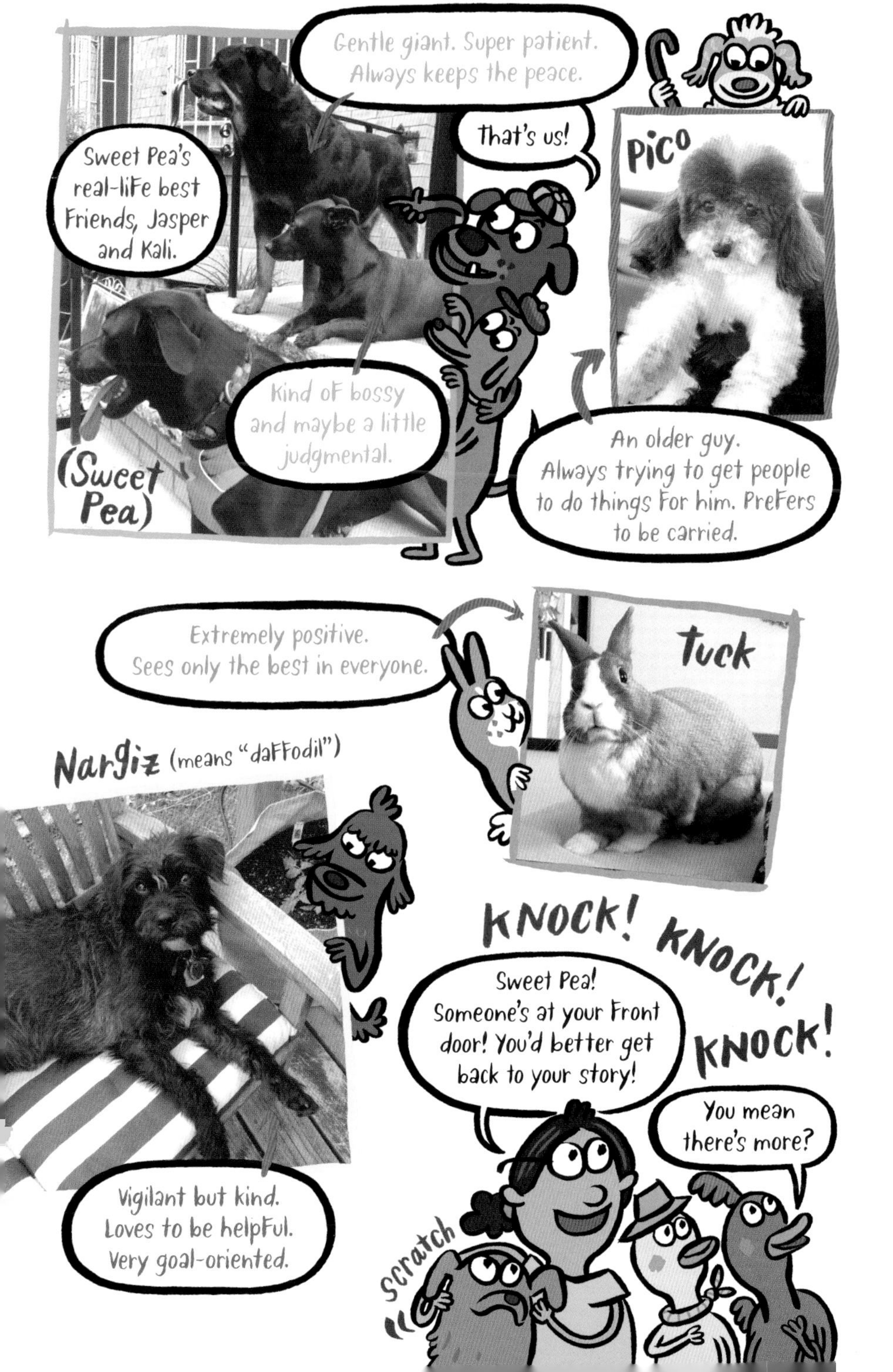

Gentle giant. Super patient. Always keeps the peace.
Sweet Pea's real-life best friends, Jasper and Kali.
That's us!
Pico
Kind of bossy and maybe a little judgmental.
(Sweet Pea)
An older guy. Always trying to get people to do things for him. Prefers to be carried.
Extremely positive. Sees only the best in everyone.
Tuck
Nargiz (means "daffodil")
KNOCK! KNOCK! KNOCK!
Sweet Pea! Someone's at your front door! You'd better get back to your story!
You mean there's more?
Vigilant but kind. Loves to be helpful. Very goal-oriented.
scratch

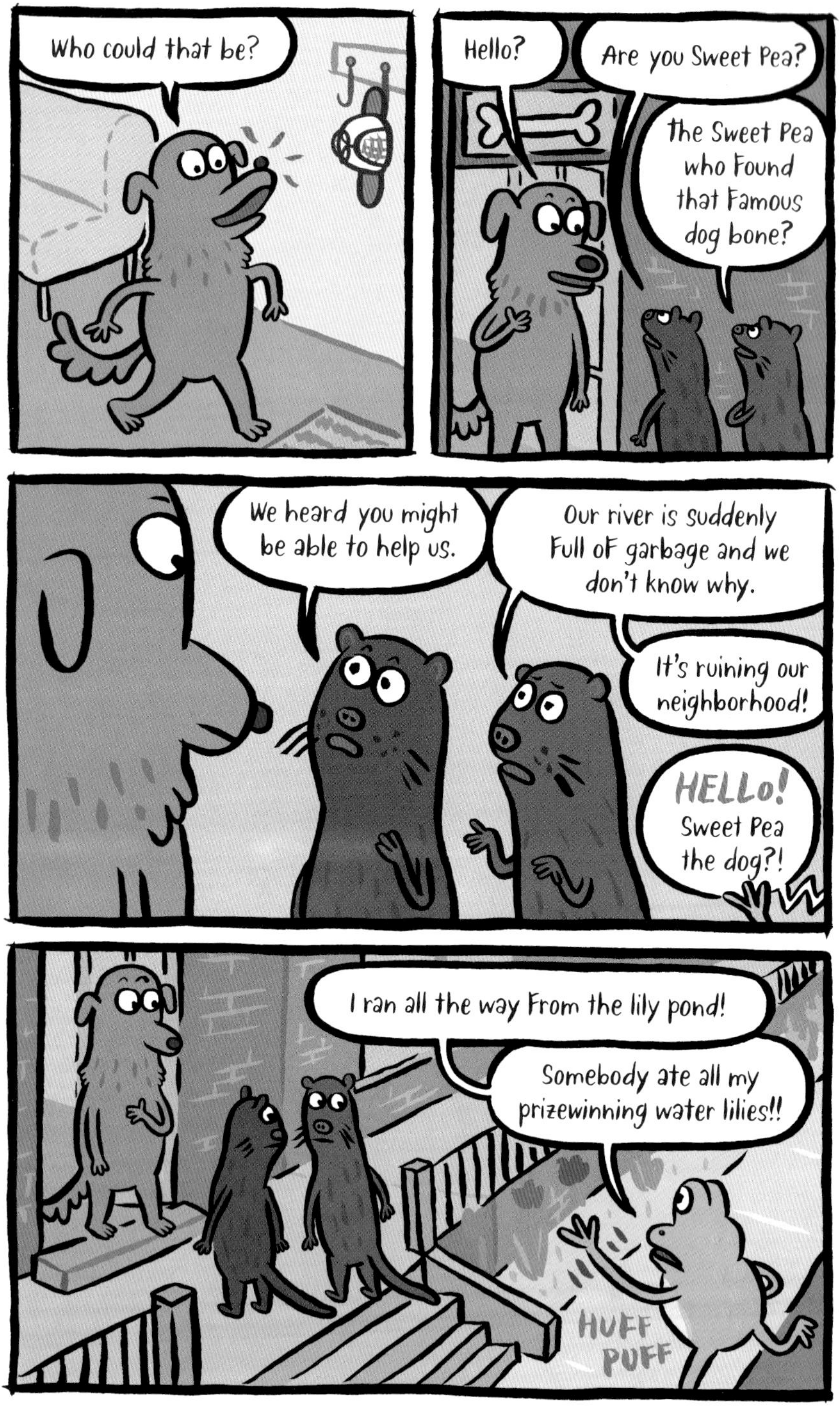

Who could that be?
Hello?
Are you Sweet Pea?
the Sweet Pea who Found that Famous dog bone?
We heard you might be able to help us.
Our river is suddenly Full oF garbage and we don't know why.
It's ruining our neighborhood!
HELLO! Sweet Pea the dog?!
I ran all the way From the lily pond!
Somebody ate all my prizewinning water lilies!!
HUFF PUFF

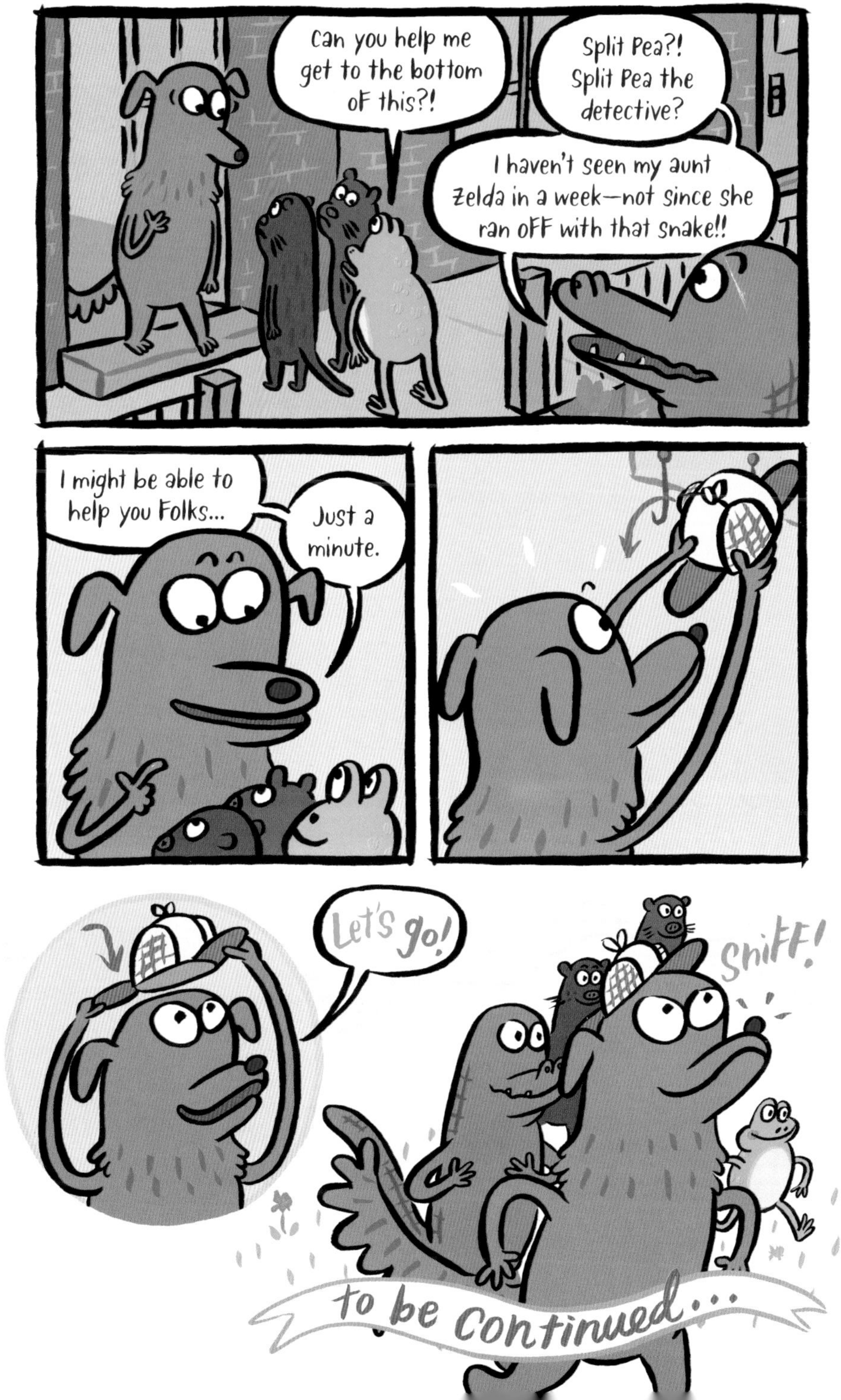
Can you help me get to the bottom of this?!
Split Pea?! Split Pea the detective?
I haven't seen my aunt Zelda in a week—not since she ran off with that snake!!
I might be able to help you folks...
Just a minute.
Let's go!
Sniff!
to be continued...

© Josh Feeney Photography

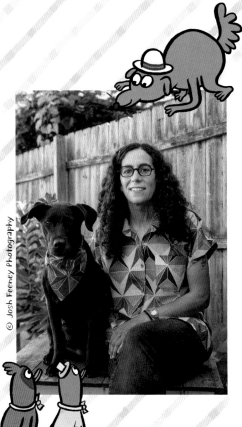

Sara Varon is a graphic novelist and children's book author/illustrator living in Chicago. Her books include *Robot Dreams*, *Odd Duck*, *Bake Sale*, *New Shoes*, *Hold Hands*, and *My Pencil and Me*. Her work has received many accolades—among others, *Hold Hands* was named a Best Children's Books of 2019 by the *New York Times*; *Odd Duck* was selected by *Kirkus Reviews* as one of the Best Children's Books of 2013; *Bake Sale* was named a YALSA Great Graphic Novel for 2012; and *Robot Dreams* was on Oprah's Kids' Reading List in 2008. In 2013, Sara Varon was a recipient of the Maurice Sendak Fellowship. **saravaron.com**

Also available

From the author of Robot Dreams
BAKE SALE
Sara Varon

ROBOT
dreams
by Sara Varon

SARA VARON
NEW SHOES

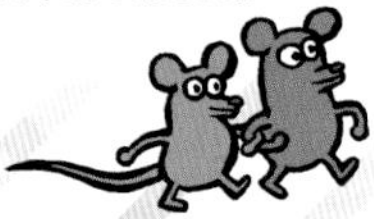

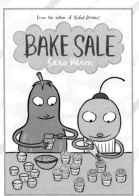

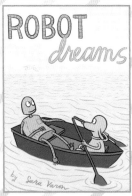

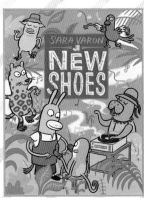